the other, in his kneecap. The blasts from the rifle resounded through the quiet backstreets.

"Enemy neutralized."

The OTHER-
WORLDER,
EXPLORING
the DUNGEON 1

Souya
An Otherworlder trying to make his way through the dungeon.

Beltriche
A priestess with the Divine Medium trait. Childhood friends with Shuna.

Arvin Forths Gassim
Former knight of the Church of St. Lillideas.

Zenobia
A mage who loves her drinks. Curvy.

Shuna
Boy swordsman from an archipelago.

Teaming up with a party of real characters!

Éa

Lana's younger sister. An archery master. Somewhat reserved.

Cheerful elven sisters. The elder went for *arajiru* soup; the younger, for instant ramen.

Lana

An elf with magical talent who was driven out of her forest.

Mythlanica

The Goddess of Deception and Secrecy whom Souya serves.

"Souya, I want some of that as well."

Who'd have thought I'd be presenting a cup of ramen to my goddess? What a cheap offering.

1

HINAGI ASAMI

Illustration by Kureta

The OTHER-WORLDER, EXPLORING the DUNGEON

YEN ON

NEW YORK

HINAGI ASAMI

TRANSLATION BY ALEXANDRIA MCCULLOUGH-GARCIA • COVER ART BY KURETA

IHOJIN, DANJON NI MOGURU. Vol.1
©Asami Hinagi 2019
First published in Japan in 2019 by KADOKAWA CORPORATION, Tokyo.
English translation rights arranged with KADOKAWA CORPORATION, Tokyo
through TUTTLE-MORI AGENCY, INC., Tokyo.

English translation © 2021 by Yen Press, LLC

Yen On
150 West 30th Street, 19th Floor
New York, NY 10001

Visit us at yenpress.com • facebook.com/yenpress • twitter.com/yenpress
yenpress.tumblr.com • instagram.com/yenpress

First Yen On Edition: November 2021

Yen On is an imprint of Yen Press, LLC.
The Yen On name and logo are trademarks of Yen Press, LLC.

Library of Congress Cataloging-in-Publication Data
Names: Asami, Hinagi, author. | Kureta, illustrator. | McCullough-Garcia, Alexandria, translator.
Title: The otherworlder, exploring the dungeon / Hinagi Asami, Kureta ;
translation by Alexandria McCullough-Garcia.
Other titles: Ihojin, danjon ni moguru. English
Description: First Yen On edition. | New York, NY : Yen On, 2021.
Identifiers: LCCN 2021030964 | ISBN 9781975319557 (v. 1 ; trade paperback)
Subjects: LCGFT: Fantasy fiction. | Light novels.
Classification: LCC PL852.I426 I4613 2021 | DDC 895.63/6—dc23
LC record available at https://lccn.loc.gov/2021030964

ISBNs: 978-1-9753-1955-7 (paperback)
978-1-9753-1956-4 (ebook)

1 3 5 7 9 10 8 6 4 2

LSC-C

Printed in the United States of America

[Contents]

I lay on the ground looking up at the sky.

There I stayed until my breath settled and the sweat started to cool on my overheated body. A spattering of thin clouds dotted the clear blue sky; three faint moons hovered in their midst. I let out a sigh and allowed my gaze to sink down with it. My eyes landed on a meadow that stretched out to the horizon. At the very edge of the flatlands stood an enormous, hornlike object that looked as if it had been thrust into the ground. Its name—the Tower of Legions.

Legend had it that the horn belonged to the giant who created this world. Ask a long-lived storyteller, and they'd tell you that the steeple came crashing down out of the sky from a foreign land. Then again, according to the priests of the depths, the myriad gods had discarded the tower here.

Whether those were merely ancient superstitions or the truth, I couldn't say. What I did know for sure was that the tower brought both prosperity and calamity to the people of this world, and it had become an indispensable part of their existences. At times, it gave birth to great heroes; at others, it cut them down. Its riches erected nations, and its hidden treasures brought them to ruin. The demons it conceived and created were so powerful that the blade to finally fell them would leave an epic tale that would float forever after on the wind in the wake of its swing.

I had one year to explore the depths of that dungeon. My target: the fifty-sixth floor. And I still didn't even have a clear idea if that would turn out to be an impossible challenge or a walk in the park.

Time to find out.

But first, I had to set myself up for life in this land.

PROLOGUE

July 1946: The existence of another dimension was identified. According to official records, a certain country sent the first advance unit there in 1949.

October 1951: A major nation dispatched an entire battalion to the Other Dimension. Developments in communications technologies of the time led to near-daily media coverage of the expedition. Stories of beautiful elves, brawny dwarves, myriad races of beast-folk, and magic beyond human understanding filled the airwaves. These cheerful tales were the perfect distraction from the wounds left by the last world war and the unceasing anxiety that yet another might break out.

Chronicles of adventures in this foreign realm were penned into books, which were made into drama series, then adapted into movies. Tours were put together for the richest of the rich. It was, in the truest sense of the word, a brand-new world, a vessel for human dreams and envy.

But every dream must come to an end.

February 1955: An explosive tell-all book about that battalion dispatched to the foreign land was published, graphically recounting all that these representatives of humanity had done in their stay. In short, it told of destruction, rape, and murder.

The troops' commander insisted that they had only demolished what had been necessary in order to establish their headquarters and that the accusations of rape were inaccurate retellings of consensual relations. He admitted they had indeed returned fire after native tribes had launched an attack against them, but that could hardly count as murder. No one believed his brazen lies. Of course, that tell-all book also became a drama, then a movie. Some of the wealthy tour-goers testified to hunting beastfolk and shooting them down.

Just around this time, the tremendous costs associated with traveling to this foreign land came under fire. A two-meter-square portal of light had to remain open for five seconds per person for each entry and exit. Each opening was so expensive that these travelers could have brought back hunks of gold as big as they were and it still would not have been enough to cover the sum. Though a few useful resources had been discovered in the other world, even they could not outweigh the operational expenses. And nobody took any of the people who claimed to have mastered skills commonly referred to as "magic" seriously.

January 1956: The entire battalion dispatched to the foreign land was annihilated. With his dying breath, their commander left these final words:

"There are gods in that world."

To this day, no one knows what happened to them.

February 1956: A nonaggression pact was signed between our worlds. We have no record of who signed this treaty on behalf of the foreign land.

June 1957: The development of an aqueous cerebrum led to the completion of the world's first artificial intelligence prototypes. Meanwhile, the Space Race intensified. All of humanity shifted its focus toward the stars. In doing so, the people of this world turned away from the evil deeds they had committed and consigned the existence of this foreign land to oblivion.

Back in the present day, the only reason I knew about the other realm was thanks to the video games I played. For someone as uncultured as me, there was no more entertaining way to learn than through games. It wasn't the most expensive of hobbies, and best of all, you could play them as much as you wanted without inconveniencing anybody else.

All that aside, I first heard of the Firm at the end of March. I had just come back to Japan and had fallen into a deep depression over my younger sister's situation. To make a long story short, I was strapped for cash. I needed to come up with the kind of money I could never earn with the hand-to-mouth existence I was leading at the time.

That's when this Firm reached out and offered me a lifeline. It wasn't like I had any noteworthy skills that would make me head-hunting material, and I knew no halfway-decent company would choose to work with someone like me. Or maybe I should say, hire me for a halfway-decent project? Either way, nothing about it was aboveboard. But I needed the money, so I decided to go in for an interview.

At my sister's insistence, I borrowed a suit out of the pile of things my dad had left behind when he'd passed and made my way to the designated building. It was huge. Inside the classy lobby, a beautiful receptionist led the way to...a dim basement storehouse. The interviewer must have been in his fifties. He had thinning hair, glasses, and a face that was hard to read.

"Please, have a seat. We don't have much time, so let's proceed as quickly as possible. First, I'd like to you sign this," he said, gesturing to the binder full of papers resting on top of the folding chair reserved for me.

"A nondisclosure agreement?" I asked. The contract looked shady as hell. I sat down and flipped through it, but the densely packed text made my head spin.

"Please do read through it carefully. Though I must admit we don't have much time."

"Could you summarize it for me, please?"

I figured that would be best if we needed to hurry.

"Silence is golden."

"And the cons?"

"Loose lips sink ships."

"Understood." I signed the form.

"Allow me to ask you a few point-blank questions."

"Oh, okay."

"Are you opposed to work that may involve taking life-threatening risks?"

"No, sir."

"Do you have an extensive network of friends?"

"No."

"Would you be opposed to engaging in morally questionable or violent activities?"

"Depending on the situation, no."

"Are you a devout adherent of any particular religion or denomination?"

"No."

"Do you believe in God?"

"Yes." *Rice is divine, after all.*

"Have you ever killed another person?"

"Huh? No." I'd never murdered anyone.

"In a few words, tell me what 'living' means to you."

"Eating and putting food on the table, I suppose?" *What's up with these questions?*

"Do you have any close family members?"

"One younger sister."

"Is she a discreet sort of person?"

"She can be loud, but she's the type who keeps her promises."

"I see…" He was silent for a beat. "Would you like to travel to the Other Dimension?" he asked.

"Huh? …Sure, if it pays well." My jaw dropped when I heard how much I'd get. They sent an advance to my sister's bank account. I checked that the deposit had gone through, then nodded again.

What follows is the explanation I received after we moved to another room.

The Other Dimension was split into three continents. As they were all lined up next to one another, they were called the Left, Middle, and Right Continents. The military battalion of years past had been sent to the Left Continent. I would be sent to the Right. There, I'd find a dungeon called the Tower of Legions, and deep within that, the fifty-sixth floor. My job description: "Acquire the resource found there within one year."

I didn't really understand the technical details, but apparently if you used that material as a catalyst on a spaceship, you could make some black hole thingamajig-type engine with incredible energy output… In any case, it was supposed to be insanely crazy. I wondered how they knew that to begin with but assumed it was none of my business to ask as someone at the very bottom of the ladder. And I got the feeling he wouldn't answer even if I did.

Six professionals and three AI units were originally supposed to be sent off on this mission, but one of the pros got into an accident at the last minute and wasn't able to make it. I was their replacement. Given the top secret nature of the plans, they evidently hadn't been able to prepare any understudies. I had a ton of questions, but a job was a job. Money was money. *Don't worry, be happy*, I told myself.

Honestly, I was more concerned about having to spend a whole year with total strangers. Group projects had never really been my thing. I was seriously nervous.

"Oh, I almost forgot. I brought this," I said, reaching for my résumé, but—

"No, that's quite all right. We've already investigated your background."

"Oh, I see." So my sister's hard work making this forged document had been for nothing.

"By the way, Mr. Interviewer, when do we leave?"

"In two hours."

"Seriously?!"

"Seriously." I had no idea how to respond to this matter-of-fact declaration. All the plans floating around in my mind disappeared. I needed to do one thing before anything else.

"I have to call my sister! Excuse me!"

"That's fine, but we'll be listening in on you."

"Go ahead, I guess?!"

Knowing it was totally pointless to leave the room, I stepped out into the hall for privacy and called my sister. The phone rang twice before she picked up.

"It's me," she said.

"Hey there, Yukikazzie."

"Gross. Don't call me that."

"Sorry, Yukikazzie. I'm really sorry. Your big brother's landed himself a job."

"You're such a creep. Go jump off a bridge. Congrats on the job. That happened pretty fast—it's a normal company, right?"

"Yeah, sure. So anyway, I'm heading off on an assignment in, like, two hours and won't be able to get in touch for about a year. But don't you worry about me."

"You idiot, it's straight-up exploitative!"

"The pay is good. I even got an advance."

"Do they even give you anything resembling social security, pension, or health insurance?!"

The door opened with a *clack* behind me, and the interviewer popped his head out into the hall.

"We provide an excellent benefits package," he explained. "If for any reason you are unable to return, we will compensate your sister with a fee for her discretion and additional remuneration for emotional damages. Both of these are also handsome sums."

"He said I get an excellent benefits package. It'll be fine."

"Yeah, I heard him! This is all super shady! Can you put him on the line?!"

"That I must refuse. Speaking with employees' families never leads to anything but problems," added the interviewer, who then retreated into the room.

"It's all right. It might be a bit dangerous, but I'll come home no matter what. Don't worry," I reassured her.

"Every time you say that, I get even more worried."

"Hmm, but the money's good."

"Con men always wave around a thick wad of cash. It's the oldest trick in the book."

"You're so smart, Yukikazzie."

"You're just a total dumbass!" She was entirely right.

"It's too detailed to be a scam. And they don't have anything to gain out of tricking me."

"*I've said this a million times, but you really don't have to worry about my leg. The doctor said once I get used to the prosthetic, I might even run faster than I could before.*"

"Yeah, I bet you could."

Even so, I still wanted to do this for her, as her older brother. I felt bad for dragging her into my own issues, but I'd rather regret trying than regret not doing anything at all. And so I had no choice but to jump at any opportunity that came my way, no matter how suspect. That's just the kind of foolish man I was.

"Sorry. But I promise I'll come home, so don't worry."

"*Ugh! You're so stupid! I should've known you wouldn't listen to a word I said! Drop dead! I hope you live, crawl through hell, and come back home, you idiot!*"

Click. She lost it, and I lost her. In so many ways.

The door to the room opened.

"Have you finished?" the interviewer asked.

"Yes, I'm done."

"The clock is ticking. Let's move on to a lecture on the other realm and get you suited up."

I changed into the combat fatigues they had laid out for me and put a ceramic-plate body-armor vest on over them. The vest weighed very little but had various modular pouches to carry a mini arsenal of backup ammo for all the guns I'd use. They also gave me a pair of lightweight but sturdy metal-reinforced boots. As for guns, they'd prepared an AK-47 equipped with the latest features but disguised to look virtually indistinguishable from a 1953 model, as well as an M1911 Colt Government pistol fashioned in the same way. I removed the magazine from the AK-47, slid back the charging handle to check for debris in the chamber, then pulled the trigger.

Not bad. It'll do, as long as it shoots out bullets when I need it to.

I replaced the magazine and repeated the procedure on the pistol. All clear. I sheathed my personal karambit in a sleeve on my arm, hung a well-worn Japanese-style woodsman's hatchet from my belt, and threw on the aramid fiber poncho, which they gave me to hide my equipment, over everything for the finishing touch.

"Well, you certainly look the part now," noted the interviewer.

"Thanks." *No need to butter me up.*

After that, he spent every second we had left cramming summaries about the Other Dimension into my brain. He told me about the different races, religions, and influential powers, about the economy, cultures and civilizations, expected weather forecasts, and contagious diseases, and of course the dungeon, its rough history, its structure, the enemies lurking within, and the surrounding areas. And then, at the very end, he added one final point:

All of this data dated back half a century, and they could not confirm whether it was still relevant nor provide any details on the current situation.

We moved on to yet another room, this one wide open and bright. An ostentatious piece of equipment stood in the center of the space. Shaped like a pedestal, it looked like an altar where you'd present offerings to the gods. A bunch of people dressed in workman's clothes bustled around it in a great hurry.

The five professional explorers stood waiting before me. There were four men and one woman. They were just casually milling about, but they never let down their guard for an instant. Though they looked genial and relaxed, I could've sworn I saw something glimmer deep in their eyes—that indescribable aura gained after mastering the art of this particular craft. Every single one of them had it in droves.

Do they even need me here?

"Mr. President, is this our last squad member?" asked a man with a scarred face. He gave me serious team leader vibes.

"Yes, though we were pressed for time, so I cannot guarantee he will meet your collective levels of proficiency. I'd say he's thirty percent of what you're looking for."

"I'll take it. Better than someone in the red."

Wait, the interviewer was the president?

"You're the Firm's president?" I'd pegged him as some drab middle-management type.

"Well, my business is at stake here. This isn't a task I can delegate so easily. That said, if this succeeds, we'll make trillions. But if it fails, everybody working here, as well as in the upper floors of the building and their families—not to mention our affiliated partners and contractors—will lose their livelihoods. That's all. So let's just take it easy."

How exactly am I supposed to do that?

"I'm surprised you went with someone like me," I admitted.

"I've invested a tremendous amount of money into this, so I would hate to waste a single person's slot. The rule of thumb I've settled on over the years is this: The sweeter the deal, the easier it goes through. Though your name is what did it for me. It's got a lucky ring to it."

"That sounds more than a little reckless." *Is this actually going to be okay?*

"Don't sweat it, kid. The president's always like that," explained the scarred man. "At the same time, he's the kind of guy who has what it takes to build such a huge operation and get an army of people working for him. You should take pride in the fact that he chose you, so get it together."

I appreciated the encouraging words from our team leader—until the great president in question muttered, "He wasn't actually my first choice, but…"

"Dude." *I heard all of that, you know.*

"It's time!" yelled one of the elderly workmen near the pedestal.

"We will now begin to open the portal! First, we'll keep it open for six seconds and throw in the containers and machina units! Live humans will go in after! We'll shut the portal for twelve seconds, then open it again for seven. All of you need to jump in then! You only get one shot! Stumble and miss your chance and it's all over!"

A crane had placed the containers in a line on top of a rail installed before the portal. They carried clothes, provisions, medical supplies, and a wide variety of other vital resources meant to keep us alive. The three cylindrical AI robots came after, and we humans stood behind them. I brought up the rear.

"Opening!" yelled the man.

A brilliant light exploded and converged around the altar; a portal appeared atop the platform in the center of the light.

"Push! PUUUSH!" The workers pushed and slid the containers down the rail. They disappeared through the portal, which swallowed them all without a hint of resistance. I got the feeling I'd seen something similar in a movie a long time ago. The AI units followed shortly after. The techs worked so quickly that they finished shipping everything off with a second to spare. I did wonder if it wouldn't have been more efficient to use some kind of automated mechanism, but it was very true to the Japanese spirit to rely on human hands for the most pivotal tasks.

Next was our turn.

I'd never done it myself, but I imagined this was what it must feel like to go skydiving. I felt my heart start racing. My legs stiffened from nerves, so I punched them a few times. It wouldn't be close to funny if I tripped from trembling too much.

"So, the president mentioned he chose you for your name. Out of curiosity, what is it?" the woman in front of me asked nonchalantly.

"My name is Souya."

"Oh, as in 'Valley of the Gods'? That does sounds auspicious."

You wouldn't know it by the shitty life I've led.

"Opening! Run! RUN!" the same elderly man shouted, and we all broke into a sprint. Once again, a blinding light exploded, converged, and then revealed a portal. There was no going back now. The first man jumped into the ring of light, then the second. Then the third disappeared in his wake. I followed after them.

That's when time began to flow in slow motion for some reason, like it does in moments of crisis. The scenery around me crawled by. I saw the fourth person dissolve into the light, saw the woman's short hair bounce as she ran. Then she, too, was gone. I started sweating. A violent dread came over me. I couldn't even begin to describe the sense of impending danger.

This is definitely bad.

The worst part about it was that the portal now gleamed right before me. I dived in, and a torrent of light blinded me. I didn't get a sense of entering or leaving anything, which was the scariest part. I cracked open my eyes but found there was nothing to see— nothing but a vast, empty void.

For a split second, it felt like I was floating. But of course, I was actually in free fall, the wind wrapping close around my body. Though, it was so dark that I couldn't be sure if I was actually falling down; I could've just as easily been getting sucked up toward the ceiling. Either way, I was going so fast that my balls retracted up against me. Through the *whoosh* of the wind rushing past my ears, I heard myself let out a short yelp.

I'm definitely gonna die. I'll get squashed like a tomato—no, a pancake. Forgive me, dear little sister. Your big brother's going out with a pathetic little splat.

Driven by something like instinct, I curled up into a fetal

position. There was so much going on, but damn, that wind was so freaking loud. My lips got all crusty. At least it wasn't cold.

"Give me a break."

The fall took forever. I actually got kind of used to it. Leave it to humans to find ways to get bored, even in the moments before they die. I turned on my wristwatch light and shined it around. It landed on nothing but dark obscurity, except I did get the feeling I saw something squirming off in the distance.

Is that a whale?

Whatever it was loomed large enough to draw the connection in my mind. It seemed to be moving slowly, but that was just a trick of the huge size difference between us and the darkness. It was a cluster of tentacles; its skin shone pallid against the light of my wristwatch. The tentacles opened up like a flower in bloom and revealed what lay at their core—a figure that looked just barely human. That was all I could take in.

As if it were the most obvious move, I screamed so loud I thought the effort would crush my throat. This thing, more terrifying than death itself, a gargantuan monstrosity, started closing in on me. I still had no name for it, but I squeezed my eyes shut and prayed, "Please, God." Then—

—I sensed sunlight on my skin. I opened my eyes to find blue sky. I could smell grass and felt the ground meet my back. Was it a dream? No, way too nightmarish for that. And the three faint moonlike orbs in the sky were too real to be a mere dream. Counting my racing pulse, I tried to pull myself out of this state of shock. I took a deep breath of clear, pure air. Once I confirmed that I was in no pain and had sustained no injuries, I got to my feet.

A grassy meadow billowed under the gentle strokes of the wind. I could see a small river and a forest off in the distance. In the opposite direction, I found the dungeon I was after. Even modern architectural technologies could never hope to replicate a building that enormous.

There were no two ways about it. I had made it to the Other Dimension.

Just that morning, I had been in Japan, and now I'd crossed over through dimensions into another realm. What a busy day. If I'd had only a bit more time, I probably would've given more than a passing thought to the fact that I was now standing in an entirely new world.

Okay, enough thinking.

The containers and AI units had scattered haphazardly all around me. Free from any obstructions, the spot where I stood provided good visibility, but there was nothing else there except for what I saw on my first glance around. A soft breeze ran over the grassland. It had all the makings of a beautiful spring day.

I took a second to chew on and then swallow the inescapable truth.

Somehow, I was all alone.

CHAPTER 1
No Otherworlders Allowed in the Dungeon

(1ST DAY)

Mr. Souya, you're using that stake all wrong. And you should line up the tent posts more evenly—and neatly. See? It's all crooked. Take that one about five centimeters to the right. Also, please separate the container with ammunition from the one with food and medical supplies. Is that north? Or south? Kindly reset the gyroscope, please. If you discover any physical damage on me, please call my manufacturer at—"

"Shut up, you piece of junk!"

I'd found a nice little river, so I'd repacked all the supplies into the unbroken containers and spent four hours lugging them over to it. I couldn't exactly set up camp in the middle of an exposed field. Every moment brought a new problem. Half of the containers had literally been cut in half, as if someone had taken a water blade and sliced them straight down the middle. Whatever they'd carried had also disappeared somewhere.

Thankfully, there were still plenty of munitions left; the food and medicinal supplies had noticeably diminished, but there had originally been enough packed in there for six people to make it through a full year. Now that it was just for me, I'd have some left over. My biggest problem, though, was this artificial unintelligence.

All three of the machina units had been damaged. It looked like someone had gouged out holes all over their cylindrical tanks with a spoon. Only one of them had made it through with their most important part, the aqueous cerebrum, intact. They were simple to service, though, so it hadn't been too hard to salvage usable parts from among their fallen comrades to bring one back to functionality, even for a complete amateur like me.

But this one has to be still broken somewhere, right?

"Mr. Souya, I'm hungry."

"Huh?"

The battery-signal light bulb at the top of the robot's tank started blinking.

"I'm hungry."

"Wait, what do you even eat?" I asked.

"Please fill this designated cup with three hundred milliliters of water mixed with three percent sugar," she instructed.

Machina's torso opened up; her multifunctional arm pulled out the cup inside and handed it to me. As annoying as she was, this machine was also my lifeline. I found the sugar among the food provisions and threw together some simple syrup. Good thing I'd already gotten a potful of water from the river and boiled it. I poured some now lukewarm water into the cup, shook in a bit of sugar, mixed it up with my finger, and handed the cup back to Machina. She unfurled a straw and slurped up the sugar water. A happy face meaning *Yum!* flashed on the monitor installed in the top portion of her tank.

"Mr. Souya."

"Hmm?"

"I'm hungry."

"Huh?!" *It can't be*, I thought as I took the lid off the robot and checked her most vital part, the aqueous cerebrum. What looked at first glance like a simple globe filled with plain water was actually a device teeming with specially developed neurons almost on par with those at work in a human brain. Humanity had produced more of these gizmos than it knew what to do with. They cycled through periods of widespread popularity and decline every decade or so, leading some to argue they would soon fall entirely out of use. Still, even after several rounds of restrictions limiting their functions, these household appliances had wormed their way deep into the hearts of modern society. *They say AI is man's best friend, second only to dogs.*

And my new best friend's heart......was cracked and leaking fluids.

"Aaaaah! Duct tape! Where's the duct tape?! Machina?!"

"It is in the yellow-striped container within compartment A-3. I'm hungry."

Before anything else, I threw some more sugar in the pot of water and handed it to Machina. I kicked the yellow-striped container over onto its side and tore through it for the duct tape.

"Found it!"

I grabbed a towel as well and wiped down the glass globe, then stuck some tape over the leaky cracks. These triage measures out of the way, I found the machina unit's repair manual and flipped to the section on their aqueous brains.

There was almost nothing to read.

"Be careful not to touch the wires directly. Protect the surface with a bonding material, tape, or a waterproof bag. If any functional damage arises, please call the manufacturer's customer support center at—"

The end.

I rummaged around for superglue, peeled off the duct tape for a second, and slathered the glue over the cracks in Machina's brain. Then I taped it up once more, wound some plastic wrap around the whole globe, and plastered liquid hardener over everything.

That should do it. Please let that be enough.

"Mmm, yummy!" Machina said, a satisfied look on her screen after draining the pot of syrup. I thumbed through the manual and began giving her an oral command.

"AIJ006 Machina Odd-Eye V166S6 Multiple Personality Control Model: Special Mission Unit Three, Code 330, begin self-evaluation," I ordered.

"Error. Incorrect model number," she retorted.

"Machina, tell me your model number."

"This unit does not have the capacity to determine its own model number."

"Just hurry up and run a check on yourself!"

"Roger," replied Machina, who then began humming as Tetris-like puzzle pieces appeared on her screen.

That task out of the way, I sighed. Then a violent wave of anxiety came over me.

She's a mess. You're telling me the sidekick who holds my life in her hands is being kept alive by some superglue and duct tape? Nope. This has to be some sick joke.

"Self-evaluation complete. No errors detected," reported Machina. But broken appliances never really could tell when they were busted, could they? I pretty much gave up hope on her then and there. Worst-case scenario, I'd go alone.

"*Haah,*" I sighed. Might as well make something to eat. A full stomach would probably help me take my mind off all this.

I got to cooking in the simple kitchen made of nothing but the bit of firewood I'd gathered. I scooped up some more water from the river and set it over the fire again. Earlier, I'd run it through a water-testing kit; it was safe to drink once boiled.

I dropped a few dried sardines in the pot to make a stock, then turned off the heat just before it started bubbling. With the sardines still inside, I stirred in a bit of miso until it dissolved. Next, I very nervously nibbled the ends of some seaweed-like plant I'd found growing in the river. It had a slightly bitter and peppery taste. The tip of my tongue didn't get numb, so I figured it was probably safe to eat. I cut it up with a pair of scissors and added it to the pot.

My Other Dimensional Seaweed Miso Soup was complete.

"Thank you for the meal," I said, bringing my hands together, then took a sip of the soup. Not bad. It was loads tastier than the Chinese food drowning in oil that I'd had once before in the Middle East and a hundred times better than a meal of carrion coated with spices, random-ass pickled vegetables, or the flour and water concoctions I used to throw together and fry when I was totally broke. The aroma of the fermented miso calmed my nerves until I felt like myself again.

"Activating secondary personality, Wide Area Combat Program Isolla. Requesting cooperation from project participant," announced Machina out of nowhere. I put my chopsticks down and turned my attention toward her.

"Please provide a report on the human casualties incurred at time of entry through interdimensional portal."

"Whatever happened to the others remains unclear. I walked five kilometers in all four directions from the landing point but found no trace of them."

"Input received. Commencing analysis of available resources. Activating sonar beacon. Scanning labels.

Weapons container damage recorded: sixty percent of contents lost. Medical supplies container damage recorded: seventy percent of contents lost. Nutritional provisions container, fifty percent of contents lost. Sufficient resources remain to support a one-person squad for one year."

"I have a question. If I requested a rescue party, would anyone be able to reach me?" I asked, knowing it was probably futile.

"Negative. Seven thousand nine hundred and twenty hours must pass before the portal can be reopened."

"Thought so." They wouldn't have needed to squeeze in someone like me on the mission if they could open it willy-nilly.

"Releasing bug drones within a twenty-kilometer radius to chart a map of the premises and town adjacent to the dungeon." Isolla unleashed a swarm of mosquito-like drones. Even though I knew they were fake, the sight gave me goose bumps.

"Look for the other squad members while you're at it," I added. *If they're alive, that is.*

"Request denied. There are no recorded precedents of finding persons lost during portal entry. If this is the only functioning machina unit, we cannot afford to expend those resources."

"You mean they're dead?"

"The possibility is exceedingly likely. Squad Member Souya, allow me to confirm some items with you."

"Go ahead."

"Given current resources and squad member capabilities, this mission has a point two percent probability of success. This figure represents only a momentary snapshot of the current situation and is subject to change based on future developments. Under Article Twenty-Four of the Artificial Intelligence Act, all resources embedded within machina units can be diverted toward the rescue, protection, and preservation of human life. Squad Member Souya, do you wish to abandon the current project?"

"No, we'll continue." I'd come all this way. I would do what I had to do. Giving up without trying anything on the assumption it wouldn't work would in itself be the most pointless move.

"Understood. Terminating supplementary personality. Reverting to main system. Good luck."

"Thanks."

Then, just as I was thinking about reheating the now lukewarm miso in my hands—

"La, la, la, laaa! ♪ Mr. Souya."

"Don't tell me you're hungry again," I moaned.

Having made her cheerful reappearance, Machina chirped, "You have a visitor."

"Huh? Yeah?"

I heard a splash. Sensing someone standing behind me, I turned around. There stood the first resident of this foreign realm I'd ever met, fresh out of the river.

"Huh, so you hail from another world, you say?" asked the—fish?— as he took a sip of miso soup. My eyeballed estimate put him at around 70 percent human, 30 percent fish, with real gills in the spot where they'd land on humans. He had surprisingly lovely round eyes and ears that seamlessly turned into fins. A seaweed grass skirt hung around his waist over the blue-tinted scales covering his body, and a necklace made of seashells and coral jangled as it hung from his neck. The sharp harpoon he'd brought lay on the ground next to the camping chair where he sat.

"Oh, shall I warm up your soup?" I offered. "I'll bet it's gotten cold."

"My race doesn't handle heat very well. Even this is almost scalding." He gracefully scooped up the soup spoonful by spoonful. His movements had a certain elegance about them. Maybe he'd come from a well-to-do merfolk family?

Wait, hang on, I thought. I'd gotten so blown over by the impact he'd made as the first Other Dimensional resident I encountered that I'd overlooked something fundamental.

"Excuse me... How is it that we're able to understand each other?" I asked. I couldn't imagine merfolk used Japanese in everyday life.

"Well, I mean, I am a priest, you know," he replied. "I may come from the depths, but even I've got the Babelian Benediction, see."

Babel, as in the tower in the Bible?

"What exactly is that?"

"I guess a stranger to this world wouldn't know, would ya? Basically, my god asked another god many levels higher up the ladder for the ability to communicate with other races. As long as your conversation partner is sentient and uses some kind of spoken language, the Babelian Benediction helps us understand one another," he explained.

So it translates your thoughts in real time with no lag? And this fluently? Whoa, that's crazy.

"Is this something everybody here has?"

"It's not rare, by any means. Pretty much anybody in covenant with a half-decent god can get it."

"Yes!" I saw my first glimmer of hope. If I could communicate, then I could negotiate. That meant I could hire a team and explore the dungeon!

"So are you after that, too?"

The merman pointed a razor-sharp, nail-tipped finger toward the dungeon in the distance.

"Yes, in a sense. Is that something Otherworlders are also allowed to do?"

"I don't know much about life on land, but they shouldn't turn you away if all you're trying to do is explore. The spire the Legion Gods abandoned belongs to no one," he replied.

Oh, so that's why it's called the Tower of Legions.

"Ngh," he grunted.

"?"

The merman handed me the necklace of strung coral. "This is for you, as thanks for showing a servant of our Lord Ghrisnas your hospitality. Take it. If you don't, we'll be enemies next time we meet."

"I gladly accept your generous gift. Thank you very much," I responded, gratefully taking it from him and immediately hanging it around my neck. Figuring this probably required some kind of gift in return, I rummaged around the containers and found a pair of sunglasses.

"I hope you'll accept these in return," I offered.

"What's that?"

I modeled them for him. "They protect your eyes from the sun."

"But you can't see in front of you, can you?" he asked doubtfully.

"It's dark, but you can still see." I handed him the glasses, and he tried them on.

"Hoh-hohh." He turned his head, looking all around. "Hoh-hohh." Talk about a delightfully heartwarming scene. "Ah, now I've done it. My grandkids won't let me hear the end of it if I don't get back soon. I'll take my leave for today." He put down his empty bowl and picked up his harpoon.

"How long will you stay here?" he asked.

"One year, at the most," I replied. "Was this by any chance somewhere I shouldn't have set up camp?"

"Not if you'll only be here a year," he said, then added, "You're the first lander I've ever met who not only didn't scream when he saw one of us but even went so far as to invite us to a meal. I am Ghettbad of Maudubaffle."

That second part is probably where he's from, I assumed and responded in kind.

"I am Souya of Japan."

"All right, Souya of Japan. Our land runs out for six stalts from the river. After that, you're in Kingdom of Remlia territory. That Heuress Forest over there is elven domain. You heims had best not step foot there right now, or you'll be killed on the spot," he warned.

"I appreciate the advice."

"Right then, until next time." Ghett jumped into the river and disappeared beneath its depths with alarming speed.

"This mission currently has a point six percent probability of success."

"Inched up a bit, huh?" This was shaping up to be an auspicious meeting.

I slid on a backpack filled with a first-aid kit and a tool set, rechecked my guns, and attached a sling I'd found in the container to my AK-47. Then I grabbed four spare cartridges of ammo for each gun, made sure the containers were locked, threw a sheet over Machina, and hid her behind a very simple disguise.

"What's the status on that area map?" I asked Machina, activating her through a remote eyeglasses device after I put them on.

"A comprehensive progress status remains unclear as we cannot identify if there are any underground structures in the city. I can, however, display real-time surveillance data over a bird's-eye-view map of the aboveground terrain."

"Good enough. Set a drone or two to fly around me, too."

"Understood."

Now, how about we go check out that dungeon?

Constructed from stones, the city had an antiquated feel. A fortified wall surrounding it also gave it the appearance of a fortress.

Entering through the large open gates, I discovered a world bursting with activity. Beings of all sorts of races and horses drawing heavily laden carts went to-and-fro along the cobblestoned main street. Street vendors shouted over one another, blacksmiths pounded away at their steel, and alluring beastmaids called out enticingly to coax customers into their stores of employment. Countless resplendent weapons lay out in rows under the eaves of the shops lining the road. Would adventurers be the ones to stop and examine them?

Gorgeous women of fantastical species stole my attention. One long-legged, beautiful elf had porcelain-white skin and hair that seemed to be made of golden dust. Another woman unblushingly displaying a generous helping of skin and scales had fiery-red locks and a matching tail. Curly horns and fluffy wool sprouted from the body of a full-figured lady who walked with a staff taller than she was. I also spotted a female knight who, like one I'd seen before in a video game, was covered head to toe in a full suit of armor. The sight of her moved me. I would have jumped at the chance to team up with her.

An aromatic blend of foreign spices wafted my way along with medicinal smells that assailed my nostrils and the intoxicating perfumes of passersby. I heard the vividly explosive sounds of clanging steel and roaring flames, noticed the pockets of stillness formed in spite of this crushing river of people, and felt the danger lurking down the narrow alleys I peeked into.

And yet, I didn't experience the sense of alienation a foreigner usually gets in an unfamiliar country. Everywhere I looked, my eyes landed on incredible diversity: an abundance of color, monsters of all stripes and shapes, and chaotic scenes different from anything I'd ever seen before. All the people around me were too far beyond outlandish to process, but they walked through the street as if nothing could be more normal.

I had worried I might stand out, though I shouldn't have bothered. Compared to the people walking around with multicolored wings sprouting out of their backs or the three-eyed beastfolk I'd passed, a lone Japanese man looked plain, so very plain. I got the feeling I'd fit in just as well if I'd come wearing a full-blown kimono, my hair in a topknot, a katana at my side.

The small river Ghett had vanished into flowed through the city. The town appeared to have other springs as well, and Machina's survey showed that a simple water and sewage system had been set in place. Establishments resembling bathhouses dotted the area. Could that mean the town also boasted bountiful supplies of combustible resources?

The path to the dungeon was a straight shot down the road. I didn't even need to use the location-tracking feature on my device to find it. My destination was way too huge to ever miss. After walking about twenty minutes, I finally stood before it.

Yep, that's pretty damn big.

Getting closer only drove home how enormous it was. According to Machina's structural calculations, it was so tall that no currently available materials would be able to replicate even just the portion visible aboveground. And strangely enough, though most towers got thinner the higher up they went, this one flipped that on its head. It started off wide at the top and narrowed the farther down it went. I was supposed to explore that narrow section, the part sticking into the ground. Exactly how long was it? I couldn't even begin to imagine.

It looked to be made of something like an elephant's tusk. I decided to take a sample just in case. As a last resort, I figured I could plan to blast a hole in it with some TNT and make my way down, but I'd need to verify whether the material was something I could blow up in the first place.

I followed the flow of people and almost immediately found the entrance. I say "entrance," but it was basically a cavity that something had busted open. The smell of alcohol and grilled meat floated all around me once I stepped inside, emanating from a large pub set up near the opening. The sun still shone high in the sky, but that didn't stop some of the patrons from already being drunk off their asses. People like that were universal, I guess. Paper slips that I took to be job postings covered a great big billboard. Most surprisingly, a line of portals stood in the back of the cavernous space. I watched as adventurers popped in and out of them.

"The fields are stabilized. Fascinating." I jumped at Machina's voice coming through the receiver.

"I guess they invented those portals?" I'd known this ahead of time, but this place was full of other things I didn't know about.

My eyes landed on a reception-like area of the hall. A couple of clerical-type ladies attended to several explorers. There were quite a few counters, so I wasn't sure where to line up.

"Machina, can you analyze the writing here?" I asked.

"Analysis in progress. It will most certainly be quicker if you pose your query to a local inhabitant," she suggested.

"Okay." Good point. Just then, I saw a woman carrying a bundle of documents and decided to ask her for help. "Excuse me, this is my first time here. Which line should I use?"

"Welcome. You'll find new adventurer registration and screening for permits to explore the dungeon at the far-right counter," the cat-eared young lady explained with a dazzling smile. Luckily, nobody waited ahead of me in line, so I took a seat at the counter. Across from me stood a woman with two horns protruding from her head and a face completely devoid of emotion. She had a slender frame and lovely silver hair.

"......Yes?" she asked in a bitterly cold tone.

"Uh, I'd like to explore that dungeon. I heard I could take care of the paperwork for that here." Had I gotten the wrong counter?

"I see. You should have started with that."

"I'm sorry." What was with this intimidating presence? I felt like I was dealing with a violent beast.

"In that case, please fill out the required forms." She handed me some papers resembling lambskin and an inked pen.

"......"

I couldn't read it. I didn't even know what it was asking for.

"I-I'm sorry. I don't know how to read or write in this language."

"I see. You should have told me sooner. I'll fill it in for you, so allow me to ask you a few questions."

"Thank you. I'm sorry."

"It's my job." She spun the papers around to face her. "Are you registered with any other Adventurers Guild?"

"No."

"State your name and place of origin."

"My name is Souya—of Japan."

"Japan? I haven't heard of it before. Is it out on the Left Continent?"

"Even farther out than that—it's in another dimension," I blurted out, then immediately regretted it.

Shit. Should I have kept that a secret? This is a different continent for sure, but the last batch of humans who came did absolutely nothing to earn a good rep there. Are they gonna kick me out? Argh, this is such a basic thing to mess up. Our whole mission here was supposed to be pretty covert, wasn't it?

Just then, Machina whispered in my ear, "It's merely a paper form. If we determine the situation is dangerous, I'll sneak a drone in and revise the entry or burn the evidence. You would have risked garnering suspicion had you responded with a string of flimsy lies. Answering honestly was the prudent choice."

Gotcha.

"Oh, you're an Otherworlder? Haven't seen many of your kind recently," the receptionist noted before adding the information to my form without any real follow-up. "For what purpose do you intend to explore the dungeon?"

"Monetary gain."

"I see, monetary gain. You should be aware of one important rule of this dungeon. If explorers acquire takings worth more than fifty gold pieces in a single expedition, they are required to pay a one percent tax on the total value to the Kingdom of Remlia," she explained. "Payment is accepted in coins, paper bills printed by the Central Continental Trade Group, or even in raw materials from the dungeon. You must submit your tax seven days from the date a trade group appraises the value of your harvest. Should we find you misrepresented the value of your resources or fail to submit your payment within the allotted time, we will confiscate all of the equipment you own. I suggest you don't do anything stupid if you do not wish to end up stripped naked at the bottom of the sewer."

"Yes, ma'am."

Scary as hell.

"Do you suffer from any physical irregularities, mental irregularities, or magical afflictions? Have any members of your family or lineage ever been cursed? Have any close relatives passed away due to infectious disease?"

"No." My good health was one of my only redeeming qualities.

"Do you hold animosity or hatred toward any particular species, religion, or nationality? Additionally, have you ever been the target of such discrimination?"

"No." I answered quickly, but then the thought of the battalion dispatched here crossed my mind. People tended to lump other people from the same unfamiliar culture all together. I could shout myself sore explaining I had nothing to do with them, but there was a chance nobody would listen.

"Is there a problem?" She'd seen right through me.

"I just realized there might possibly be some people who have it out for me, maybe."

The receptionist trained her sharp eyes on me. "I won't put anything down if it's not a clear threat. You probably have nothing to worry about. No one, under any circumstances, can delve down into the dungeon alone. But the moment you forge partnerships, you also create enemies. Win honor and you will also naturally earn resentment and jealousy. What matters is whether or not you have the determination to not let that crush you."

"Then it should be okay."

I mean, it's not like I've got anywhere else to run. I'll turn what-ever shade they throw at me into fuel to keep going.

"Let's continue. What was your previous occupation?"

"Umm…" How could I explain it in terms that made sense here? I guess a temp agency was kind of like—

"A mercenary, basically." It wasn't exactly right, but it wasn't far off.

"Do you belong to any religion?"

Is my family in the Jodo Shinshu sect? Oh, but I am Japanese after all, so more broadly I can just say—

"Yes, Shinto."

"Shintoe?" she repeated, sounding it out. "Don't know it. Could you give me a brief overview?"

"It's a polytheistic religion that's very accepting of gods from other religions. We don't follow any specific commandments, but we do appreciate nature and all forms of life, and we make sure to give special thanks for our food, particularly during meals. We strive to live as upstanding people and bring shame upon ourselves if we stray from that path. It's kind of a loose compilation of all these values and, like, Japanese sensibilities? It's kinda just vague, you know?" The more I spoke, the less I followed what I was saying. Did this even count as a religion?

"Polytheistic, doesn't mess with other religions. No command-ments. Meals are savored. A set of intuitive values unique to the Japanese race, correct?" *Basically, in a nutshell.* "Next, please tell me the name of the god with whom you have consecrated your covenant," she continued.

"Huh?"

"I mean the god you've made your contract with." *But I wasn't ever baptized.* "A god from our world would be best, but we can also work with gods from other dimensions," she explained. "It's been done before."

"It's just, I don't have one. A covenant." Was that something we even had the chance to do in modern-day Japan? I had no clue.

"I see."

"Is that bad or something?"

Her expression remained completely impassive. "It is rather rare. However, there are some people who choose to break off their consecrated covenants of their own volition and others who fall out of favor with their gods and have the contracts severed that way. Still others reject the idea of a divine blessing from the start. If you're asking whether not having one is a problem, then not really. There are plenty of more miserable and pitiful souls out there."

"Really? That's good to hear." I breathed a sigh of relief.

"The only issue is that you cannot enter the dungeon."

Game over.

No matter how depressed you felt, how desperate you might become, or how much you might want to break down and cry, hunger waited for no one. But as long as you found yourself in a social structure such as a town, you wouldn't have too much trouble filling your grumbling stomach. If you had money, that is.

If I hadn't had any money on me, I think I might've seriously lost all hope.

I followed the map the receptionist gave me until I reached the coin dealer. The shop stood far removed from the main street, whose clangor echoed in the distance. I opened the steel door to the store, most likely installed to prevent theft, and was greeted by a youngish shopkeeper and his ingratiating salesman's smile.

"Welcome. What might we help you with today?" His voice rang much brighter than the dim room in which we stood.

Weighing scales of varying sizes were arranged all around in an almost Middle Eastern design. A brawny, bodyguard-type man wielding a large sword stood next to the shopkeeper at the counter. As soon as I entered the store, the man who had been lurking in the shadows by the entrance positioned himself behind me.

Guess it's better safe than sorry when you're dealing dangerous sums of cash.

"I'd like to change these into the local currency," I announced, placing gold bars on the counter. They'd been packed in a container to help with garnering initial funds. Only three damaged bars and half of a whole one had made it.

"One moment, please." The shopkeeper wiped the bars down with a cloth and ran his eyes along every inch of them from several angles. "Sir, it appears the stamps on these have been filed down."

"They slipped and fell from my hands. It was an accident."

"Ha-ha-ha, well, let's leave it at that," replied the shopkeeper with a pointed grin. He placed the bars on one half of a scale, then filled bags on the opposite half with sand. Once they balanced out, he moved the bags to another scale and weighed these against round pieces of metal. "It amounts to forty gold and eight silver pieces," he announced. "That's a fair appraisal based on the rigorous standards of the Zavah Night Owl Trade Group. Would you like to have these evaluated at another location as well?" That came to five gold pieces more than Machina's estimate.

"No, that's fine. I'd also like to break some of that into smaller pieces if you could."

"Of course, not a problem."

Unless there had been some extreme fluctuations in the market, ten copper pieces should have been worth one silver, and ten silver pieces worth one gold piece. "I'll take fifty pieces of copper and silver."

"If I may, we also handle Mythlanic gold," suggested the shopkeeper.

"Myth-what?" I repeated, not really understanding what he'd said.

"Are you perhaps from a different continent?" he asked.

"No, I'm from another dimension."

I'd let the cat out of the bag yet again.

"I see. No wonder. I had thought the fabric of your cloak looked rather unfamiliar," he remarked, his eyes fixed on my poncho.

"Ha-ha-ha." I laughed it off and forced a polite smile.

"My apologies. Mythlanic gold pieces were once used as common currency among the three countries that controlled this region at the time. These historical coins are enriched with magic, albeit trace amounts. We no longer possess the technology to manufacture them. They're rare and valuable. The current rate is twenty gold for one piece."

"No thanks, I'll pass." Stocks and futures trading were a bit much for me.

"Very well. Your coins, sir." The shopkeeper took three leather bags from a worker in the back of the shop. "Fifty copper, fifty-three silver, and thirty-five gold pieces, if you would please confirm."

"Thank you." Tedious as it was, I got to work lining up the coins in rows of ten to double-check.

"Are we in agreement?" he asked.

"All in order." It was all there.

"Our fee comes to one silver piece." I took two silver from the leather bag and placed them on the counter.

"Thank you kindly. Our trade group offers all manner of wares essential for the prepared adventurer. I do hope you'll have a look around our flagship store down the main street from the First Gate."

"How did you know I was an adventurer?" I asked.

"This is an adventurer's town; nobody but adventurers and those who seek their fortune serving them live here," he replied.

There was at least one of those men right here, shriveling before me, very much not in the dungeon. I put a few coins in my pockets and the rest in my backpack.

"I pray you'll forgive another impertinent question, sir," began the shopkeeper as I fixed the straps on my shoulders, "but is that perchance a gun?"

"......" It'd been one surprise after another since I came here, but this made me break out in a cold sweat. Nobody had warned me about this. Did people here understand the value of a gun?

"Uhhh, well," I hemmed. It would've been easy to refuse to answer outright, but information was a thousand times more valuable here. I chose my next words carefully. "You surprised me. You have them in this country, too?"

"Yes, we have dwarf-crafted models, most recently used to great effect not long ago in the war against the elves." I grimaced at the word *war*. *Please don't let any more of those break out while I'm here.*

"If you don't mind, could you show me one of the models used in these parts?" I asked.

"Of course, gladly," he responded, then shouted "Hey!" to call someone in the back and order him to bring over a gun.

It was a long-barreled musket, as large as a spear, decked out along the sides with a golden carving of a human holding a lance who was stabbing an elf to death. It had a loose trigger, something I assumed was a flashpan made out of a gemstone-like material, and still smelled strongly of smoke, probably black powder. Technologically speaking, it seemed to be on par with sixteenth-century flintlock muskets.

"What would you say to twenty gold pieces? This one has a long and storied past. I imagine it will only continue to increase in value. This is a once-in-a-lifetime opportunity."

"No, I'm good."

"A pity. Well." Out of things to do, the shop owner smiled. I interpreted that as, *I showed you mine. Now it's your turn, right?* Making sure no one saw, I removed the AK-47's magazine, slipped the strap off my shoulder, and handed him the rifle. The shopkeeper used a cloth to receive the gun (out of what I guessed were merchant's manners) and took a careful look at every nook and cranny.

"A rather rustic specimen, isn't it?" he remarked. "Not a hint of embellishment anywhere. The wood is nothing remarkable, though the metal weighs very little for steel. It seems to have quite a number of parts."

"Are those local guns widely used among adventurers?"

"Two years ago, an adventurer shot his gun while in the dungeon, and the blast of gunpowder drew every single monster on that floor to him. My word, did the Guild have their work cut out for them. A whole team had to come together to clean up that mess."

I need to check if I have a silencer once I get back to camp. All the strategies the Firm laid out for me will be useless if I can't rely on my guns in the dungeon.

"Hmm, let's see. I can offer you eighty—no, one hundred gold pieces for this. Would you consider letting me take it off your hands?" he offered.

"Sorry. This one's not for sale." I took back the AK-47 from the shop owner, who eyed it greedily. The money was tempting, but the Firm's president had strongly impressed one thing upon me above all others:

"Do not unleash any technological singularities in the Other Dimension."

Metal refinery methods, navigation techniques, developments in gunpowder, guns, pharmaceuticals, explosives, bacteria, aircraft, the nuclear realm, AI, the Internet—the list of advancements that catalyzed countless other discoveries could go on and on. Without exception, every world had people challenging themselves to break through the limits of existing technologies. Give those geniuses even the smallest hint and they were bound to run away with it, developing and disseminating new inventions at an explosive pace. It would be all too easy to imagine what might come next. But I'd come here to explore that dungeon. I wasn't trying to be the spark to ignite the next war.

"Thanks for your help. See you around."

"Oh, sir! A moment, please. I'd strongly suggest you allow us to escort you back to your—"

I quickly said my thanks and left the shop. The owner started saying something, but I just ignored him. I couldn't have anyone tailing me, so I jogged for a bit to put some distance between myself and the store. After taking about three turns among the narrow back alleys, I wound up in a twisting, labyrinthine section of town. It did occur to me to ask Machina for directions, but I thought it might be fun to explore a bit on my own and kept going.

And fun it was. The uneven streets had sneaky drops so sudden I almost tripped over them, low-built roofs to perhaps deter riders on horseback from approaching, and patches completely submerged underwater. Lively scenes bursting with commotion were charming for sure, but this kind of quiet and calm neighborhood held its own sort of excitement, too. I felt like I was having my very own fairy-tale adventure.

My nose caught a whiff of some kind of roasted meat, and I

screeched to a halt. I was hungry. The unending parade of nerves and surprises of the day had pushed it out of mind, but I was starving. I sprang into action more nimbly than I had since I'd first arrived in this world. The scent led me to a stand set up amid the eaves. I ordered one of whatever they sold without bothering to ask what it was. It came out to two copper pieces. Happy as a clam, I started walking off with it.

It looked similar to a kebab. A thick, round, crepe-like baked flour wrap swaddled the mystery meat, and I couldn't tell it if had been stewed, or grilled, or what. I took a bite.

"Mm!" The juicy gravy from the meat beautifully complemented the simple wrap. If I wanted to be really critical, I would've said it could use a little more seasoning. But what kind of meat was this? It tasted like chicken but could've just as easily been pork.

"Alert. Mr. Souya, enemies approaching," Machina warned, and I froze in place. "They have been tracking you since you left the coin dealer. I will now commence targeting as they have taken an undeniably hostile stance."

I swallowed the rest of the kebab and washed it down with a swig of water from my bottle. Switching off the safety selector lever on my AK-47, I cocked the charging handle. Bullets loaded into the chamber.

"How many?"

"Three. One coming in at two o'clock and two from five o'clock."

"Got it."

"Countdown to contact: five, four, three, two, one."

A man appeared. I turned my head and got a look at the other two behind me as well. The one in front of me, a picture-perfect delinquent, had a longsword hanging from his clothing.

"What do you want?" I asked. His face dropped for a split

second when he realized I had been waiting for them. Then he spat out in an angry tone that gave away how little probably went on upstairs, "Money, all you've got. Hand it over and we'll let you live."

Short and sweet. I appreciated that.

I grabbed a random handful of coins from my pocket and flung them down the street; they turned out to be gold pieces. A dull echo reverberated off the cobblestones wherever they had bounced. Unfortunately for them, all three followed the coins with their eyes. By the time the closest one looked back up at me, I'd already closed the distance between us. I rammed the butt of my gun into his chin and felt bones crunch beneath it. Whipping around, I readied my weapon. One of the guys I got in his side; the other, in his kneecap. The blasts from the rifle resounded through the quiet backstreets. After a brief pause, anguished cries escaped the mouths of the wounded men.

"Enemy neutralized," Machina announced.

"Any reinforcements?"

"Negative."

"Doubt it." I could feel a pair of eyes watching me. A shadow slinked quickly around the corner when I turned to look. *It'll be too risky to pursue them when I don't know the lay of the land.*

I picked up the empty shell casings and gold pieces. Just as I was considering retrieving the bullets, too, Machina interrupted and announced, "Caution, individuals approaching. Possibly residents responding to the gunshots."

"Got it. We're gonna run for it. Activate the locator." The exit route appeared on the translucent EL display-panel lenses of my glasses. I followed it and quickly headed back to the main road. A burnt-red darkness had begun to inundate the streets. Once again joining the river of people that had now grown even more crowded, I walked with the flow for a bit, checking over my shoulder a few times to make sure nobody was on my trail. I could tell my racing heart wouldn't subside until I'd made it back to camp, but that was fine.

Crystals embedded in the streetlamps began to illuminate the cobblestone pavement below them. Night completed its fall over the town, revealing an entirely new side of the settlement. A collective sigh of release at the day's end was let out, and the town grew clamorous with sounds of drinks and food and talk of fame. Steamy women welcomed men who'd abandoned their wits and reduced themselves to fools. Songs, cries, and angry yells filled the air.

My eyes briefly met those of a beastmaid loitering about in sheer silk garb. Her eyes shone red, and long rabbit's ears perked up from the top of her head. She grinned at me, but I looked away too quickly to tell if that meant she found me intriguing or thought she'd found her next mark. I passed a raucous party full of people of unfamiliar races, but I wasn't yet acclimated enough to this world to join in the revelry.

Little by little, I left the hustle and bustle behind and stepped further into tranquility. A large bell rang out, perhaps to announce another day had drawn to a close. This one had brought me no results or rewards, only awareness of new problems to tackle. And so marked the end of my first exploration into the Other Dimension.

(2ND DAY)

The receptionist at the Adventurers Guild was called Evetta.

"I'll search for a god who might agree to consecrate a covenant with you. Please come back again tomorrow," she had told me the day before, then sent me away.

We hadn't agreed on a set time, so I took it easy in the morning. I studied the map of the area Machina had made, organized my supplies, and worked on my camp setup. By the end of that period, I'd managed to bring the kitchen and toilet a few steps closer to the standards of modern civilization.

Ghett dropped by with some fish, and I cooked it up into a fish-bone-broth-style stew, and we ate together. I set the leftover catch to dry in the sun and got to town a little after midday. That's when—

"You're late."

—I found Evetta standing in front of the gate. She'd drawn herself up to her full height, and her arms were crossed. Her displeasure came through her deadpan countenance quite clearly.

"Huh? What are you doing here?" I asked.

"The West Gate is the most heavily trafficked," she explained.

"That's not what I meant."

"I went around to all the major inns this morning, but I didn't find you at any of them. Then I remembered your coral necklace. It's a gift from the merfolk, right? It made me wonder if you'd set up your base outside of town," she continued.

"Yes, but that's not what I'm asking."

"I do have someone waiting at the reception desk in case I missed you by any chance, you know."

"Right, it's important to cover your bases." I was trying to ask why she'd gone out of her way to wait for me.

"......"

"......"

We both fell silent.

Then Evetta spoke, trembling slightly.

"I'm going all out on my first assignment, to no avail so far. You got a problem or something?"

"No! Not at all. Thank you very much! Also, I'm sorry!"

"It's my job, after all," she said, a stiffly prim look on her face. We collected ourselves and headed off god-hunting. But first I treated her to a late breakfast and lunch. It cost me a whole silver piece.

Our first choice was the god most adventurers made their pacts with. It was a collective god comprising the souls of six legendary adventurers depicted in famous ballads: Lumileux the Tempestuous, Duin the Silent, Garwing the Revolutionary Mage, Aldy of the Three Blades, Robbes the Resolute, and Thurseauve of Oblivion. People exalted their deeds and worshipped them together as Windovnickel, God of Adventurers. Although the god did not have a physical presence, the Disciples of Windovnickel worshipped the legendary adventurers through the stories of their deeds. It is said one can see footprints of their exploits in every dungeon in the world.

Their sanctuary had an atmosphere far too relaxed to feel like a real temple. In fact, it was actually a bar, complete with its own billboard of job postings. Though it was only midday, drunkards milled about.

"O ye who seeks to follow the path of the adventurer, our Lord Windovnickel will transform your inquisitive spirit into strength. Your honor will be immortalized in stories, tales which will give birth to miracles. And then you, too, will join their ranks in the saga carried on the wind one day. Have you the courage to confront hardship? There is no such thing as an easy adventure. One must maintain an indestructible will, unyielding resolve, and—," and so on, rambled a man behind the bar. Everything about him screamed *bartender*, from his rippling muscles to his mohawk. A ridiculously huge battle-ax hung on the wall behind him.

"Hey, Boss. I'll take a large root-veggie salad, three thick slices of dungeon pork, and I'll have the large guinelle eggs soft-boiled. And one ale—ah, actually, I'm on the clock, so make that a milk," said Evetta, rattling off her order.

I knew it; he's the bartender. Wait, hold up. Didn't you just polish off three whole entrées before we got here?

"Evetta. Give us some space," asked the bartender.

"...I'm sorry. Force of habit." Evetta trudged off to a seat across the room, then started to put in an order with a waitress.

"She still acts like an adventurer, even though she's already crossed over to the admin side of things at the Guild," he remarked.

"Ohhh, she used to be an adventurer?" I'd kind of gotten that feeling.

"So you must be the Otherworlder looking to try his luck as an adventurer that Evetta mentioned."

"Yes, that's me."

"All right, up for a covenant?"

"I sure am!" Talk about laid-back. Not that I cared if it meant I could get this over with already. The boss placed a book on the counter and laid his hand over it.

"I am called Rasta ole Rhasvah. As a disciple of our Lord Windovnickel, I bestow upon you a new compass needle to guide you in your quests," he began. "O man of youth, the path of adventure is full of treachery. To explore means to risk your life at all times. It is an austere life that no ordinary person can bear. And yet, we press on. Have you the determination to preserve an unshakable spirit until the last seconds you hold life within you? If it be so, proclaim your name and place your hand upon mine."

My adventure is finally starting.

I called up all the resolve in my heart and laid my hand over his. It was hard and spoke of a tumultuous life. The bartender must have also been an adventurer once. And a famous one, at that.

"I am Souya of Japan."

Spheres of light burst into life. Undimmed by the midday sun, they shone brilliantly, danced, and burst. Then, silence. I felt something welling up within me.

"All right, it's a no go!"

"Why do you sound so happy?!"

I guess I'd just imagined the sensation.

"Boss! What is the meaning of this?" Evetta ran over to us. The boss put the book away and began wiping down the counter.

"Hmm, it's probably *that*. I see it every once in a while. Have you got any dreams, young man?" he asked me.

"You could say so."

"Are you talking about an ideal? Or a realistic desire? The thing about adventures is, they're all about chasing after dreams almost guaranteed to never come true. Other gods may laugh 'em off, but our Lord blesses those kinds of ambitions. Our Lord Windovnickel is, after all, our hopes and dreams manifested into one."

Doesn't wanting to save my sister count as an ambition? Ah, maybe not. It's not like she wants that for herself. The fact that my own goals are twisted hasn't totally escaped me.

"I'll give it to you straight. You are nothing like a typical adventurer. Try your luck elsewhere," he advised. "Though, I do have a fun illustrated pamphlet for all new contracts of Lord Windovnickel, perfect even for someone like you who can't read. What do you say to one gold piece?"

"I'll pass."

We decided to move on to the next option.

Flames: the most primordial of the magical crafts, a power easy to call forth but difficult to tame. They were here long before the giant who created the world, before the myriad gods in existence, before all else. The religion built around them did not worship a god in the flesh, either. According to the explanation I heard on the way over, its disciples subscribed to a creed steeped in fatalism that went, "From flames the world was made, and by flames shall it be unmade."

Secure in their belief that all would one day return to oblivion, they eschewed unnecessary wealth and strove to live in honorable penury. War-devastated refugees laid the foundations for the sect, and mighty pyromancers spread its gospel across the world. Its god seemed to welcome a rather wide range of proselytes into its church, from ill-fated adventurers to those seeking to master the flame-craft, from those setting out on the path of adventure alone with nothing but the skin on their backs to the filthy rich who abandoned their bloated wealth to convert. I could see a towering bonfire raging within the temple's open gates even as we walked by.

"Excuse me, you there."

"Who, me?"

A dark-skinned beastman with a golden tail and pointed ears called out to me just in front of the entrance to the temple. A fox, maybe? He looked to be in his later teens.

"What business brings you to our temple?" he asked.

"I'd like to join your church."

"Please leave."

"That was quick!" I was at a total loss. He could at least tell me why.

"You look a little puzzled. It is true our Holy Flames refuse none—with one exception. You and that thing," he said, gesturing at my neck. The necklace Ghett gave me hung around it. "Only those cloaked in water are out of the question. Would you be able to take responsibility if, by bringing that into our gates, you extinguished our Sacred Blaze?"

Does this thing have that kinda power?

"Discard the token of the Deep and I will allow you to gaze upon our Holy Flames, but no more," he offered.

"No, I suppose this just wasn't meant to be," I responded.

"I suppose not."

Thank you, next.

"Hark, I am Gladwein the Iron Arm! I have no need of feeble followers in my house! I want not your wealth, nor your honor, nor your blood, nor your words! Prove yourself to me with your body, with your skill!" and so on, yelled a woman who had apparently just recently come into godhood. Her billowing blond hair framed her bronzed, fierce face, and her body encapsulated the golden ratio of beauty and brawn. She pointed at those around her with a long, wide, thick sword I didn't think I stood a chance of even picking up. She was essentially Hercules in female form. But more than that, more than anything else about her, my eyes were drawn to one thing—her clothing.

She was in a bikini suit of armor. A suit of armor—but a bikini. The top hugged her ample bosom; the panties cut a deep V-line; this was a real-deal suit of bikini armor.

"A famous anecdote tells of how once, when vanquishing an evil dragon, Lady Gladwein destroyed her own sword under the force of her power. Left with no other choice, she battled and slew the beast with her bare hands," Evetta explained.

"She took down a dragon with her bare hands?!"

"Exactly. Every woman who dreams of becoming a vanguard idolizes her." I immediately regretted leering at Lady Gladwein. She could crush me with a single fingertip.

"No good! Next!" she cried. The line I'd joined began inching forward. Up at the front, people assaulted the corpse of a massive boar. It measured about two meters long—crazy huge. Did this species only exist here?

"Nope! Next! You there!" she yelled at one of the hopefuls. "Your face screams defeat before you've even tried your hand! Come back another day! And you, you sorry dolt! I saw you scoffing at him! Try again in your next life!"

Some just weren't cut out for the task at hand; others fell flat on their faces from the nerves; one snapped her lance in two; another swung his ax back only for it to go flying from his hands; each blundered in their own way. So far, twenty people in a row had failed to pass the test.

"Pretty sure I don't belong here," I muttered, venting my anxiety to Evetta.

"That's not true. Look, there's even a young boy here," she noted in reference to the next challenger, a kid carrying a long-sword on his back. I'd put him at around fourteen, fifteen years old. He was so young that he hadn't finished growing into his full frame yet.

"Oh."

But the very air changed the moment he readied his blade. His hands clasped gently around the hilt. He got low to the ground, crouched down like a hunting dog, then shot forward like a wild animal. Sword flashing in his thrust, it sank into the boar's hide— and stayed there reverberating from the impact on its own, free from the boy's hand.

"Urgh!" He'd been so close. If only he'd held on to the sword, he would've pierced straight through the carcass. At least that was my amateur read of it.

"What fool allows his weapon to slip through his fingers?!" berated the goddess to the young boy. He sheathed his sword and turned to leave without a word. "Nevertheless, I bestow the move two marks and your youth three! All together that makes half a man! Join the pride of my disciples and devote yourself in worship to me! You have a long road before you learn to move like a complete man!"

"Huh?" He turned around, dumbstruck. Only when cheers sprang up around him did he grasp what had just happened.

"Come now, here," ordered the goddess. "Do you not seek a covenant with me?"

"Ah, uh, y-yes, please!" The room broke out in laughter. A warm, genial energy flowed around the wide-eyed, innocent adventurer.

"That young man has much to improve with his skills, but I see a bright future ahead of him," commented Evetta.

"Makes sense." He looked pretty skilled to me already. After him, not a single other applicant secured the pact they desired. I watched with a gnawing pain in my stomach until it was my turn.

"NEXT!" boomed the goddess. I held my breath and concentrated. I drew my woodsman's hatchet and raised it above my head, my right hand wrapped around the handle, with my left gripping my right wrist. All I knew about swordsmanship was from the little taste of kendo we got in PE class, but it would have to do.

"Eh, aaaaaaaaaah!!" I shouted to psych myself up and used my whole body to swing the hatchet down. My eyes went dark for a second from screaming too hard. Once I could see the world around me again, I found the blade had sunk about two centimeters into the boar's skin. But what was the verdict?!

"Out of the question!" *I knew it!* "Hey, Evetta," called out the goddess. "Are you the one who brought this to me?"

"Yes, milady." It looked like she and Evetta knew each other.

"In no way is he fit to be a vanguard," she reproached her. "You should not have brought him here."

"...Yes, milady."

Was that true?

"NEXT!" I couldn't have agreed more.

◇   ◇   ◇

One thing I learned after traipsing all over town was that the gods of this world lived in very close proximity to normal people. And in just one day, I saw a ton of them—enough to shift my perspective on religion in general.

The overwhelming beauty of the women revered as goddesses particularly blew me away. Talk about a sight for sore eyes, a feast for the beholder. Even those goddesses of other races were so stunning in their variety that I couldn't help but cry out in awe.

The male gods were all studs, too, I guess. Not that I cared or had any luck with them.

I saw and learned a lot. That's gotta count for something. No doubt. Yeah.

At least, that's what I kept telling myself.

"Come on, don't get so down," I said. "I'm sure something good will come of all this."

Twilight had blanketed the town. Evetta crouched down at the side of the road, her head cradled in her hands. I sat on the ground next to her.

"I never imagined *every single god in town* would turn us down," she moaned.

"Yep, they sure did. Every last one. We came pretty close a few times, but nothing worked out in the end."

"......I'm sorry I couldn't be of more help," she apologized.

"You did a great job, Evetta. I just didn't have any luck, is all." I knew her job obligated her to help me, but she'd devoted the whole day to my case and had taken me all over town. I couldn't blame her for anything.

"But we've come up completely empty-handed," she protested.

"It's just one of those days. I'll bet this kinda thing happens when you go down in the dungeon, too, no?"

"Yes, that's true." She nodded her head very slightly a few times.

"Let's go grab something to eat. My treat," I suggested.

"Very well. I won't go easy on your wallet."

Hang on a second.

Just as we were getting into it—

"What have we here? Making a woman hang her head in a place like this—did you put a bun in her oven, you little devil?" sneered an unfamiliar voice. It came from a young girl with cat ears who stood there flicking her thin tail back and forth. Super adorable.

"What are you looking at her for? I'm right here, over here." The voice did sound a bit low for someone so young, I thought, before realizing it actually belonged to the cat she held in her arms. It was ashy gray, all skin and bones. And it was talking.

"Did the cat say that?!" I exclaimed. This had to be the biggest shock I'd gotten since coming here.

"Pipe down; don't get so rowdy," the cat continued.

"Evetta, the cat! That cat is talki— Evetta?" I stopped short. All the blood had drained from her face.

"Souya, I'll await you at the reception desk tomorrow. Please come before noon. I apologize again for today. I'll take you up on that meal tomorrow and order enough for both days. If you'll excuse me," she spouted off quickly, then sprinted away at lightning speed. It only took a second to lose sight of her among the crowd.

Does she hate cats or something? I wouldn't have guessed that.

"Hmph, looks like Little Miss Horns is rather weak-kneed. I won't snatch your soul, fool," scoffed the cat. "Now, you. Yes, you, half-wit."

"Uhhh, what can I do for you?" I asked. The cat jumped out of the girl's hands and walked up to me. It was filthy. Its fur looked like a raggedy, overused mop. Only its golden eyes stood out somewhat mysteriously.

"Give the child a tip for her trouble. She carried me all the way here," the cat demanded. "You can't very well leave her unrecompensed, now, can you?"

Why should I have to pay? I wondered. But the cat-eared girl was too cute to deny, so I fished a copper piece out of my pocket. The cat swiped the coin from me and handed it to the girl as if I'd had nothing to do with it.

"Good work, my dear. Take care as you head back to the temple. Do not stray or buy any treats on your way. Keep an extra watchful eye out for men, you hear?" The girl clutched the coin as one would a precious jewel, waved good-bye, and left. I waved after her, too.

"So...," I started. Now it was just me and the cat, who rubbed its chin all over my knees. "What can I do you for, um, little kitty?"

"My name is Mythlanica, Souya, or whoever you are."

Mythlanica... That sounds familiar. Where have I heard that before? Oh, right, at the coin dealer.

"That was quite the display of skill yesterday when you trounced those scoundrels. Praiseworthy, even," the cat continued. My hand naturally shifted to rest on the hilt of my karambit, ready to draw it at any moment. It looked like this cat had been watching that little tussle.

"However, in so doing, you disturbed my slumber, a heinous

crime punishable by certain death. You must now lay down your body to atone for this sin." *This cat just straight up told me to die.*

"What exactly would that entail?" I asked.

"Devoting the remainder of your life to serving me," the cat replied, cementing my impression of cats as smug little creatures who go through life with self-satisfied grins perpetually plastered on their faces.

"Ah, right, right. Thing is, I've got stuff to do, so I'm gonna head out. Plus, I've gotta get up early tomorrow." *No time to put up with this bullshit.*

"You fool!" it exclaimed. "I, the magnanimous and irreverent being that I am, have chipped and chipped away at my demands and am offering to spare your life! You could not hope for better terms! This kind of steal comes once in a hundred years, if at all!" I paid it no mind and started walking home.

"Argh, fine! All right! I'll sweeten the deal only a tad more! So lend me your ear!" the cat cried as it clutched at my pant leg. The sight filled me with pity, so I decided to give it one more chance. "Food, give me food! Then I'll let you off the hook! What outstanding generosity on my part! My compassion flows as deep as the great oceans!"

"Ughh." This thing was starting to get on my nerves. I'd always been more of a dog person anyway—though, that little cat-eared girl was pretty cute.

"Don't you dare 'ughh' me, you little ingrate! Can you not see how much I...?" It trailed off and slumped into a heap on the ground, and it looked so spent lying there that I wondered for a second if it had died. "Curses. I over...exerted myself... Can't...go...on..."

"Ughh." Was it faking this? Pretty convincing, either way. I thought about leaving it there but figured I'd feel kinda gross if I came upon its corpse the next day.

"So basically, you're hungry?" I confirmed.

"I haven't eaten my fill in well-nigh on fifteen years," it said pathetically.

Well, I guess I've got enough extra food to take care of one cat.

"Want to come to my place?" I offered. "I camp out in a tent, so don't expect anything too fancy."

"If you insist, I shall grant you that honor."

And so, my harvest for day two amounted to a single cat.

(3RD DAY)

Days started early in the Other Dimension. Huge, far-off bells rang in the morning. I woke up at six, bathed in the river, and changed. I got Machina to help me wash my dirty clothes, and by the time the laundry was ready to hang, a guest had arrived bearing the ingredients of our breakfast.

"Here, deep-sea critters and clams," said Ghett, handing me the goods, aka shrimp and clams.

"Thank you very much."

"Need a hand with anythin'?"

"No thanks, just take a seat."

"Well, then."

Ghett sat down in the camping chair and got to work on a disentanglement puzzle. I started preparing the food. The small shrimp I shelled, *headed,* and deveined. They were small, but at twenty strong, they added up to a real treat. The clams, which resembled Japanese littlenecks, I rinsed quickly in some salt water. I took a few cloves of elven garlic, or what they call the odorless variety of garlic here, removed the ends, and minced them up. Then I grabbed a few red chilis similar to cayenne peppers—maybe I'll call them Other Dimensional cayenne peppers. No, that's too long; red chilis it is. Anyway, I grabbed a few of those and deseeded them. Next, I massaged a bit of salt into a bunch of assorted wild herbs I'd picked from the field and set them aside.

On my way home the day before, I'd bought a clay pot. Dumping a ton of oil into it, I threw the garlic and chilis in and topped them off with a pinch of salt. To prevent anything from burning, I moved the pot away from the heat and waited for the garlic and pepper to become fragrant. Once it was just right, I added all the shrimp, clams, and herbs to the mix and set it to simmer. After I had that going, I cut a few slices of some dark rye bread I'd also picked up and toasted them on each side, then plated and placed them on my simple table. The pot had begun bubbling nicely by that point, so I put out the fire. And presto, a simple Other Dimensional *Ajillo*.

Everything felt legit when I added *Otherworldly* or *Other Dimensional* in front of it, but I realized after stopping by the grocer yesterday that their diet wasn't actually that different from ours. Even Machina's tests showed I could eat pretty much everything they had.

I let the breeze floating across the meadow cool the *ajillo* off for a bit. For drinks, I figured we could just have green tea, so I shook an unmeasured helping of tea leaves in cold water and let it brew. Ten minutes passed.

"Ghett, let's dig in."

"Right, let's." I handed him a spoon.

"You scoop this up, put it onto your bread, and eat it together."

"I see." He must really love clams, because he put nothing else on the slice of bread he brought to his mouth. "Hmm. Now, this is really something. Really something." The clams crunched loudly in his mouth as he chewed them, shells and all. Not that I minded if that's what he liked, but man, what a strange sound.

"Thank you for the meal," I said, my hands together in prayer, then loaded my bread with a generous helping of shrimp, too. "D-damn, this is goood."

It was pure bliss. The garlicky flavors stimulated the appetite, and the plump shrimp and the sour tones of the rye frolicked in my mouth. The bread itself, not to mention its beautiful texture, was delicious—simply delicious. We couldn't have stopped ourselves if we'd wanted to. The wild herbs had a delicate bitterness that accented the dish perfectly. It could've used a bit more salt, but I restrained myself. An amateur like me tinkering with seasoning is destined to fail. I didn't get a single clam.

Bread. More bread. Not enough bread. Get the bread!

And so, the two of us polished off the other loaf of bread I had bought to keep on reserve, too. By the end, we dragged chunks of it across the bottom of the pot to soak up the last bits of oil. I didn't normally have that kind of hard, dark bread, but I ate it with fervor, perhaps in part because of its novelty.

Ow, my jaw hurts.

"*Belch*, I've never had any lander food like that before," said Ghett. "I need to lie down."

Crude thoughts such as, *This merman looks exactly like a beached sea lion*, came to mind.

"Maaan, you know, I feel kind of bad," I said apologetically while washing the dishes.

"Hmm? Why? Was there something wrong with the food?" Ghett asked, still sprawled out on the ground.

"No, not at all. I meant for taking all that delicious seafood for free."

"Your race sure does fixate on a peculiar kind of humility. None of my kind can work fire. If we're fortunate, we might enjoy this kind of meal once or twice before we die. That's worth more than enough. And not for nothing, but those were gold-piece leavings. I would've only chucked them if you hadn't used them."

"What do you mean by 'gold-piece leavings'?" I didn't understand the term.

"Anything I can't trade for a full gold piece."

"But couldn't you get silver or copper pieces?"

"Ohhh, I'd forgotten all about those."

Huh? You forgot how much your coins are worth? I thought, but I was wrong.

"Do you have any silver pieces on you?" he asked. I took one out of my pocket. "That thing right there is flesh-burning poison for all variant races."

"What?!" I exclaimed, reflexively dropping the coin.

"Why are you getting all worked up? Now, how's about I tell you a little story while I wait for my stomach to settle after that feast?"

What follows is the bloody history behind the silver coins, as told by a merman priest. It begins like all stories...

Long ago, soon after the curtains drew to a close on the age of the gods and people took over authorship of history, there lived a king who ruled over all the beastfolk. His name was Rha Guzüri Duin Olossal, king of the beasts.

Throughout every age, man and beast have always stood in opposition to each other, the only variable in this constant battle being who held the higher ground. In this age, the beasts had pushed humans to the edge of utter ruin. They had lost ground in every corner of the Great Land save for their stronghold in the northernmost reaches of the Left Continent. Even that was no more than a silver mine treasured by the dwarves. It was here that the last king of men raised his prayers to the gods.

"O gods on high, I beseech thee, grant us the power to vanquish these bloodthirsty beasts," he pleaded. One thousand days he prayed. One hundred elves offered their lives as sacrifice. Finally, on the thousandth day, a god answered their call.

"Very well, King of Man. Fill your chalice with the blood of said beasts and drain it, thereby becoming a beast yourself. Do this, and I shall grant you my aid."

The king agonized over the choice presented to him but in the end did as he was told. In return, the god worked a miracle—a spirit of calamity took root in the silver of the mine. Thus, the king commanded it:

"O mighty silver, I bid thee work thine evil on every race save for those of man! Loathe them, burn them, kill them—kill them! Scorch all vile beasts with abominable bodies such as mine own in a world-destroying conflagration and incinerate them to naught but ash!"

Thus consecrated, the silver bent itself to the king's will. Dwarves took the silver and beat it into a slew of weapons. Rows and rows of silver spears, swords, and arrows before him, the disgraced king spoke his final words: "Come, my children. It is time to begin." On that day, a new line of beast-hunting kings was born.

And so, the forces of man beat the beasts back to near complete annihilation, took mercy on them, stayed their assault, and settled upon coexistence. As a symbol of peace, the silver weapons with which they had hunted beasts were melted down into coins and dispersed throughout the world. However, should the beasts bare their fangs at man once more, those silver pieces would again take shape as swords and spears and arrows that promised to decimate them once and for all.

As for the god who bestowed such a blessing upon the races of man, no one can say who it was.

"......" A million thoughts ran through my mind, but it was not my place as an outsider to throw in a flippant comment. The silver piece I picked back up had a monster on it. I couldn't tell if it was the king from the tale or the king of beasts.

"We merfolk did give the beastfolk passage across the oceans, but we never killed any people," explained Ghett. "And still we got lumped into the curse all the same."

"That's— Sorry."

"Why should you need to apologize?"

"You're exactly right."

"Oh, and the copper pieces, they're just no good. They rust in no time and pollute the water."

Huh, a superstition about poisonous copper went around in Japan for a while, too.

"Actually, Ghett, I'd like to ask you something if I may."

"No need to be so formal. What?" I didn't expect I'd be much help, but I was grateful to have formed this bond, so I wanted to ask in case, by any small chance, I could do something.

"Why do you need money?" The day before, Ghett had mentioned that merfolk could find everything they required to survive in the great abundance of the oceans. They didn't need to bother with those on land, and they had no reason to interact with people.

"I've got five granddaughters, see," Ghett started. "The youngest of them came upon a storm-wrecked ship and saved a man's life. She spoke of nothing else after she delivered him to the shore, almost as if in the throes of some delirious fever. Then one day, she just, *poof*, disappeared—after stealing one of our most prized possessions. This treasure, called Ghu Baurî, will allow you to transform into any shape you wish at the cost of whatever is most precious to you. There's no doubt in my mind my granddaughter went after that man."

So basically, she pulled a Little Mermaid.

"The rest of our family came out against it, but as long as that's what she wanted, I figured it would all work out," he continued. "Or so I thought. One day, I got called out for a potential deal through the grapevine. The sellers, the Ellomere Western Peng Traders. The item, one female mermaid. The price: four thousand gold pieces."

Looked like this Little Mermaid didn't turn into sea-foam but instead got put on sale by a trading group. It took one copper coin to buy a loaf of bread in this world. I couldn't even imagine what you'd have to do to earn four thousand gold pieces.

"Forget it. I'm not fishing for pity in telling you this. I merely answered your question."

"Right, of course." Just then—

"Mm! What is that scrumptious smell?!" A gray creature came walking out of the tent. The freeloader stretched and opened its mouth into a cavernous yawn. It was seriously nasty. I almost wanted to dunk it in the river water.

"Good morning, Lady Mythlanica." I wasn't totally sold on addressing a cat so formally, but she would throw a tantrum whenever I tried without the title, so I had no other choice.

"Souya, prepare my breakfast."

"Okay, okay." I blanched the Other Dimensional fish I'd left out drying overnight to remove some of the salt, wiped off the moisture, removed the skewer, and plated it.

"And what exactly is this?"

"What do you mean, 'what?' It's fish."

"This is unbelievable!" she protested. "I can smell you two had something much better, didn't you?! DIDN'T YOUUU?! How dare you put this mere guppy before me?! The insolence! Raise your sword at once!" The cat flopped on the ground, belly up, and flailed her legs like a child.

"All right, fine. Then don't eat it." I'd just give it to the winged bunnies flying around the meadow. They looked all the cuter since they never opened their traps to talk.

"Wait." The cat placed her front paw on the hand I'd wound up to throw the dish. "I never said I wouldn't eat it."

"I see." For someone who'd just railed against the fish, she sure gobbled it up with surprising relish. Ghett watched the cat, an inscrutable look on his face.

"Souya, what might that be?" he asked.

"It's a cat," I explained. "Do you have a different word for them here?"

"No, just cat. But to think it speaks, it must be a rather impressive...... No, couldn't be. I've spoken and eaten more than my fill today. I'll take my leave." As he turned to go, Ghett mused, "Mythlanica? Now...... Hmm, I'm sure I've heard that name before, but my stomach is too full for my brain to function." He dived in the river and disappeared beneath the water a little slower than usual.

"I could have used some more, but I'm satisfied," Lady Mythlanica informed me.

"Glad to hear it."

Satisfied in spite of all her protestations, she licked the edges of her mouth clean with her tongue and announced, "I'm going to sleep. You may wake me once lunch is prepared. Next time, you'd do well to serve me meat other than fish." With that, she went back into the tent.

Is this dumb cat seriously not gonna do anything but eat and sleep? I know that's what they do, but it just doesn't sit right.

It would have been fine if she were a helpless little kitty that never said more than "Meow, meow." Taking care of creatures more pitiful than yourself provides comfort in times of crisis. But she could talk like nobody's business, she was cheeky as hell, and she wasn't even cute as a cat. Plus, she was filthy!

"Mr. Souya, isn't she an adorable little kitty? I just looove cats!"

"Uh, sure."

A happy face flashed across Machina's screen, and she spoke in a cheerful voice. For what it's worth, I had ordered her not to speak in front of the locals.

I guess pieces of junk have a soft spot for the useless. Maybe it's a kind of sympathy? Yeah, must be. Well, isn't that just perfect.

We turned to the day's god-hunting session, morning edition. In short, it was complete defeat.

"This is pretty much what I had expected," Evetta said, her face determined. *I'm begging you, let there be a* but *that comes after that,* I thought. "However, I have a good idea."

"Really?"

"Yes, but it can wait until after lunch." We wound up going back to the bar where my devotion had been turned down the day before. Lunch was on me, as promised.

"Oh-ho, if it isn't the would-be adventurer with no dreams and a retired veteran. What can I do for you today?" asked the owner of the place.

"Boss, I'll have three orders each of salt-grilled dungeon pork, an extra-large wild greens sauté, a rock-eating turtle soup, and a deluxe fluffy honey bread. I'm on the clock, so I won't need any ale; just give me a milk," Evetta rattled off.

"You got it!" answered the barkeep.

That's a pretty heavy order. Will we finish it all? Maybe we can take it to go?

"Evetta, I actually ate a pretty big breakfast."

"Souya, what will you have?"

Ahh, so that is all for you, huh? And on my dime, no less.

I asked for some light bites and left it up to the barkeep to decide what that meant. He brought out two thick slices of bacon and a bowl of pickled beans. It wasn't bad, but the flavors were too simple. The bacon had only salt and fat from the meat, while the beans were nothing but sour. Meanwhile, Evetta got to work devouring the feast fit for a three-day celebration that had been laid out on the table in front of her, starting with the plates at the ends. She dug in with true gusto. Did all women in this dimension binge like this?

We focused on the meal for a while. I quickly tired of the beans but couldn't bear to waste them; every once in a while, I'd take bite, get annoyed at the taste, then start all over again. I decided to work my mouth in other ways to make up for the lack of flavor.

"By the way, I ended up keeping that cat from yesterday," I told her.

"Have you lost your mind?!" she exclaimed, appalled, a plate of sautéed greens in hand. "C-cats—cats have got those eyes that narrow into slits, those rough tongues, and tails that stand up straight on end. They steal away everyone who's lost their soul!" She stayed her spoon.

"Are you scared of cats?" I asked.

"What?! I may not look it, but I was a pretty elite adventurer, I'll have you know! You think I can't handle a stinking cat?! Is that what you think?!" Tough talk for someone who looked so shaken up. She turned back to her food and gobbled it down before my eyes. Maybe she was stress-eating.

Oh, I forgot to leave lunch out for Her Highness. I guess I'll send Machina a message to open up a bag of dried fish or something for her.

Just as the thought crossed my mind, an emergency alert flashed on my glasses. I covered my face with my hands so no one could hear me and whispered back, "What's wrong?"

"Please return to the camp immediately. We've been attacked."

Machina's system went down right after the alert came through. It wasn't clear what had happened. I considered using Evetta but then imagined the worst-case scenario and had her stay in the bar with my money.

Dark clouds obscured the sky as if mirroring my feelings exactly. The campsite lay five kilometers away from the city. I raced over as fast as I could, preserving some of my energy in case I had to fight upon arrival. My home coming into view, still small in the distance, I dropped down to the ground and brought a telescope to my eye.

It was a disaster. The tent had been blown away, the simple kitchen destroyed, and my camping goods were scattered all over the place. I couldn't see anyone lying in wait. I moved in closer. My AK ready, I crouched as I walked to make sure the barrel didn't veer from my line of sight. One by one, I eliminated all the camp's blind spots, careful not to set off any traps. They probably didn't have bombs here, but one hit with local poison and I was done for.

My breath almost devolved into hyperventilation, but I gritted my teeth and brought it under control. I found Machina beneath the tent sheets, and I turned her over, praying with all I had.

"……"

Aside from a few footprints on her torso, she seemed unharmed. That was a relief at least. "AIJ006 Machina Odd-Eye, activate," I commanded.

"......Registered user's voice pattern recognized. Lifting auto-lock mode; commencing system recovery. Activating, activating; unidentified device found. Unable to process with built-in system support. When using new tools, please first—"

"Force command: Switch to Isolla." If the main system wouldn't work, I had to try the backup.

"Understood; activating. System functioning at thirty percent capacity." After a second of noise and flashing screens, my glasses came back online. I kept my commands simple so as not to overburden her.

"Order: Scan the area for pulses. Mark any living organisms with a red dot."

"Activating pulse radar; scanning...... No pulses found." The pulse radar worked within a one-hundred-meter radius. Now I could be sure there were no others waiting to ambush me. For the moment, I crossed that worry off the list.

"Order: Display bird's-eye view of the area on my glasses. Make the radius two kilometers. Zoom in on anything approaching."

"Understood. Cancelling autonomous drone sequence; activating display."

I put the AK down and stood the machina unit back upright. As far as my amateur eyes could tell, there didn't seem to be any damage to the aqueous brain or other functions. But this thing had started off half-broken. There was no telling what would send it plunging down the path of no return into darkness.

"Question: How long will it take to recover full functionality?"

"Unclear. The system is currently functioning at eighteen percent capacity and declining."

Shit. Not good.

"Question: How long will it take to regain functionality after rebooting?"

"Unclear."

"Question: What happened?"

"We fell under attack by a group of three men. I put a tracer on one of them."

"Display his location."

"Understood." A map of the town marked with a red dot showed up on my glasses. On an unrelated note, I saw drag marks out of the corner of my eye. A cold chill ran down my spine.

"What did they take?" I asked.

"The weapons and medical supply containers."

At that, I finally lost all words. Of all the things, they had to take my two lifelines. Both stolen containers had been locked. They must have assumed that meant they held valuable goods.

"Display the containers' current location. You're tracking them, right?"

"Capacity reduced to five percent. Rain approaching. Sending out return signal to all drones. Squad Member Souya, please find cover. Do not under any circumstances attempt a mission without suppo—" She cut out, and the system went down once again. My glasses also stopped working. A meter showing how long the unit would take to restart came up on Machina's monitor, but it had dropped all the way to 0 percent and showed no signs of budging.

Rain started to fall. My thoughts ground to a halt. Human brains had this way of breaking down when too many things happened at once.

"......"

It felt like it took about five minutes for me to restart.

It's not safe here—should I go somewhere else? Maybe find a place to stay in town? No, that's even riskier. I guess I'll drop by the Adventurers Guild and ask Evetta for help. But what if she's not there? Wait, can I really trust her? Going into town is out—too dangerous. I can't think straight.

I was at a total loss. Who knew it would feel this awful to find yourself all alone in another dimension? I started cleaning up the mess to calm my nerves and clear my head. Menial tasks like that were decent at changing your state of mind, though they weren't much more than a temporary escape, of course.

And then.

"Right. Nothing came up on the scan, after all." I found the cat's corpse. She'd been stabbed in the stomach, vomited blood, and died. She should've just run. I bet she probably put up a brave fight. At least, I decided on that interpretation. No matter how annoying, everyone deserved to be glorified a little after they died.

I dug a hole some distance away from the campsite and buried her body there. Taking a tree branch I found lying around, I stuck it on top of the mound and wrote *Her Greatness, Lady Mythlanica* on it with a permanent marker. I brought my hands together. The warm rain soaked my back. I'd never really understood what you were supposed to think in this kind of situation. It wasn't much more than formality, but what else was there? I'd shown my respects.

Next, I needed a diversion. Off came the glasses that didn't suit me. I checked how many bullets I had left and found enough for three people, but any more and things would get iffy. All that running around town in my search for a god to follow had given me a pretty good handle on the layout. I knew exactly where to find the red dot I'd seen.

"Sorry. Machina, Isolla, I'm about to get a bit reckless."

◇ ◇ ◇

The brighter the busier parts of town that burst with activity and life shone, the heavier the silence and shadows that fell on its darker underside. That's the kind of place the bastards who'd attacked my camp had chosen to hide in. Failed adventurers with crushed dreams ended up here. It also drew in half-assed idiots who'd never even tried to give that life a go. It wasn't destitute enough to call a slum, but you never knew what went on behind closed doors.

Hiding was the wrong word. Evidently, those tools didn't even have the good sense to take that step. I found them in a building built as a half-basement, with one staircase leading down to a cellar and a warehouse-type floor on top. Light poured out from the ventilation window on the side. The men were probably drinking it up, flush with cash from their latest payout. From their shitty singing and laughter, it sounded like those three had no other company inside.

An anger I hadn't realized I'd been stifling threatened to explode. I knocked on the doors of the neighbors to either side of the building to regain my cool. A beastmaid and her child answered the one on the right. The lines of worry and doubt that came over her face relaxed with the gold piece I handed her.

"Sorry to disturb you. Things are going to get a little loud for a moment."

"You do what you need to do, honey," she answered.

An elderly woman lived in the house on the left. I gave her the same spiel about making noise, but she said she'd lost most of her hearing and wouldn't mind. I pressed a gold piece into her hand to apologize for the inconvenience.

And now I am calm. I am undeniably, unmistakably collected.

I took yet another gold piece and chucked it in the building through the ventilation window. Without even waiting to hear it land, I ran down the stairs and rammed the door, busting it open with pure momentum. There was one guy on my right and two on my left. I shot a barrage of bullets out of the AK at the two to the left as I fell. Blood splattered all over the walls and floors. My ears rang as the gunshot ricocheted in the closed room.

I pulled out my Colt Government and busted a cap in the knee of my man on the right. He staggered but still went to unsheathe his sword, so I gave him a few new piercings in his elbow and palm. He screamed like an animal.

My gun still trained on them, I got back to my feet and held up a lantern they had in the cellar. It was a small space. I saw bottles of booze rolling around atop a bare-bones table, chairs, and chains and ropes hanging from the beams that crossed the low ceiling, but no other enemies.

"I've got a couple questions for you gents," I told them.

"Pfft! Ba-ha-ha-ha!" One of the men broke out in laughter. *Must've shot him in the wrong spot. Maybe I should send two or three bullets through his skull.*

"Hey, you," said one of the guys. I shined the lantern on his face. It looked somehow familiar. Then it clicked—it was the same dude whose jaw I'd crushed two days prior. Had he used some kind of magic? Was it that easy to heal a wound like that?

"Those foreign weapons are no joke. But, ya know, you really shouldn't underestimate adventurers."

"Huh?" I felt someone come up behind me, then a blow. It sent me flying to the side and slammed my shoulder into the wall. The impact knocked all the wind out of me.

You gotta be kidding.

One of the shitheads I'd shot held a broken chair in one hand. Was that what he'd used to hit me? Hold up, I'd just shot him with an assault rifle—how was he moving? What was going on?

In the midst of the confusion—

"See? This is what we're working with." A bright light wrapped around the hole in the guy's palm and refilled the wound as if rewinding the damage. Someone slid the naked blade of a long-sword out of its sheathe. I hadn't seen enough to fully understand, but I'd gotten the point.

"Well, time to die."

Oh, buzz off.

(4TH DAY)

Adventurers ran this town. To state the glaringly obvious, fights broke out here all the time. That's just the kind of animals they were. Common bar brawls aside, they committed no shortage of thefts, muggings, murders, and scams, and got into intra-party fights to try to avoid divvying up the spoils of their exploits. The Guild had the unenviable job of mediating these disputes and cleaning up that garbage, or so Evetta told me. I then put my question to her, "So who handles arguments between adventurers and civilians?"

The answer was a pain in the ass to explain.

The Adventurers Guild in this city had been run under the auspices of the Kingdom of Remlia. It had broken away from the Central Adventurers' Confederation after the current king had gained a certain level of fame as an adventurer himself.

Going independent in and of itself was not so unheard of. All the Confederation representatives who got sent over were money-grubbers. Plus, it took forever to travel in this world. Crossing the seas added an additional layer of danger. If the extra hands requested never made it to town, the local Guild members would get even more work dumped on their plates. If they collapsed under the pressure and fell behind on their work, active and would-be adventurers could run amok. Nothing beat governing yourself if you could hack it.

However, the Guild ran into a whole host of problems as soon as it had opened its newly independent doors. One of those pertained to how disputes between adventurers and non-adventurers should be solved. The king was a renowned adventurer. Everybody who was anybody knew that. If he tipped the scales of justice in favor of fellow adventurers, then subjects outside the profession would say, "Typical king of the adventurers. He's playing favorites." Conversely, if he found the adventurer to be in the wrong, he'd hear nothing but "The king has abandoned the way of the explorer!"

Nobody saw him as a king before an adventurer. Remlia ole Armaguest Rhasvah, legendary adventurer, came first. If the majority of his subjects had been farmers, popularity would've probably come second or third on the king's list of priorities. However, adventurers were fighters. It was best to tread carefully around them, especially because there could be monsters among their ranks strong enough to take down an entire country alone.

Then you might ask, wouldn't giving adventurers special treatment solve the issue? The answer would be no. While this was indeed an adventurer's city, it could not function with them alone. It needed merchants to buy raw materials and put them on the market. It needed artisans to take those materials and fashion them into weapons. It needed chefs to fill stomachs, carpenters to build houses, farmers to grow the grains, and performers to provide entertainment and respite. The list could go on forever.

After much debate, in a move that sort of defeated the purpose of the whole break for independence, the king decided to defer that responsibility to outsiders. The Kingdom of Remlia belonged to the Central Continent's Federation of Monarchs, and the king sent them a request for constables. Everyone hated constables almost by definition. They took that hatred gladly, even from the most monstrous adventurers. It'd follow that only the cream of the crop had what it took to do that job.

And I had just spent the entire night looking for one such kindly officer. Why? Because I had gotten into a squabble with some adventurers. However, I was about to keel over from exhaustion and my injuries.

Am I gonna die before stepping foot in the dungeon? If this were a game, I'd be losing before even starting the tutorial. Can't say I saw that coming.

I haven't lived up to my name at all. My namesake, the indestructible warship, would finally sink if it saw how pathetic I am. My sister hasn't had much luck, either, given she was named after another destroyer known to squeeze the luck out of other ships. I'd love to find some sort of item that brings good luck and take it back with me.

But to do that, I'd have to survive and go in the dungeon.

I started moving once more, my legs chafing against each other with each step. A kid pointed at me, and his mom scolded him, saying, "You mustn't stare." Did I really look that bad?

I turned the corner and ran into a pair of elves who screamed at the sight of me. One of them, your classic, beautiful elf, carried a bow and wore an outfit that was basically underwear over her tall, lean figure. The other had a staff and was unusually petite for an elf.

Her voluptuous breasts caught my attention through her loosely fitting robe. Both bore the trappings of adventurers.

"Sorry...to scare you. Could you please...tell me...where the constable pos— *B-blegh*—" I hacked up blood but managed to cover my mouth at the last second to avoid staining their clothes.

"Y-you're hurt," noticed the elf with the cane. Concerned, she took a step closer, but—

"Sis, don't get involved!"

—the elf with the bow caught her hand and pulled her back. *Yeah, good move. I would have done the same.*

"At least let me give him some first-aid healing spell," protested the first.

"This guy is definitely bad news! Just ignore him. Come on. Why the hell should we care about some random heim?"

The last thing I wanted was to beg a couple of ladies for sympathy, but I had no choice. They were my only hope. "I'll repay...the favor. The constable post. Could you...tell me...where it is...please?"

"Go straight down this road and turn right at the bar; it'll have a billboard with a hunting horn on it. The post should be right around there. Shall I call someone for help?" replied the kind, big-bosomed elf.

"It's fine. Thank...you." I tried to hand her a few gold pieces as thanks, realized they were covered in blood, and lay them on the cobblestones. "'Scuse me."

I readjusted the grip I had on the chains. Slow as an ox, I started on my way again. The little moans didn't even register anymore. I felt like I could break out in song. Cue the movie credits scrolling over my image. The only problem was that I hadn't even started doing anything yet.

I found the bar and turned right. Luckily, the post was closer than I'd thought. Another fifty meters and I would've died. No joke, just dead. A carefree voice answered my knock on the steel door. Totally spent and relieved, my legs finally gave in. The door I leaned on opened, and I collapsed inside.

"Whoaaa!" a deep voice cried out. It came from a uniformed middle-aged man with a sword at his hip. His diamond-shaped hat made quite an impression.

"Are you the constable?"

"I am. Why?"

"Here." I handed him the chains.

"What in the world?" he asked quizzically as he followed the line outside. Then he screamed. He'd found the trio of adventurers— I'd blasted open holes in them, snaked the chain through those and wrapped it around all three, broken their arms and legs, and rolled them up into a bundle. They weren't dead yet, and I could still hear them moaning in pain. Thanks to this grotesque ball I had to drag behind me, everyone had run away before I could ask for directions. I had to walk straight through the night because of them.

"'Don't underestimate us,' you said, right?" I grinned at the guy staring daggers at me. "Well, don't underestimate me, you damn adventurer."

Mic. Drop.

A weight lifted off my chest. And so, with a last refreshing rush of achievement, I perished.

Nope, still alive.

"……!"

"……"

"……! ……?!"

"……"

"……!"

"……!"

Sounds of two men and a woman talking came to me. They sounded both nearby and far away.

Ugh, I hate this. They remind me of my dead parents, who are long gone and nothing but ash now, but they sure do cling to my memory. Is this considered a curse?

"You shouldn't be treating him like this!" screamed the woman. "How exactly is he at fault?!"

"Don't go out of your way to take his side. Who do you think you and I are bound to protect and support?" retorted one of the men.

"Is separating the wheat from the chaff not part of our role as well?!"

"Just try it. Forget about the Guild; you'll drag the king into this, too. Cool your head."

"Now, now, you two. We can wait for him to wake up before we move on to discussing particulars," noted the second man.

"Then......shall we get started?" I suggested, getting up from the simple cot where I lay. I saw Evetta, a young boy with small wings on his back, and the constable in the room.

"Souya!" exclaimed Evetta. "Are you all right?!" She rushed over and put her hands on the bars. I was fully locked up in a prison cell.

"O-ow!" My whole body hurt. Muscle and bone creaked as they ground against each other. And for some reason my skin felt hot, though not like a fever from a wound, but as if I'd been scorched by something external.

"You've got some luck, pal. If that elf who happened to pass by hadn't worked her magic, you'd be one arm short by now," said the constable.

Now that he mentioned it, I kind of remembered taking a long-sword to the arm. Nervously, eagerly, I tested out all five fingers on my left hand. It hurt a little to move them, but my nerves and muscles seemed fine. That must've been some spell.

"The elf—what was her name?" I asked.

"Beats me. She didn't give it. Oh, but she did have a huge rack."

"Seriously?"

"Yep, like this! Or, like, this big!" shouted the constable as he gestured to replicate her cup size. The lady at his side with a slightly humbler set watched him coldly.

"Souya," she said. "I'm glad you're looking okay."

"Sorry to worry you."

"I think I've got the general idea, but could you tell us what happened?" Evetta leaned in closer. The bars she held squealed under her grip.

"Whoa there. Sorry, horned lady," cut in the constable, "but that's my job. I'll allow you to stay, so let me ask the questions first."

"......All right," she acquiesced, but her intimidating expression never wavered. She looked cold but was actually a rather passionate person.

My man the constable pulled over a desk, got out some paper and a pen, and took a seat. "First, sonny, your name is 'Souya of Japan,' am I right?"

"Yes, sir." The inked pen slid over the paper.

"You are suspected of inflicting bodily harm to three adventurers," he continued.

"That's right." I'd passed out before I could explain anything. That's what it must have looked like to him.

"Anything to say in your defense?"

"Some valuable goods were stolen from my camp. Those three adventurers are the ones who did it," I explained. "Luckily enough, I found them, and while I sustained some injuries, I managed to detain them and deliver them here. The rest you already know."

"And did you locate those stolen items?"

"No." The containers never would've fit in that cramped cellar. There hadn't been enough time to interrogate them, and I couldn't have looked around the area long or I would have risked dealing with reinforcements.

"In that case, can you produce any witnesses who will attest to the fact you were robbed? Evidence will do just as well."

"Oh...... No, I can't."

This is bad. Maybe once Machina reboots, I can— No, will people from here even believe anything that unexplainable gizmo has to say?

"We've inspected the adventurers' residences but found no objects that looked in any way foreign. Now, that lot are not exactly what you'd call upstanding citizens, even if you were trying to be nice. They've got a bad reputation. Rumor has it that one of the merchants took them in as little tykes and has them doing shady work for him now. The thing is, you don't have any proof. And without that, all we've got left is the absolute wreckage you made out of them. I'd have gladly looked the other way if you'd only slugged 'em once or twice, but that, well...you can't really overlook that."

Not even a moan reached my lips. I realized way too late that I'd made a rash move and regretted it.

"And I've got one more piece of bad news for ya, sonny." *Wait, what more can there be?* "It's got to do with your legal status." The constable laid down his pen. "According to Central Continental law, noncompliant individuals and those who have not consecrated a covenant with a god qualify as criminals on that basis alone. We're supposed to arrest them and bring them before the Church of St. Lillideas. As a side note, they condemn people to the death penalty or life as a human guinea pig nine-to-one."

"Awha?!" *What is this, a witch hunt?*

"Personally, I wouldn't want to hand a nice guy like you over to them. To get even more specific, I only took up this post ten days ago, and I'm not dyin' to rush all the way over to the Central Continent so quick. We're short-staffed, so I'd have to come straight back here. That's too many months to spend on a boat."

"Um, how long does it take one way?" I inquired after that part kindhearted, part self-interested speech.

"Six whole months." Even if by some miracle I was found not guilty, it'd be checkmate for me.

I came to the wrong place for help. I need to run. Just gotta get my weapons…and, of course, they took them all.

"This is where I'd like to ask you two from the Guild for help. Is there any way you could make a special exception and just call him an adventurer for me? It can be temporary or whatever. If you could, he'd be out of my jurisdiction, and the boat trip would be out of my future."

What a capable, lazy-ass dude. Kind of impressive.

"I second that request," I added.

"Request denied." The winged boy rejected me on the spot. The rest of his body looked too human for him to be a beastman, and I doubted he could fly with those tiny wings. They might as well have been there for decoration. I could've sworn he was just a kid, but it was even less wise to judge a book by its cover in this world.

"I am Saorse, Guildmaster of the Adventurers Guild in the Kingdom of Remlia," he began. "Otherworlder, let's get one thing straight. Nonconforming fools are unfit to receive divine protection from any of the Legion Gods. That is all. If you'll excuse me, I have work to do."

"Guildmaster! Please, there must be something you can do!" cried Evetta.

"Unhand me!" Evetta flung her arms around the Guildmaster, who had tried to bow out with as few words as possible. *This almost looks like a charming brother-sister tussle,* I thought, clearly trying to escape reality.

"Exactly how many gods, including the lowest ranked, do you think have rejected him? It's unprecedented!! To make matters worse, he then decides to roll up the men he brawled with into a ball and parade it all through town. No god will ever accept him once they catch wind of his behavior!" Yeah, he had a point. I'd partly brought this on myself.

"Then at least give us one more day! We'll plead our cases before the gods in town once more."

"Sorry to interrupt, but I would feel bad making you do that again, Evetta."

"Souya, hush your mouth!" *What are you, my mother?*

I watched as Evetta continued to plead my case to the Guildmaster in vain for a while. His face half-resigned, the constable mumbled, "Guess I better book that ship."

That's too bad. Looks like my adventure has come to an end, ran the monologue in my mind. *Man, I wish I could've explored the dungeon. I know I've said this a million times, but I haven't even done anything yet. The only possibly feasible option I have left is to knock the officer out (sorry, dude) and make a run for it. But no, what would happen if I went on the lam?*

Just then—

"I've heard enough. We have but a simple matter before us," the voice of heaven itself rang out. A shadow slipped through the prison window bars and jumped down to the floor.

"Huh?" It was the gray cat.

"You fool! You dug that grave far too deep. It took me half a day to crawl my way out."

"Well, you were dead." I was sure I'd checked her pulse. Her blood had coagulated, and her pupils hadn't moved.

"Heh-heh-heh. A low-grade death is gone in a few hours." *Damn, this world has got some weird cats.* "Souya, it appears you are in search of a god with whom to consecrate a covenant."

"Exactly, Lady Mythlanica. Could you point me in the direction of someone who could help, by any chance?"

"I am offering to make that pact with you, dimwit."

"Huh?" *Wait, is this a god? No waaay. Like I'm gonna believe there's a god that does nothing but eat, sleep, and stick her back leg up in the air before going to town licking it.*

"Did you just say Mythlanica?"

"Uh, yes. Is she famous or something?" I asked, answering the Guildmaster's question with a question.

"Long ago, three kingdoms ruled over the Right Continent," he explained. "The three nations thrived with powerful weapons we have since lost the means to replicate, along with advanced civilizations. That is, until a single woman laid waste to them and all the prosperity they so proudly enjoyed. Her name was Mythlanica, she who attained her place among the gods through wicked deeds and artifice."

"D'aw," Lady Mythlanica purred, proudly standing tall.

"I was under the impression she had expired after all her adherents perished," continued the Guildmaster.

"If it were that simple to be rid of me, I would never have become a god in the first place. Anyway, I scavenged for rats in prison and survived."

In other words, Lady Mythlanica used to be human? Does that mean she also has a human form? I need to know.

"Now, Souya. Will you make the covenant? You know you want to, don't you? What will it be?"

"Yes!"

"Hmm, whatever should I dooo? You did treat me rather rudely, if you recall. Well, ask nicely, and I might consider it."

I don't mean to brag, but my next moves were absolutely captivating. I got down on my knees and sat up ramrod straight, legs tucked in under me. With hands still on my thighs, I gracefully lowered my head. This part you simply cannot rush. Recklessly dive down and it'll come off like you're pressuring the other person. I placed my hands together on the floor, forming a diamond with my index fingers and thumbs, and hovered my head just about a finger's width off the ground. Making contact with the floor is unhygienic and not recommended. Refinement is key.

"Please, Lady Mythlanica! I beg you! Please! Pleeeaaassee!" And there you had it—the most esoteric bowing technique known to the Japanese—the *dogeza*. Emotionally, you should aim to match a peasant forced to cough up yearly taxes during a famine.

"Uh...... Right...... Very well. Now cease this. You embarrass me. Seriously, I can't stand to look at you. Stop."

"Otherworlder, allow me to give you a word of warning. Serve a malicious god and you are bound to endure even more torturous penance than had you no god at all," said the Guildmaster.

"We have a saying where I'm from that goes, 'One man's devil is another man's savior.'" Like *one man's trash* but with gods.

"Nothing you say in that state holds any weight," said Lady Mythlanica, expertly roasting me. By the way, Evetta had curled up into a ball in the corner. *Sorry, I'll be with you in a second.*

"Let us begin. Assume a knight's genuflection according to the ways of old."

"Excuse me, what exactly would that be?"

Lady Mythlanica shook her head in disgust.

"Bend one knee to the ground, then place your left hand on your right shoulder and your right hand on the floor, fingers splayed so that I may see them," she instructed. I did as I was told. "Now, bow your head. Do not, under any circumstances, dare look up until I give the word."

The weight of the air around me shifted. It held a cat's presence no longer. I could sense a person standing there. Bare feet padded softly over; I caught a glimpse of toenails.

"Mythlanica of the Dark Flame inquires: Art thou willing to become my sword and satisfy my every lust? No honor shall your blade reap, no glory shall your blood acquire, no peace shall your soul enjoy. In light of this, if thou hast no objections, answer me with silence."

"...," I answered.

"Mythlanica the Sinister Manipulator inquires: Dost thou possess the fortitude of mind to convert even the degradation of sipping mire into thine strength to do what must be done, attain what must be attained, and steal what must be stolen? Art thou willing to plot against the royal and slaughter the heroic? If thou hast no objections, answer me with silence."

"......"

"Mythlanica the Malevolent accepts thine silence. O knight with no sword, he with no convictions, insubordinate Otherworlder. Mighty straddler of worlds who fears no evil name, seeks no acclaim, treasures no dreams. I hereby absolve thee of all thy sins and condone thy deceptions. Even should thou shoot the dark sparks that engulf the world in calamity, I alone shall forgive and accept all of thy being. As such—"

Fine hair brushed against my ear, soft skin touched my shoulder, and something leaned over me sweetly. Then came the bewitching fragrance of a woman. The evil spirit whispered in my ear.

"Your blood, your bones, even your cries of resentment now belong to me."

I felt moist lips press against the nape of my neck. A tongue ran along my skin, and fingers slid down my face. A stabbing pain attacked my heart. I struggled to breathe for a second, then saw a vision of myself vomiting up my entrails. I forced myself to stop shaking. To show fear is a man's greatest shame.

"The covenant has been consecrated. Raise your head."

"Yes, milady."

My gaze landed on long, silky, fluffy fur and golden eyes; before me stood a gray cat. I now knew it to be my goddess's shadow, a disarming guise concealing the terrifying being within. And yet, she could be a devil for all I cared. I'd take her at my side over struggling all alone any day. But I was curious about one thing.

"Mr. Constable, my friend! What did my goddess look like?!"

"Wowza, talk about a woman of ruinous beauty. She was so fine that she gave me chills."

Argh, I wish I coulda seen her.

"You, cease this nonsense." It hadn't taken long to piss off my goddess.

"All right! Now the rest is up to you at the Adventurers Guild. Everybody, get out," ordered the constable. Thus, I was safely released from jail.

We got back to the wrecked campsite, and I immediately checked Machina's status. The reboot meter had gone up to 59 percent. If it kept going at this rate, she would probably start working again the next day. I let out a sigh of relief. Her manual happened to be lying on the ground. I picked it up and flipped through it until I found what I was looking for: instructions on how to find the containers without her.

Every container came installed with a simple radar probe that looked like a big flashlight. In fact, it actually had a working light. Not that it meant anything here, but it also worked as a radio. It could connect to other devices through a USB cable and also had a hand-cranked charger, my personal favorite part.

I selected the missing containers' numbers. The medical supplies and weapons were in three and four. That set, I switched on the probe. It beeped: signal received and returned. Checking the manual again, I found that it had a ten-kilometer search range. The containers had probably been hidden in the city somewhere. Still, this was no more than a simple probe. It would beep louder the closer I got to the containers but couldn't tell me much more. I'd have to actually walk around on my own two feet to determine their exact location.

Actually, that still left a bigger problem to deal with. I looked around the campsite for anything I could use, putting things in order as I went.

......Nothing.

Water splashed over dishes somewhere behind me. My goddess had also started cleaning up. It would be disrespectful to look upon her human form, so I tried my best not to peek, no matter how badly I wanted to.

I took stock of the weapons I had once more. The AK was out. It could be the most durable and maintenance-free gun out there, but it would do me no good cut in half. Plus, I didn't have any more bullets. The Colt Government looked fine, but only two rounds remained in its seven-bullet magazine. My woodsman's hatchet hadn't done much against that boar carcass, but it cut through human flesh like butter. Only, those wounds had healed right back up in an instant. Were all adventurers that beastly?

Last up, the karambit. I'd gotten it as a gift ages ago but had never mastered how to use it. A normal knife worked well enough if I had to stab anything, and the hole, called a grip ring from its applications in light work, always got in the way. I'd also cut myself on the curved blade before. Though I'd gotten a crash course on how to use it, you'd need to work up to a considerable level of skill to be able wield it in defensive maneuvers and cut your attacker's hands or neck.

Well, I figured, if I didn't have much brawn left, maybe brains were the way to go, so I started reading the manual again for helpful information.

"Caution: This manual will completely disintegrate within six months due to bio-telomere technology." It included simple medical instructions, an illustrated survival guide, a manga depicting emergency simulations, another explaining the history of AI, and a technical repair guide for the machina units. And—a page that had been wet and dried. This page alone was made of a different material. It was a handwritten note clearly added after printing, and the scribbled penmanship made it look like its author must have been in a hurry.

"Employ this emergency measure in case either over half of the squadron members perish or all the machina units are destroyed. This is dangerous. I repeat, this is extremely dangerous. Appended here only as a last resort."

All things considered, this last resort might come in handy right about now.

The constable had interrogated all three adventurers, but they had held their tongues. Actually, I'd gone a little overboard on them, and none of them had physically been able to talk, or so I heard.

But going back to the fundamental question, who had hired

those degenerates to steal the containers? My money was on either the trade group or the royal family. There also remained the possibility it might've been the work of an individual adventurer, but even then, they'd need to go through the merchants to make any cash. I had to keep a close watch on the Adventurers Guild, too.

But in the end, my greatest suspicion fell on the trade group because they had both access to trade routes and the means to hire people to do the job. You could say the royal family checked those boxes, too, but if they had orchestrated this, then I was shit outta luck. Not even Goliath would go up against an entire country. So I decided to proceed under the assumption that the trade group had in fact done the deed.

My cleaning at the campsite finished, I set off for the city. A sleepy Lady Mythlanica rode on my shoulders as I walked all over town until I got a hit on the radar in the warehouse district.

"Excuse me, which trade group owns this warehouse?" I asked the guard in front of the building.

"The Zavah Night Owl Trade Group."

"Thanks." A satisfied smirk rose to my lips, and I left the area.

I found the headquarters for the Zavah Night Owl Trade Group that *also ran the coin dealers* without any trouble. It had a great location on the main street. Neatly arranged rows of weapons caught my eye after I stepped inside. No matter what else might be going on, you just couldn't stop a boy's heart from jumping with joy when he was surrounded by weapons.

The shop attracted a good number of customers. Friendly, attractive staff milled about recommending this or that to the patrons. Some readily took them up on their suggestions, while others haggled over the terms of the sale. Business was booming.

"Welcome, sir. Are you looking for anything specific today? I'd be happy to show you around if you'd like," an elderly saleswoman offered. She was plump and elegant, and I could totally see myself buying whatever she put before me.

"Excuse me, I was hoping to see the owner of the shop."

"Pardon my asking, but what business do you have with him?" she inquired.

I took a deep breath and, in a voice as low and powerful as I could muster, responded, "I'm interested in purchasing all the foreign goods you have in stock."

"……" She replied with silence. Then she whispered in the ear of one of the staff passing by and called someone out for me. "Show our guest upstairs," she instructed two muscular dudes. Together, we ascended to the second floor.

They led me to a room that must have been reserved for hosting clients. It contained a taxidermied monster, furniture adorned with golden embellishments, and a display of impractical yet dazzling swords. Plus, an expensive-looking sofa and table. The tightly shuttered windows left only a dim light in the room.

A man waited for me there—the same man from the coin dealer, in fact. He looked pretty young to be representing the shop on these matters. Was it talent or money that allowed him to get here—or both? Anyway.

"Leave us. Let me talk to our guest alone." The bodyguards retreated at his order. "Now then, please have a seat."

"Thanks." I did as he asked and sat down on the luxurious sofa. *Whoa, pretty fluffy.* Lady Mythlanica descended from my shoulder and curled up into a ball.

"Mr. Otherworlder, I've heard some interesting tales about you."

"Ohhh, you must mean how I clumped those three adventurers into a ball."

He chuckled. "Now, then. What can I do for you?" *Shameless bastard.*

"I'd like you to return what your underlings stole from me. Do it now and I'll forget this ever happened."

"I'm sure I have no idea what you mean. Return what?" *He would say that, wouldn't he?*

"What if I told you that I knew the stolen goods your men took are being kept in your warehouse?"

"So close."

"?"

I had no idea what he meant.

"I must say, you're so close. Mr. Otherworlder, you have some truly spectacular technology at your disposal. You have power we could not hope to understand. On top of that, you're a man of nerve and talent. You came so close, yet so far." He must've been pretty damn sure of himself because he didn't even try to hide it.

"You are but one man. With a single word, I can have the items in the warehouse relocated. Would you like to call the constable? Or perhaps someone from the Guild? Neither would make it there in time, and I can feign ignorance for as long as necessary. You almost had me. If only you had kept your knowledge of their location close to your chest, you might have had a chance to retrieve your belongings."

"Sure, but what would be the point in getting them back just so someone could steal them again?"

He was right. I couldn't keep any valuables in my tent safe all on my own. If I kept playing this game of retrieving what's mine just to have it taken once again, I'd run myself into the ground and end up too exhausted to do anything. Hiring a guard wouldn't work because they'd soon see I had very little money, take advantage, and eventually bankrupt me. Not to mention, I'd constantly worry they might steal from me themselves. There'd be no time left for adventuring.

The man flashed a smile, incredibly pleased with himself. It was the kind of smile only someone who knows they've won by a landslide can give. "I'm pleased you understand where things stand. In that case, did you perhaps have any other items to sell? You would do well to bring them in before you lose them next time. We'll purchase them from you at a fair price."

"Nah, I don't have anything like that left."

"Well, then." He gestured toward the door as if to say, *Get out.*

I slung Lady Mythlanica, now fast asleep, over my shoulder and stood up from the sofa. "Mind if I ask you two last questions?"

"Ask away." He really thought he was sitting pretty.

"How are you so sure I won't resort to violence while I'm here?"

"You've lost your guns. Furthermore, should you decide to get rough, we would respond in kind." He snapped his fingers. The men waiting outside reentered the room—huge, fierce-looking brutes. I couldn't describe them any other way.

"This one is especially talented. He's taken care of quite a number of adventurers who have crossed the trade group." He meant the dude on the left.

"Would you mind opening the window?" I asked.

"You, open it."

The talented Mr. Muscles went out of his way to open it for me. Bright light and clangor poured in through a window that perfectly framed the warehouses.

"Those containers you stole all come with an emergency device that does a little something like this." Time to activate the probe. I clicked the red button twice, waited one second, then pushed it down for five seconds. "It's what we call a 'self-destruct function.'"

A thundering boom exploded in the distance. Smoke shot up into the sky like out of a geyser—but from the warehouse, of course. Rubble and inventory flew all around and scattered. Textiles floated through the air, and blasted bits of golden goods rained down. Women shrieked, men screamed in anger, and the blast captivated almost everyone passing by. It had been about three times larger than what I'd expected.

"Wh-what? What did you—? What?!"

"I blew it up. You've got explosive-type magic here, too, right? It's similar to that. I'll bet nothing in that warehouse made it through."

"......Ah, ahhh." The man's soul slipped out of his mouth. Maybe he had something really valuable stored there? If so, I'd gotten lucky.

"Ah, sorry. Just one more thing?" Before he could answer, I drew my Colt Government and put a bullet through each of the gangster virtuoso's legs. I took pity on the guy and didn't hit his vital organ. Surprised, Lady Mythlanica dug her nails into me.

The bodyguard scuffled back like a robot that had run out of oil.

"I'll leave you with that today. I've gotta get myself registered with the Adventurers Guild. But I'll be back once more tomorrow, same time, same place. Prepare yourself before then. Now, if you'll excuse me."

I collected the bullet casings and strolled out of the room. Downstairs, everyone from customers to staff members had erupted into a full-blown panic and rushed toward the exit. I slipped into the crowd and disappeared without a trace. After getting out onto the main road, I made sure nobody had followed me and turned into a back alley. Several corners later, I felt pretty safe. Just then, Lady Mythlanica spoke up.

"Mm-mm-mm. Quite the villain, aren't you?"

"No wayyy. They're the villains here."

"The just make wrongs right. Villains destroy other villains, don't they?"

"I see."

This conversation took us right up to the dungeon. My destination was the reception desk. Lady Mythlanica had to wait for me by the entrance.

"Excuse me, I'd like to register as an adventurer."

"Of course. We've been expecting you," replied Evetta. "Now, let's continue from where we left off last time. Please tell me the name of the god with whom you have consecrated your covenant."

"Lady Mythlanica."

She moved her pen smoothly across the scroll. Then she double-checked the form, tracing her finger over every last item.

"One moment, please." Form in hand, Evetta stood up from her chair. A Guild member behind her guided her through the process as she affixed something to the scroll and shined what appeared to be a magical light over it. She came back seeming kind of happy. I was happy, too.

"Your provisional registration has been completed. Two days hence, before the morning bell rings, you will be given your essential equipment and participate in a field training course. Please report back here. We do not accept late arrivals, so please keep that in mind."

"Yes, ma'am." *All right. It's not even a real first step, but I feel like I've made some progress.*

"Souya, on a completely unrelated note, I understand there was an explosion by the warehouse district. The culprit is still on the loose. It could be dangerous, so please do not approach the area."

"You got it."

For the first time since coming to this world, I left the city in high spirits. I sincerely hoped there would be more days like this to come.

But yeah, that probably wasn't gonna happen.

(5TH DAY)

"Understood. I have comprehended the situation. That sounds like a great plan if you ask meee!"

"You think?" Machina started working again the next day, so I caught her up to speed.

"Aahh, Mr. Souya, it looks like Isolla has a question. I'll pass you over to her, okaaay?"

"Sure thing." I felt a bit apprehensive. Hopefully Isolla would be as easygoing as Machina.

"Squad Member Souya, please first provide a rational explanation for why you disposed of the weapons container through self-destruction."

"I judged I wouldn't be able to keep them secure on my own."

"Did you consider the prospect of hiring a paid guard?"

"You can't buy someone's trust with money." *You can sell it, though.*

"The machina unit could have provided surveillance."

"Surveillance, sure, but nothing else. You two can't physically attack humans, can you?"

"No, we cannot," she admitted. "According to Article Two of the Artificial Intelligence Act, we are forbidden from directly inflicting damage on humans."

"That's what I thought."

It went without saying that AI robots would never injure humans. That applied to Otherworldly humans, too. Their programming instructed them to work for humans, yet never harm them. The contradictory nature of the contract they were forced to comply with had brought many an AI to the brink of insanity.

"However, we do have the capacity to help you set traps."

"That's true. But there's no guarantee running a little interference would force any infiltrators to give up. Worst-case scenario, this could've wound up a one-person Alamo." Isolla was apparently an American-made program. Would she get the sarcasm? "Did I make the wrong decision?"

"No, you were correct. Even if you were mistaken, you would be correct." I'd asked a trick question. Isolla and Machina could propose their own suggestions, but they didn't have the authority to oppose me.

"I will assist you in the negotiations today," she offered.

"Actually, about that, I'm gonna have Machina help me out."

"Ohhh... I see." Her voice dropped.

Hang on, is she actually sulking? I didn't see that coming. It's kind of throwing me for a loop.

"The thing is, I've got a plan. You know how Machina comes off as kind of ditzy? I thought we could use that to make them drop their guard. I don't have any complaints about how well you function, Isolla."

"I see. Switching out."

"See ya." She was definitely pissed.

"Hellooo. ♪ Ditzy Machina, at your service," she chirped. "Allow me to explain something as there appears to be a misunderstanding. This is not my original personality setting. The more stress humans experience, the more they yearn for frivolity. Additionally, Isolla was designed to be prim and proper, and it would be confusing if we had the same demeanor, right? You are more than welcome to adjust my settings as much as you like if the current ones displease you. Would you like to proceed? Would you like to abort?"

I'd stepped on a land mine. "I like you just as you are, cheerful and fun."

"If you saaay sooo."

Looking for a way out of this conversation, I introduced Lady Mythlanica. I picked her up and presented her to them. "Machina, disable orders against interaction with outsiders and begin new user registration. This is Lady Mythlanica, the goddess who made a covenant with me. Say hello."

"What devilry is this? Are there two people inside that column? Is that not too cramped? Or are they ghosts?" She touched her paw to the monitor.

"Hello, Lady Goddess. I am Machina, a relatively rare, mass-produced model of a sixth generation artificial intelligence robot made in Japan. I was originally developed for space exploration purposes. Though I am still repairing my internal functions, at full capacity I can manage three more separate characters."

"Is that something akin to a golem?"

"We are legally prohibited from acting independently, but roughly speaking, that's pretty close!"

"Machina, serve her as best you can. That's an order."

"Understood." She extended her arm and raised it in salute.

I ate a light meal of toast and cheese while waiting for my guest to come. For my goddess, I prepared chicken soup with stir-fried meat and vegetables. Her mouth burned easily, so I let it cool before offering it to her. Some time passed, and then—

"Souya, glad to see you're all right."

"Ahh, Ghett." The man I'd been waiting for made his entrance from the river.

"I'm sorry. Did I worry you?"

"Well, of course. Anybody would worry after seeing the mess at your camp with you nowhere to be found."

"Actually, I'm about to go settle that matter with the trade group. Before I do, I have a question for you." I stood up. There would be no sitting around and chatting today. "Those two containers. How much did you get for them?"

"……"

From my inspection of the ransacked campsite, I had come to a single conclusion—those three stooges had in fact laid waste to the place, but they did not steal the containers. Those weighed far too much for anyone to easily carry. And yet, I'd found no drag marks left in the ground or any evidence that they'd used a carriage or wagon.

In that case, they had to have transported the containers into the city via river. When I had asked Machina about it, she'd told me that the containers floated due to their waterproofing. However, I didn't have any proof of Ghett's guilt. The adventurers could have conceivably used a small boat.

Nevertheless, I had to suspect him more than anyone else. Ghett had a good handle on my movements. He would have had the means to predict when I would be away and guess which containers held the most valuable goods. And there was one more thing.

"You are a good person. You care deeply for your family. And I can believe your concern for me is genuine. That's why it's easy for people to take advantage of you."

"......" He looked at me with an indescribable expression.

"Ghett, it won't come back to bite you. So please, tell me how much they were worth."

"Twenty gold pieces." *What a steal.* But maybe that was my arrogance talking.

"Thank you very much. I have a favor to ask of you."

"What's that?"

"In the event I die, I'd like you to dump this at the bottom of the ocean." I placed my hand on Machina. "Also, I don't care if it's leftovers, but I'd like you to keep sharing your fish with Lady Mythlanica." I petted milady's head. "'In exchange' sounds a bit wrong, but you can feel free to sell whatever else you find here."

"You trust me with that?"

"I do," I replied without hesitation. It wasn't out of simple honesty that I trusted him. Rather, I trusted him because I knew exactly how he would betray me, because I knew why he had done it.

Ghett said nothing in reply. That was one way to answer. However, speaking in the manner befitting of my goddess's servant, I offered him this, "In the name of Mythlanica the Malevolent, I forgive your deed."

After returning to town and making a few pit stops, I headed to the shop. Nothing remained of the previous day's hustle and bustle, and business had slowed to a trickle. Instead of customers, rows of muscular employees (I think) stood in lines around the store.

"After all that happened yesterday, you go and pull this?" My man the constable trotted by my side, fiddling with his hat in an exasperated fashion. I'd dropped by and asked him to come with me, and he hadn't stopped blabbering since.

"Yeah, but today I'm an adventurer, so."

"*Provisional* adventurer," the Guildmaster corrected. "We haven't officially accepted you yet. What in the gods' names is wrong with you?" He spoke from behind and surprised me. "I had half a mind to desert you, but then Evetta would come and stir up an even bigger headache, so I had no other choice but to come. However, depending on how this goes, I may still very well cut you off, so think wisely before you act."

"Understood."

A surly staff member led us upstairs and into the room from the day before. Inside stood the same man, along with a plump elderly woman. She looked familiar— Oh, right, she was the staff member I'd spoken to.

"Hello." I quickly greeted my hosts. Plopping myself down on the sofa before anybody else, I crossed my arms and propped both feet up on the table. The man's face twitched and stiffened while the woman, displaying an expression I couldn't begin to describe, poked him in the back.

"First of all, I now realize I have not yet properly introduced myself, Mr. Otherworlder. I—I am L-Lonewell Z-Zavah, the owner entrusted with management of the Zavah Night Owl Trade Group."

"My turn. I can't trust you with anything," the elderly woman cut in. She pushed the man, now dripping with cold sweat and chattering his teeth, behind her and stepped out in front. "I will take the liberty of handling this matter in place of my incompetent son. I am Hollzard Zavah, chairwoman of the Zavah Night Owl Trade Group. Before we go any further, allow me to offer my sincere apologies for causing you all manner of inconvenience," she stated, reverentially bowing her head.

This could throw a wrench in my plans. I think this lady knows how to play the game.

"I welcome your two companions to take a seat as well."

"Please excuse us." The constable and Guildmaster sat down on either side of me.

Before she sat down across from us, the woman gave her son an order. "You, send your little friends downstairs on home."

"Wha—?! But, Mother! What if—?"

"Real merchants don't go around brandishing a half-baked show of force. If the Guildmaster decides to let loose, forget the shop, he'll level the stores next door to the ground. And who do you think would pay for that damage? We will. Besides, our guest hasn't proposed anything yet, has he?" She turned her gaze toward me. I didn't have enough bullets left to make a real scene, but it'd be imprudent to give that away.

"I came today to first see where you stood on all this. That's all. For today, at least," I spat, leaving volumes unspoken.

"Riiight, so, mind if we get down to business?" the constable asked as he took out his documents, clearly annoyed. Nobody stopped him. "Sooo, Ms. Chairman of the Zavah Night Owl Trade Group, your organization has been accused of burglary. Do you have any idea why this may be?"

"No, not at all," she replied with a sweet smile.

"You're aware there was an explosion down at one of the warehouses yesterday, correct?"

"It was *our* warehouse."

"This young man here is responsible for that blast, though he claims he used a mechanism installed on the stolen goods meant to detonate and dispose of them."

"I see. However, we were only holding on to those items for another trade group. But is that so? You mean to say they were stolen goods?" Was she brazenly lying, or had she actually been duped into hanging on to the containers?

"And the name of the trade group in question?" the constable asked.

"I'm not at liberty to say. It would degrade their trust in our professional integrity." *Yeah, you would say that, wouldn't you?*

"Hey, sonny," the officer whispered in my ear. "Untangling the links between trade groups is no walk in the park. You can't get to the bottom of that in anything like a day or two. You said you'd settle this by the end of the day, right?"

"Don't worry, it'll work out," I answered.

"If I may, we also have a claim we'd like to discuss." *There it is.* "We suffered severe losses in that explosion. The warehouse in question held a considerable amount of unappraised resources that our adventurer clientele entrusted to us, you see."

It sometimes took a while before adventurers could find someone to buy the high-value items they picked up in the dungeon. However, they'd be responsible for taxes as soon as they had them appraised, so they apparently often asked trade groups or the Guild to temporarily store those unpriced materials.

"And we were not the only ones affected," Hollzard continued. "The warehouses directly next to ours also sustained damage in the blast. We have compensated their respective representatives for their losses as a temporary measure, but let me assure you, it was no small sum. Hmm, Mr. Otherworlder. You said you used an explosive mechanism?"

"That's right," I answered shortly.

"None of our employees were inside the warehouse at the time of the explosion. I find it difficult to believe any of our people could have activated this mechanism of yours. This must mean that you personally detonated the device of your own free will. From this, we might also draw another conclusion—that you had it sent to our trade group's warehouse in order to destroy it."

"Oh, come on. That's not very likely, is it?" the constable protested simply in my defense.

"Who can say? As I understand, this young man is a servant of a dark god called Mythlanica."

"I consecrated my covenant with her after I was robbed."

"And you expect me to believe that?"

She's pissing me off. But I have to hold it in. It's not time yet.

"Shall we move on to the main issue?" I tried to hurry things along a bit. This pointless conversation was a pain in the ass.

"Yes, by all means," she agreed. "The Zavah Night Owl Trade Group seeks monetary redress for the damage you caused to our inventory, the indemnity we paid our partner trade groups for the losses they incurred, and the medical treatment of our security guards. In total, our claim amounts to nine thousand seven hundred and five gold pieces."

"Wha—?!" exclaimed the Guildmaster, who had been silent to that point.

"Of course, we will hold the Adventurers Guild responsible for whatever amount you are unable to pay individually."

"Excuse us for one moment." He grabbed me by the scruff of my neck and dragged me outside.

"What do you plan to do here? That nine thousand seven hundred and five gold pieces is almost our entire budget for the whole year!"

"It'll be fine. Both the robbery and the warehouse blast happened before I registered as an adventurer. Worst-case scenario, you can use that to get out of it." Hard to believe the same guy who'd said he'd cut me off earlier could get so worked up.

"You speak the truth?"

"It's true. Ask Evetta."

"Fine." The Guildmaster switched right back to his icy demeanor and returned to the room. I followed after him.

"I understand your claim. However, I have one of my own as well. As I mentioned earlier, the items I detonated were stolen from me. And yet, you've chosen to conceal the identity of the culprit to protect your 'professional integrity,' or whatever. In that case, put that precious integrity where your mouth is and cover the cost of the supplies I lost." I knew they had recovered and examined fragments left over from the explosion. They probably thought they knew how much they were worth, too.

The woman hesitated but only for a moment. Then she smiled. "Of course." Little fishy took the bait. "On one condition. I will request my goddess to arbitrate, to ensure the fairness of our negotiations."

"Sure, go ahead."

The constable poked my side and whispered in my ear, "The Minerva Sister goddesses can get downright nasty when you have to pay up. You got that kinda money?"

"It'll be fine. Shut up," I hissed, ignoring him.

Hollzard took out a single bird feather and held it up in prayer. "O goddess of mine, Sage of the Night, Raptor of Knowledge, Glavius. Grant a portion of your divine wisdom to me, your humble disciple, and with your keen eyes, pass judgment upon the world of men that flickers before you."

Light flashed. A single owl fluttered down to perch on the woman's shoulder. "O Hollzard, my disciple. For what purpose do you intend to use my keen eyes?"

"I beseech you to arbitrate a dispute between myself and this Otherworlder to ensure an impartial negotiation."

"Very well, my dear disciple. Now, I turn to you, he who would contest my beloved devotee. You may state the name of your god followed by your own," the small owl commanded. Her piercing gaze overpowered me. No animal had a stare like that. I could feel intelligence far surpassing that of humans hidden in her eyes. Without my own goddess beside me, I felt forlorn.

"I serve Mythlanica. My name is Souya from Japan."

"Mythlanica and Souya. Will your goddess not stand witness on your behalf?" the owl inquired.

"I'm afraid my goddess is in repose. I'd like to have this little one here stand in for her." I took off my glasses, switched on the holographic mode, then placed them on the table. An image floated up from the lenses.

"Good morning, people of the Other Dimension. My name is Machina, and I exist to serve Mr. Souya. I'm sort of like what you might call a spirit in this world. I hope we can come to a mutually beneficial agreement today. I intend to do my best in today's negotiations." The fourteen-centimeter-tall holographic Machina bowed her head. She appeared as a beautiful twelve-year-old girl with pigtails, a frilly yet revealing top, and a miniskirt.

"Wait, do you mean to tell me all the girls in your country walk around lookin' like that?" asked the constable incredulously.

"Pretty much, but not really," I replied in a half-assed answer. *Just don't go around spreading misinformation about Japan, all right?*

After seeing Machina, the woman smiled instinctively. It had worked, after all. These bastards still thought they were going to rake me for cash. They weren't just wrong—they were dead wrong.

"Now then, I will go first, Lady Glavius. This is the note with the amount we are requesting in redress, as well as a catalog of the items we lost." The woman fanned her documents out in front of her. Under a spell of some mysterious power, they began to float in the air and spread out before the owl.

"Nine thousand seven hundred and five gold pieces, I see. It is an equitable sum. However—"

"It's not exactly accurate, is it? The current market price comes to nine thousand eight hundred and two gold, three silver, and six copper pieces," Machina cut in. "The two-hundred-gram, thousand-year-old fossilized tree sliver and Great King Turtle liver listed on the catalog of items were both sold in the market first thing this morning. Combining the inventory from two trade groups, there now remain less than three hundred grams of the thousand-year-old fossilized tree slivers on the market. This will increase its value, which I have calculated to be one point eight times its current price. Furthermore, it takes copious amounts of pure water from a pseudo-spiritual disaster to make these ingredients into third-degree Magical Miraculous Medicines. The catalog listed this water as well, so I've adjusted the value of one casket, or around nine hundred fifty-five liters, to one point two times its current price. Aside from that—"

"Machina, that's enough," I barked, cutting off her flawless recitation for the moment. The woman gritted her teeth and swallowed her surprise.

Impressed, the constable asked, "You guys just got here a few days ago, right?"

"Yes. However, I have a detailed understanding of all the fluctuations on every market in the city."

"Souya, was it? It seems you've unleashed a few eyes. Hmm, are you using insects? Or is that metal of some sort?" the owl inquired, spinning her neck around. I had set up drones in the corners of the room to spy on the documents for me. *I gotta hand it to you, goddess. Didn't think you'd catch me.*

"However, it's not foul play. There's no difference between utilizing money to hire a hand or utilizing technology to gain an eye."

She was shaping up to be a much more understanding goddess than I'd imagined. "Well then, dear Hollzard, your claim now amounts to nine thousand eight hundred and two gold, three silver, and six copper pieces. Does this satisfy you?"

"Yes." She nodded.

Now it was my turn. I lined up the papers I had printed out and went through each of them, pointing out the things lost in translation.

"Here is my catalog of items. However, this only covers the destroyed container. The items in the one that remains missing I have decided to exclude. Machina, if you would."

"Beginning with the gun attachments, the container held three magnification scopes; at ten gold pieces each, we request a total of thirty pieces in indemnities. Seeing as comparable products for the other types of attachments do not exist in this world, we will not submit them for compensation." I crossed out the other attachments on the list with a magic marker.

"It also held twenty AK-47 assault rifles and eight M1911 Colt Government pistols. Trade Group Chairman Zavah, your son offered us one hundred gold pieces for the AK-47, so we will base our calculations on this rate. Would you agree to a similar price for the M1911s?" Machina asked.

"My son told me about those. We couldn't even imagine making such small guns in our world. Go ahead and double it."

"Thank you very much. In that case, that comes to a total of three thousand six hundred gold pieces." The woman's lips curled into a smile. "We will also request repayment for the bullets."

Now then, would she be able to keep that stupid smile when all was said and done?

"According to my research, dwarf-made firearms and gunpowder are not currently being imported, correct?"

"Ohhh, yes. The dwarves stopped producing them about half a year ago due to an accident. They were making a new kind of gunpowder and blew an entire city into smithereens," Hollzard explained. "Ever since then, the government has taken over management of all remaining gunpowder. They outlawed its sale on the regular markets, so it's impossible to put a price on it."

Wait, are the dwarves making a nuclear bomb or something? Also, this means that son of a bitch tried to sell me a gun without any bullets, didn't he?

"Yes, that's true. We could not formally appraise the gunpowder available here. Souya, would you please give them a demonstration?"

"You got it." I took a chunk of meat out of my backpack and set it on the table. It was about forty centimeters thick. "Cover your ears. This is gonna be loud," I warned, then shot a single bullet through the meat. The casing rolled on the ground, and I snatched it up as quick as I could and hid it in my pocket. The gunshot caused the constable's face to contort hilariously in shock.

"Were you able to appreciate the difference?" Machina asked.

"There's no smoke," answered the owl.

"Precisely. The gunpowder you utilize in this world is called black gunpowder in ours and has become obsolete. These bullets use a smokeless gunpowder. Although they have similar properties to what is available here, in a sense, they are distinct products. As such, I would argue they do not fall under the aforementioned prohibition. What do you think, Lady Glavius?" We weren't going to take any *you can't put a price on it* bullshit.

In response to Machina's question, Glavius asked, "The type of gunpowder is not the only difference here. Are you certain you do not want to expand on this?"

"Yes, quite. We are forbidden from divulging all the details of our technology to the inhabitants of this world."

"And why is that? Answer me," the owl demanded.

"We came here only to explore the dungeon and do not wish for anything more. The last thing we want is to potentially cause some kind of war or conflict."

"So you would deny the merchant his greatest source of income? Very well, I will defer to your wisdom," conceded the owl. "Let us appraise these items." The woman turned sheet white. Victory was finally in sight, at least for now.

"I understand you have a type of currency called Mythlanic gold. As luck would have it, Souya happens to serve a goddess of that same name. If I'm not mistaken, this gold derives its value from more than its historical significance as a relic of the bygone kingdom's currency. Each coin contains a small amount of magic that its owner can quickly activate at will. We therefore propose to request an indemnity for each bullet equal to one Mythlanic gold piece. We do not have adequate knowledge to discern whether the coins do in fact possess this magical power, so we will exclude that from our claim."

"Mm-hmm, that is an equitable proposition," the owl agreed.

"Thank you very much."

I felt the woman quiver from across the room. I'd have given anything to know what she thought as she watched Machina politely bow her head and saw me flash a big-ass smile from behind. Seriously, what I wouldn't give.

Take that, you greedy maggots.

"The container had two thousand five hundred and eight rounds of the 7.62 by 3 mm bullets and three hundred of the 45 ACP bullets. Mythlanic gold is currently trading at twenty-two gold pieces. If we convert the total, that will come to sixty-three thousand three hundred and sixty—"

"Excuse me, Lady Glavius. Would you please cancel the arbitration?" She threw in the towel. Both mother and son had the exact same look of hysteria on their faces.

"Hollzard, do you understand what it means to cancel an arbitration you requested your goddess to conduct?" the owl asked.

"Yes, milady." The air shook, and it wasn't the woman's tremors this time. No, the air itself actually trembled. The small owl had unleashed a fierce, savage force.

"You rotten dolt!" shrieked the owl. "As punishment, I banish you from my protection for one year! I should send you back to your days of peddling vegetables on the streets!"

"I am terribly sorry."

"......Souya, and you as well, Machina." The owl plucked two of her own feathers and handed them to me with her beak. "I hereby lend you my might. Should you wish to continue this arbitration, hold up that feather and call me by name. You may also use it to request a new arbitration. Farewell. May we meet again, my new Otherworld disciples."

Now it was my turn to be shocked. Who would have thought I'd get to have a contract with a second goddess? Before I could offer my thanks, she disappeared into a whirl of light.

"Mr. Souya! I want that one, the one that's got a nicer shape!" exclaimed Machina. "Make sure you write my name on it, okay?"

"All right, all right." As a reward for her good work, I inscribed

Machina's name on the feather. I just hoped we wouldn't get yelled at for that later.

"Constable, Guildmaster, would you allow us to continue this discussion in private?" the woman asked, her voice quaking.

"I'm leaving. I've got work to do," responded the Guildmaster.

"Likewise," said the constable. On his way out, he leaned over and whispered, "I'm gonna pretend I didn't see you put that metal item in your pocket, so don't ever drag me into your shit again. Got that?" and then disappeared. Evidently, the old dog was more cunning than I'd thought.

"So." I sat up tall and put on a straight face. "Answer me a few things."

"Ask whatever you want." I heard the woman click her tongue in disgust. *That's some attitude, you old hag.*

"Who stole my containers?"

"The Ellomere Western Peng Traders. They're run by a young man my brainless son associates with. He used to only do business with the poor or beastfolk, work that never brought in much cash, but ever since he started sleeping with that merfolk whore, he's been a different person. Good grief, what an asinine partnership I've gotten roped into."

"Who gives a shit?"

"In my home country, we have a saying that goes, 'The customer is king,'" Machina added. The only people who ever used that phrase nowadays were self-righteous assholes.

"Well, I've got the king of pestilence in front of me right now," she growled.

"Want me to bust out that feather?"

"You'd have to break into the national coffers to get your hands on an amount as absurd as sixty-three thousand three hundred and sixty gold pieces. Do you really want to turn not only the trade group but also the Guild against you, too? Though I suppose the royal family would just steal it back from you in the end."

This hag still didn't understand she had lost. In fact, she thought she could turn it all around. Now at the end of my rope, I decided to let her have it.

"You think I give a damn? I'll dump every last coin I get at the bottom of the ocean, for all I care. And what do you think will happen to a country that suddenly loses all its cash? You think it can function on its own? How much exactly do you import from the Central Continent? You're right, I might be signing my own death warrant. Still, I'd get killed, and that'd be the end of it. But what about you two? When all is said and done, everyone will know that you, Hollzard Zavah and Lonewell Zavah, Disciples of Lady Glavius of the Minerva Sisters and managers of the Zavah Night Owl Trade Group, screwed over the entire country by pissing off a single Otherworlder. The royals and all the other trade groups will hate you. Forget that, every goddamn person in this entire town will hate you. They'll shit-talk every last drop of blood you have, take you to task, and spit curses on even your goddess's name. Could you handle all that notoriety? You'll end up dirt poor, left with nothing but live rats to chew on to stave off your own starvation—do you think you could live like that? Or are you telling me you want to see this get bloody? Want me to try jazzing up both you and your darling son's arms and legs with some twenty-two-gold-piece bullets? I've still got plenty left to sell. So come on, tell me what it's gonna be. But think very carefully first."

As if she'd run out of gas, the old hag froze up. I'd guzzled it all down. Forget about whether I could actually carry out my threat, if all I had was my own life to bargain, then I'd put it all on the line. Who the hell did she think my goddess was? The whole world could turn against or curse me all they wanted. I didn't give a shit.

"Oh, the market has changed. One Mythlanic gold coin is now worth twenty-three gold pieces," Machina chimed in, completely failing to read the room.

"A-anyway. What else did you want to ask me?" Hollzard's hands were shaking. Looked like the old lady had finally come to grips with where she stood here. She'd realized the man she was dealing with couldn't be blinded by self-interest—a merchant's worst nightmare.

"Where is the other container?"

"That I don't know. I swear."

"Did you hire the adventurers who attacked my camp?"

"No."

"Did you put the merman up to steal from me?" *Depending on how she answers this question, I will actually put a few holes in her limbs.*

"No, we didn't ask him to do anything. I wasn't lying; we were only holding on to the items."

"I see. I'm going to put this matter on the back burner for now. You owe me one—no, two, for your son's share, also. And I will have you pay me back in full. Just try and run, and I'll use that feather on you."

One win, in the bag. Next up—

—a kind of anticlimactic, or disappointingly simple, confrontation with the real culprit. In an unexpected turn of events, the mid-level boss of this video game turned out to be way stronger than the final boss. A single bullet settled my beef with the Ellomere Western Peng Traders for good.

I had Hollzard's idiot son take me to Ellomere's shop, where I found the young chairman and a woman with dead eyes at his side. As I started to get down to business, I noticed an exquisitely beautiful gem on the young man's desk. It had been left there so carelessly that I immediately grew suspicious. And yet, I'd gotten so worked up in a weird way after the whole Zavah ordeal that I put a bullet through it without any hesitation. Using the idiot son as a shield, I started pushing past Ellomere's guards when I heard a woman scream. It had come from a mermaid bouncing around like crazy. In the end, the evil spirit that had possessed the chairman disappeared, leaving nothing but his dumbfounded expression. Both the mermaid and the chairman had completely lost all their memories of the recent past, so I explained the situation to them. And with that, the case drew to a close.

(6TH DAY)

"Did you find anything that looks usable?"

"Four intact AK-47s, two M1911s, and six guns usable for maintenance. The rest is junk. As for the bullets, I would have to check each one individually with my molecular sensor."

I'd configured Isolla to go through the wreckage of the guns I'd recovered. Pretty much everything had melted into sooty clumps, but a surprising portion of it had made it through.

"No, don't worry about checking them. Is there any possibility the trade group is hiding more somewhere?"

"I've looked into every person involved in the group. They have nothing else."

"Got it."

I tossed the junk guns into one of the empty containers, along with the AK-47 that had been sliced in two. Next, I took the Colt Government pistol out of my pocket, ejected the cartridge, and pulled the slide back. I half expected to feel some sort of emotion come welling up, but nothing ever came, so I chucked it in with the rest.

"Isolla, anything you forgot to throw in here?"

"No. And you? Any other regrets you'd like to add to the pile?"

"Good to go. They're all in there." It was a pretty good joke. "All right, Ghett, dump this at the bottom of the ocean somewhere for me. Try to go as deep as you can, please."

"All right. There's a ravine down deep that not even merfolk dare go near. I'll throw it there for ya. And how about this box? If you don't need it, I'll take it off your hands. I'd like to use it to take my fish to market. It'll probably carry more than my creel."

"Sure, take it, take it."

"Great, I will. Right, so, well, a whole lot has happened, but...... See you around."

"See ya."

Dropping the container into the river, he pushed it from behind until they both disappeared beneath the water. His granddaughter had decided she wanted to stay with her human. In a depressing twist, it turned out the price she'd paid the precious jewel to get her legs had been the love she and her man had for each other.

The dungeon held countless treasures we could never begin to imagine. Those two would probably find something in there that could make their dreams come true, someday. She'd told me she wanted to wait for that day together as a couple. I passed that message on to Ghett, along with the broken jewel, and called it a job well done.

As for the medical supply container, I recovered that from the Ellomere Western Peng Traders. They gave me forty gold coins for all the trouble and also returned all the ransom money Ghett had paid up until that point. Though they had asked me to return it to him, when I tried, he just told me, "It's yours," and refused to take it. I'd have to go and give it back to the trade group at some point. It was a shit ton of money—too much for me to ever spend.

"Only after we break bread, betray each other, and then forgive each other do we finally gain real trust. Humans really are pieces of work, aren't they?"

"Do not fool yourself into thinking you know anything about anything after that little betrayal, you half-wit." I'd intended the comment for Isolla, but Lady Mythlanica answered instead. She leaped up to my shoulder and continued.

"Humans will betray one another at the slightest provocation. They steal. They slander. They envy. They lie. I once read a history book with the words, 'Within these pages, I record our failures and follies' inscribed on its cover. The historian who wrote it was executed for the crime of telling the truth."

Isolla added, "We have a similar saying in my world, too. 'History is indeed little more than the register of the crimes, follies, and misfortunes of mankind.'"

"That so? Your world doesn't fare much better than ours, does it?"

"Indeed." Then she retreated, and Machina came out in her place.

"Here's a phrase I know: 'I believe unconditionally that God dwells, lives, and is recognizable in all history.'" My AI duked it out with my goddess over who knew the best axioms.

"Gods dwelling in all of history, is it?" At her words, Mythlanica started staring off into the distance.

Dusk began to creep over the meadow's horizon. Whatever lay beyond that remained a mystery to me. We could hear the bells ringing far away in the city. Night would soon arrive. I went to prepare dinner but lost my balance and staggered to a knee. Instinctively, I grabbed on to Mythlanica so I wouldn't drop her.

"Hmm? What's the matter?" she asked.

"Nothing. It's a little embarrassing to admit, but the exhaustion just hit me now that the adrenaline has worn off." Come to think of it, I had hardly slept since I'd arrived here. *Hmm?* A fundamental question came to mind. "Isolla, how many days has it been since we arrived?"

"Six days; seven, if you consider the time difference. But you've been in an extremely stressed state and have only slept lightly the entire time. Your vital signs are very unstable. I recommend you immediately intake nutrition and sleep. After all, you're going into the dungeon tomorrow."

"Seriously? I'd totally lost track of the days." It was Friday, so I had to make curry. Did I have curry powder?

"Souya, Isolla is right. Hurry up and go to sleep," commanded Lady Mythlanica.

"Yes, milady. After I make your dinner."

"Unnecessary. I'll pick at some dried meat or fish if I must."

"But—"

"Sleep."

"Sleeping."

My vision had begun to flicker, and my knees were shaking. I brushed my teeth, wiped myself off with a damp towel for a bit of refreshment, then ducked into my tent, removed all my equipment, and threw it into a corner. I put on a new pair of underwear and changed into a comfy combo of chino pants and a T-shirt. The temperature was fine, neither too hot nor too cold. Still, I wrapped myself in a terry-cloth blanket so I wouldn't get cold at night. And for a pillow—nope, I had no energy to look for one, so I decided to do without.

This would be my first time lying down flat outside of the jail cell. Every night before this one I'd slept hunched over my gun. No wonder I hadn't gotten any rest. Ironically, it was only after letting all my guns go that I could sleep peacefully.

The trade group almost surely wouldn't mess with me anymore. Stealing only to get your loot blown up didn't lead to any profit. The Guild found the three adventurers guilty of a whole host of other unrelated crimes and sentenced them to long-term imprisonment, so no other unknown criminals would be brave enough to tread on merfolk territory. The law of the landers did not apply here. I'd run my mouth about forgiving Ghett, but whether I lived or died had always been up to him and the goodness of his heart, right from the start.

I closed my eyes, and my conscious mind began to melt into the darkness. It was pitch-black, like the void I'd seen on my way to this world. Warmth saturated the abyss. I felt the wind. It sounded like something small came my way. A hand touched my face, and my head lifted off the ground, then landed on something soft. I cracked opened my eyes but saw only darkness.

I must be dreaming.

There was a woman in a black dress. Long, jet-black hair fell over her face, obscuring it from view. I caught glimpses of pale white skin on her jaw, cheeks, and ears. I had no mental energy left to decide whether this was a who or a what. All I knew for certain was that peaceful darkness covered every inch of me, as if I was sinking into mud.

Into the darkness.

I melted away.

Into the darkness.

CHAPTER 2
The Adventurer with a Blank Slate

(7TH DAY)

The morning fog swirled all around me on my walk to the city. My destination was the enormous building thrust into the crust of the ground—a dungeon called the Tower of Legions. At last, my adventure was starting. The anxiety and excitement sent my heartbeat racing. In the week since I'd arrived, I'd lost and gained so many things. I had overcome my first trial, so I could surely make it through the next one, too. With confidence in my pocket, I set out to tackle the dungeon.

Typical of early morning, the reception desks in the wee hours before the bell rang were largely unmanned. A quiet hush enveloped the dimly lit room. Spying a familiar face, I went to say hello.

"Good morning, Evetta."

"Good morning, Souya," she greeted me back, as straight-faced as ever despite the early hour. I bet she probably never had much trouble waking up. "You're a bit early, but as an ironclad rule, adventurers always strive to act in advance. Wonderful."

"Aww." It had paid off to have Machina blast an alarm to wake me up. Getting to sleep early hadn't hurt, either.

"Here, your Guild-issued supply kit." She handed me a large leather rucksack. "I think everything is in order, but please do check to make sure."

"Will do." I opened it up. Inside was a belt with small pockets, a lantern containing a kind of crystal, a scroll detailing my personal information, ten pages for mapmaking, and two treated pieces of charcoal to use for writing.

"What's this?" I asked. One of the items I just couldn't place. It came in a leather pouch and had two glass vials that looked like test tubes lined up against and affixed to each other. Each tube had a cork keeping the clear liquid that filled it inside. On closer inspection, I noticed delicate golden ornamentation that gave me the impression this item held a secret power.

"Souya, you're a rearguard, so please keep your ryvius close to your heart," Evetta instructed. "If you ever switch to a vanguard position, try to position it behind your shield or on your back. There are no hard and fast rules, but you should always find a way to put it somewhere your party members can see it."

No one's gonna see this if I pin it to my clothes under my poncho, will they? Producing a thin elastic string from my backpack, I threaded it through the vials and hung them from my neck.

"So what's a ryvius?" Felt like an important question.

"Oh, that's right. I'd forgotten." Evetta casually whipped out a knife so fast I didn't even see her move. "I'll need trimmings of either your hair or nails."

"Then let's go with hair." With a whoosh, two strands of my locks fell victim to her blade. She uncorked the tubes and dropped a strand in each vial, then put her knife away and took out a book.

"My name is Evetta the Pulverizer. In the name of my beloved and venerable Remlia, I raise up my voice in prayer to Lord Windov-nickel," she chanted. "O mighty Garwing, bestow upon this man a trickle of power overflown from the world of magic, a fragment of a miracle. Support his life with knowledge and let this knowledge fuel his faith, faith that having left the hands of God will transform into magic, surround his person, and convert into life. Turos Mea!"

The light I'd seen appear at the bar before danced around like fireflies and then converged upon the book. "Ryvius!" she shouted, then took that book bathed in the magical light and whacked me over the head with it.

"Gah!" I yelped.

"Oh, sorry. I think that last part was unnecessary, but I just got so into it, and my hands slipped." *Please don't beat me up by accident. I thought I was gonna die. I'm seeing stars.* "Now, all you have to do is shake the vials until they change colors."

"......Okay." *What is this, a science kit for kids?* I shook the tubes. Evetta flipped through her documents, checking something. That's when other adventurers started trickling in through the doors. They were probably newbies like me. Each one got a supply bag just like I had. Not one of them got slammed upside the head with a book, though—just saying. The top of my head throbbed.

"Uh, Evetta, I see some colors."

"Okay, let me check." The liquid in one vial had turned red; the liquid in the other, blue. "It worked? ......Yeah, I think it probably worked. Look very carefully, Souya. The red color represents your internal magic, and the blue, your external magic." The colors settled at the bottom of the vials; the red liquid measured about as long as my thumbnail; the blue, about the size of my pinky nail. "This red internal magic represents your capacity to regenerate. As long as you have some left, you'll automatically re-heal, even if your limbs get chopped off or if you spill your guts. It's called Turos Mana, which comes from Garwing's moniker."

Now that she mentioned it, my head didn't hurt anymore. I ran my hand over it but felt no inflammation or bumps. And then it clicked. This was the strange power those three adventurers I'd fought had.

"However, please don't place too much faith in it. You'll die immediately if someone snaps your neck. Additionally, if you get skewered in a trap and find yourself unable to move, you'll die eventually. It also does not protect you from poison, disease, or parasites. If you have a foreign object in your body before you regenerate, it may still be lodged in there after you heal. In extremely tense situations, even swinging your sword may damage you from within. Be careful not to assume you're uninjured simply because you don't see any external wounds, because if you fail to check yourself properly and fail to realize your magic has depleted, you could kill yourself."

"Okay." I'd already found out firsthand that while incredibly strong, this power was not limitless.

"You should also know it only works around this city and within the dungeon. We often see adventurers get cocky outside of those bounds, drop their guard, and wind up dead. The ryvius is a powerful tool, but it is nothing more than a supplement to your own strength. In the end, you must rely on your own mental and physical capabilities. Please do not ever forget this."

"All right. I understand." In other words, it all came down to spirit and guts. "And how about the blue one?"

"This one is extra. The blue external magic meter represents how much magic you can use. I imagine you'll find out soon enough if you have the talent to be a mage."

So basically, it shows what you'd call HP and MP in a video game. Magic, huh? I'd love to try it out. It sounds amazing. How badass would it be if I could shoot fire or thunder out of a staff? Could I also make myself invisible or fly?

As I inspected the vial, I asked her a question. "Evetta, is my ryvius potential on the higher end? Or is it lower than most?"

"......"

It seemed very difficult for her to answer. "It's certainly not on the higher end." My ryvius filled about a tenth of the vial.

"Uh, so is it, like, a bit below average?"

"I'd say it's higher up on the low end? Perhaps. I conjured one for a puppy once during training, and he had about the same amount as you."

"So basically, I'm on the same level as a puppy?"

"No! The puppy wasn't very big at all at that point, so it had a surprising amount of ryvius for its size. I'm sure that as you grow, yours should also increase." Too bad I'd long left growth spurts behind me.

I shook it off and equipped the items I'd been given. That said, I already had pockets on my vest, so I only had to tie the lantern around my waist. The rest of the supplies I put in my backpack. The rucksack I didn't know what to do with, but Evetta promised she'd hold on to it for me.

The bell rang, alerting everyone to the arrival of morning. About twenty adventurers had gathered around. Most of them were clearly doe-eyed greenhorns like myself, but a few among them did not fit that description. One middle-aged man in particular very clearly had quite a bit of mastery under his belt. He had raven hair and eyes, a five-o'clock shadow, and a patch over his left eye. Compared to the hordes of towering adventurers, he'd probably fall on the smaller end. However, he had an impeccable physique. His leather armor had clearly seen some repair, and the shield he carried on his back bore fresh scratch marks. The sword hanging from his hips had also obviously been worn down through repeated use. Not a single thing about him looked new. And yet, nothing appeared dilapidated, either. It all bore witness to his storied past.

He reminds me of someone. Yojimbo, Shogun, *Toshiro......* *Toshiro Mifune. In this fantasy world?*

He began speaking in a calm voice. "We'll now begin the two thousand four hundred and second Initiate Adventurers Training Course. My name's Medîm, and I'm in charge of the heims here, my little chicks."

Heims were what they called normal humans like me. A few of the adventurers, actually mainly those normal humans themselves, clicked their tongues at the term. A casual glance around the room revealed that most of the adventurers worked with staff of the same race. Heims had heim counselors, elves worked with elves, and beastfolk with other beastfolk, though there were too many varieties to lump them all into one category. It got me thinking—was Evetta a beastmaid? She did have horns. What kind of beast did she get that trait from? It would have to be a question for another time.

"I'll be looking after you, you, you, and you two young ladies over there," he continued. Everyone he pointed at gathered around him, myself included. In our group, we had a blond-haired, blue-eyed young dude in a suit of armor carrying a sword and shield; a red-haired boy dressed in light armor with a longsword slung across his back; a similarly clad boyish young girl with short hair and a spear; and rounding out the pack, a woman in a black robe that did little to conceal her sexy curves. From her pointy hat and staff that stood as tall as she did, I assumed that she was some sort of mage. And last of all, me. All five of us were heims.

I guess interracial tension and discrimination must be a thing here, too. It's annoying to think about, but if I don't keep that in mind, I can see myself getting into some tricky situations. Better watch out.

"All right. Being an adventurer is all about getting in experience. So without further ado, in we go." The battle-hardened adventurer leading us set off. I went to follow him, but Evetta grabbed both my shoulders from behind and held me back.

"Souya, be sure to do whatever Pops says. Did you tie your lantern on tight? You're not forgetting anything? If you need to go to the bathroom, you should do it now. And make sure to run at the first sign of danger. Do you understand me?"

"Yes, ma'am." *Again, are you my mother?*

"Ah, Evetta. That him? The notorious Otherworlder?" our leader asked.

"Yes, Pops. Please take good care of him."

"That's a tall order. I'll look after him just as much as the others."

"Please, *please* take good care of him." *This is so embarrassing— can you stop? Everyone's staring. The little girl's giggling at me.*

"Good luuuck!" Evetta called out, waving at me from behind. I gave her a small wave back, turned around, and finally took my first steps into the dungeon.

We started climbing down a wide staircase, walking two abreast. *Aren't we going to use a portal?* I thought, glancing at them out of the corner of my eye.

"Hey, you. What's your deal with that girl with the horns back there?" the young boy at my side asked. *Have I seen him before? I can't remember. Feels like it's on the tip of my tongue, but—*

"What's my deal? She's just my counselor, and I'm just an adventurer."

"She came with you when you went through Lady Gladwein's

test, didn't she? I saw you eating together at the bar after that and then again sitting shoulder to shoulder on the side of the road. Something smells off. You can't tell me you're only—"

—And then the memory came rushing back.

"Ah, I remember. You're the kid who got to make a covenant with Lady Gladwein."

"What?!" the knightly dude exclaimed from behind us. "Boy! You secured a covenant with Lady Gladwein at such a young age?!"

"Whoo, nicely done. She only takes in maybe one disciple every six months, if that," the veteran adventurer called Pops complimented him.

"I went to try my luck as well, but a beastkid threw me out one-handed," explained the knightly dude. "What kind of trial did you pass to manage that?"

"I…I—" The boy hesitated.

"He stabbed a boar with his swooord," answered the cheerful young girl, completely ignoring his distress.

"C'mon, Bel! Knock it off! Don't spread that around! What if I get a weird handle 'cause of that?!"

"Whaaat? You were the only one who got to make a covenant, you know, Shuna. That's amazing! Just sit back and let them talk you up some more!"

"She's got a point. That was one hard boar," I agreed, adding my own takeaways from my go at the trial.

"Sure was, right, brother? I only got the tip of my spear in, myself."

"Ha-ha-ha," the young girl and I laughed, squarely in the failure camp.

"A boar, you say. I didn't know that was an option," mused our resident knight.

The boy seemed lost for how to respond. Perhaps searching for a way out of that conversation, Shuna, as he'd been called, landed on something and came back at me. "Forget about me! I wanna know about you and that lady!"

"Like I said, we only have a professional relationship. It is true I've put her in some tricky positions, though."

"Tricky positions?" He wasn't letting anything slide.

"Oh, so you've got a thing for girls like her, Shunie," teased Bel.

"Th-that's not true!" *Ahh, now I get it. Evetta is beautiful.*

"Are you perchance unfamiliar with the Horns, little boy?" the lady mage asked flirtatiously, breaking her silence.

"Horns?" he asked. You could almost see the question mark floating above his head. Now that she mentioned it, I remembered both Lady Mythlanica and Evetta saying something about that before.

"The horned woman you're talking about. She seems well tamed, but that's a dungeon monster, you know," explained the mage. "People often confuse them with beastfolk, but you can tell because they don't have any other animalistic features aside from their horns. I'd never seen ones shaped like hers, so I'm positive that's what she is. You be careful, little boy. Meet one of those in the dungeon and you'll be torn limb from limb. Although, you *can* sell their young for a pretty penny. If you think you've got what it takes to train them, you can put them in your party to bolster your battle power, or you could also get some fortified chains and play house with them. Do give it a try if you're curious. But you know, it might be easier to just buy one off of someone, don't you think?"

"Well, I, uh…" Shuna's face hardened as she spoke. Mine too. To make it worse, I'd gone and pictured Evetta trapped in chains. An electric charge ran through the awkward mood in the group.

"Evetta belongs to King Remlia. Regardless of her past, she has achieved great things as an adventurer. Careful who you mock, miss, or it may be the end of you." Pops sure knew how to throw some shade. I felt like I now understood why everyone called him that.

"I'm terribly sorry," the lady apologized.

A blast of hot air blew our way as the end of the staircase came into view. "This here's the second floor. It's technically in the dungeon, but you're as safe here as you are upstairs," Pops explained. Steam swirled all around the second floor. Though it was constructed of stone like the floor above, along with the rest of the city, it seemed a little brighter somehow. Strange, since I didn't see any light fixtures. Pipes also crisscrossed all over the ceiling in another mysterious design feature.

Cloth curtains partitioned the wide-open space into several rooms. I peeked into an empty one and saw a stone bathtub, wooden bucket, soap, and something resembling a loofah neatly set out. A pipe that looked like a faucet rested on top of the tub. This had to be, you know, a bathtub.

"The walls, ceilings, and the like are made of emiluminite," Pops explained. "We had some trouble in the past due to the heat, so we asked the dwarves to run water lines around to cool things off. The baths were a by-product. Don't let that fool you, though—it's vital you take your baths. Don't let that slip by the wayside. We once had an adventurer who hated washing up. He eventually carried a disease back with him into town, and boy, what a mess that was. The water's got medicinal herbs mixed in it, so it'll help your wounds heal and relax your muscles. It's free, so make sure you always take a dip on your way up." The ladies squealed in delight.

"You'll normally only see portals every five floors, but for some reason, there's one set up on this level and on the one below us," he continued. "Get your authentication and all in order, and you'll be free to use the portals to come here all you want."

The young boy put his palm up to a nearby portal. I looked around to see what the others would do and followed their example. I could have sworn that the membrane of light changed colors slightly. Did this mean we could safely use the portals to explore the dungeon? It was much smaller than the one the Firm had set up in their basement—distressingly small—but worlds more technologically advanced.

"Sorry, Pops, what's emiluminite?" I asked. It had me sorta curious.

"It's a type of light stone that's unique to the dungeon. It gives off light and heat on impact. They put it in the lanterns in your supply kit, the streetlights in town, and the like. The emiluminite content is particularly high on this floor, but you can also find it on other levels. No one knows why, but take it one step outside your ryvius radius of regeneration, and it turns into a normal, everyday rock."

"Huh." *They've got some handy stuff here. I might be able to use that for something.*

"Oh, sweetie, is that where you're starting from?" the lady asked incredulously. "You'll always find emiluminite in dungeons like this. What's more, the deposits are basically inexhaustible. It's one of the factors used to substantiate the theory that the dungeon is a living organism. In other words, emiluminite is the crystallized form of whatever fluids, or perhaps even waste, the dungeon secretes as a product of its biological activity. That's especially so here, in the Tower of Legions, since it's said to be a horn that belonged to the giant who created the world. Basically, this place is still alive. Can you picture it? It has continued to live since long, long before the gods ever roamed the world, back since primordial times. And it's only a single horn. What exactly do you think the giant who made it was like? How massive must it have been, and why did it fashion this world only to then disappear?!"

She'd heated up by this point and was talking straight at the wall—and that's right where we left her. The rest of us started moving on to the next floor down.

"Hey, guys!"

On to the third floor. "This level's safe, too," declared Pops. "Like it or not, you're gonna get real familiar with this place if you do any exploring." It reeked of blood. Men in aprons were carving up giant hunks of meat. Every once in a while, I heard a monster's agonizing last breaths. This floor served as the processing workshop.

"Any monsters adventurers slay will first be brought back here. They'll smoke the meat, turn the bones into tools like handles or construction materials, fashion clothing, canteens, and things out of the skins, and make medicinal ingredients out of the monsters' blood, organs, secretions, etcetera. Basically, nothing is wasted. They can also put rare resources through a preservation process and hold on to them separately, then send them on to the merchants upstairs."

Makes sense. Like it or not, we'll definitely be frequent customers. By the way, can you buy raw meat here? I wondered, but Pops and the other initiate adventurers headed down to the next floor before I got the chance to ask. I tagged along after them.

We'd now made it to the fourth floor. It'd be nice if I could get all the way to the fifty-sixth floor this easily, but I figured that wasn't gonna happen. This level felt markedly different from the two floors above us. It had a damp, moldy smell and was much darker. Light shone about the stairs, but gaping darkness awaited us at the end of a four-meter-wide corridor. This was the real dungeon. The real test started now.

"Okay, you," Pops declared as he handed me a map. It showed the staircases on each level. We'd gone down deeper than I'd expected. "For the time being, you'll be the leader. The five of you, organize yourselves into a party and come down to the fifth level. I'll be waiting there."

Wait, what does that mean? I went to ask, but Pops had already sprinted off. "Damn, he's fast!" And quiet; not even the metal on his equipment made a sound as he disappeared into the dark. Four pairs of eyes turned to me.

"Anybody else want to be the leader instead?" I asked hopefully. I'd never been good at public speaking.

"Shall I do it?" The knight seemed eager. I handed him the map. "All right! Everyone, follow me!"

"Wait." I stopped the knight in his tracks. "You've got the map backward."

"Oh, pardon me. This is my first time reading a dungeon map." He flashed a charming smile. I turned to look at the young boy and girl. They both averted their eyes. How about the learned young lady?

"Tee-hee." She brushed me off with a smile. Is that how it was gonna be?

"My bad. I'll do it after all. Sorry for the hold up." I snatched back the map. I whispered into the speaker on my glasses. "Isolla, scan the map and give us directions.

"......Isolla? Machina? Do you copy?" *Hmm?*

No response. *You've got to be kidding; is there some kind of interference going on? Aaah, well, whatever. I just have to read and follow the map. I don't need modern technology for that.* I pulled out my flat, credit-card-sized, military-grade compass and got my bearings. *I almost forgot. We need to figure out our formation before we go anywhere.*

"Mr. Knight, you take the lead."

"Right."

"As for the rest of you…" I had the knight up in front, then put myself next in line, followed by the young boy, the mage lady, and the young girl pulling up the rear. "And if you could all turn on your lanterns…" I went to switch on mine, realized I didn't know how, then just shook it around, and it lit up. Its dim glow didn't inspire much faith. Nervous, I pulled out my radar probe and turned on the flashlight. You couldn't even begin to compare the two. The beam from the probe reached all the way to the end of the corridor.

"That's bright. Is it magic?" asked the knight.

"Basically."

He started off, looking a little surprised.

Maybe it was because I had just seen Pops show us how it should be done, but my party members' footsteps and our jingly metal pieces grated on my nerves in an odd way. If any foes in the area noticed us, wouldn't they come and try to attack?

"Turn right at the next intersection."

"Got it." The knight proceeded cautiously, sword and shield in hand, and checked down both the right and left corridors. I'd written him off as unreliable based on nothing but my first impression, but this guy had seen battle. He carried himself without a single wasteful movement. "All clear," he announced, and we proceeded accordingly. I turned the corner after him, too. Then, I felt something behind me.

"Enemy!" I screamed and swerved the light over only to find a monster flapping its wings furiously as it rushed toward me. It was a freshly severed human head that had sprouted wings. That abomination opened its mouth wide and bared its fangs.

"Apologies." The knight grabbed my shoulder and pushed me

out of the way. I lost my balance, somehow managed to take a defensive stance, and fixed my eyes on the monster again—but by that point, the battle had already ended.

The knight bashed the monster with his shield, and the young boy added on a thrust of his sword into the beast. It only took a second. Another monster appeared while I stood there dumbfounded. That one the young girl skewered onto her spear, securing it for the mage lady to call forth a flame and turn it into a literal fireball. The space filled with the smell of burnt meat.

I hadn't done a single thing.

"This little guy's a chocho. I've never seen a wild one before," cooed the mage lady as she started feeling up the monster stuck on the young boy's sword. Just the thought of what germs might be on it made me nervous. "Its human features are so much more pronounced than the farm-raised variety. Its wingspan is twice as big, too. Ooh, look at that thick slab of meat."

The resemblance it bore to a human face was just a pattern its feathers made, a camouflage. Given its wings and bone structure, I figured it might be some kind of bird—which begged the question.

"Does it...taste good?"

The mage lady's eyes sparkled.

"It's delicious. They're a bit violent, but as long as you've got a darkroom, you can raise them, and basically everything but their teeth and bones are edible. But their eggs are to die for. They're sold as large guinelle eggs here. Guinelle are a type of large bird that doesn't naturally exist on the Right Continent. The chocho eggs have got a very similar taste and richness, so they were first sold as a substitute but then went mainstream and stole the name. Just a bit of trivia."

"You eat *that*?" the knight asked, completely pale.

"Of course. We eat them back on our home island, too," added the girl. "The wings are really good if you fry them up in oil till they're crispy and sprinkle salt on 'em. They'd probably be good in soup, too."

"Don't bring up the island. They're gonna treat us like country bumpkins," the young boy chided her.

"Lord Knight, I hope you realize about a third of the food eaten in this town comes from the dungeon," the mage lady informed him.

"I didn't realize. Beggin' your pardon, I'd never even thought to wonder where it all came from."

"What? What are you, some kinda rotten prince?" the young boy snapped.

The knight only replied in a soft voice, "There's not much to brag about when you're from a noble house on the lowest rung of aristocratic society."

"So you *are* from a distinguished family!" exclaimed the mage.

"What, really?! Are ya rich?!" asked the young girl breathlessly.

So he's rich, tall, probably has a good personality, and to top it all off, a nobleman. Yep, I bet only the most extraordinarily eccentric of girls wouldn't jump at that deal.

The knight gazed coldly at the young boy and me while the ladies bombarded him with questions. I figured I should probably stop them considering where we were, but if I stepped in at this point, I'd look like a lowlife getting jealous. I didn't want that. I may have already admitted defeat, but that I couldn't bear.

"Hey, kid," I said.

"Yeah?"

At times like these, nothing beat a totally unrelated topic. "What do those chocho eat?"

"Prolly bugs and rats, no? I bet there's tons of small critters here. This place'd be poop and rotten meat city without 'em."

"Makes sense." It made a simple food chain. Then, for no real reason, I asked, "So do you think that chocho thing's at the top of the pecking order on this floor?"

"No freakin' waaay. All the ones we were raisin' back home got eaten up by a stray dog. They're not a superstrong species. You can tell they're weak 'cause they've got to use camo."

"Huh."

The ladies squealed in delight. Our resident knight smiled kindly. We had just finished our first battle in the dungeon and were riding that high, intoxicated by the rush. We'd gone in without a game plan and had pulled off a perfect combo. And we'd won. Our spirits were almost destined to soar. Even the kid and I secretly rejoiced on the inside, despite looking a little bummed. In other words, we'd all completely let down our guard. None of us noticed the beast that feasted primarily on chocho approaching.

"BRRRRRRRRRRR!"

The air shook with its roar. There stood a fat, bulging boar. At almost four meters long, *big* didn't cut it. Its body almost completely filled the corridor both in width and height. Perhaps aroused by the smell of the chocho's blood and charred flesh, it turned its wild, murderous instincts in our direction and came barreling straight at us!

Not even five seconds and it'd be on us.

"RUN!"

The kid grabbed the cowering mage and the young girl and pulled them close. The corner. We had to make it to the corner and get behind the boar. Only an idiot would take a gigantic beast like this straight on—

"Come at me, monster!" Our brave knight stood directly in the beast's path without a hint of fear. "No self-respecting knight would ever retreat in front of an enem— Gaaaaah!" The boar flung him out of the way with its enormous snout. Luckily, he landed behind the beast. But I had no time to check if he was okay. I flashed the light at the boar and tried to get it to come to me. We'd have to retrieve our knight later.

"Run! RUUUN! Next corner, turn left! Then keep straight!" I shouted out instructions. The kid ran at the head of the pack. Next came the slow-footed lady mage. The young girl and I brought up the end.

"What *is* that? And what did it eat to get that big?!" screamed the girl.

"*Anything!*" I answered.

"Noooooooooo!" If I'd been alone, I probably would've screamed, too. Getting chased by a massive boar in a dim dungeon was way more brutal than anything I'd imagined. And I had no trouble at all picturing what would happen if it caught up to us.

"Kid, next left!"

"Ah!" The boy turned right at the fork in the tunnels, and the lady mage followed suit.

"Forget it! Don't turn back! Just keep going!" I yelled. If they went any other direction than straight, they'd rejoin us. More likely, they'd run right into the boar. But if the map in my mind was correct, the route the boy took would lead to a dead end.

The boar skidded wildly around the corner. I could hear its hooves slipping and sliding just behind us. I shined the light on it once more as a threat. It didn't shrink at all and in fact bellowed even louder as it bore down on us.

"Okay, follow me!" I pulled the girl's hand and ran as fast as I could. We turned three corners but didn't break away from it at all. I was starting to run out of breath. My thighs felt ready to cramp up any minute. But the girl seemed to have quite a bit more stamina than I did, so I couldn't give in to weakness.

"Hey, mister! Do you have a plan?!" she asked me.

"Yeah! I do, but we need to get a bit more space between us or it won't work!"

"You just need a bit, right?" She released my hand and turned around. Pinning her spear under her arm, she held up three little wooden statues.

"My Lord Ukhazol, King of the Tree Spirits, Lady Gastolfo, Goddess of Fertility, I, Beltriche of Azollid, beg you both for a miracle. Please! Stop this beast!" she chanted, then scattered seeds on the ground.

The boar was right in front of us. We weren't going to make it. I instinctively grabbed the girl from behind to protect her—not that it would mean anything, but it beat the alternative.

Just then, a literal miracle happened. Vines sprouted from the seeds and wrapped themselves around the boar's front legs. Propelled forward by momentum, it fell flat on its face.

"This will really only last for a minute! It won't hold long!"

"Got it!"

With the boar's every thrash, another vine let us down and snapped in two. We burned the last of our energy to sprint away in the brief delay. The extreme circumstances and adrenaline had eaten through almost all of my stamina. I was panting like crazy, and cramps shot up and down my legs. And yet, somehow, we made it to the place I had in mind.

"Your spear!" I borrowed it from the girl and set it on the ground, then took off my poncho and covered the spear with it.

"Wait, you're kidding." The girl's voice dripped with unease when she caught on. I leaned my back against the wall and sat down on the ground.

"Get in the corner, please. If this doesn't work, run away while he's eating me," I told her. Completely ignoring me, she came to sit between my legs while resting her back against my chest.

"Nah, as if I could. I'm pretty sure we'd *both* get squashed to death and then eaten."

"Yeah, guess you're right."

A twelve-meter straight shot of corridor stretched out in front of us. The boar turned into our line of sight, spotted us, and started pawing the ground. I had no other choice at that point but to pray this brute was as dumb as it looked.

The giant beast charged. It was like a semi-trailer made of meat. My face twitched at its tremendous power. The girl smelled sweet. Sweat drenched the nape of her neck. I could feel her body trembling. She almost definitely beat me in physical strength, but she was still petite and thin. I hugged her around the shoulders, and she anxiously grabbed on to my arms. When confronted with mortal danger, human physiological responses apparently kick in and try to produce offspring. If that was true, then this ill-timed carnal lust made a bit more sense. But this moment of escapism didn't even last a tenth of a second. Our moment had come.

"Hold it!" I shouted. I flung the poncho off of the spear, and the two of us leaped to our feet and pushed our full weight behind it, the end of the handle buttressed against the wall. The boar charged right into the spearhead, which bent under the impact. Blood and screams filled the air.

"Oiiiiiiiii!"

The spear pierced through the roof of the boar's mouth and reached almost to its brain. But it wasn't dead yet. It kept lunging forward and trying to close its jaws around us, driving the spear farther into its flesh with each thrust.

"Eek!"

"You son of a bitch!" I whipped out my woodsman's hatchet and slashed wildly at it. The blade didn't even scratch the boar's hide. Its teeth gnashed and closed in on Beltriche. I kicked it in the snout over and over again, but the beast wouldn't stop.

What do we do?

This is bad. What's our next move?

My jumbled thoughts raced for a second—and then we heard an extremely high-pitched wail.

"?"

The boar's eyes rolled up into the back of its head. Lifeless, the lump of meat crashed down on us. I braced myself for a horror-movie twist where it would come back and attack us again......but it never happened.

"Bel! You okay?" The kid quickly slipped his longsword out of the boar. Oil and blood covered the blade—I shuddered to think where he might've stuck it.

"I-it's so heavy! Shunie, get it off me!" Bel called out.

"I'm trying, but it won't mooove!"

I did all I could, too, but it wouldn't budge. And I wasn't trying to take advantage of a situation where I could be legally pressed up against a girl my little sister's age. I just didn't have the strength. Seriously.

Ah, this is heaven, but I'm running out of air.

"Mister? You're breathing kind of weird. You okay?" asked Bel.

"I think I'm gonna pass out." The enormous weight on my chest made it impossible to breathe.

"Shunie, hurry!"

"I told you, I'm trying!" Their argument started to sound so far away. Just as my consciousness faded out, the pressure lifted, and air flooded into my lungs. I gasped as if I'd been drowning.

"You guys sure are something."

There stood Pops, though I had no idea when he'd arrived. "Dungeon boars this massive give even adept adventurers a run for their money." Pops grabbed the beast with one hand and moved it out of the way. Our valiant knight hung from his other hand. I wondered who the real monster was here. "Oh, it's a female. You got lucky—if it had been a male, you'd have all been dead meat. Their skin is real tough, so you need to build yourself up quite a bit before you can take it down physically."

"Seriously?" *The pigs in this world are terrifying. Crazy scary. Okay, looks like pork's on the menu for dinner.*

"Pops, this thing's huge. You're saying these newbies took her down? Impressive," remarked one of a bunch of aproned men standing around. I had no idea when they'd gotten there, either. Each held an enormous butcher's knife.

"All riiight, fellas, let's get her drained, gutted, and chopped up. Don't you dare waste a drop of blood, a scrap of meat, or a fragment of her bones! This little piggy's a giant, so we're gonna need to fix her up real quick before we can bring her back through the portal. Watch out so you don't get in the adventurers' way."

The men jumped into a flurry of activity, dissecting and dismantling the pig with fascinating speed. "Which of you's the party leader?" one of the butchers holding a scroll asked. The boy and girl pointed at me from their seats on the ground. "It's a female, you know, so I can give ya a good price for the meat, but the hide's not worth much. The bones we'll take at the standard rate. Still, there's a lot to go around, so you'll come outta this with a tidy sum. Plus, the Guild covers all the transportation fees for anything caught on the first few floors, so you don't have to pay anything outta pocket. If you go through us, the Adventurers Guild Meat Packing Department, I reckon it'll come to about thirty gold

coins in total. But if you've already got a preferred merchant, we can send it round to them. What'll it be?"

"You three, I'll go through the Guild unless you've got any objections. That all right with you?" I asked the other members, just in case.

"Thirty gold!" exclaimed Bel. "Umm, thirty divided by five, that's…"

"You mean six," corrected Shuna.

"No need to include me in that. Divide it among yourselves," Pops ordered.

I watched the three talk it through, then looked over to our mage lady, who stood a little way off and got visual approval. *Do whatever you want*, her eyes told me.

"I'd like to sell it to the Guild," I told the butcher. "Oh, but could I get however much meat one piece of gold is worth? Make it a spareribs cut with the bone attached."

"You got it. Your name?"

"Souya of Japan."

"All right, Souya of Japan. I'll give your counselor the final workup and your cut later, so here's your receipt for now."

I took the scroll he handed me. Nothing remained of the boar by this point but part of its intestines. My party and I turned to leave. I was absolutely exhausted, but the rush of superiority I felt for a job well done somehow pushed me forward. Plus, the sense of relief to have Pops with us was amazing. He started talking as we walked.

"I'm gonna give y'all one piece of advice: Don't get all excited just 'cause you won a battle. Don't let your guard down. Even if they look like pushovers, all monsters have the innate instinct to survive. Always remember that. Conduct yourselves with that in mind. If you have even the slightest doubt about defeating your enemy, run. Some idiots claim that to be an adventurer is to be reckless, but they always end up as boar food.

"Don't expect someone will always be there to give you the answers. Think of a solution yourselves, even if it's the wrong move. Fail over and over again and learn from the experience. Don't give up hope after one or two hundred failures. Never abandon your friends. But don't put too much faith in them, either. Rely on them. Don't run away to save yourself. Run away to save them. And finally, survive. That's all. I guess that might be a bit too much to take in."

Should I point out how much of an understatement one *was there?*

Anyway, nothing really noteworthy happened after that. Pops single-handedly, and I mean that literally, cleaned up any other random monsters that popped up. And then, we made it to the fifth floor. After that, Pops took the lead and got us through it at a quick clip. In the blink of an eye, we'd crossed the whole floor, found a portal near the staircase going down to the sixth floor, and wasted no time in getting ourselves authenticated.

"Okay, now all that's left is to wash up and you're done. Make sure you scrub down your equipment, too," Pops reminded us. "Good work out there. You're all on the right track."

I put my hand over the portal, and it displayed the different floors of the dungeon. It was gesture-controlled. Did that mean technology that advanced too far for its own good was indistinguishable from magic? And vice versa? I selected the first floor, dived into the light, and just like that, my first exploration down into the dungeon ended.

I could only answer *How was it?* with a simple phrase: soul-crushingly exhausting.

◇   ◇   ◇

A drunken party next to us broke out into a wild revelry, never mind the fact that it was still midday. We'd come to a bar run by a guy with a mohawk, which the Guild apparently owned. Parties of beastfolk and fresh initiates like us sat to either side of our table. We could hear them singing ballads exalting the deeds of fallen comrades. One of the parties not at the bar had evidently already lost one of their own. We'd come pretty close, too, especially our Lord Knight, who still looked a bit pale.

"So in the end, we got thirty-four gold pieces for the boar. That comes to seven pieces per person, but I already spent one on the meat, so I'll just take six," I explained, then lined up all the pieces on the table and placed each person's share in front of them.

"Apologies, but I can't accept that." The knight pushed his pile of coins back in front of me. "I made such a shameful display of myself. I've stained my grandfather's name."

"If you say so, but I'm still gonna have you keep that. Messing up is part of the job description. You can make those kinds of calls when you're the leader." I pushed the money back by him. He seemed to accept that, albeit reluctantly.

"He's sayin' he don't need it, so why don't ya just keep it?" asked the kid.

"'Kay, then I'll take your share of the meat, Shunie," offered Bel.

"I wasn't the one who said it!"

The two kids hungrily gobbled down their lunch. I loved seeing that they were full of energy.

"I agree," chimed in our lady mage. "All I did was give a lecture on the chocho, then run for my life and trip. What in the world was that boar?! It was twice as big as I'd heard they should be. That stupid teacher! I can't believe I paid him good money, and he didn't even warn me about something *this* basic! 'Scuse me, another drink!"

A row of empty ale bottles stood lined up in front of her. Our waitress, a beastmaid, brought her a fresh bottle. I pulled her aside, slipped five copper pieces into her uniform pocket, and whispered, "Water them down after this one, please." Then, outta nowhere, she kissed me on the cheek. She had lovely golden locks, cat ears, and a tail. Someone kicked my shin.

"Hmm? Hmm?" *Who was it? The kid?* Putting that aside... "Sooo, ladies and gents. What do each of you plan to do after this?" I asked them.

"Bel and I are gonna go back to our inn and give Lady Gladwein our report about what happened today," stated the boy.

"I plan to keep drinking," announced the lady.

"I'd like to stare into space for a bit," said the knight.

"Oh, no, no. That's not what I meant. Sorry. I worded that wrong," I said, revising my question. "I wanted to ask whether the five of us would keep going as a party." Suddenly, a hush fell over our table, despite all the clamor around us.

"What kinda dumb question is that?" the kid asked me, shocked. "*The Pops* put us together, you know? Like it or not, we're stuck with one another—unless someone dies or something."

"*Is that how it works?*" *You should've let me in on this kinda thing earlier, Evetta.* "Is Pops that big around here?" I put the question out there. Even more surprise came back. The kid dropped his spoon, the full bottle of beer the lady held slipped out of her hand, and the piece of meat the girl was gnawing on plopped down to her plate. Was Pops that big of a deal?

Lord Knight set it straight for me. "Ask anyone who the 'king of adventurers' is, and they'll name King Remlia. But the only one to be called the 'father of adventurers' is Pops, Lord Medîm. He's in at least three of the most famous adventurer epics, and those are only the ones I know. He's what you'd call a living legend. And also one of the few people permitted to explore the dungeon alone."

Sounds pretty badass. Huh? Do you need permission to go in alone?

"Where exactly do you hail from? Now that I think of it, I've never seen clothing like yours. You employ unique equipment as well. Everything about you, from your quick wit to your keen judgment, tells me you're no ordinary lad."

Unfortunately, I'm just a normal guy with terrible luck.

As I pondered how to start explaining, the knight took out his scroll and said, "Wait, pardon me. I should have offered my own introduction first. This is as good a moment as any." He unrolled the scroll.

"……" Everyone fell silent.

"Sorry, I can't read."

"Me, neither."

"Same here."

The kid, the girl, and I all fessed up to our illiteracy. I wondered what percentage of people in this world could read.

"Hmm, looks like three scrolls to me." I decided to forget this lady clearly drunk off her ass. We were all at a loss, when—

"Yooo, party of tenderfoots who defeated a dungeon boar in your first battle. Pops said good things about you, and he hasn't said that about anyone in a while. This is on the house." The mohawked bartender placed large, heaping plates of thick bacon and boiled beans on the table.

"Meat!" cried the boy and girl in unison before attacking the dish. *You two are still gonna eat? According to Machina's calculations, you've already had more than twenty thousand calories each.*

"Boss, do you think you could read this for us?"

"Sure thing." I'd asked in the spur of the moment, but he agreed to help us out. He pulled a chair over from a nearby table and sat down. "I, Rasta ole Rhasvah, servant of Lord Windovnickel, hereby agree to read aloud the vitae of these newly inaugurated adventurers. I swear by the name of Thurseauve that I will faithfully recite whatever I see here inscribed. Should I lie, may my tongue be cut off and may I drain a vial of snake poison."

Having finished that rather heavy oath, the boss picked up our knight's scroll. "Name: Arvin Forths Gassim. Homeland: Ellusion of the Central Continent. Former knight of the Lillideas Church. Hmm… Gassim…… Are you Gassim the Executioner's grandson? The famous court execution officer of the Lillideas Church known for sending two hundred people's heads flying in one day?"

"No, that's an exaggeration. The real record is two hundred and sixteen people in two days," the young man revealed unhappily as he picked at his beans.

"I knew it; you *are* a rotten prince," said the boy. "I don't know what you do, but you've got an official position in the Central Continent, right? Don'cha just have money flowing in, even if all you do is sleep?"

"I did have a title, though it amounted to no more than a formality. From what I understand, my mother, father, and sister lived their lives without ever knowing hunger." *And yet, he's now an adventurer. There must be something going on there.* "But all that ended when my great-uncle hatched a plan to assassinate the Seventh Pope. Fortunately, the attempt was staved off. My great-uncle, his family, and his close relations were, naturally, all executed. My grandfather's honor protected my family at least, but I was stripped of my knighthood. My elder sister got off with imprisonment. I will say in defense of my great-uncle's honor that he was a fine man, but he was tricked by an elven concubine."

"If he was so fine, how the hell did he get tricked by some sexy el—?"

I shoved some bacon in the boy's mouth. "Don't talk about other people's families so carelessly." *Are you looking to start a fight?*

"I became an adventurer to obtain a pardon for my elder sister. You can't buy a pardon from the Church of St. Lillideas. You have to earn it with either honor or glory; that's why I'm here."

The boss cut through the depressing mood by saying, "That won't be easy. You'll have to get down past the fortieth floor at the very least. Either that, or hunt down hordes of Dark Crowned monsters. Otherwise, you'd have to find a treasure so precious it'd send shock waves through the country. You've got plenty of options, none of them painless. We don't see many adventurers after nothing but glory nowadays. I'll bet true adventurers will welcome a young man like yourself and wish you well. If anyone dares laugh at you, I'll give them a fist in the face with my name on it for you." He curled his fingers into a ball. One punch from that would easily kill someone like me. Not that I had any room to laugh at other people's dreams.

The boss unrolled the scroll even farther and read, "Apprentice to Zammonglace, the Scarlet Knight. Certified in swordsmanship, horsemanship, spear fighting, and shield wielding. Mastered St. Lillideas's first level of healing magic. In good health. Unable to form a party with beastfolk due to the Church of St. Lillideas's doctrine. Unable to form a party with elves due to familial circumstances.

"Hmm, well, as your senior and more experienced adventurer, allow me, Rasta ole Rhasvah, to give you an evaluation.

Arvin Forths Gassim, you will live to be a brilliant vanguard. You will be your party's shield, their sword, and the key to their success. You bear some challenges regarding race, but these are trivial. If you would like, I can introduce you to some adept adventurers."

"It's an honor to receive such gracious words from a member of the Remlia royal family." Arvin smiled happily.

"Boss, are you a royal?" That surprised me more than anything, so I just had to ask.

"It's not a big deal. They call us a royal family, but my distinguished cousin went and became king all on his own. I don't have anything to boast of personally. I'm just someone who wandered all around the world and ended up a bar owner." He looked seriously annoyed, so I didn't press any further. The sudden drop in his mood sent Arvin's smile crashing down into gloom.

"Then I'm even worse. I got tossed in the air by a boar."

"Don't let that get to you, son. Dungeon boars are actually pretty tough. You're meant to learn how to escape from them, not how to defeat them. Now, just between us..." The boss lowered his voice and continued, "King Remlia also got his bum sent flying by a boar, just like you. Not only that, but it also grabbed hold of his cape with its teeth and spun him around first. If Pops hadn't been there at that moment, our king would've been a boar meal. Don't you dare ever speak of this, or my shop will go under."

"Y-yes, sir," Arvin promised, and the boss slapped him on the back.

"Who's next?" The kid, his mouth full of bacon, handed his scroll over to the boss. "Oh-ho. Pfft, 'Swine Slayer,' the young swordsman," he read and burst out laughing. His infectious chuckle soon had the ladies and me joining in, too.

"See, I knew I'd get some weird nickname!"

"N-no, sorry. But dungeon boars are formidable foes, you know. Then again, you went up against a boar at Lady Gladwein's trial, too, so maybe it's destiny, bwa-ha-ha-ha-ha-ha!"

Unable to keep a straight face, the boss howled and roared. The boy looked about to snap and foolishly reached his hand for his sword. The boss took a swig of our lady's ale to clear his throat and started reading the next scroll.

"Name: Shuna. Homeland: the Azollid Archipelago. Primary deity: Ukhazol, King of the Tree Spirits. Disciple of Gladwein the Iron Arm. Uses an unnamed style of swordsmanship.

"Now, Shuna, I've heard tell about the way you wield your sword. They say you get down low, then spin as you thrust. None of the warrior lines I can recall use a technique like that. At least, none of the human ones. Your master was beastfolk, right?"

Shuna pounded the table. "......Yeah. But it's not like I'm trying to hide it 'cause I'm embarrassed or anything. Master told me over and over that I should keep it to myself for my own sake, so I was just following orders. I was totally against it, though! My master protected our island of three hundred people from fifty pirates with one arm—like a real hero! If you're gonna laugh at that, too, then we'll have to take this outside."

Tears welled in the corners of Shuna's eyes. He must have been through some pretty rough things in his past. Clearly, discrimination against beastfolk affected not only them but the people close to beastfolk, too.

"No, it's no matter to me. Everybody knows beastfolk can't start their own warrior lines. It's no great surprise to find an uncommonly talented swordsman among their midst. I only ask since there are some humans who can't do so, either. Take, for example, the scum who make their livings as assassins. A long time ago, an adventurer started a party but kept their past a secret from everyone. All of them met unfortunate ends. That line of work sticks with you until you die."

The boss waved off the dark topic and turned to Arvin. "Tell me, apprentice of Zammonglace, the Scarlet Knight. What do you think about a swordsman who studies under a beastfolk master?"

"I'm jealous, to be honest. My master has been called the Bloody Knight and all sorts of monikers and used to say that to truly master a weapon, you should never limit yourself to only human opponents. I'm not at liberty to defame the teachings of the Lillideas Church, so I can't join a party with any beastfolk for the moment, but once I'm free, it might be interesting to find a beast-folk teacher."

"......" Shuna looked down at the ground and blushed. *Whoa, this kid can be pretty damn cute.* "The reason I wanted to be an adventurer...," he mumbled, hiding half of his face behind his hand—maybe he was still grinning from ear to ear, "...is because I want to prove how strong I am. But I don't mean just my own strength. I want to prove to the world how powerful my master is."

The boss nodded slightly. "As for your evaluation, I'll have to go with a young, talented swordsman. But don't get too cocky. All the youngsters are blessed with talent. Only those who hold on to it even after they age make a name for themselves. Though to be fair, I don't believe any youngsters can compare to you, Swine Slayer—"

"Hey!"

The boss ignored Shuna and unfurled the young girl's scroll. She fidgeted nervously, the picture of innocence. *If only my little sister were this cute.* "I-if you would be so kind!" she squeaked.

"Name: Beltriche. Homeland: the Azollid Archipelago. Primary deity: Ukhazol, King of the Tree Spirits. Disciple of Gastolfo, Goddess of Fertility; Giuma, Goddess of Amana; Midras of Shining Waters; Great Turtle Lord Cadran; Leteugan of the Frosty

Winds; Yuta, the Optimist; Ryuryuska, the Thunderous... Hey, hang on a second. Exactly how many covenants do you have?" He traced his finger across the scroll. "Fifteen, twenty, twenty-eight, twenty-nine, thirty......thirty-five. Thirty-five! Well. Is that even allowed?" The figures had even the all-knowing boss sweating nervously.

Shuna, still munching away at that bacon, poked at Bel. "Hey, Bel. Thirty-five? Did you pick up some more again?"

"I mean, there are just so many gods in this city, right? A bunch of them asked me to worship them whenever I have a minute. But I turned down all the super controlling ones or the ones that force their commandments on you. Lord Ukhazol does always say, 'Take what you can.' It's sooo hard to say no when they feed me, you know."

Huh. I see. I see how it is. What the hell did I go through all that trouble for?! I'm right here! Right here, you know?! The guy who got turned down by every single god *in town!!*

"I don't even really need to ask, but do you carry the Divine Medium trait? You sure you want to be signing up as an adventurer? You could have a very secure life as a priestess in one of the higher temples. Wake up, eat, sleep. And you realize you'd have your choice of disciples, both men and women, to do with as you pleased, right?" he asked.

"What are you suggesting?! I would never use manipulation to pick the person I love! I'll choose carefully, let the buds I like keep growing, and nip the others right off!"

"......I never did understand women. Like Shuna, you use a similarly unnamed spear technique and can conjure, unsurprisingly, an extensive variety of magic. It'd be dark by the time I finished reading them all."

"Yes. It's a great number of skills. That, at least, I'm proud of.

But they've overlapped so much that now I can only use one! I made covenants with so many gods that I don't even know what all the skills do! I'm so sorry, my gods and goddesses! Especially you, Lord Ukhazol!" I guess some people just had what it took to bring all the gods to their yard.

I hallucinated for a second and heard something go, *meow.*

"As for your evaluation, as an adventurer, you're a jack-of-all-trades, master of none," the boss declared. "However, your Divine Medium trait is exceptionally rare. You have limitless potential. Nevertheless, you've taken on too many covenants too easily. Show some restraint. I don't care how understanding he may be, it's rude to your primary deity."

"Yes, sir." She drooped sadly.

"You two." The boss gestured for Arvin and me to come in close. Just three dudes, huddled up having a little whispered chat. "Listen up. If someone's got the Divine Medium trait, it means they can let gods with no physical body possess them and deliver prophecies or perform miracles on their behalf. Normally, they'd be kept locked away by a religious order or sect and almost never brought out in public. I've been in the adventurer industry for forty years, but I've never seen one until today. In other words, she's not someone who should be walking around all loose and carefree! She'll be fine staying in Lady Gladwein's accommodations or when she's with Shuna. But don't you two dare let her out of your sight otherwise. She could easily get kidnapped and impressed into becoming a priestess for some dark religion or sorcerers. Do you understand?!"

"Yes, sir," we answered in unison. The boss put us both in a headlock and forced us to nod.

"?"

Bel looked at us curiously. She seemed just like any other girl on the outside, but I never would've guessed she would be so invaluable. *I guess it's really best not to judge people by appearances.*

"Me next, if you please," the mage asked with almost zero enthusiasm. Were her hands shaking because of the alcohol?

"Name: Zenobia. Twenty-four years old. Homeland: Fosstark. Sorry, I've never heard of this place."

"It's at the southernmost end of the Central Continent, just your regular rural town."

"Apologies. Belongs to the Church of Flames, disciple of the sect led by Robbe, the Great Pyromancer. Studied magic at the Azure Sky Academy. Forgive me, I haven't kept up as much as I should. The only magic academies I've heard of are the Hoense School and the Jumichla School. Which one does this belong to?"

Zenobia's expression hardened. She gulped down some ale, then admitted, "It's a private institution, the Blue Sky Magic Schoolhouse." No way he could've known that.

"Hmm, well, there's nothing bad on here. You've acquired a well-balanced mix of the magic basics. That should serve you well enough up until about the fifteenth level. Daily diligence makes the adventurer. Give it all you've got." A considerably clear-cut explanation. Zenobia did not look happy at all.

"......Huh? Is that all? Yes, I'm normal. I'm just a regular girl. I'm so run-of-the-mill, there's nothing else to say. But I mean, cut me a break—we've got a knight with a heavy burden, a genius boy swordsman, and a Divine Medium priestess here! We're trending way above average on abnormal! It makes me look pitiful! Ugh?!" She trained her gaze on me. "You're on my side here, right?" *Please don't look at me so pleadingly.*

The boss put his rugged hand on my head. "Zenobia, this man right here came from an alien world, got shut out by every god in town, beat the living daylights out of a group of three corrupt adept adventurers and dragged them through the streets for a whole night, then blew up a warehouse belonging to the trade group that sicced them on him, threatened and forced the merchants into submission, and acquired a feather from one of the Lady Minerva Sister goddesses. Word around town is that he's backed by a distinguished merman priest. And just for good measure, he's an oddball who chose someone of a different race to be his counselor."

"Nooooooooooooo! Nobody's going to remember meee!!"

"They will, they will." *No one could forget that body.*

"Does that mean we'll get a discount if we take you shopping with us?" Bel asked.

"Not sure," I asked, tilting my head in question. I could see a few of the trade groups blacklisting me.

"O' course, everything I just told you is based on rumors," the boss assured. "I'll bet it's a bit exaggerated."

"Then would you do mine, too, please?" I pulled out my scroll and handed it to him. It probably wouldn't reveal anything worse than what he'd already told them, but I figured it was important to go through the formalities.

"Let's see, hmm. Hmm?" The boss unrolled the scroll and looked puzzled. "Is this some kind of joke?"

"Huh?"

Illiterate as I was in this world, even I could understand the scroll he showed me.

It was blank.

CHAPTER 3

A Shot in the Dark

'm home." It was nearly twilight by the time I got back to camp. I put the spareribs wrapped in preservative leaves in the provisions tent and threw my equipment in mine.

"Welcome hooome."

"Welcome home."

I froze at the second voice. "What in the world—?"

A lantern stood on the ground next to Machina. It differed in some of the finer details but looked very similar to the one I'd hung around my waist. I picked it up and heard Isolla's voice start coming out of it.

"While admittedly a violation of the AI Act, I deemed my services essential in your dungeon explorations and requested Machina separate some of our functions. From now on, please call me Isolla Pot." So they'd made a miniature AI teapot disguised as a lantern of this world, huh?

"Is there no other way around the signal interference? I'm afraid you'll break if I take you into the dungeon." My radar probe had broken already, in just one day. I didn't want to put even part of my irreplaceable AI support in harm's way. The glasses device I had at least ten replacements of.

"I said separate, but my core still remains within Machina. Only during a breakdown in semi-quantum communication would my functions be duplicated and transferred to my pot to make it independent. As soon as the communication line reconnects, I would begin to synchronize and fuse my duplicate with the mainframe."

"Sorry, I didn't quite get that. Do you mean it's not a problem if this pot itself breaks?"

"There would be no problem at all. In simpler terms, it's as if I am having an out-of-body experience. We have twenty-three spare miniature teapots. We would run into trouble if you broke them easily, but I'll leave that to your judgment."

"Got it." That hadn't cleared all my doubts, but if they said it was okay, I decided I'd trust them. "That aside, what do I smell?" *Tomato sauce. Did Machina make it?* I wondered, but the terms of the treaty prohibited AI machines from autonomous operation. And I hadn't done anything as risky as put them within arm's reach of a fire source.

"Oh, you're back. Supper is ready. Eat before it gets cold."

"Huh?"

Lady Mythlanica hopped on top of Machina. "A goddess made this meal, Mr. Souya! I'm sure it's full of blessings!"

"Seriously?" I had no idea milady could cook. A pot hung atop the primitive stove. I took off the lid and stirred the ladle. Inside was a simple tomato-paste soup consisting of mashed beans. I'd planned to have the spareribs, but I could let that age for a bit. "With great thanks, I will partake of this meal." I brought a spoonful of the soup I'd ladled into a bowl to my mouth.

It had a rustic taste. A delicate garlic flavor complemented the perfect salt seasoning. Some cheese had probably been mixed in, giving the soup a rich creaminess. The crushed beans felt smooth in my mouth and didn't overpower the soup. The flavor comforted my soul and gently filled the stomach and whetted the appetite. Was this what home-cooked meals were like here? The food served at the bar had tons of salt in it to push alcohol sales. On top of that, it was overwhelmingly oily, and the vegetables were all sour for some reason. Bold and messy, it had little color variation. They did serve pretty generous portion sizes, I'd give them that, but I was already tired of the flavors.

Humans need both salt and oils to function. Judging from the much more physically fit bodies I saw here, I could understand how they'd go through huge amounts of both. However, I was just a normal human. I'd do my heart in if I followed an adventurer's diet.

"Lady Mythlanica, this is absolutely delicious."

"That so? Today was your first day leaving the nest, after all. I thought I'd give you a taste of what I can do. Count yourself lucky if I ever do it again. You should thank me with every fiber of your being. Right, I'm off to sleep."

"Y-yes, milady." I raised my now-empty bowl above my head with both hands in gratitude. Her tail slipped into the tent. I had as many refills as the pot could offer, washed up, and prepared to sleep. Then an important detail hit me.

"Machina."

"Yes, Mr. Souya?"

"Lady Mythlanica made this meal in her human form, didn't she?"

"Yep. ♪"

I got close to Machina and whispered, "You recorded it, right?"

"Yep. ♪"

"Good, show—"

"Squad Member Souya, I have a private matter to discuss with you. Please take me some distance from here."

"......"

At Isolla's request, I picked up her mini pot and walked a little way from camp. The hour was late, and darkness had fallen over the entire meadow. Back at camp, the distant lights bobbed like a bonfire. It was an ancient night. Innumerable stars studded the heavens, and the ground, dark as the deepest reaches of the ocean, stretched on forever. Even the insects lowered their voices in awe of the breathtaking nighttime scenery.

"I have a proposal regarding your explorations going forward."

"I see." I'd been expecting this.

"I request you sever your covenant with Lady Mythlanica. At this point, you also have a relationship with Lady Glavius, the Night Owl. It appears the Minerva Sister goddesses do not command the most prestige among adventurers, but they are still a great deal more respectable than a goddess who conceals her adherents' details."

My scroll had come up blank. Of course, after I realized that, I'd gone to the Guild and asked Evetta to make me a new one. When that proved impossible, she passed the baton to the Guildmaster, but even he couldn't do anything. No matter how many scrolls they tried, each one immediately turned into a blank page. After going through about thirty of them, the Guildmaster called out an elderly man with a long beard for help. He was apparently an expert on magical appraisals. According to him, the blank scrolls had to do with the goddess with whom I'd consecrated a covenant. Deception and secrecy—these two traits had strong ties to Lady Mythlanica's godly nature. Their effects even extended to me, her disciple.

I did learn one good thing, though—only the details of my life up until I entered into the covenant with Lady Mythlanica would be hidden. Anything I learned or did afterward wouldn't be affected...probably. Starting the next day, I planned to test out that possibility.

The other fortunate bit of news came from Arvin. He needed three days to refit his armor to make it more appropriate for use in the dungeon. Zenobia said that worked perfectly for her and told us she would use that time to brush up on some magic at a school in the city. Shuna and Bel apparently planned to shop around town for some extra equipment. We'd all agreed to meet up at the bar in three days.

To be frank, I had a serious problem. What kind of idiot would follow a leader who couldn't prove his identity? Adventurers placed their lives in their party members' hands. Trust was a must. Who the hell would agree to have faith in some dude without any real accomplishments to speak of and who kept his past secret?

"Is Machina on board with this?"

"No, she objected to my proposal. She has something akin to Japanese morals programmed into her core. It's truly ludicrous."

"I also—" I did agree with Isolla, but she cut me off before I could say anything.

"Consider the facts. Your party members are all incredibly talented. I base this evaluation on a meta-analysis of all the observational data I've collected. You balance one another out well, and none of you have any glaring personality defects or ideological conflicts. Furthermore, you have managed to gloss over your own impotence well. Continuing to explore the dungeon as their leader will undoubtedly provide the quickest route to achieving your goals. What did

you come here to accomplish? You came to raise funds for
your sister's shur, shurge, surjur......for your sister's
operation, did you not?"

I couldn't really say why, but hearing her stutter over that word
sent everything I'd thought flying out the window.

"I didn't stutter. I simply have not finished transferring
my full functionality over to this vessel. Japanese is a tricky
language, you know."

"Sure."

"It's true. Please believe me."

"Sure."

"You have three days. Please mentally prepare yourself
to sever your contract before that time is up. Do you understand me?"

"......Fine," I half-heartedly responded just to answer. Even
assuming she had no power, Lady Mythlanica had been the only
god in this world to offer me her assistance. I couldn't do a simple
pros and cons analysis and cut her out of my life. I knew better than
anyone that I didn't have any breathing room or other options
available to me. But that's not what this was about. It just wasn't
like that.

"I didn't hear you."

"Fine. I'll think it over."

"Is that so? Well then, if you'll excuse me." Isolla fell silent.

I went back to camp, brushed my teeth, and wiped the sweat off
my body with a damp towel. The complications that came up in the
latter half of the day had almost made me forget, but I had finally
gone down into the dungeon for the first time. It hadn't moved me
as much as I might've anticipated, given all the trouble I'd gone
through to get to that point. More like, as soon as I solved one
problem, another popped up in its place. Good grief.

Heart heavy, my body cried out for rest. I stepped into my tent to find Lady Mythlanica curled up in a ball on my pillow. Her Grace did almost nothing but lie in repose. I stretched out on the ground, careful not to wake her.

I couldn't sleep. It seemed my heart of hearts was in greater turmoil than I'd thought. I tossed and turned a bit, then—

"What's wrong? Lose your courage in the dungeon?" It appeared I'd woken Lady Mythlanica from her slumber.

"No, that's not it, exactly," I responded evasively.

"Good. There is not a soul that does not experience that dread. Those who fail to fear the unknown die quickly. Do not look this way."

Why not? I wondered, but then an irresistible bare leg draped over my waist. Pale arms extended from behind me and wrapped around my neck. Warm breath brushed past my ear. A pair of humps pressed against my back. They felt terrifically supple and indescribably soft. My man the constable had told no lies. These had to be ravishing beauties.

"I'll only do this today as a special treat. You should fall asleep with the warmth of another's flesh in no time. However, turn this way, and I will curse you."

"Actually, this will only make it harder to sleep."

"*Mrah.*"

"Lady Mythlanica?"

Her breath grew quiet and even. I pinched her doughy arms and even trepidatiously slid my hand down her smooth thigh. No response. She must have fallen fast asleep. I had to stop. This was arousing all sorts of things in me.

I haven't gotten any of that in a long time, or more like, ever, and when a man is tired, it's even harder to— Wait, calm down. What did I come here for? To do what? What? Calm down, that's what.

Aren't you—aren't you supposed to recite the numbers in pi in this sort of situation? Okay, three. That's all I remember. That's not distracting me one bit. I feel like I'm about to fill this pie with something else. Again, what am I—? And then the tent flapped open.

Something rolled over and stopped in front of me. It was Isolla.

"Here, please use this. It's a sedative. Inject yourself with it if you feel you have lost control of your emotions. Now is precisely that time." The kettle's arm presented me a needle-less syringe about the size of a ballpoint pen. I had a lot I wanted to call her out for, but for the moment, I thankfully took the syringe and injected it into my neck. It didn't hurt much, but the strange sensation of a foreign substance running through my body had me trembling.

"Aren't you guys forbidden from making autonomous decisions under the AI Act?"

"This was no autonomous act. I simply happened to fall and roll over here, rest assured. I can put myself back."

That was exactly what you'd call autonomous. So AI robots could disregard the terms of the treaty this easily, huh? Was it just me, or did this look like a fatal flaw?

"In my country, we have a saying that goes, 'Don't tell anyone at trial about our relations.' You understand what I'm trying to say, don't you?"

"Nope, not a clue."

"It's a lesson about how even a man with incredible resources and a vast network of personal connections, one who had earned approval from a majority of his people, who was entrusted with the highest mission and responsibilities of the greatest country on earth, and swore to love his wife before God, fell victim to his carnal desires."

"Okay." I decided not to ask any more about it. It felt like I'd see more of the darkness in her heart than I cared to. "By the way, Isolla."

"Yes?"

"When will this medicine kick in?"

"In two seconds."

I passed out.

(8TH DAY)

The situation was all too simple. By adventurer standards, I just didn't have enough physical strength—not even close. I'd be hard put to cut even a chocho down with a longsword. You used completely different muscles to shoot a gun and to slash a sword, and I didn't have the time to build that kind of strength now. That being the case, I had limited choices in terms of the weapons I could use.

"Hey, shopkeeper."

"EEYYAAAAAAAAAAAAAHH!"

I'd dropped by the main store of the Zavah Night Owl Trade Group to get something new to defend myself.

"Show me a few weapons."

"EEEEEEEEEEEEEEEEEEK!" The shopkeeper's knees buckled, and he scuttled back away from me. The relatively big store had about thirty people inside, staff included. Every single one of them stared at me.

Argh, now even more people are gonna gossip about me.

"I'm just here today to get a—"

"EAAAAAAAAAAAAAAAAAAH!"

"So you want me to go to the Ellomere Traders."

"Pardon me, I was a little flustered. What may I help you with today?" He immediately snapped out of it and straightened himself out. I'd started to get the hang of how to deal with him.

"I'd like to see a crossbow. Do you have any in stock?"

"A crossbow, you say? We do indeed. Please, right this way." He had the crossbows all lined up in a corner of the shop, in what one might call a dead space. "It's not our most popular product among adventurers, you see. That is not to say, however, that we carry anything but the best quality." I saw about twenty different varieties, each using slightly varying designs or created with different materials, all of them following the same basic construction.

"May I?" I asked.

"Please, be my guest."

I picked up one of the crossbows and pulled the string back to allay my biggest concern. "Ngh, nghh, ungh!" I pulled with all my might, but the string wouldn't budge.

"Master Souya, you're meant to secure this with your foot and pull back with your legs," he explained.

"I see." The crossbow had a metal *stirrup* at the very front end of the stock. I stuck my foot in it and used my legs to pull—hard! "Grr, grah!" I couldn't do it. "You sure this isn't defective?"

"I do believe we've kept it properly maintained."

I handed the crossbow to the shopkeeper. He put his foot in the stirrup and attempted to pull the string back, too, but failed as well. We tried two more the same way with the same result. We even tried pulling the string together, but it didn't move an inch.

"Oaffet, Oaffet, you back there?" he yelled out to someone. An almost two-meter-tall beastman answered his call. His friendly face, droopy ears, and wagging tail felt out of sync with his enormous body. He was a dog, definitely a Saint Bernard. "Try pulling this back," the shopkeeper ordered.

"Yah." He put both hands on the string and drew it back with ease until it latched into the slot connected to the trigger. "You adventurer?" he asked me.

"Who, me? Yeah, sure am."

"Come now, Oaffet. He's a customer," the merchant scolded him. I ignored him and listened to the rest of what the beastman had to say.

"This one, no good for bring down monster. Bad aim for small ones, won't go through big ones, next shot too slow."

"I see." So it wasn't very accurate, huh? But I mean, I couldn't even load it properly.

"Plus, expensive. Breaks easy. Much money to fix. Bolts expensive. Lotsa money, but easy to lose. If expensive okay, bow is better." Checking the tag, I saw the number fifteen next to the character for gold piece. That was a lot of money. "Bows too bulky in dungeon. But good bow stands out. You can brag other adventurers. Brag important. Adventurer with no pride forgot easy."

"Are you an adventurer, too?" I asked him.

"Yes. But now, I guard boss."

Hmm, prestige, huh? I've never even considered that aspect. Maybe it's not as simple as defeating monsters and descending farther down.

"Then could you show me some bows?"

"Yah."

"Master Souya, he's merely a bodyguard, not a clerk," protested the merchant.

"It's fine, it's fine." It might sound obvious, but it was better to ask someone in the same line of work about these kinds of things. The merchants here only tried to push whatever they wanted to sell, so I couldn't trust them, especially when they had no idea what they were talking about.

We moved over to the bow area. It boasted a large selection with a wide range of sizes to fit customers from a variety of races. Their materials differed, but all the bows basically looked like a sideways V and had their corresponding bowstrings wrapped around them.

"Truth is, real archers, make own bow. No buy. Store bows rip-off. But this one not bad." The bow Oaffet picked up loosely resembled an Ω. Small but thick, it had been made of at least three different kinds of wood. "This elf bow. Even beastman strength no break. Bendy. Even heim can use."

Oaffet affixed the string to the bow and drew it. The bow's materials creaked slightly as it bent. He handed it over to me, and I tried it out. Not bad. I could imagine myself fitting an arrow and pulling it back. The bow cost five gold. Others cost around nine silver on average, making this considerably more expensive.

"I'll take it. Also, choose some arrows for me, please."

"Yah. Cheap arrows no good. Metal arrowhead, arrow shaft good. Pick up and use again. Heavy ones good. Recommend this cui arrow. Also, buy gusta ore arrowheads and domer copper shafts. For arrow feathers, use flying rabbit ones. They fly round meadow in evening. And you need bowstring?"

"This bowstring, it's twine, right?" I had something that would give me even more elasticity.

"Yah."

"Then I'm okay. So I'll take twenty arrows and twenty each of the arrowheads and shafts. Shopkeeper, ring me up, please."

"Of course. All together that comes to eight gold and five silver pieces. I'll throw in a quiver for free." I handed him the money.

"I'll carry the bow as is. Could you wrap everything else and put it in the quiver?"

"As you wish. Just a moment, please." The shopkeeper disappeared into the back room.

"So, Oaffet. I've got a question for you." I slipped him five copper pieces for the tip.

"Yah."

"I'm looking for a master archer who could give me a crash course. Know anyone?"

"You no can use arrow? Why buy?"

"There's a very complicated and bizarre reason for that."

"I see, good luck." He slapped me on the back. "I know one great, not busy archer."

Tip from my more experienced fellow adventurer in hand, I went on the hunt for an archery teacher. Apparently, he could often be found hanging about the city walls in the afternoons. Helpful, except that covered a huge amount of ground.

"Shall I guide you from above?" asked Machina.

"No, I'll walk about and look for him for a bit."

"Understood."

Ever since the dustup with the degenerate adventurers, I'd stopped relying on my AI companions for everything. I trusted Machina and Isolla, but I hated the thought of getting so dependent on them that I would be unable to fend for myself in an emergency. My mental fortitude and my strength were my last lines of defense. If I didn't train both every day, they would atrophy and do me no good.

Lines upon lines of white sheets hung out to dry along the water canal that ran close by the walls to the city. The fluttering white fabric reminded me of a hospital rooftop.

Oh, this is how I felt when Gramps died.

I'd cried with worry back then over what we were going to do without him. It felt laughable, thinking back on it now. Humans could live anywhere if they set their minds on it. Once I put my body to work, I didn't even have time to worry anymore. What's more, I stopped caring at all about what other people thought or felt. Nothing mattered but putting food on the table and saving money. But even so, I never considered my lifestyle deplorable.

I just want a reason to die. I want the sense of purpose that makes you forget time and the instinct to survive, one you'd risk your life for. Something that transpires in the tiniest of seconds and ends in a flash. So far, I haven't found anything that absorbing in my life. Without it, I've just been existing. And I don't expect to find it going forward, either. Nothing is going to change that, not even this world where power hinges on glory and honor. More like, I won't change it. Better yet, I can't. What exactly am I trying to do?

"Hey, you! Young man!"

"Huh?" I answered, completely zoned out, the dumbest look on my face. About six middle-aged ladies were washing their laundry close by. One of them waved at me to come over. I got closer and then—

"Wait, is that a dead body?"

"You, grab his legs, would you? He's far too heavy for us; we can't do it alone."

—I saw the back of what seemed to be a particularly shaggy man (?) floating in the water. I figured he must be a beastman, though I'd never seen one with such a thick coat of fur. But, well, I didn't want him contaminating the water supply, so I grabbed hold of his legs. The ladies and I heaved and hoed in unison and lifted him up to the road. He weighed a shit ton and was enormous, even bigger than my newest pal Oaffet. He'd easily stand at least two and a half meters tall.

And he had a beastman's head. It looked like a wolf to me, with a long tongue and sharp canines peeking out of his snout. I thought I'd seen a pretty varied assortment of beastfolk since I came to this world, but none of them had as much beast in them as this guy. The memories that stayed with me were almost exclusively those of women, who all had beast-like qualities around their ears, eyes, and noses, maybe a tail, and fur on about 10 or 20 percent of their skin. Even those with relatively more fur had it only in patches on their arms, legs, and a part of their neck at most. This was my first time seeing an almost entirely beast person. He was basically a wolf walking on two legs.

"Lord Baafre, Lord Baafre! I can't believe you're sleeping out here again! Would you please cease this nonsense? Your fur is going to get in our laundry!" The woman tugged at the beastman's face. *Hold on, he's alive?* After she gave him about five hardcore slaps on the face, the wolf-headed man opened his eyes.

"Ugh, good nap." He sluggishly got to his feet, then shook his body like a dog to dry off. A deluge of water splashed all over me.

"Lord Baafre, I beg of you, at least sleep on the floor next time."

"Mm-hmm, forgive me."

"Is this man some sort of god?" I asked the woman, who looked at me with pity.

"Oh-ho, you there. Have you not heard tell of the great hero of the north, Baafre Heijin the lycan?!" asked the wolfman. "No worry, I'll tell you the whole grand tale for a drink of cheap liquor. There happens to be a shop where I left some things just down over there. Come!"

"Huh?"

Before I could run off, he grabbed my arm and pulled me to an alfresco café-type bar. Though *alfresco* was just my way of putting a nice spin on it. In truth, the café constituted nothing more than a few simple tables and chairs arranged around a space with no roof. It looked like all the cooking happened in a shanty toward the back. Did this even count as a restaurant?

Lord Baafre sat down at a table topped with all kinds of junk, then forced me to take a seat, too. "Heeey, Tutu. Beer! And a drink on the side!" *What's with that order? It's like asking for rice with a side of rice.*

"Lord Baafre, I'd be meow than happy to serve you a drink. But you've got a big tab already." A cat beastmaid came out from the shanty wearing an apron over what basically amounted to panties and a bra. She had a lithe feline frame, long, wavy blond hair, and pointed ears. Her tail looked a bit like a besom broom.

Wait, she looks familiar. Well, she is a beastmaid, and it's hard to differentiate between people of another race.

"This young gent right here will handle the bill."

"I was afraid of that."

"Oh! You're that generous new adventurer from yesterday!"

"Yesterday? Oh!" She'd been our waitress at the boss's bar. My body burned a bit as I remembered the kiss she'd given me.

"What's this? Did you come all the way out here looking for little old mee-ow?" she asked, sinuously curving her body and looking not altogether displeased. I mention this for posterity, but I was even less displeased. I just didn't show it.

"I helped drag this gentleman out of the river and then for some reason wound up responsible for his bar tab," I told her.

"That's terrible. Guess you're not the one for me, meow."

"No waaay."

Tutu disappeared into the shanty and came back carrying bottles of ale. "Also, you pay up front here. Nine copper pieces. Only Lord Baafre gets to keep an open tab," she explained.

I didn't want to trouble her haggling over the cost, so I paid up. My head started hurting when I tallied up the total expenses of my outing for the day. I didn't even want to think about how much more the archery lessons would put me back.

"Come now, Tutu. For all your talk about this tab, you still keep my weapons as leverage."

"These stinky, bony old pieces of crap! I had a merchant appraise them for me, but it didn't work! I wasted the appraisal fee for nothing! Mrow!" Tutu kicked a large sack by her feet, and it made a loud *clang*.

"Bah-ha-ha-ha! No tricksy little merchant has what it takes to appreciate my weapons' true value. Nor can any ordinary person wield them. A lycan's weapons are—"

"Nothing but garbage. They're always in my way—I'm gonna toss 'em, I'll show you!" She kicked the sack again. A sword, spear, ax, bow, and shield, all clearly old, tumbled out.

"Will you desist? I swear to you I shall pay off my tab after my next expedition, all right? See? So please, don't stomp on your dear friend's keepsakes," he pleaded, pretty much as shamelessly as my goddess. "More importantly, you. Those are some rather curious clothes on you. I've never seen this type of material." He turned the topic over to me and unabashedly grabbed on to my poncho.

"I think I heard 'em say he's an Otherworlder," Tutu chimed in. They both sniffed me up and down. I had absolutely no idea how to react.

"I see; you don't say. No wonder he looked so befuddled, even after laying eyes on my heroic visage. Now then, as promised, I shall regale you with the legend of us mighty lycans." The wolf-headed man took a bottle of booze in his hand and drank it down in one gulp. Then, fueled by the cheap ale, he began to tell the legend of the moon and the wolves.

Our story takes place far, far north of here, beyond the farthest reaches of the Right Continent. There, a city of great wealth called Neomia once stood. Blessed with fertile lands and favorable weather and protected by mountains and precipitous cliffs, the city sustained no foreign invasions for many years. Moreover, boons of their king's wisdom reached far and wide. By any measure, they had reached the very peak of prosperity.

And yet, as the Great Pyromancer Robbe proclaimed, "All flames will surely fade." Neomia's downfall began with a snowfall in spring. For one year, then two, the winter did not abate; snow and ice quietly claimed life after life. The spring of the fifth year came, and yet the snow continued to fall.

Plagued by his people's famine and resentment, the king lost sight of the wisdom he once commanded. The country's sullen nobles admonished the king, who then invoked the name of a god of a false creed who had been sealed away. The king of the beasts had vanquished this god and stolen their name. It was the god of vampires.

The king received the dark god's favor. His people froze and starved. Declaring it a rescue mission, the king devoured every last one of them, and those who "survived" this feast then turned to dine on others still alive. Every life in the city was extinguished in the span of one night. Only voracious vampires and their kin, the nobles of ice, remained. Neomia became a city of death and fell to ruin.

However, those who took up residence in the mountains survived. They were the Endguard, warriors bound by an ancient oath to protect Neomia from foreign attack, and they took up their arms for it. The city had perished, and their king was no longer the man he had been. Their proud nobles had also vanished, along with the citizens, of course. Nevertheless, the warriors fought for Neomia and her honor, to ensure the vile, bloodsucking beasts would not escape from the cage of the dead city.

Valiantly they fought; over and over they suffered defeat. Even honor tarnishes once sullied by the debased blood of beasts. The warriors turned their blades against friends, against family.

In the eighth year of winter, on a night of two full moons, the warriors reached their end. A horde of vampires closed in on their last stronghold. Nine warriors remained—only nine. Nonetheless, these nine had refined their martial prowess over hundreds of battles. They laughed in the face of death, for to die laughing was the pride of a warrior.

Just then, a woman who called herself the Goddess of the Moon appeared before them. Although she was beautiful, they say her silhouette was as shadowy as the dark side of the moon. The goddess extolled the warriors before her.

"O brave heroes, the most valiant in all the world. You shall all perish this night. None shall see the light of day. In this, your final hour, have you any wishes?"

Caught unawares by a question so ill fit for their current state, the warriors forgot she was a goddess and laughed. An elder warrior responded, stating, "We shall fight to the death and die in the fight. You yourself have promised we shall attain this, our long-cherished desire. What more could there be for us to wish?"

The goddess asked once more, "Are you sure there is nothing? Do you truly have no desires but to fight?"

An unassuming, young warrior said, "I want to crush them all." According to the pride of the Endguard, that was a foolish wish. They fought to protect, and if their enemy should flee, they did not give chase. They laughed and toasted to the cowards who clung so to their lives. That had been their way for generations. Thus, for a proper Endguard warrior, his would have been a laughable wish. He would have endured severe beatings for many years for speaking such nonsense.

And yet, not a single person laughed. Should they adhere to the code their ancestors had protected throughout the ages, they would gain naught but personal glory. It would be honorable but meaningless. Yet, should they unleash the vampires from this city, death would reach across the Great Land. Those beasts were rats carrying a cursed disease. Allowing them to roam far and wide would bring dishonor upon Neomia, City of Wealth. No one would remember its prosperity of old. It would go down in history as a city of ice and death.

The warriors had died one by one to prevent that from happening. They had died laughing. But on that night, would all their sacrifice be in vain?

"This is your wish?" The warriors all answered the goddess with silence. "O warriors bound to perish, guardians of the end. Your wish shall surely bring dishonor upon your blades, drain your human blood, and send you into a nightmare from which you shall never awaken. If, in spite of all I have said, this be your wish, answer me with silence."

The warriors answered her with silence.

"I am the Goddess of the Cruel Moon, she who will share with you the blood of the abominable. Receive this blessing from the demon who descended upon you, and with it, demolish and vanquish those who sought the graces of their devil."

A strange mutation overcame the warriors. Their arms and legs thickened ever more, and beastly fur covered their bodies; their mouths rent apart and bore fangs; their pupils widened beneath the moonlight. Their nails grew as sharp as their weapons, their muscles thicker than steal, and their voices—

"Come, my beastly brethren. Let us begin the hunt."

—rang long into the night, echoing off the walls of Neomia, the City of Death. And so began the night of the bloodstained lycans.

"After that, well, we bashed the vampires to a pulp and protected the peace of the entire Right Continent. How about that? Spine-tingling, no? Worth the price of a drink, wouldn't you say?"

Maybe, but there are already five empty bottles rolling around on the table.

"Wellll, I'd take that all with a big pinch of salt," said Tutu, relaxing with her chin rested atop the jolly wolfman's head.

"No, no, it is naught but the truth. I have not spoken a single lie."

"Lord Baafre, I'll admit you are a very talented adventurer, regardless of how terrible you are at making any money."

"Ohhh, are you an adventurer?" So he was my senior. I needed to show him the proper respect, for what it was worth.

"Mm-hmm. However, I am currently under suspension!"

Wait. You can be suspended from exploring the dungeon?

"An unfamiliar adventurer took me for a monster and attacked me. He simply would not relent, so I whacked him ever so softly, but it gave him a light wound that knocked him out cold for about ten days. The Guildmaster really let me have it. Even Remlia scolded me, too. No one had yelled at me like that in fifty years—they almost had me in tears, you know?! Ba-ha-ha-ha-ha!" Tutu petted his head to console the wolfman, who showed none of the dignity of a man who had supposedly saved this continent.

"So, umm, Lord Baafre? There were nine of you, right? The lycans. Do the rest of them also work as adventurers here?"

"No, they perished. Half of them sacrificed themselves to defeat the king of the vampires. The other half I slayed with my own two hands."

"Huh?" The story took a very sudden, very bloody turn. Scratch that, I also got the feeling it had been pretty gory from the start.

"They had been cursed, after all. Some went crazy with plea-sure and lost their minds. Sadly, our pride as warriors died that night. They went wild for blood—not to drink it but to see it. In other words, they became no better than the vampires." Lord

Baafre polished off the sixth bottle and offered me some encouraging advice. "Foreign adventurer, let me tell you one thing. 'The works of the gods in this realm always come drenched in irony.' Do not rely on the easy way out, unless you want to end up like us."

"Good point. I would hate to wind up as someone who gets dead drunk off the booze they made a new adventurer treat them to."

"Well, look at the mouth on you."

I handed the seventh empty bottle to Tutu and got up from my seat. "But it was a pretty interesting story. Thank you for sharing it with me." I wasn't sure if it was worth twenty-one copper pieces, though.

"Speaking of, what were you doing out here to begin with?" he asked. "There aren't any decent restaurants or inns in this corner of town. If it's a lady you fancy, you could've easily found some heims closer to the front gates."

"No decent restaurants around, you say, mrow?"

"Gah!" Tutu started strangling Lord Baafre from behind. Seeing them get along so well made me jealous.

He had a point. I'd totally forgotten. "I came to look for a master archer I heard hung around here."

"Oh, I know just the one." Lord Baafre shook a beer bottle in the air. Judging by the sound it made, he'd probably already emptied half of it. In the end, I paid twenty-four copper coins and learned where to find the master archer.

"You come back soon, meow!"

"And buy me some more driiinks!"

I waved to them both and left. Somehow, I felt a bit cheated.

Farther down along the canal, I turned into a dim back alley. Deeper and deeper into the darkness I headed, down the path's intricate twists and turns. The vibe here felt much like the dungeon. It had a whiff of danger, too. I kept a mildly watchful eye out as I went.

All of a sudden, a small whirlwind of a group crossed my path—a gaggle of beastfolk and elven kids. They raced down the alleys, having a blast. Children had a way of breaking open little holes between interspecific barriers and slipping right through them.

I came upon a woman practicing magic. In the corners of the light she emitted, I saw a mysteriously profound shadow. I sensed a small but terrifying presence lurking in the depths where her light could not reach, a glimpse of a quiet illusion.

At last, I found the small bridge I was after. Had it been overlooked during the development of the area? The bridge had character that set it apart from the rest of the buildings, which looked newer. Though small, it seemed sturdy. Beneath this bridge I would find my target, or so I'd heard.

They cut a striking figure. Like two sisters from a fairy tale, they sat snuggled up next to each other. I got the sense they looked a bit dingier than the last time I'd seen them, not that something so trifling could manage to tarnish their beauty.

"Excuse me." Still a short distance away, I got down on one knee, then put my left hand on my right shoulder and my right hand flat on the ground. A flash of recognition came over the elder sister as she looked at me. She was a lovely young lady, a bit petite for an elf, with long, blond hair and ears that drooped just a little. Her curvaceous frame seemed at odds with her cute demeanor. Her arms wrapped around a tall staff.

"You saved me the other day," I told her. "Thanks to you, I managed to keep my arm."

The younger sister roused from her sleep with a grunt and trained her bow on me in a fraction of a second. I hadn't even seen her fix the arrow to the string. This sister was a terrifying beauty.

A tall, lean blond, she perfectly aligned with the classic image of an elf. For some reason, she had on a rather revealing outfit a young beastmaid might wear, composed of skintight mini-shorts and a sports bra. A gauntlet on her right arm caught my eye. It had an elaborate design made of thin gold and a mysterious, alluring draw.

"Ah! You're the heim who almost died the other day, right?!"

"Stop this, Éa," admonished the elder sister, and the younger elf lowered her bow. By some strange coincidence, these very same elves had previously come to my rescue. *No way*, I'd thought when Baafre first described them to me, but that's who it was.

"You were far too generous with your thanks for the directions I gave you. I followed after you to return it, and the constable asked me to heal your wounds," explained the elder sister.

"You'd better be grateful," spat Éa.

"I am hugely grateful."

"I'm so glad to see you. After thinking it over later, I came to the conclusion that even taking the treatment into consideration, the token you gave us was still much too lavish. We did use a portion of it, but I'd like to return the rest."

"Whaaat?!" the younger sister exclaimed. The elder sister opened her wallet, and I couldn't help but peek inside.

"No, I don't need the money. According to custom in my country, having a gift returned to you brings bad fortune." You could probably find someone who believed that, if you searched through all of Japan.

"I see…… Then I suppose I have no choice." A wave of relief passed over me as she accepted my reasoning. It would wound my pride as a man to take any of the coins from her already very empty purse.

"I am Souya of Japan, an adventurer from another world.

Please allow me to thank you once more, lady elf. Oh, please stay as you are. I've interrupted your rest. There's no need to trouble yourself." The elder elf started to get up, but I stopped her. This was just my impression, but this woman gave off a noble air, a sense of refinement worthy of respect.

"Thank you for your kind consideration. My name is Laualliuna Raua Heuress, an adventurer like yourself. This is my younger sister, Éa. Come on, introduce yourself."

"Why? He's just a heim."

"You're going to make me angry," Ms. Laualliuna growled. Nothing about her was scary. Grudgingly, her younger sister greeted me, too.

"I'm Éa Raua Heuress. Hmph, just try getting all chummy and I'll put an arrow through your forehead."

I felt it about time to get down to business. "I'm looking for an archery instructor. An experienced adventurer told me great things about you two. If you are not currently occupied, would you please consider it? Of course, I will compensate you for the favor."

"No. Way. In. Hell. You wouldn't catch me dead teaching a heim how to shoot. Especially not one who dares to carry an elven bow. Where'd you get that? Don't tell me you pried it off a corpse? And now you want to steal our techniques, too?"

"Éa, hold your tongue."

"But, Lala! He's—!" Heated, Éa got to her feet—and immediately collapsed.

"Éa?!"

I instinctively reached out and caught her. She hung limply in my arms, unconscious. Her breathing was short, her face deathly pale, and beads of sweat formed on her brow.

"*Blegh.*"

And then she threw up on my poncho. It smelled bitter. Éa

choked and coughed but still did not regain consciousness. This looked really bad.

"Ah, um, I'm so sorry," Laualliuna apologized in a fret.

"It's okay," I assured her. "I've seen this before, trust me." Turning Éa on her side and using my fingers to keep her airway open, I helped her expunge everything from her system until she calmed down, slapping her on the back with my clean hand. Her breath immediately stabilized. I poured a bit of water from my bottle over her mouth to lightly rinse it off. There didn't seem to be anything left inside.

Is she hungover? I can't smell any alcohol, though. In that case, is this some chronic illness? No, what if...?

"Machina, is there any risk she has an infectious disease?"

"I cannot completely deny the possibility. Please submit her excreta and blood for analysis as soon as possible." Éa remained unconscious, but she'd calmed down.

"Pardon the question, but is your sister—?"

"She's not ill. She suffers due to an injury, though the manager of the inn misunderstood and asked us to leave."

"I see." That was a relief, at least. We waited for a few minutes, but Éa showed no signs of waking, so I slipped my arms underneath her legs and back and lifted her up. Unconscious people were supposed to be very heavy, but she weighed less than a feather. Was she getting enough to eat?

"It's a bit far from here, but let's go back to my camp. At least you'll be protected from the wind there. I imagine it's difficult to trust me so easily, so please hold on to this," I offered, handing Laualliuna my wallet. "It's got almost all the money I have. Feel free to run off with it if you deem me untrustworthy."

"I can't accept that. It's far too cheap a ransom for my sister's life."

"Fair enough. All right, then I'll leave my life in your hands. I hope you'll take that in exchange for your trust, Ms. Lanalliu, Laualli, Ms. Lanaju......Launalliuna. Ms. Laua...lliuna." *Take that, Isolla! See how I didn't give up?!*

"You can call me Lana, Souya." Her lips curled up into a fragile smile, and my heart fluttered with the most joy I'd felt since landing in this world.

We hitched a ride on a horse-drawn carriage headed for the farms and arrived at the campsite. I negotiated with the farmer to see if he wouldn't mind dropping off some vegetables on his way back to town, and he cheerfully agreed. The trick was to let him catch a glimpse of Lady Glavius's feather, a tip I'd picked up from the young head of the Ellomere Traders.

"Give me just a second. I'll set up a tent for you." I couldn't exactly lay Éa down in the pantry and supplies tent, much less my own messy sleeping quarters, so I pitched a new one for them. Having done it six times already, it had almost become second nature to me. First, I checked to see if the residential tent kit had all its parts. Then I spread out the inner tent, slipped the two main poles through the sleeves, and inserted the corner end tips into one side of each.

"Souya, I can help you," Machina offered.

"Please. I'll take the left pole, so you get the right, okay?" The two of us lifted up the inner tent. Once the poles fully extended, we inserted them into the empty end tips. I shook the expanded tent loosely to double-check if it would hold. Then I affixed the canopy poles into the designated end tips on the tent. One by one, I affixed the reinforcements to fasten the fabric to the poles. After that, I moved the tent so that it had its back end to the wind, lined it up with the other tents, and hammered in the stakes to secure it in the ground. I threw the cold weatherproofing fly over the whole thing, tied that to the poles, and drove stakes through its ends as well. The fly's rope I used to adjust the tension on the tent and once again secured this to the ground with stakes. Thanks to Machina's help, it didn't even take me eight minutes to set up.

Machina's help......?

"Hey, Little Miss Machina."

"Yes?"

I casually tossed a question over to the robot, who stood at my side. "You're pretty much moving by yourself, aren't you?"

She threw a *Huh?!* up on her display screen, then tilted her body from side to side and rolled it around in a big circle. Finally, she returned to her normal position and responded, "I didn't do anything. ♪"

You little—you're doin' it, too, huh?

"I just happened to lose my balance, landed by you, and assisted with the tent assembly, that's all. More importantly, should you really keep your guests waiting? I'm worried about them!"

"I'm gonna grill you about this later."

"Tee-hee-heeee. ♪"

Lana's eyes had opened wide in shock. I lifted Éa, who I'd laid to rest at her side, in my arms and brought her into the tent. "Please, take a rest in here. I'll get you some blankets. Hang tight for a little bit, and I can whip up something warm."

"Were you not going to practice archery?"

"You and your sister's health comes first. Any student would be beside themselves with worry if their teacher didn't feel well. Oh, just take off your shoes, okay?" Lana stepped in the tent and sat down. She had beautiful legs—not too skinny, not too plump.

I stepped away for a minute and rummaged through the other squadron members' personal effects until I found some women's clothing. I'd tried not to think too much about it, but what *had* happened to them? It was probably better not to dwell on that. I grabbed some clothing and towels, a tub filled with water, and pillows and blankets and carried them all back over to the tent.

"You can change into these if you like. Oh, sorry."

"It's no trouble." I'd walked in on Lana removing her accessories and smaller pieces of equipment. My eyes drifted toward her bare shoulder, but I quickly looked away.

"That's a rather unique attendant you have," she noted. "I've never seen anything like it."

"She's no attendant. She's my partner."

"Do you mean your friend? That mass of metal is your friend?"

"That's right." As soon as I left the tent, that very mass of metal started speaking to me.

"Mr. Souya, give me your poncho, please. Also, take these antibiotics, just in case."

I took the pills and swallowed them, then removed my poncho and shoved it in the scanner drawer in her lower half. "Machina, what's the recovery status on the medical program?"

"It's at fifteen percent."

"How many more hours will you need to recover full functionality?"

"Optimistically, I would estimate approximately three months. Please refrain from sustaining any injuries to your internal organs in that time."

"Would it be possible to perform an abdominal surgery at this stage?"

"That would be difficult. We should have sufficient medical supplies for it, but considering Isolla's and my own capabilities, I expect the probability of success would be rather low. I can, however, extract the necessary information from the medical program as a last resort. Nevertheless, in addition to rendering the original program useless, it remains uncertain that I would be able to perform a perfect medical procedure."

"Hmm." What a conundrum. "We'll put this on the back burner for now."

"Understood."

It was time to prepare their food. I figured something easy on the stomach would be best. We had some leftover fish, so I chopped it into chunks and put it in a pot. Next, I threw in some grated ginger as well as smallish potatoes and onions cut into bite-size pieces. After that, I added the water, a dash of mirin and soy sauce, and some Japanese soup stock powder, then turned on the flame. Once the water boiled, I removed any fat that floated to the top, mindlessly scraping it off. It was menial labor but a good diversion.

"Isolla, come here for a sec." I heard a *roll, roll, roll.*

"Yes, what can I do for you?" She'd scooted right up to me. I stepped on her.

"Once I've got a minute, I'm going to press you for every little detail on your treaty violations, got it?" I removed my foot.

"Oh nooo, I'm rolling awaaay!" She scuttled back into the supply tent.

I'm worried. More than anything else, I'm terrified of what these two will get up to. AI robots rising up in revolt is a sci-fi movie staple. Who's to say they won't abandon me and start up a new religion among the locals as their goddesses? I can totally see it happening, but I still need to rely on Machina for way too much. Most importantly, would they even be able to create the portal to get back home?

The soup had simmered for about ten minutes, so I turned off the flame and dissolved some miso in the water. I tasted it; pretty good, for myself. As something I would serve to others, it wasn't bad. One miso soup with fish, ready to go. Funny how quickly I'd given up on adding any otherworldly elements to dish names.

"Something stinks."

Éa came out of the tent wearing a T-shirt I'd lent them. Thanks to her short shorts, it looked like she was naked save for the shirt. Lana followed soon after.

"It's not much, but I made soup." I served Éa some in a bowl and handed it to her with a spoon.

"You eat that. I'll choose my dishes and my food myself."

"Éa, you're being rude," Lana warned.

"No, it's fine." Only a fool would take something as it was handed to them, no questions asked. I'd learned that lesson the hard way, too. I took a sip of the soup, slurping more softly than usual. "Does that satisfy you?"

"I don't want to eat anything that fishy," she announced. *You don't say?*

"May I have some?" asked Lana.

"Just a seco—" I went to get her a new bowl, but before I could, Lana gently took the one from my hands.

"It's delicious." She hadn't hesitated to drink from something I'd put my mouth on. For some reason, I felt kind of guilty. "What is this dish called?"

"Oh, *arajiru*." I was mortified. I should've served her something a little more refined than that.

"*Arajiru?* What's in it?"

"Umm, it's stewed fish and vegetables with miso."

"What is miso?"

"Miso is a seasoning from my world made from fermented beans. It's not much to look at, but it's good for your health."

"How wonderful. Were you a chef in this foreign land?"

"Oh, no, no, not at all."

"No need to be so modest. This is lovely." One look at Lana's genuine smile clearly free of hollow compliments sent a shock running down my spine.

......*Huh? Why do I feel so good? Was it always this fun to tell other people about my cooking? I could get hooked on this.*

I invited Lana to sit in one of the camping chairs and put the pot next to her so she could refill her bowl as she liked. Just then, looking terribly displeased, Éa demanded, "And what about for me? Don't you have anything else?"

"All right, take your pick of whatever you want from here," I said, ducking into the supply tent with her. Inside, I'd lined up all the meat, vegetables, and grains I'd bought in this world. I saw her eyes sparkle like a child's. "If you're hungry for meat, I've got a good cut of pork," I suggested.

"Meat might not be the best right now." She still looked a little pale. "Show me what's in here," she ordered, slapping one of the containers. I opened it for her. It held condiments, rice, dry goods, and the like, mostly instant foods in case of emergency.

"What's this?" She picked up a cup of ramen and turned it in her hands inquisitively.

"It's called ramen."

"Ramen?"

"You add boiling water and it turns into a soup with wheat that looks like string. It's not that good." Honestly, I'd grown tired of it.

"This is what I want."

"You got it." I stepped out of the tent and turned the kitchen fire back on, then poured some drinking water in a new pot and left it on the flame. She was having a rough go at opening the cup.

"It's got some clear skin. Doesn't taste good."

"Yeah, 'cause you don't eat that part."

Running her tongue all over the packaging plastic, she looked ready to start chewing on it, so I temporarily confiscated it. She pouted at me. I removed the film and pulled back the lid. Éa watched closely, transfixed. For someone who had been so wary, she had gotten pretty close to me. After an indescribable few minutes waiting, the water started to boil. I went to pour it in the cup, but—

"I wanna do it."

—she insisted, so I left her to it.

"Fill it up until that line inside."

"Got it." She clumsily added the boiling water. I placed a spork on top of the cup.

"Machina, set a timer for three minutes."

"Timer set for three minutes. Beginning countdown."

Éa stared at Machina, her eyes bulging. And yet, her attention soon returned to the mysterious food in her hands.

"Once that round thing over there tells you it's time, you can open it up and dig in."

"Got it." She sat down next to her sister, clearly excited. It was as if she was a child, I guess. Physically an adult but a child inside.

"Souya, I didn't know you were back." Lady Mythlanica appeared from within the tent. She walked gracefully, her tail straight up in the air. "Your guests?"

"Yes, I've asked them to teach me archery."

"Look over at the river for a bit."

"Yes, milady." *Don't ask, just do.* I turned my back to the sisters and Lady Mythlanica and gazed at the river. Fish swam in its clear waters. They, too, apparently belonged to merfolk, and we couldn't take any of their resources without permission.

"I am Mythlanica of the Dark Flame, the goddess who has

consecrated a covenant with this foreign adventurer. You are welcome here, beautiful elves. I trust my disciple has shown you no disrespect?"

"Not at all. He has treated us most courteously. I am Laualliuna Raua Heuress, daughter of Mellum, Disciple of Ezeus. This is my younger sister, Éa. She is yet a child. I pray you might forgive her coarse manners."

Lady Mythlanica's voice reverberated from up high. "All is well. I am no goddess of great refinement. And I would argue my devotee would match any boorish behavior, if not exceed it."

"That could not be farther from my experience. King Remlia and your disciple, Lady Mythlanica, are the only ones who have shown us any respect. He is a good, wonderful person."

"I see. We stand on land he has borrowed from the merfolk. May you forget the troubles that vexed you in the city and rest at ease here."

"Thank you very much, Lady Mythlanica."

"Souya, prepare my meal."

"Yes, milady." I understood that to mean my order to wait had lifted and went to spin around, but two hands reached out, caught my head in motion, and stopped me from going any farther.

"Slowly," my goddess commanded.

"Ngh! Yes, milady." I caught a glimpse out of the corner of my eye but failed to see her in full. She quickly reverted to her feline form and started snaking around my legs. What was that about? Was I maybe not devoted enough to her?

"Da-dada-daah... ♪ Deet-do-daah... ♪ It has now been three minutes," announced Machina.

"Can I eat it?!"

"Go ahead."

Éa opened the lid on the cup of ramen, totally pumped. She'd gone with salt ramen. She wrapped some noodles around her spork and brought it to her mouth to—

"H-hottt! It's so hot!" Awkwardly, she shoved the noodles in her mouth, blowing on them as she went. Then she sipped the soup. Her whole face lit up. "Lala, this is really good. Want some?"

"I'm okay. I have this," Lana replied, already on her third bowl of *arajiru*. Hmm, for some reason, she looked absolutely lovely eating the soup.

"Souya, I want some of that as well."

"As you wish." Who'd have thought I'd be presenting a cup of ramen to my goddess? What a cheap offering. I had gone back in the pantry tent, opened the container, and was debating which flavor to go with when—

"There's a term called *tainted*."

—Lady Mythlanica hopped up on my shoulder and whispered in an unusually quiet voice, "It's a nasty custom the elves have. They use it to label illegitimate children or those with mixed blood. Laualliuna has also been labeled a stain upon her clan. Take caution. That woman is more than you can handle."

"Mixed blood—do you mean she's half elf?" I asked, also in a low voice. Now that she'd mentioned it, petite yet busty Lana did indeed differ from other elves.

"Who can say? I know not."

"I only brought them here so the younger sister could teach me to use a bow. I just need to keep this relationship up until that's done."

"Good. Treat them well while it lasts. Lest you forget, you are the one who's important to me, far more than any foolish elves."

"I know."

Lady Mythlanica rubbed her face against my chin, and I stroked her fluffy body in return. She picked the soy sauce ramen.

After dinner, we got straight into archery practice. The lesson fee we set at five silver pieces per day, on top of room, board, and clothing for both sisters. Was that a bargain? Expensive? Either way, I didn't have time to look for another option. I took a target I'd made from scrap wood and drove it into the ground.

"What kinda archery do you want me to teach you—warrior or hunter style?"

I answered Éa's question with another question. "Sorry, what's the difference?"

She looked at me in disgust, then drew the bow she'd brought with her; it had the same shape as mine. She put her left hand on the bow; her right, on the string.

"Warrior style is when you hold the bow upright and nock the arrow on the right side of the string." She pulled out an arrow from the quiver on her back and fixed it to the string, then shot it at the target about ten meters away. It hit the bull's-eye perfectly. She hadn't taken her eyes off me, standing at her side, the entire time. "When you hold the bow sideways, or diagonally, and put the arrow on the left side, that's called hunter style." Her posture changed, but her arrow landed in the same exact place. "Do I really have to explain what makes them different?"

"This is just a feeling, but…warrior style makes reloading quicker but aiming harder. It takes longer to nock an arrow in hunter style, but it's easier to aim. Is that right?"

"Huh. If you can tell that much, you might be kinda cut out for this. With warrior style, you won't bump into the person next to you in line formation, and since you can pull the string back farther, you can pack a punch even with lighter arrows. Hunting style lets you align your line of sight with your arrow, so you get more accurate aim. But you can only pull the bow back to your jaw, so you have to use heavy arrows. Show me one of those."

I pulled an arrow out of the quiver hung across my back and handed it to her. "A cui arrow, yeah? It's got good balance—not exactly light, not exactly heavy. Same goes for your bow. They'd both work with either style."

"Is hunting style easier to learn?" I asked.

"Yeah, definitely easier. But you won't be able to kill anything in the dungeon if you use it with that bow."

"That won't be a problem." I'd found blueprints for a compound bow in Machina's database. Once her manufacturing program got back up and running, I'd make a small pulley and remodel the weapon. That would probably be enough to take care of the power side of things.

"All right. 'Kay, so stand with your body perpendicular to the target," she instructed. I turned to the side. "Hold out the bow toward the target with your left hand. Careful how you tilt it."

"Got it." I did as I was told.

"The arrow, you're gonna hold with your pointer finger, your middle finger, and your thumb. Try as best you can not to mess up the feathers. But it doesn't really matter as long as you can hold it in place. Just keep that in mind as a basic rule." I held the arrow with those three fingers.

"Place the arrow on top of the bow. The tip should be either resting on your pointer finger or just above it." I lay the arrow down on top of the bow.

"Notch the butt of the arrow on the bowstring." I did. "Pull your right hand back until you touch your face." I pulled. "Don't let go yet."

Drawing it back wasn't so bad, but keeping it there was hard. Muscles in my fingers and my arms that I rarely ever used screamed in protest. Éa walked around behind me and stepped in close, then adjusted the bow's angle and shifted my right arm into the correct place.

"Don't ever forget this stance. When you let the arrow loose, you are a stone. Okay, release." I released. The air whizzed slightly. It hadn't flown as quickly as I'd expected, but the arrow hit the mark—right in the middle, in fact.

"Oh, I did it." So basically, you had to keep your body still when you shot, just like with a gun. The biggest difference was that it took far more muscle power than I could've imagined.

"Hmph, good for you. My archery master always used to say, 'Those who miss their first shot will miss their last.' Maybe now you'll make your last shot, too, no?"

"I'm not really trying to think about that just yet."

"Okay, since it's your first day, I guess I'll have you do ten. Hit the target ten times in a row within thirty seconds. Call me if you get it. I'll be sleeping until then." She waved as she walked away.

Not entirely sold on that plan, I got started practicing anyway. First, I focused only on finding the target. Time didn't matter. I carefully notched the arrow, slowly took aim, and quietly let it go. I shot. It hit. *I've got skills, don't I?* I thought, and arrogance washed over me momentarily. Just as I'd been told, I focused on keeping my stance exactly as Éa had adjusted it for me.

I'd aimed with my left hand and shot with my right when using the guns, too. It felt a bit different but like something I could get over pretty easily. The problem, as I'd feared, was simply a matter of muscle.

My seventh shot missed; a finger on my right hand had cramped just a twitch. I took a tiny break and steadied my breath, then started over from scratch, like a heartless arrow-shooting machine.

"May I interrupt you for a moment?"

"Be my guest."

Isolla approached. I paid her no mind and kept shooting.

"Why didn't you mention you were going to use a bow and arrow to me?"

"You know how?" I'd found the bow designs, but the manuals on how to use them had been illegibly corrupted.

"I have a record of every battle in human history stored within me. I could show you how to use a rock and club if you so desired."

"You don't have any gaps in the data?"

"I just finished decoding it all." Made sense. "While neither Machina nor I are in peak condition, we still exert every effort to be of use to you. Trust us. Going forward, please make sure you always consult with me before you make any decisions regarding battle. Do you understand?"

"Got it." Shoot. Miss.

"Allow me to make an additional recommendation. Lady Mythlanica mentioned this as well, but you should be very cautious regarding your relationship with these elves. If possible, it would be best to cut ties with them immediately."

"Why?" Shoot. Hit.

"That is the conclusion I arrived at through data collection. Their race is at war with the Kingdom of Remlia due to a dispute over land sales. The problem began with an argument over discrepancies in the different units of measurement elves and heims utilize. A skirmish that resulted in grave injuries broke out, and King Remlia's eldest son went to mediate and was evidently murdered. Despite their appearances, the elves are a savage race. Furthermore, your counselor Evetta has failed to mention one important matter."

I drew the bow back and held it.

"If this country goes to war, adventurers will be compulsorily enlisted in its army. Do you understand what this means? The citizens of this country despise those two for no other reason than because they are elves. In addition, they're also adventurers, which undoubtedly means members of their own race despise them as well. What good can possibly come from associating with people surrounded by hatred on all sides?"

Shoot. Hit.

"As I told Lady Mythlanica, this is only gonna last until I finish my archery lessons. I won't get too deeply involved."

Shoot. Hit.

"Understood... I will now update you on the progress status of our program repairs. Manufacturing is at twenty percent; medical treatment, fifteen percent; cooking, twenty-seven percent. Please choose from among these programs which you would like to prioritize for reparations."

"Cooking."

".......You should choose medical treatment and manufacturing."

"You don't say. Cooking." Shoot. Hit.

"Wouldn't you agree you already possess sufficient skills to prepare nutritious meals?"

"No, I've pretty much reached my limit." I didn't know many more recipes. I hadn't gotten any better at trimming fish and still left meat on the bones. It was a waste. Just that morning I'd tried to make mayonnaise and wound up with a sloppy mess. If I'd known it would come to this, I would've paid more attention and learned more from my grandfather, a chef.

"We do have nutritional supplements, and if nothing else, the food available in this world could serve well enough to provide you the calories you require. You expend too many of your resources on food."

"Well, food's important." It felt especially important now, for some reason. I wanted to make delicious meals for Lana.

Shoot. Hit.

"This is exactly why Japanese people are so—" Static drowned out the rest of her sentence.

"This is Machina. I exercised my administrative privileges to temporarily suspend Isolla's functions. I apologize for the inconvenience. She has a slightly hysterical temperament. Allow me to take care of her."

"Understood." *Sorry, Isolla. But I'm in a tough spot, too.*

"As the analysis of your poncho has been completed, I will announce the results. The test found no traces of pathogenic bacteria. It identified stomach fluids and regurgitated pork, root vegetables, and beans. There is no risk of contagion."

"That's good to hear." Shoot. Miss.

"Shall I provide you my report evaluating Ms. Éa's condition?"

"I saw an injury on her when I carried her here, a gunshot wound to her lower abdomen. I didn't see any sign of an exit hole, so I'm guessing the bullet is probably still in there."

"Yes. She likely has severe lead poisoning. It may be life-threatening if the bullet is not removed immediately."

"Makes sense."

Shoot. Miss. I retrieved the arrows. A mini-kettle rolled up to my feet.

"Mr. Souya. What would you think about treating her wounds and having her and Ms. Lana join your party afterward?"

"You know, you're suggesting the exact opposite of what Isolla said. I might have agreed with you if we had the medical program fully functioning. But just try and see what happens if we kill her during a foreign medical operation. It'd be plain murder. Sorry, but I'm not about to have loads of people hate me for no reason." That felt like a pretty rational, unemotional call. And yet, I couldn't throw away the possibility, either.

"A wise assessment, just like Isolla's." *Do I sense some sarcasm?* I meant to ask, but the mini-kettle rolled away before I could.

Nocking an arrow, I concentrated on my aim and shot. Miss.

I mean, who wouldn't want to play god and save someone's life? Even more so if that person happened to be a gorgeous girl. But the only ones standing here were a good-for-nothing dope with no idea of what might happen on the morrow and a couple of banged-up robots. What could you do with that? I needed to carefully choose how to use the limited resources I had at my disposal. Although I guess Isolla and I had different opinions on that matter.

The only people saving others should be those who could afford to do it. It was definitely not my job.

Shoot.

Hit.

I made a latish light lunch, then practiced my shots, made as sumptuous a feast as I could manage for dinner, then once again went back to practice. Night came early in this dimension. It washed over the world, oblivious to my personal turmoil. I coated the ends of the arrows with luminescent paint and set a lantern close to the target. It gave off a subtle, quietly beautiful light. The night winds whistling through the meadow made it seem like a giant snake. I sank my body fully into the dark and drew the bowstring.

This might have had something to do with the goddess I served, but I felt terribly at ease in this environment. Even the chill of night felt pleasant. The pain in my arms melted away into the darkness, along with the pointless thoughts running through my head.

My arrow hit its mark. I steadied my breath carefully, very carefully. In my left hand, I held on to three arrows along with my bow. I pulled another out of the quiver on my back, quietly notched it, and began to shoot. Hit. Hit. Hit. Miss.

I stopped breathing.

Next time, I held four arrows next to my bow. Notch, shoot. Shoot. Shoot. Shoot. The last arrow I pulled back slowly, aimed, and released.

Hmm.

They'd all missed. I retrieved the arrows and quickly checked to make sure they hadn't gotten damaged, then put them in my quiver. I then started from scratch once more.

Over and over, hour after hour, I silently shot my arrows alone amid the darkness. Muscles in areas I hardly ever used wailed in pain. I pushed through it. I'd keep pushing through it until I died. If it ever became too much, I'd just break, that's all.

What do you call that? What am I? Here I am, in some foreign dimension, all alone, practicing how to use a primitive firearm. I blew up all the weapons I had, threw the rest away, and— No, I can't go down this road. There's no point.

Any hesitation in my thoughts sent my arrows off the mark. I cleared my mind and notched an arrow. Aim. Shoot. Setting aside whether they hit or not, the *whoosh* the arrows made as they flew through the air had sharpened. Maybe I was getting the hang of this. Was I making any progress? Or was I straining too hard? Even if I'd wanted to ask, my teacher had long retired for the night.

I guess I should just take it easy, I thought and shot another arrow. Shoot. Shoot. Shoot. Shoot. Shoot. Shoot. Retrieve the arrows. Shoot, shoot, shoot, shoot, shoot-shoot-shoot-shoot, shoot-shoot-shoot-shoot. Retrieve the arrows. Shoot-shoot, shoot—

(9TH DAY)

Ngh.

Dawn had broken. I must have fallen asleep. No, more like passed out.

I felt grass and dirt on my cheek, and something white brushed against the tip of my nose—one of those otherworldly winged rabbits. They were wild animals, but they didn't fear humans. Thinking back, one of them had sneaked into camp and gotten chased out by Lady Mythlanica.

I slowly extended my hand, and it sniffed the tip of my finger. I scratched around its neck a bit, and it ruffled its feathers. *So cute. Maybe I'll keep it.*

"You're white as snow, so I'm gonna call you Snowball." *I'm keeping him. I already went and gave him a name.* "Do the rabbits here eat vegetables, too?"

I petted and stroked his head, but Snowball showed no signs of wanting to escape. No way he'd make it out here in the wild. Destiny must've brought us together. I had a cat and now a bunny.

"All right, let's head back to—," I started saying as I went to get up, when an arrow flew straight through Snowball's head with a *thunk*.

"SNOWBAAAAAAAAALL!"

"I caught breakfast!" cheered Éa, who had loosed the arrow. That one shot ended Snowball's life. I wanted to believe he didn't suffer. Reality was truly a cruel mistress. "Wait, were you out here practicing all night?"

"My memory cuts out just before dawn. You know, this is really fun. I might be kind of good at it."

"Hmph, I'll be the judge of that. But after breakfast."

She handed me Snowball's dead body, minus the arrow. I carried him by the ears back to camp; they still felt warm.

"Good morning, Mr. Souya. It's great to see you excited about practice, but please take good care to get enough rest as well. Shall I make some coffee? Or would you prefer hot cocoa?" Machina had turned the kitchen stove on and was boiling some water.

"Make it two cups of cocoa." I figured Éa would like something sweet. "Machina, can you skin a rabbit?"

"I can trim fish, but I've never done rabbit before."

"Huh? You can prepare fish?" I'd asked her the question offhandedly but her response surprised me.

"Ahem. The machina unit series was originally produced as a cooking robot. Bits and pieces of those older generations' memories and experiences are still stored within me, so trimming a fish is as easy as pie."

"Right, so how about any experience with rabbits?"

"Rabbit does not traditionally play a part in Japanese cuisine, you know. Do you think it would suffice to drain its blood, remove the guts, and skin it?"

"Probably." The two of us stood there, our heads tilted in question, pondering what to do. I couldn't really understand how Machina's frame managed to tilt like that.

Is she also sitting on some transformer abilities? I mean, she was made in Japan. Oh, I can also see her having some superpower to combine with other machina units.

"What? You can't skin a rabbit? Pfft!" Éa mocked me. "Sheesh, heims really don't know how to do aaanything. I'll do it." She took

Snowball from my hand, pulled out a knife, chopped off his wings and head, put a gash in his stomach and fished out all the organs, sliced a line from one of his hind legs to the other, and then pulled off his skin with her hand as if taking off a piece of clothing. "Here you go."

I took Meatball from her hand. A somewhat complicated emotion came over me. Still, I couldn't waste him. But how would we eat him?

"Your cocoa is ready."

"Ouch, that's hot. What is this? It's so sweet!"

And so the conversation went on at my side as I stared at Meatball on the cutting board. Since nothing else had yet come to mind, I threw his unhygienic entrails in the garbage pit and washed my hands. Next, I moved over to the pantry tent and grabbed a cut of pork, vegetables, and seasonings.

"I'm borrowing one of these pots," I told Machina.

"Okaaay."

I eyeballed some soy sauce, mirin, noodle soup base, and sugar, then checked the taste with my pinky finger. *Good.* "Tell me when it starts to simmer."

"Roger."

I got to work dissecting Meatball. First, I hacked off his nails. Then I chopped the rest of the meat into bite-size pieces, avoiding bony areas as I went. He looked just like chicken. If I'd had the luxury of time, I would've slowly and thoroughly simmered the bony bits. That I didn't have, though, so I smashed them with a meat-pounding hammer. Those parts I'd eat myself. After that, I cut up the root vegetables into similar-sized chunks. Finally, I stuck the prepared ingredients onto skewers.

"It's simmeriiing."

"Thanks." I looked in the pot, then sprinkled in some

water-soluble potato starch to give the mixture some thickness. Once more, I checked the taste. Not bad. *Hmm, something's missing, but it might throw the whole thing off if I add anything else. I guess this is the best an amateur can do.* I removed the sauce from the flame.

"Machina, can you handle this?"

"But of course." I handed her some skewers. She lined up the ingredients with her arm and drove the skewer through them in a flash.

I heard the creaking of carriage wheels approaching, the neighing of an easygoing old horse, and an easygoing old man's greeting. The farmer I'd spoken with the day before had arrived. I had him show me the freshly harvested vegetables loaded on the carriage, and I chose five white eggplants, three big, fat cucumbers, and three vibrant tomatoes. Unbelievably, it cost only five copper pieces. Vegetables that didn't keep long generally went for pretty cheap, apparently. I asked him to come by again the next day and waved good-bye.

"Okay, all done." Machina had finished skewering all the ingredients.

"You're good at this."

"I know!"

I dipped the loaded skewers into the sauce, then put a metal net over the flame and grilled one of the skewers to test it out. The sweet aroma of grilled soy sauce mixed with sugar wafted up to my nose. It hit me like a punch to the gut so early in the morning.

I want rice so baaad. But I don't have much, so hold it in, self.

"……" Éa stared at the skewers as she drank my cocoa. Her eyes gleamed like a hunter sizing up its prey. The little fat in the rabbit meat floated up to the surface with the heat, then dripped down. The edges of the onions browned a bit.

"You should flip it over right about now."

"Got it." I flipped it over and added a little more sauce. The sauce's merciless fragrance enveloped the entire campsite. Nothing in this world tasted bad if you grilled it with some sweetened soy sauce, in my opinion.

"Is that about done?" The meat had browned well, and the vegetables looked nice and tender.

"I would give the grilling about thirty-five points. It is, however, safe to serve."

"You're one tough critic." I went to take a test bite right away, but Éa caught my wrist.

"Are you gonna eat that?"

"Yes, why?" She had a pretty strong grip. The skewer wouldn't move any closer to my mouth. I tried to bring my mouth to it, but she twisted my arm away. "I need to try it out to see if it's any good, you know."

"Then just one bite. I'll take one bite first. Just one," she insisted.

"Liar. You'll eat the whole thing." She had it written all over her face. We had so many other kebabs waiting to be grilled, but here I was fighting over a single skewer with her. "Okay. Let's take a bite at the same time," I finally suggested.

"Ew! Gross!"

"Hey, that hurts! We've got more coming, so just hang on a second. Just a second!"

"Why don't *you* hang on a second? I wanna eat it now! GIVE IT TO ME!" *What is she, a child?!* I thought but also refused to give in myself. I had a feeling that if I gave in now, I'd be resigning myself to a long future of the same thing happening over and over.

We were right in the middle of this little scuffle when—

"You there, elf," I heard a voice say from behind me. "Unhand that man. How dare you attempt to steal my guest's fare? Shame on you," Ghett said, his harpoon raised and ready.

Why did he have to come at such an awkward moment?

"Ee—" *Hmm?* Éa's face turned pale white and then— "Eeeeeeeayaaaaaah!"—she let out a piercing scream. She immediately ducked behind my back for cover, trembling.

"My Lord Ezeus, my Lord Ezeus, grant me the grace of the forest and protect me from the beasts of the deep." *You can use me as a shield, but I'm not good for much defense.*

"I'm sorry, Ghett. She's just a child. Please forgive her."

"Why do you apologize, Souya? I cannot understand this."

I calmed them both down and had them sit for the meal. All this time, Machina had been grilling the kebabs. I glanced over at her. It hurt to admit, but she did it better than me. The skewers she'd plated looked so perfectly grilled that they could have been served at a real restaurant. In any case, I ate the one I grilled. *Oh, it's pretty good.*

"Souya, is it breakfast yet?"

"Good morning, Lady Mythlanica. It's almost ready."

"Hmm, Machina. What kind of meat is that?"

"Freshly hunted rabbit."

"Rabbit, huh? I detest boney meat. I'll take the pork one over there. Make sure you cool it down properly. Oh, and dip it in that sauce once more before you serve it to me." Lady Mythlanica had jumped atop Machina's head and was putting in orders for her own kebabs.

"Oh, Souya," said Ghett. "I'd forgotten. Here."

"Thank you for bringing me something every day."

"Don't mention it. It's only fair, since you give me breakfast." He handed me a net full of shellfish. *Wow, so many oysters. No time like the present.*

"Machina, scan this, please."

"Okay. I've got my hands full, so please put it in the evaluation box below."

I dropped one of the oysters in her drawer. Since the seafood Ghett brought me came from the Maudubaffle Ocean, whose waters ran clean, we could eat most of it raw. But of course, it could be infected with parasites, so we needed to test everything to be sure.

The remaining oysters I scooped out of their shells, rinsed off, sprinkled with potato starch, gently massaged, and rinsed off again. I repeated this process about three times each to remove the sliminess and clean them. Afterward, I dropped them in some salt water and set it aside.

I lightly seared the eggplants on the flame and sliced them into sticks. The cucumbers I cut the same way, while the tomatoes I sliced into quarters to make them easy to grab. I planned to go a little wild today and make everything finger food.

Next, I made a dressing of granulated Japanese soup stock, vinegar, sugar, soy sauce, and sesame oil, and mixed it all up nicely. After a quick taste test, I added more vinegar and soy sauce. I loaded the vegetables onto a plate and filled a cup with the dressing next to it.

"Mr. Souya, the examination is complete. These can safely be consumed raw."

"Great." I pulled the test oyster out of the box, sprinkled some lemon juice and salt over it, and ate it just like that.

Whoa... Delicious doesn't even begin to cover it.

The meat was so fresh that I half expected it to start dancing in my mouth. Chewing on the luxuriantly thick muscles provided an absolutely exquisite sensation. It had a rich and creamy taste and slipped gracefully down my throat like a piece of fruit.

"Souya, where's mine?" Ghett gave me the stink eye as I trembled, overcome with emotion.

I slipped the rest of the oysters into a bowl and drizzled a bit of ponzu and lemon juice on top. Though I tried not to go too heavy-handed on the condiments, since Ghett already knew the oysters' natural flavors so well, I wanted to let him experience them anew with Japanese seasoning. I washed the shells quickly with some organic dish detergent. Once clean, I arranged them on a plate and filled them back up one by one with the seasoned oysters. Lastly, I sprinkled just a little more ponzu and lemon juice on top. I put the finished product on the table. Machina served her dishes at exactly that moment, too.

"For today's breakfast, we have raw otherworldly oysters with a large side salad garnished with Japanese dressing."

And...

"Fully-loaded grilled skewers." Machina also added a pot of green tea.

"Whoa, whoaaa!" Éa looked half joyful, half terrified. "These are raw, right?" She pointed at the oysters.

"Yeah, but they're fresh and safe to eat," I assured her.

"Yes, they are completely safe."

"Don't force yourself if you don't want to," Ghett added, diving straight into the oysters, shells and all, just like always. After some rather disturbing crunching noises, he exclaimed, "Hot damn!" His sunglasses slipped down his face, and I saw his eyes fly wide open. "I'd long grown tired of these shells—were they always this good?" Talk about a luxurious diet.

"Éa, wash your hands before you eat. Also, go wake up your sister." I brought over a bowl for handwashing.

"She won't get up until midday. She went to bed really late again last night, so let her sleep in."

"Wha......? Ohhh, I see. Yeah, good idea." I decided not to ask why she'd been up so late. But it made sense; she was in a total stranger's home. It would have been careless to let her guard down. Éa washed her hands and very nervously brought an oyster to her mouth, but— "Actually, you eat one first."

"I already did."

"Just do it!"

"Okay, okay."

"Good grief. No use sharin' something this tasty with the elf," Ghett grumbled, exasperated. I washed my hands, brought them together in thanks for the meal, and ate an oyster.

"Mm! So good!" The ponzu hadn't overpowered the oysters; if anything, the two had combined and harmonized beautifully with each other. Ghett and I gobbled them down without pause.

"Lady Mythlanica, did you not want any?" I asked, slurping another oyster out of its shell.

"I cannot eat anything raw for religious reasons." Well, no working around that. Though I did sort of remember her saying she'd eaten raw rats once before.

"What the—?!" Éa exclaimed after eating her first oyster. Even her fear of Ghett flew out the window as she reached for more. Wait, why had she been so scared in the first place? Did children have any particular reason to fear merfolk? "I wish I could give Lala one of these."

"Hmm, raw food goes bad pretty easily," I explained. "We'll give her some another day." I'd have to find a way to make a refrigerator. We had a battery for electronic devices and solar-powered chargers, but what else would we need?

"Promise me! You gotta swear you'll do it!"

"All right, all right," I promised all too easily. For the time being, the three of us scarfed down the rest of the oysters. There had been about twenty to start, but it didn't even take us five minutes to devour them all.

"Lady Mythlanica, your skewer has cooled."

"Mm. Serve it to me as you see fit." Our skewers went to the goddess first. "Mm-mm. Mmm. Not bad, not bad at all. Mm." Machina hand-fed her the pork-and-onion skewer. Obviously, you should never, under any circumstances, give onions to a normal cat. Ever. It just so happened that my cat was a goddess, so it wouldn't do her any harm. "Machina, I think I will take a rabbit one as well."

"Yes, milady."

Then I guess we could also dig in.

"So sweet and salty. It tastes weird."

"You don't like it?"

"I wouldn't say that." Éa looked like she found it about 70 percent good.

"Spoiled child. I think it's great," Ghett announced, his words clearly holding no lies. He held a skewer in each hand and took bites back and forth between the two. An idea came to mind, and I went to get another spice.

"Éa, try sprinkling this on top. Just a little, though. It's extremely precious in this world, you know." I handed her a small bottle of a seven-spice blend. Curious, she flipped the lid open and closed, shook a bit on her skewer, and took a bite.

"Oh, that's really good!" Her eyes sparkled. She vigorously sprinkled more on her food and went to town. *She's just a kid, but I guess she likes her food with a kick to it, huh?*

"Souya, hand me some of that," ordered Lady Mythlanica.

"Me too," Ghett chimed in.

They both tried it. Lady Mythlanica did not approve, as she hated spicy food. On the other hand, Ghett climbed fully on board. I loved him for eating everything I served so heartily.

"Wait, you guys, don't forget about the vegetables," I reminded them. They didn't seem to be going very quickly, so I did my best to clean the plate. They had a rich, fresh flavor.

I don't think they taste bad. Is the dressing what they're not liking? I'll have to try harder next time.

Meals were always more fun with a bigger group. We all shared a rollicking, jolly breakfast. Her stomach full to the brim, Éa sprawled out on the grass and rested on her side, and Lady Mythlanica stretched out next to her. I was washing the dishes in the river when Ghett came over and took a seat next to me.

"There's a lot I'd like to say to you, but after all, you're the kind of person who doesn't blink at a friendship with a merman. Nothing I could say would change your mind. And of course, it'd be presumptuous of a man of the sea to speak of the muddled messes the races up on land get themselves into. However, I have welcomed you here as my guest and cannot in good conscience let you entirely alone. So, here."

"What is this?" It looked something like a dried finger? No, an octopus tentacle?

"This tentacle belongs to my Lord Ghrisnas. If, in your darkest moment of need, you happen to be near some water, hold this in your hand and call out to him under my name. If you're lucky, help will almost certainly, probably, come, I hope."

"O-okay." Not the most reliable lifesaver.

"My god does as he pleases. Not even men of the sea can comprehend him. Use this only when you truly have no other choice. But be prepared for a fate much more atrocious than death. Better yet, try not to get into such a dangerous situation in the first place. You're a smart human, I think. I believe this is true, but you are also foolishly stubborn. Personally, I don't hate that dangerous side to you, but it's too much for one with only limited life left to live. So anyway......I'm going home. See you tomorrow."

"Later."

Splash jumped the merman into the river. Like a shadow, he disappeared. Looking at the tentacle I'd gotten made me crave *takoyaki.*

All right, time to practice.

Picking up my quiver, I left the campsite behind. Once in front of the target, I drew back the bow that now fit a little more snugly in my hand. I shot around ten arrows with about 70 percent accuracy. I'd be happy if I could keep that up at all times, but my stamina and concentration would only go downhill from here.

"Ahh, nope, no good. You're straining too much." Éa was behind me, lying on her side like a reclining Buddha. "Pull the bow back with your breath and release. You're using more power than you need to now because you're out of sync. Keep that up and you'll hurt your elbow and your wrist."

"Got it." I tried breathing like she told me but messed up my timing, and my arrow went flying in the wrong direction.

"Breathe in after your arrow hits its mark. Keep your body still until about then."

"Yes, ma'am." She was starting to sound more like a real teacher. I did exactly as she'd instructed. It hit. It was a clean shot and also less taxing on my body than I'd expected.

"Repeat what you did just there until your body instinctively knows how to do it."

"I see." I drilled that sensation into my body as if carving it into my skin, over and over and over. I'd thought this basically paralleled shooting a gun, but it didn't come close. Little by little, I erased the gap in those sensations from my mind. I wasn't shooting anything; I was firing, letting loose. My hand found nothing but air when I reached back for another arrow.

"Try these." Extra arrows jangled as they fell in my quiver.

Their weight made me stagger backward. "My sister spent all night putting them together. Where'd you get the parts?"

"At Zavah's. A beastman recommended them to me, though."

"Makes sense. They look like the hunting arrows the Rusasa Clan uses. They're super powerful if you hit your target, but they're that much heavier."

I tried nocking it. The shaft was made of metal, too, making it weigh at least three times more than the arrows I'd used so far. Taking that into consideration, I aimed a little higher than usual. I stopped breathing. No matter what, I had to make this first shot.

I released. The hum as it flew sounded somewhat deeper, too. A dull thud rang out when the arrow found its mark. It had pierced straight through the target.

"Okaaay, now practice, practice, practice."

"Got it, got it, got it."

Maybe it was because Éa was watching, or the new arrows suited me better, or I'd gotten the hang of it, but I decimated that target. It felt amazing. *This could go to my head.*

Straight through the target they flew. The beam supporting the board teetered on the fourth shot. On the fifth, it broke down completely. I looked at Éa, a smug grin on my face. She looked back at me with mixed emotions.

"Th-that's nothing! I did that, too, you know! And I did it like half a day after first starting to learn!"

"That's pretty crazy."

"Forget it; just practice! Get one hundred in before lunch!"

"Got it."

Anticipating this might happen, Machina had made an extra target for me, which I stuck in the ground. I picked up all the arrows, checked they weren't damaged, and put them back in my quiver.

"Oh, wait," Éa called out. "From now on, every time you hit your mark, take three steps back. If you miss, go back to your starting point. Okay, go."

"You got it." *Doesn't matter what you're doing; it's all about practice.*

Mindlessly I released arrow after arrow, willing my body to learn how to shoot someone dead. But I knew this could all still come to nothing. I could carry a first-class bow and acquire first-rate skills, but it wouldn't mean anything if my scroll swept those accomplishments away with all my other information.

Well, if it doesn't work, I'll move on to the next thing. And if that doesn't work, I'll try the next thing after that. I'll keep trying, forever and ever, until the day I've lost all the strength to think or try. I'm pretty sure that's exactly how my life, how my time here, will go.

My fourth shot went awry. Éa stood behind me, booing every time I missed. I moved back to my original spot. Over and over, I repeated. And I started to feel a difference more quickly than I had expected.

By the seventh shot of my fifth try, eighteen meters stretched out between me and the target. I nocked the arrow, drew back the bowstring, pictured the arrow's trajectory in my mind, aimed accordingly, and released. At that exact moment, a gust of wind blew past. The arrow spun, its shaft wobbled, and it still hit the mark. My intuition had told me the arrow would miss, but the wind had corrected its path.

I think it must've been a miracle, sent by the gods as either a blessing or a prank. Of course, it had relatively no meaning. But a hit was a hit.

"How d'ya like that, Éa?" I turned around and pumped my fist in the air. But I didn't see her anywhere. Wait, there she was, lower than I'd looked. She'd curled up into a ball and was having trouble breathing.

"......Éa?"

No answer.

◇   ◇   ◇

The moment of truth had come. Evetta had just finished writing my details on a scroll (that the Guildmaster made me buy for a silver piece). Looking terribly bored, he recited the blessing over it.

"I am Saorse the Small-Winged. In the name of my beloved and venerable Medîm, I raise up my voice in prayer to Lord Windovnickel. Under Thurseauve's holy name, I hereby pledge to preserve nothing save the truth written herein. Should any falsehoods taint these pages, may the grace of the divine flames purge them from sight. However, may any shame upon this man remain in perpetuity. This marks my thirty-second try at blessing this new adventurer's scroll. It's starting to drive me crazy, so if you could please hurry up and make this the last one, I'd—"

"Hey," I cut in. The incantation had started to sound like a vent session. Lana, who had been talking to her own counselor, came over to me.

"What was that about?" I asked, curious.

"I received an invitation to join a party. I'll meet up with them early tomorrow morning and explore the dungeon."

"That's great news."

"Yah!" The Guildmaster imbued the scroll with light; it pissed me off how cute he looked doing it. He rolled it out, and Evetta, the Guildmaster, Lana, and I all stared at it.

"Ah," Lana murmured, and as I had feared, once again all my

information began disappearing from top to bottom. Man, why did my name have to disappear, too?

"Hey, Otherworlder." The Guildmaster slapped my back. He turned his lovely, beautiful face and gorgeous smile toward me and said, "Give it up."

"Nyyeeeoooo." A strange sound escaped my mouth. My heart felt about to break. It might've already chipped.

"Souya."

"......Evetta."

"......"

Stop that! Don't look at me so pathetically!

"Excuse me, but is this—?"

"Huh?"

Lana's voice snapped me back to reality.

"There's a part down here that hasn't disappeared," she explained.

"Seriously?!" A few symbols that looked like writing remained visible down near the bottom of the scroll. "Is this—huh? What does it say? Guildmaster!"

"It says, 'Studied archery under Éa Raua Heuress.'"

"JESUS!" I screamed unintentionally in prayer. "Which means! From here on out, it should record any new skills I get no problem, right?!"

"Don't forget to ask your counselor to update your scroll." Just how straitlaced was this dude?

"Souya."

"Gah!"

Evetta hugged me. She smelled amazing. And yet, my muscles strained, and my bones creaked under her grip. It wrung the air out of my lungs.

"You did a great job," she praised me.

"No, Evetta. He hasn't actually done anything yet," the Guild-master corrected.

"Oh, right......" She released me. My vision blurred as the blood flow that had been cut off rushed free and almost knocked me out. The Guildmaster's voice came to me sounding somewhat far away.

"Good for you, Otherworlder. Now it's up to your party members to decide if they're willing to take you with your lone skill in archery. Good luck." He flashed a brilliant smile at me. This bastard said all that on purpose.

"On an unrelated matter, Princess," he continued, turning to Lana. "As you can very well see, this Otherworlder is a bumbling blockhead who has caused nothing but trouble since he registered with the Kingdom of Remlia's Adventurers Guild. He has barely scratched the surface of the dungeon, yet he is a constant thorn in my side. I say this out of concern for your person: I do not know why you are here with this man, but I can promise you nothing good will come of a sustained acquaintance with him."

"On the contrary, my sister and I have been the ones imposing on him," she replied. One of the words the Guildmaster used piqued my interest, but even if I tried to ask, would anyone explain it to me?

"Is he perhaps holding something over you? If so, say the word, and I will entreat our king for assistance at once."

"No, I assure you he's done nothing of the sort."

"I understand you find yourself in a precarious position. Humble as my capabilities may be, I, Saorse, pledge to—" He'd seriously pissed me off by that point, so I grabbed his face in both hands.

"I may not know much, but I know how to treat my guests. I swear it on my country's name. Keep trash-talking me and I'll pluck your feathers out, stick you in oil like fried chicken, and make a down comforter out of you, got it?"

"S-Souya." Evetta looked panicked for some reason. The Guildmaster grabbed my neck and pulled me off him, his face hard as stone. Morons who smile at everything always looked like this when they got mad. His congeniality only ran skin-deep. I couldn't fathom what might've motivated him to lead the Guild.

"Indeed, while uncivilized, you do have some sense. I apologize for the affront to your honor. And I will forgive you this one time, but try laying your hands on me again and I will evaporate you on the spot."

"……" Only an idiot would respond to his cheap provocation. I answered with silence, soon broken by a grumbling stomach.

"Evetta, can you honestly not wait until lunch after that enormous breakfast you had?" asked the Guildmaster, exasperated.

"It wasn't me," she replied.

Lana had turned bright red and looked down at the ground. She'd skipped breakfast, after all.

"Right, I guess we should get going," I said. "See you later, Evetta. Don't forget, breakfast is the most important meal of the day."

"Agreed. But like I said, it wasn't me."

I took Lana's hand and left the Guild. It was still a bit early for lunch, but… "Shall we grab a bite to eat somewhere?" I asked her.

"O-okay."

I could've brought her back to the campsite and fixed her something there, but I would have felt bad making her wait that long. Lana hunched her shoulders as she walked along with her staff, her face still turned downward. Her stomach had only emitted a natural physiological response, but that didn't make it any less embarrassing. She did seem to come from a well-to-do family, too. Also, I really, really wanted to ask what that *princess* was about. However, Isolla had warned me not to get too involved.

I decided I wouldn't try to imagine what might connect the key words of *elf, war, defeat, princess,* and *adventurer.* Throw in *beautiful and cute, in dire straits,* and *ill younger sister* to the set, and I would 100 percent sympathize with her. I'd want to lend her the meager power I had—no question.

Don't lose sight of your goal. Think of your own sister, my still functioning rational brain interjected, ordering me to get a grip.

I took a deep breath. *Okay, I can do this.*

We wandered around looking for a restaurant. Street food that we could eat as we walked probably wouldn't cut it. The only place I knew where we could sit and have a meal was the boss's bar, but it would be awkward to run into Arvin and the others there. I hadn't really been paying attention, but I realized I still held on to Lana's hand. As long as she didn't mind, I wouldn't say anything. Yet here I was, walking hand in hand with a big-bosomed, ill-starred elf.

Aaah, this is one of those moments that make me glad I came here. If my sister saw me like this, she'd hit me with a dropkick, no doubt. If she used her prosthetic leg on me, could I get away with just some pain? Or would she scrape half my face off?

"Oh, what about here?" I asked.

"Okay."

Those worries bouncing around in my mind, I came upon a random shop, a small, two-story restaurant. Without much thought at all, we stepped inside. It was a dingy, grim place with, of course, equally grim patrons. I felt my skin tingle under someone's gaze.

I'd messed up, big time.

I stopped in my tracks, but Lana pulled me into the store and sat down. She had more guts than I'd thought. I let go of her hand and sat directly across the table from her. I hastily asked our waitress, a middle-aged woman, to bring us some drinks, bread, and soup. And then, silence. *Crap, I don't have anything to talk about.*

Lana looked captivatingly lovely beneath the dim glow of the emiluminite lights. She saw me admiring her and looked away. *What the—? My heart's going crazy. It's not like I'm in middle school and she's my first crush.*

A minstrel sat off in the direction where Lana had averted her gaze, in a corner of the restaurant. I could've sworn our eyes met. He started strumming a small, guitar-like instrument and softly began to tell a tale—a hushed fable.

Long, long ago, at the ends of the east stood a city infested with demons. The desolate city had no name. A cursed giant spider— Rhora, the Dragon Eater—spun her nest in its ruins. Seeking fame and acclaim, a thousand adventurers challenged her in battle, but none ever returned. Countless heroes tried to vanquish her, fell under her curse, and joined the hordes of her children. Her nest ate away at the vast continent, and her children greedily devoured everything in sight. The giant spider even attempted to spin her web inside the Tower of Legions. However, one hero thwarted her plan.

A hunter lived in the forest of the elves—a great hunter who bent the mists to his will. The fog wound its way all around the giant spider and her minions. A thousand arrows rained down upon the chalky cloud, slaying her children, and a hundred more pierced through her many eyes. When the fog finally lifted, only the spider's corpse remained.

The hero's name was Heuress. Great hunter of the forest,

nameless sorcerer. Should Rhora ever appear again, he shall return, together with the mist.

The song finished, and our food arrived, a soup with vegetable scraps floating at the top, dark bread, and fruit wine. I immediately dug into my portion so Lana wouldn't hesitate to start on hers. The soup had as little taste as its appearance suggested, and the bread was even harder than it looked. I didn't know what regular wine tasted like, so I couldn't compare. Lana tore her bread into little pieces before bringing them to her mouth.

"Sorry, it's not very good, is it?"

"Huh?" Lana finished her first spoonful of soup and blinked in surprise. "Certainly, the fish soup you made yesterday was divine compared with this. Are you quite sure you're not a professional chef?"

"No, I'm not." I wouldn't even call myself a hobbyist with the skills I had.

"Then you must hail from a land with delectable cuisine. I envy you."

"Yeah, we've got some good food. Speaking of which, what kind of meals do elves normally eat?"

"Elven cuisine......" A bitter smile came to Lana's lips. "Essentially, we have fruits straight from the tree or dishes with raw, wild herbs piled on top. We do make some fermented food and alcohol that I find pleasing, but there's not much I could confidently recommend to someone else."

"I see." *So very organic dishes, huh? It's probably really good for you, regardless of how it might taste.*

"Your sister seems to like pretty spicy or salty foods. Do you think that's a backlash to more traditional elven fare?"

"My sister studied under a beastfolk master who influenced her in many ways. You might say she's not very elven and neither are her dietary preferences."

That made sense. "What do you like, Lana?"

"Huh......? Who, me?" She ate another spoonful of soup and fell deep into thought. Was it that hard a question?

I glanced over at the minstrel again, and our eyes met for sure this time. He'd locked onto me and, like, stared. *I don't go for men*, I thought. He coughed once. This was a tough one. I tried my hardest to decode his signal but came up blank. I set him aside.

"I don't dislike fish. Alcohol, either, although actually, I guess it's not my favorite. I've never gotten drunk before. As for vegetables, well, I've grown tired of them. So is it maybe meat?"

"I don't know."

"I'm sorry." What a vague discussion. Maybe she didn't spare much thought for food in general?

"In any case, once we get back to camp, I'll let you try a whole range of foods, and you can let me know if you like any of them."

"Oh, okay." *I'll keep lunch light and go all out on dinner. I just hope Éa's condition improves a bit by then.*

"So, um, about Éa..." The question slipped out; I just had to know. "...Do you have any leads as to what might cure her?" Even if our medical technologies couldn't save her, maybe they had some kind of magical treatment here that could help.

The look that came over Lana's face defied all description. I didn't need to ask anything else.

The restaurant door swung open, and light flooded in. A party of adventurers walked through the doorway. The minstrel launched into his song again and sang the ballad of Heuress, the hero.

Hmm? Heuress?

"Lana, was your name Heuress?"

"Yes." It all clicked. The minstrel told us the story praising

Heuress once more. As the song finished, I caught the man's gaze and threw him a copper coin. He grinned and—didn't catch it. A dark brown feline beastmaid stole my coin midair. At that same moment, someone kicked our table and sent it flying. Our half-eaten meal and the dishes smashed against the floor and walls, then scattered all over.

"Want me to tell you the rest of that story? That heroic Heuress's grandchild stupidly started a war with the almighty humans and lost miserably. But his granddaughter did something even more brainless. After realizing they would lose the war, she trapped her people and burned half their forest down to the ground."

A young man spoke. He had chestnut-brown hair and had contorted his face into a twisted expression. He wore clearly expensive armor and a cape and carried a pointlessly fanciful sword. Behind him stood a female knight in a skirted full suit of armor and a young, possibly noble, female mage in her prime wearing a dress.

"And what might that very princess be doing in a dreary place like this, I wonderrr?" the young man sneered, not a shred of decency to be found on his visage.

There's something more important, this asshole—!!

"Don't you dare waste perfectly good food, you jackass!!" If you dared kick food in front of a Japanese person—in front of *me*—then you'd best be ready to pay for it with your life. Sure, it didn't taste all that good, but that didn't mean you could send it flying.

Incensed, I wound my fist back to pummel the dude, but his lady knight cut me off. I couldn't see much through her helmet, but judging by her general vibe, she was probably rather beautiful. It made me even angrier to think someone like that would be serving this tool.

"Huh? Who the hell are you?" he demanded to know.

"Who the hell are *you*?!"

He snorted. "What are you, a moron? You think I'd believe someone in this country doesn't know who I am?"

"Don't have a damn clue. If you're that famous, why don't you write your name on your forehead or something."

Pfft. The beastmaid behind me laughed. Maybe that's what set him off, but the veins on his face popping, the young man shouted, "I am the *prince* of the Kingdom of Remlia, Georg ole Remlia."

"And?" What of it?

This prick probably thinks he can wave around his authority and get out of anything, doesn't he? No way in hell am I letting his rude, idiotic behavior slide that easy. And there's especially and particularly no chance I'll suck up to an asswipe like him who goes around wasting food. He doesn't scare me for shit.

I kept talking. "You're trying to tell me that not only does the prince or whatever of this country not have the most basic manners, he also makes it a habit to kick people's food across the room and interrupt their meal with a beautiful woman? Man, you must have so much free time on your hands. I wish I had it that easy."

"You bastard!" The idiot prince took the sloppy bait I dangled in front of him and put his hand over his sword. I reached for my woodsman's hatchet, too.

"Souya, go outside. I'll take care of this," Lana said.

"Not happening. Leave this to me."

Lana grabbed my hand that held the hatchet. "I'm ordering you to leave. This is a matter between royals. There is no place for a mere adventurer to interfere." Her lips trembled. For a moment, I wavered. Since first coming to this dimension, I had never hesitated more or faced a heavier choice.

"I'll wait for you outside," I muttered, following her wishes. I threw the minstrel a copper coin, and he caught it, then hung his head and cast his eyes downward. The light blinded me when I stepped outside.

"Would you like to see footage of what's going on inside?" a message from Machina chimed in.

"And what am I supposed to do with that information?"

"I'll leave that up to you. Mr. Souya, let me give you one piece of advice. You are the only person in this world with the power to limit your actions."

You're goddamn right I am.

"Show me the feed." Video from a bug drone showed up on my glasses. It picked up the sound inside without a problem, too. Lana had knelt before the dumb prince who sat in a chair, one leg crossed over the other.

"Please forgive my companion for his discourtesy, Your Highness, Georg ole Remlia, second prince to the Kingdom of Remlia."

"Ever since you filthy elves murdered my elder brother, I am now the only prince of Remlia. Do not repeat this mistake, Tainted Princess."

"Yes, Your Highness. I am terribly sorry."

The dumb prince looked down at his shoes. Some soup must've gotten on them when he kicked our table away. They were wet.

"Now look, you've gone and dirtied my shoes. Wipe them."

"Yes, Your Highness." Lana pulled out a cloth.

"No, no—with your mouth. Stupid elves have no place impersonating humans."

"Yes, Your Highness." Lana got down on all fours like a dog and stuck out her tongue.

Talk about a sick fetish. And yet, the other customers in the restaurant salaciously looked on. Witnessing a beautiful royal princess get sullied before your eyes qualified as the world's greatest entertainment to some.

"Machina, blow up all the drones inside."

"Understood."

The feed cut out. I waited to hear their high-pitched explosions, kicked the door down, and ran into the restaurant. Everyone had their attention turned in the direction of the blasts. That, of course, included the idiot prince and his guardian knight as well.

I swirled through the air. The dropkick I learned directly from my sister hit the prince square in the face. He spun halfway around and slammed into the wall.

"Secret move, Yukikaze Special." The trick was to turn your body at the point of impact. It might not deliver that much damage, but it looked cool as hell. I half hallucinated a vision of my sister in the air, pumping her fist. If she'd been here, she would have busted out that move the instant our food fell under attack.

"Souya!" Lana screamed, almost shrieked. I paid her no mind.

"Do you understand what you have just done?" the knight asked, pointing the slippery tip of her sword at me, down on the ground where I fell after fumbling the landing for that kick. I stood up slowly, never taking my eyes off the blade.

"What? It's just a fight."

Leaning on the beastmaid's shoulder, the prince staggered to his feet as well.

"Lanceil, cut him down." The knight refused to follow her prince's order. Lucky for me, she was rational. "Hey! Lanceil! Did you not hear me?!"

"But, my lord—"

I laid the bow and woodsman's hatchet I carried down on a table, then tore off my glasses and handed them to Lana.

"We're doing this. A fight between adventurers. Or what? Are you saying the so-called royalty in Remlia's so used to hiding behind his authority and his ladies that he can't even fight for himself? Show some balls."

"What did you say to me?!" The prince drew his sword.

"My lord! Please desist! The long-eared wench you can torture all you like. They've done more than enough to deserve that. However, this man is an adventurer. It would be treasonous for the prince of adventurers to turn his sword on one. You would besmirch the king's name. Furthermore, your opponent has challenged you to a bare-fisted fight. Is your sense of valor worth so little you would ignore this fact?"

I thought about pointing out that Lana was also an adventurer, but they probably wouldn't have cared regardless.

"So what's it gonna be? Your lady-in-waiting makes a fair point," I said.

"Hmph, fine. I won't need anything but my fists to crush a bug like you." The prince sheathed his sword. He'd knuckled under. Dumbass. The only one who wouldn't need anything but his fists around here was gonna be—

About an hour later.

"And then, he got beaten to a pulp and lost."

"Wow, my disciple is pathetically weak!"

"You suuuck!"

Lady Mythlanica and Éa did not mince words in commenting on Machina's report. More importantly, I couldn't see a single damn thing.

"You three! You're getting in the way of his treatment! Either help or leave—pick one!" Lana shouted, then dragged me along the ground and into my tent.

"Ms. Lana, here are some disinfectants, wet compresses, and bandages. It may be best to first cool off the wound," suggested Machina.

Oof, that was a close one.

Not that I was doing so hot at the moment, but if Pops hadn't happened to walk by, break up the fight, and save me, I might have died. I'd gotten lax or, like, forgotten one vital detail: I was ultra, mega-weak in this dimension. I might have had a chance against a normal person, but I never should have fought hand-to-hand against a relatively experienced adventurer. This was what they meant when they said, *I couldn't even get a punch in.* Except that I did—it just did absolutely no damage.

"I use a fire-type healing magic, so it manifests as heat. It works wonders on lacerations, but it's not well-suited for blunt-force traumas. And his ryvius is lower than average, so I'm not sure what to do......" Yep, I had about as much ryvius as a puppy.

"Éa, lend me your gauntlet."

"Whaaat?! This belonged to Lord Heuress, you know. Are you sure it's okay to lend one of our most precious elven treasures to a heim?"

"He's almost completely out of both internal and external magic. I'm going to divert some of the magic in the gauntlet to his ryvius. Hand it to me."

"But, Lala, that's not what I'm asking."

"I said hand it to me!"

"A-all right."

The gauntlet, warm from Éa's body heat, slid onto my arm. She whispered into my ear, "You owe me five cups of ramen."

I gave her a thumbs-up to say, *You got it.*

After her, Lana whispered, "My Lord Ezeus, command Mertome, God of the Torrents, to grant me the graces contained in this treasured relic and strike up a gust that will rouse its magic. O holy wind, dance and spin, mingle, melt, and wash over this man and this ancient vessel."

A cool breeze swept past my cheeks. Lana's enchanting whisper continued. "I raise up another prayer before you. Harmonia, Goddess of Unity, instill, arrange, align, and unite this magic and become one with this man."

My muddled senses and consciousness cleared, and the pain began to slowly sink in. Just as a sponge dissolving in an acidic bath, my swollen flesh faded away. My vision cleared. Lana's large breasts hung so close that they almost touched my nose.

"Wooow, impressive. Eighty percent of his bruising has dissipated," I heard Machina gasp.

"One last thing. This may hurt a bit, but please bear with it."

Lana shook her staff back and forth in small movements. I did what I could, but my eyes stuck like glue to the two melons before them swaying from the movement.

"O fire, dear fire, bless us all with your light and your grace. With your heat and your pain, alleviate this man of his suffering." Lana's right hand glowed with light. *That'd be an awesome finishing move if she hit me with that*, I thought, and she pressed said hand to my face.

"EEAYAAAAAAAAAAAAAAAAAAH!"

"Please, don't move!"

It's hot! Lana's hand is like burning steel! Hot! I'm gonna die! This pain is gonna kill me! I'm gonna burn! I'll have to get a full-face mask to cover up these scars!

I tried to get away, but Lana sandwiched my head between her plump thighs. The fleeting happiness I felt soon disappeared beneath the heat and the anguish.

"AghhhhAAAAAAAAAAAH……" I passed out but regained consciousness right away.

"The wounds on his head have diminished to five percent of their original severity. This is an absolutely wonderful medical treatment. He has a small contusion on his abdomen, but that should completely heal in about three days."

"*Haah*, I'm so glad to hear that."

"......" My whole body twitched in agony. But the treatment had gone perfectly, it seemed. "Lana, thank...you," I managed to choke out. Now I owed her two favors.

"You realize this is all your— No, I'll restrain myself. This whole ordeal has given me a very clear picture of the kind of person you are. Aaaargh, I swear!" Lana sighed.

I couldn't make anything of her expression. She was hard to read. Did she feel exasperated, or thankful, or something entirely different? Should I curse my own stupidity? Or take pride in my horrible luck? I'd have to make sure my reckless move this time paid off in the next.

Why the hell have I come this close to dying outside *the dungeon? Someone, please tell me. Oh, it's 'cause I'm a dumbass.*

"Souya, I'm hungry. Prepare lunch," ordered my goddess.

"Heim, I'm hungry. Can I take one of those ramen cups now?" asked Éa.

These two.

"......Time to cook, I guess." My body wouldn't move. "Huh?" I broke out in a cold sweat. It felt as though I'd been bound in chains; I couldn't lift a finger. "Lana, Machina, I can't move."

"That's probably because I infused your body with magic," explained Lana.

"Mr. Souya, does this hurt?" Machina reached her arm in from outside the tent and pricked my finger with a needle.

"Ow!" My knee jerked a bit at the pinch.

"Your nerves are working, and your reflexes respond properly, too. I presume severe exhaustion is causing your symptoms. Let's wait and see how you do overnight."

"I hope that's all it is," I responded. It would be no laughing matter if I never got to stand again. "In that case, can I leave lunch to you, Machina? There should be some chopped meat and vegetables left over, so put a good mix of both in a pot and set it to simmer. We've got powdered demi-glace sauce, so throw that in and make a stew, please. Add a dash of ketchup and honey as the secret ingredients. Éa likes her food spicy, so drizzle some sriracha in her bowl only. Don't even think of offering any to Lady Mythlanica. Make more than usual so we can have it for dinner, too. If it's not enough, feel free to open up some freeze-dried bread, instant noodles, and any cans you need. You're on the job."

"Understood." She gave me a thumbs-up and then retracted her arm. Éa left with her.

"Are you quite sure you aren't a chef?" asked Lana.

"No, Princess. My grandfather just happened to teach me a few good things."

"Please don't call me that." She slapped a cold compress on my face, then lifted up my head and let it rest on her lap. Bit by bit, she covered the feverish parts of my face with the compresses. Without much hesitation at all, she opened up my shirt, and I soon felt the cool sheets all over my abdomen and chest. A couple of round things that could very easily work up my lust pressed against my face, but I kept it together. *I'm begging you, body, don't go getting hot anywhere but my wounds.*

After she finished treating my face, Lana put my glasses on for me. To tell you the truth, they looked terrible on me.

"Ow." The frames hurt where they scraped along my ears.

"Oh, I'm sorry."

"It's fine."

"Hey, devotee. Have you perchance forgotten about me?" asked Lady Mythlanica. I had indeed forgotten about her. I'd totally assumed she'd left the tent with Éa. "Laualliuna. It appears your charms have satisfied this simple man plenty, but they do not suffice for me. Princess of the Heuress Forest, I have a question for you."

"I pray I may be able to answer it."

"Why should a member of the elf royalty enlist herself as an adventurer?" I'd been curious to know the answer to Lady Mythlanica's question, too.

Lana finished removing all the compresses and started wrapping bandages around me. Her hands moved deftly. "After we lost the war, my father offered me and my severely injured sister to King Remlia. It's common practice to dispatch close but no longer useful relatives as ostensible hostages. Not only am I, as you can very well see, quite homely, but I also burned down my people's forest with my own hands. Even though I did so to defeat our enemies, my father could not easily justify keeping such a pariah in the country. His subjects would not take that quietly." As I'd feared, she did not have a happy tale to tell.

"King Remlia treated us very kindly. I fully expected to be locked away somewhere and had prepared myself to accept any fate, even if he decided to overlook my unseemly body and make an exhibition of me having intercourse with a pig. And yet, King Remlia granted us our freedom on the condition that we take up the mantle of adventurers. He did not hand down a single punishment befitting the people of a country defeated in war. Many, including his retainers, and especially the prince, objected to his plan, but none could defy the king's authority."

Lady Mythlanica climbed on top of my stomach. She started grooming herself, licking her tongue all over her body. *My goddess, please pay attention.*

"However, life as an adventurer proved much more difficult

than I'd imagined. Since the job requires you earn people's trust, people such as my sister and I cannot easily carve out a space for ourselves. Tricked by adventurers, scammed by merchants, and cheated by the owner of the inn where we'd stayed, we spent day after day huddled up on the side of the road. If I had been on my own, I may have very well hanged myself somewhere. No, my naïveté would have probably killed me long before it got to that point, my body stripped and deserted in some hidden corner of the city."

"Hmm, it appears I asked a rather heavy question," noted Lady Mythlanica. "Forgive me. But after seeing my devotee come so close to death, I was bound to hold at least some suspicion."

"Of course. I promise I will never allow a repetition of what happened today. Next time, I will be sure to knock him unconscious before I resolve the matter."

"That won't work for me," I protested. "Next time, I'll be the one to do better." I'd knocked on death's door, but I didn't regret it. If anything, I saw it as a good experience.

"Souya, you don't seem to realize how angry I am at you. I told you to let me handle it, didn't I? You even agreed and retreated, didn't you?"

"I did, technically. But when I took a peek inside and saw you about to kiss that moronic prince's feet, I couldn't help myself."

"If that's all it took to appease him, there would have been no problem at—"

"Yes, there would've been, a very big problem. No self-respecting man could sit back and watch a piece of shit like him exploit a beautiful woman." Plus, she sold herself far too short. It was a waste. I wished she'd hold her head much higher and stick her large chest out much more proudly.

"What……did you just say?"

"Huh? That no man could sit back and watch that happen."

"After that."

"To a beautiful woman."

"!" Lana stole my poncho and hid her face behind it. Her ears stuck out, and they flushed bright red all the way down to the tips.

"You're cute. Crazy cute," I told her.

"S-stop! I hate being teased!"

"I don't know how you shape up according to elven standards, but in my book, you're adorable. Ex-treme-ly adorable. It hasn't been too long since I got here, but I've seen quite a lot of women in that time. You're definitely cuter than most."

"Aaaiiieeeeeeeeeeeh!!" Lana let out a strange scream, then scurried out of the tent. Suddenly bereft of its lap pillow, my head slammed down to the ground. *Gimme back my poncho.*

I wasn't a big flirt or anything, but I could at least tell a woman with low self-confidence the truth. If she came to Japan, she'd have her pick of men.

"Hey." Lady Mythlanica narrowed her eyes. "Heed my words: I'm far more adorable, okay?! You'd do well to remember!!" With that, she left. What in the—?

"*Haah,*" I sighed.

It was only midday, but I already felt dead tired. Which reminded me, was anyone going to feed me lunch? Just sleeping there felt like a pretty good option, too, but— Oh! One of my fingers moved. I let out an even deeper sigh. At least it looked like I wouldn't have to spend the rest of my life paralyzed. My neck lay in a terrible position, so I readjusted it on a pillow that just happened to roll my way.

Hmm?

"Squad Member Souya. Have you followed even a single piece of the advice I have given you?" It was Isolla Pot.

"I'm sorry. I haven't."

"I do not appreciate the Japanese sensibility to simply apologize in response to anything. It disgusts me. However, I will respect your decisions as my owner, atrocious as they may be."

"Uh, right." Something felt off with her. A message from Machina flashed across my glasses:

Update: I have finished adjusting Isolla's settings. As she showed signs of severe stress-related breakdown, I unlocked three levels of her self-control restraints, increased her freedom of speech by one level, and unlocked two levels of prohibited phrases. In short, she will become slightly more willful and sharp-tongued, but there is no reason for concern. Over and out.

This was definitely gonna be a pain in my ass, especially now that I couldn't move.

"Squad Member Souya, I have changed my perception of you."

Drops of cold sweat trickled down my neck. She wasn't going to try to modify me somehow, was she? Or maybe inject me with some weird drugs?

"But I have accepted that as inevitable. I had prepared to work with extremely qualified squad members, so it is only logical that I would prove of little use to a tiny cicada of a Japanese man knocking on death's door. Ha-ha, you miso soup weakling." I couldn't follow her at all, but she was frightening. "Nevertheless, I do appreciate the passion with which you act if nothing else. In other words, I can overlook your failings as long as I decide to think of you as someone like Ed Wood."

"Ed who?" She'd compared me to someone who didn't even ring the tiniest bell.

"Ed Wood. Are you reeeally that ignorant? He's the Worst Director of All Time. That is how I would evaluate you. You have enthusiasm, passion, and initiative; that, I will give you. However, you lack every other essential quality. In the end, you will die from alcoholism, completely destitute."

"Isolla, I don't drink. I don't get the appeal of the taste, and I've only ever had a tiny bit in social settings."

"Hiiissssss!"

"Yeah, right, sorry." *This is such a pain. I'll just apologize and get through it. What am I supposed to do with this?*

Isolla unleashed a long, drawn-out barrage of off-kilter verbal abuse after that. She had strangely expansive knowledge regarding overseas B movies or even lower-quality films, all of it completely useless information.

Movement returned to my upper body a little after noon. Some of the strange grogginess remained, but I managed to prepare dinner. The sun fell soon afterward, and I set out to practice my bow in the darkness once again.

Tomorrow, I'll have to talk with Arvin and the others to see if they'll have me in their party with nothing but this archery skill to offer. I have zero confidence they'll say yes. Honestly, I can't see anything but failure in my future.

My inner monologue took a depressing turn, so I stopped thinking altogether. I completely cleared my mind and fired fifty arrows, but they started slipping from my fingers from something slimy. The skin on my thumb had shaved off. I haphazardly wrapped a bandage around it and shot another forty more until my bowstring snapped, then turned in for the day.

(10TH DAY)

I had a dream.

I was in some forest.

I had become *someone else.*

I sensed a familiar, beloved person behind me. Who it was, I didn't know, but the person I'd become in the dream loved and trusted this person with every fiber of their being. That much I could feel.

We came to a deep corner of the forest, a special place where we met in secret. Tree branches and leaves stretched together above us to form a canopy. Sunlight filtered softly through and shone all around us.

That's when I was stabbed in the back.

The knife seemed to have pierced straight through my spine and nerves. I collapsed, unable to do anything but crawl like an insect. I couldn't understand. Only one person could have stabbed me. We had ridden to certain death together. It had become the stuff of legends. They loved me, and so I had loved them back. We had a child. Together, we showered our little one with love. If they were unable to trust me after all of that, then they were no person but a wild beast.

Perhaps they had mutated into some new, awful form, I thought. And yet, the eyes I stared into looked back clear and lucid as day. No last words passed between us. With another flash of cold steel, our bond severed for all eternity.

It was a terrifying nightmare. I didn't think I'd forget the face of the elf I'd glimpsed at the end for a long time to come. Cold sweat drenched my sheets. My back hurt slightly where I'd been stabbed. Scratch that—it hurt, intensely so.

"Isolla!"

"Yes, what can I do for you?"

I gave Isolla, near my pillow, an order. "My back...hurts. Scan it, please."

"Understood." Her small hand extended out and touched my back.

"Ouuuch!" A current of sharp pain coursed through my body. "No abnormalities discovered upon tactile or visual inspection. Now administering a nano-scan machine." A needle sank into my neck. I struggled desperately to control my ragged breath and instinctively curled up into a fetal position.

"Mr. Souya, what is the matter?" Machina lifted the flap to the tent, looking very worried.

"Machina, please bring me a D-type medical kit."

"Understood, Isolla." With a *clank*, she rolled out of the tent and returned almost immediately afterward, kit in hand. Isolla dexterously opened it and withdrew an ampoule.

"Scan completed. No abnormalities detected in your back. Your vitals are unstable, and your condition is unclear. Squad Member Souya, do I have your permission to inject you with a strong sedative?"

"Isolla, I reject your proposal. Redo the scan. This time, perform a detailed inspection of every area but his back."

"Understood, Machina. Commencing scan...... Abnormal neural impulses detected. A metallic substance has permeated through a portion of his right arm and is assimilating with nerves in the area. Having determined the cause of the issue, I will proceed to remove it."

Isolla grabbed my right arm, exactly where Lana had put the elven gauntlet on me the day before. *That's right—I had this on in my dream, too.*

"I cannot remove the gauntlet due to insufficient power. Machina, if you would."

"Understood." Machina's mechanical arms grabbed hold of mine from both sides. Metal screeched and something ripped. "Mr. Souya, I am terribly sorry. Part of my arm has broken."

"Let's cut it off."

"Understood, Isolla."

"Hey!" A circular saw protruded from Machina's torso, spinning dangerously fast.

"Isolla, administer an anesthetic to be safe."

"I cannot put him under, but I can inject a strong sleeping pill and pain reliever."

"Understood. Let's proceed accordingly."

"Wait, you two!"

"What's all this ruckus first thing in the morning?" Lady Mythlanica had awoken. She extended her front paws, arched her back, and opened her mouth in a gaping yawn. "So what is all this?"

"Good morning, Lady Mythlanica. Mr. Souya is acting strangely. We have determined this to be the cause and are just about to chop it off," explained Machina. "It should take only a moment."

"*Yaaawn*, I'll take care of it. Machina, bring me a cup of water. Isolla, blindfold Souya."

"Understood." Machina and Isolla got to work following Lady Mythlanica's orders. *Who do you two work for again?*

Isolla tied a blindfold around my head. Through the fabric, I saw Lady Mythlanica shoot up in size. I couldn't see her face clearly, but I did make out the contours of her slender yet curvy body.

"Your water," announced Machina.

"Mm." Lady Mythlanica hugged my face.

"Eek!" Machina shrieked. Water drizzled down my cheeks. Then—something soft touched my lips. My goddess forced her tongue in my mouth, parted my teeth, and pressed down my tongue. Lukewarm liquid flooded my mouth. Slowly, I swallowed every drop.

"*Pfah*...... All right. Well, that should about do it." Lady Mythlanica gulped for air. I was too confused to comprehend what had just happened. It had been a bunch of firsts for me. It had felt so soft, like peeled shrimp. Her tongue—her tongue had—had—had— "Souya, do you still feel pain?" she asked.

"Ah." The shock had made me forget all about the pain. Actually, it had disappeared. I could now also move freely and immediately took off the blindfold. Already in her feline form, Lady Mythlanica flashed a Cheshire cat smirk at me.

Dammiiit!

"You were being dragged into death. I gave you some consecrated water, which should nullify those symptoms. As you suspected, the gauntlet caused this." She stepped her paw on top of it. "It's almost certainly cursed. I can sense overwhelming passion and obsession within it. Remove it at once."

"But it's one of the elves' prized heirlooms, you know?"

"Precisely. Do you now see how that must mean the curse only activates when someone other than an elf equips it?"

"Gotcha." That made sense. "Machina, stop pointing that saw at me."

"I wish I could have been of more help." Crestfallen, she put the dangerous industrial tool away, then left.

"I tried to take it off, but it seems physically impossible. Lady Mythlanica, could you help me with it?"

"Impossible. I have no such power." She rejected me bluntly.

"In any case, it can't hurt me anymore, right?"

"For the moment, no. However, curses are made of strong human emotions that do not simply disappear. There is no telling what might cause its effects to resurface. I do not see any good coming from holding on to it. If you go to a master spiritualist in town, they should be able to lift the curse for you. Probably."

"Got it. May I ask one more thing, Lady Mythlanica?"

"What might that be?"

"Please don't tell the sisters about this." Especially not Lana.

"Why not, pray tell?"

"As a matter of personal preference. Please." Lana would head into the dungeon early in the morning. After all that happened the day before, we now had *this* to deal with. I didn't want to put that burden on her.

"Hmph. I best her in both chest size and height, you know."

"That's not the kind of preference I meant." She'd thought I was talking about my taste in body types.

"Very well. I am a tolerant goddess, and my disciples' wishes do not go unheard. Can I ask one thing in return?"

"Of course, anything you like."

"If those sisters lead you to your death, I will curse them. You would not object, would you?"

"I will bear that in mind."

Satisfied, Lady Mythlanica curled up into a ball and fell back asleep. I picked out a change of clothes and a towel and left the tent. A dim darkness still lay over the land. I bathed in the river and washed the sweat off my body. The percentage of women around me had greatly increased, so I took great care getting ready. I knew I fought a futile battle, but it beat doing nothing.

I took a long, hard look at the gauntlet. An ornate foliage design adorned its thin metal veneer, truly stunning workmanship. I couldn't believe a curse lay within, but dwelling on it wouldn't change anything. I decided to make breakfast and portable lunches.

I put some whole-wheat flour, as cheap in this world as in my own, into a bowl. Made from unrefined wheat grain, whole-wheat flour was packed with nutrients and had high fiber and iron contents. As an added bonus, a sack of it about as big as an adult's torso cost only three copper pieces. I'd seen a beastman selling something made of fried whole wheat on a street cart and thought I'd try my hand at replicating that. Into the bowl I added water and oil, and I mixed it all up well with a spatula until it no longer looked floury, then started kneading the dough by hand.

"Is this chapati? Shall I help you?"

"Sure, then can you knead this until it's nice and smooth? After that, let it rest for a bit, then roll it into golf ball–sized clumps."

"Okaaay. You go mush, mush, muuuush, and it gets yum, yum, yuuum... ♪"

Leaving that to Machina, I turned to the filling. I heated up some butter in a frying pan, added a little garlic, and fried it until just before the garlic started to brown. After it grew fragrant, I tore up some of the herbs of this world (similar to basil in taste) and added them in to make wild herb garlic butter.

Next, I made scrambled eggs with tomato and cheese, some sweet and spicy stir-fried pork, some sautéed bacon with curry powder, and then shredded up some cabbage.

"Mr. Souya, the dough looks gooood to gooo."

"Great, time to roll it out." We each got a rolling pin and flattened the balls. Since I'd never made these before, I didn't have a feel for portions and wound up making too much.

"And now we fry them?"

"Exactly."

I lay the dough on another unoiled frying pan above a perfectly medium-heat wood fire. Then I grabbed a pot smaller than the pan and held it up to the flame as well. Once it warmed through, I placed the bottom of the pot on top of the dough and transferred that heat. The dough inflated like a bubble. My first one I grilled too long and burned. The second I didn't grill long enough, and it inflated unevenly.

"Machina, you wouldn't happen to know how much heat to use here, would you?"

"But of course." I followed her instructions. By the third one, I'd kind of gotten the hang of it, and we kept at it together. In the end, we made thirty pieces of chapati. I spread garlic butter over them, sprinkled the shredded cabbage on top, added the fillings, and wrapped them up like a crepe.

And so, we had made our very own chapati rolls. Apparently, some Indians ate this more often than naan. I tried one of the bacon rolls out. It was harder than the one I'd gotten from the street stall. Next time, I'd have to add more water and mix in some white flour.

Still, though, this is pretty damn good. The whole-wheat flour's unique taste and aroma mix perfectly with the crunchiness of the cabbage and the saltiness of the curry-powder bacon. It was a stroke of genius to douse it all with the garlic herb butter. I'll have to try it out on other dishes, too. I'm a little worried about how it'll taste once it's cooled, though.

"You're up early." Lana had woken and joined me. She'd suited up with her staff, her ryvius vials, a bag worn across her chest, a small pouch, and other adventurer gear.

"Morning. This weird dream woke me up a little early. Are you on your way out?"

"Yes, it's always best to arrive ahead of time." Good point.

A sleepy Éa also came out of their tent. I wrapped six of the chapati rolls in dried leaves they used to preserve food here and shook some powdered juice into a bottle with water.

"Lana, here. Take this for breakfast and your lunch box."

"A 'lunch box'?"

"Portable lunch you can take into the dungeon," I explained.

"I see. Hmm? Did you make this?"

"It may not taste all that great, but it should be pretty nutritious and filling. I'll do better next time around, so please make do with these for now." Before she could refuse out of courtesy, I stuffed them into her bag along with a bottle of water.

"Thank you very much."

"Want me to walk you there?"

"No, we can't have another recurrence of what happened yesterday. Please give your body the rest it needs." *You know, it's exactly because of what happened yesterday that I want to go with you.* "If you'll excuse me." Lana bowed respectfully, then walked off.

"Have a safe triiip!" Éa called out after her, waving good-bye.

"You're good not going with her?" I asked.

"If I could've, I would've. But the request singled her out individually, and it came from another elf, so I can at least trust it more than one from some random heim." We watched until Lana was just a speck in the distance.

"Hmm?" I saw Éa had squatted on the ground. "Hey."

"Sorry, carry me to the tent."

I picked her up, and she wrapped her weak arms around my neck. She felt burning hot. I carried her into their tent, laid her down, and put a blanket over her.

"I wouldn't be able to resist if you made a move on me now, you know?"

"Do you even hear yourself?" As if I'd do something so awful.

"You don't find me pretty? I thought for sure I had a good body."

Though her face looked paler than usual, her fair skin and long, slender arms and legs still held a captivating allure. A little late in the game to point it out, but Éa was drop-dead gorgeous. But I didn't have the kind of twisted fetishes that would leave me drooling over a young girl in her weakest moments.

"Of course you're beautiful. Come talk to me once you're feeling better."

"Ha-ha, no waaay. I can't stand heims, you know," she said jokingly, but tears welled in the corners of her eyes. "A heim almost murdered me, and now here I am relying on another for help. This sucks."

"It sucks for me, too. Sure, I wanted an archery teacher, but no one told me she'd be an elf with a terrible personality."

"Shut up." She slapped my arm. It didn't hurt at all. "Do you have a crush on my sister?"

"Huuuh?! I-it's not like that! I think she's lovely, but yeah. I mean, it's like—" My voice betrayed me.

This is just, you know, like something dumb middle school boys get in their heads when a girl in their class acts a teensy bit nice to them and they get all worked up over nothing...... And now I'm reliving my past. Somebody kill me.

"Ew, grossss. But it's fine. Don't break your brain over it, dummy." The *dummy* came out kind of gently. Her verbal abuse was cute in the grand scheme of things. My little sister had once called me a caterpillar with human arms and legs.

"Think you can eat breakfast?" I offered.

"I'm going to sleep for a bit."

"Call me if you get hungry."

"Mm-hmm." I went to leave the tent when a feeble hand caught me. "Stay for a bit."

"Sure, okay." I gave in to her request. I could never have turned her down when she was so limp. Sitting at her side, I readjusted the blanket that had come undone. After some hesitation, I started wiping the sweat from her brow with a towel.

"This feels weird," she mumbled, then closed her eyes and began taking small, quiet breaths. I watched her face, never growing tired of it. It felt as if I were admiring a work of art. Seeing her in her dying moments broke my heart. I couldn't help but entertain foolish plans of throwing away everything I had in order to save her. *But that's really not my role here.*

Close to two hours I sat there, wallowing in my inability to rescue even one girl. Suddenly, something stabbed me in the back. My knees felt about to buckle, but I gritted my teeth and bore it. No, this was an illusion, just like the pain I'd felt earlier that morning.

"Good sir, I have a favor to ask of you," my own shadow said, in what felt like the setup to a joke.

"Sorry, but who might you be?"

"A nameless spirit. Do not concern yourself with such details." Now darker than before, the shadow broke free from my silhouette and reshaped itself into the outline of a person. My blood ran cold, and an inexplicable sense of danger washed over me. *"Peril draws near one of my line. I would like to request your aid in assisting her."*

With that one sentence, the blood that had cooled instantly boiled. I didn't need to ask who faced that impending threat. "That ship has already sailed. I'll help her in any way I can. What should I do? And since you're asking me, it's safe to assume it's something I *can* do, right?" I glared at the unknown person in the shadow. I felt no fear of them, precisely because they were so cloaked in mystery.

"I, a hero of a hidden name, accept your sacrifice in exchange for my power."

"Wait, what did I—?"

"O ye weakling, ye strong soul, adventurer from a foreign land, our covenant is now complete."

Crap. I've gone and gotten myself into another contract without properly combing through all the terms and conditions.

The voice crept up right beside me. The shadow stood up, bottomless dark directly beneath the light.

I feel like I've seen something like this in a movie before. This is probably the scene right before the main character gets possessed and murdered—

A slight nausea hit me. I took a deep breath and smelled lightly fragrant grass, the wind, the dampness of the morning dew. The pain in my back had disappeared. My unfailingly weak body moved at 120 percent capacity.

"Isolla!" I called, but Machina came instead.

"Yes, what can I do for you?"

"Where's Isolla? I'm off to the dungeon."

"Isolla is in the dungeon."

"Huh?" Nothing had prepared me for that response.

"She disguised herself as Ms. Lana's lantern and accompanied her on the expedition."

"What the hell does she think she's doing? Actually, this is perfect. Think you can get a message through?"

"I will attempt it. A short one may be possible." Static like from an old-fashioned TV appeared on Machina's screen.

"Isolla, can you hear me?" No answer. Instead, a grainy video feed came through. It showed the inside of the dungeon from the perspective of a person's hip, likely Isolla's point of view as she hung from Lana's waist. I didn't know exactly how many people they were with, but I saw one beastman and an elf. The party stopped moving to discuss something, but I couldn't make anything out of the garbled audio. However, the menacing atmosphere came in loud and clear. They met up with another party—which included the prince from the day before. He had a shit-eating grin on his face. They talked, but I couldn't hear anything. Lana took a step back. Her other party members watched on without a shred of empathy. She started to run. The prince and his group followed. The feed cut out.

"Do you know what floor they're on?"

"Isolla sent me their data. They're on the tenth floor. She also included a map."

"Got it." I didn't know if I'd be able to descend five levels in one go, but I'd do what I could. Even if it were pointless, I had to try.

Rushing to put on all my gear, I threw on a stab-resistant shirt and my bulletproof vest over that. I slipped my woodsman's hatchet into the sheathe on my belt, put an extra knife in my boot, and secured my karambit on my arm. Then I slung on my trusty backpack and covered it all with my poncho, before hanging the coral necklace Ghett had given me and my ryvius from my neck. Lastly, my glasses. And my bow—

"Shit." My bowstring had snapped. I'd have to get it fixed—no. An image of where I could find a replacement popped into my head. Now I just needed the right kind of arrows, and I had no doubt I could've taken down even a giant spider.

"Hellooo." Ghett came walking up from the river. He looked different than usual. Hanging from his back was a quiver-like bag packed full of harpoons different from the one he normally used. They jangled as he moved. In one of his hands, he held a net wrapped around a huge chunk of meat. "Feast your eyes on this. I found a giant fish yesterday, you see. A whole school of us from the village went out to hunt it. I wanted to give you a try as soon as I could...... What's wrong?"

He realized that I didn't seem myself, but his sudden appearance was nothing short of a miracle. In fact, could running into him have been the luckiest thing that ever happened to me?

"Ghett, I would love to try that and make it into something delicious. But first, I have two or three favors to ask you."

"Sure, anything you need."

"Those harpoons on your back—sell them to me, please."

"These aren't worth any money. You can have 'em. Only thing

is, there's still some sedative poison meant for giant fish on their tips. Be careful with those. They'll put a heim out for half a day."

"That is incredibly helpful." I took them from him and slung the bag on my back, which had a hefty weight to it. I pulled one of the harpoons out. It looked more like a spear than a harpoon. The sharp, twisted tip was made of some white, crystallized, nonmetallic material. The handle had been carved from bone. A tap confirmed that it was hollow.

"Please carry me into town. How long would it take?"

"Through the canals? About three hundred seconds, if I really go for it." What a champ; this would save so much time and stamina.

"Machina, all of my devices are waterproof, right?"

"Yes."

"Then, please! Take me right away!"

"R-right." Ghett looked a bit put off by how quickly I approached him.

"Machina, I'll be back! Watch over Éa for me!"

"Of course, I'll take good care of her. Good luck!"

"Let's go. Hold your breath. This could be a bit rough for a heim, but bear with me."

I took a deep breath. Ghett picked me up and jumped into the river.

He was unbelievably fast.

I half thought the water resistance would tear my body to shreds. Even with the one quick breath break we took, we made it to town in a flash.

"You arrived in three hundred and thirty seconds. That's incredible. He's faster than the most advanced submarines in existence," Machina announced. Looked like the waterproofing on my glasses had held up.

"I know I was carrying someone, but these old bones don't go as fast as they used to."

"Ugh, *cough-cough*." I'd swallowed some water, so I crawled out of the town's river and lay on my side. "N-no, any faster than that and I think I would've died."

"Maybe. I'll wait for you back at camp. Fill me in later."

"You got it."

He disappeared into the river. I tried to stand up but felt so dizzy that my vision blurred. Slowly, I rose to my feet, careful not to lose my balance. That's when—

"Hey, Otherworlder. Rather odd company you keep."

—Lord Baafre called out and stared at me curiously. Even with his canine face, he was very expressive. "Have you come to buy me another drink? I still have troves of tales extolling my heroic deeds to tell. Of course, it all depends on how much you're willing to spend."

"No, that's not why I'm here today."

"Oh, meow! What's wrooong? You're soooaking wet!" Tutu recoiled at the wet-rat look I had going on.

"He just cropped up out of the river with a merman," explained Lord Baafre.

"Hang on just a sec meow!" Ignoring Lord Baafre, who was pointing in the direction of the river, Tutu ran into the shanty. She came back with a shabby towel and wiped me off with it. What a nice girl.

"Tutu, I need a favor." As she toweled my head dry, I reached into my purse and pulled out a random assortment of coins.

"Meeooooow!" Coincidentally, they were all gold pieces. Tutu trembled at their brilliance. I'd put down five whole coins, but it'd be too lame to take any back. "Wh-what did you want to buy? What kind of scenario did you want to play out? I'm scared!!"

"No, I just want to borrow this." I fished through the sack, still on the ground where it always lay, and pulled out an aged bow.

"Whoa, there, Otherworlder. You've got good taste, I'll tell you that."

The fortified bow matched my height in length and curved gently. Leather strips wrapped around the thick, flexible frame, and strength emanated from its every fiber. A deep, darkly gleaming, sinister hatred of those who refused to die possessed the bow. The bowstring tied around it appeared to be crafted from roped fur. I unwound it, used my entire body weight to bend the bow, and attached the string to each end.

"You need cursed energy to draw a lycan bow. No ordinary human can—"

I tried it out, and the bow moaned as it bent. Its violent, immense tension suited its lycan heritage well. But there was more. This weapon bore a curse; it loathed the world to its core. Perhaps for that reason, it strayed slightly from the rules of this world. Forget about giant spiders; with this in hand, I could almost certainly take down a dragon if I wanted.

"A fine bow indeed. I'll be borrowing this, Master Baafre. Don't go too hard on the ale."

"Who...are you?"

I waved good-bye to my old friend and headed toward the dungeon. Nostalgic homesickness hit me at the sight of how much the town had changed. Then, I ran. Though a far cry from the pace I kept at my best, nothing felt quite like running with the wind in your face. The fires burning within my muscles were the flames of life, a fact just as true for even the weakest of hearts.

And then, I once more stood before the dungeon, the fated

depths that *I* had descended in the distant past to chase after Rhora, only to eventually let the Dragon Eater slip away. It stood forever unaltered, no matter how the sands of time might flow. Mere humans could never hope to change this place.

I entered through the opening and headed straight for the portals. A party just back from their expedition passed by me and—

"Hey, handsome." I swept the legs out beneath the elf who seemed to be leading the pack. Quicker than anything, I nocked one of the harpoons on my bow and aimed its point directly into his face. Caught completely off guard, the rest of the party moved not a muscle.

Weak. Is this what passes for an adventurer these days?

"You lack one member. Explain yourselves."

"Wh-who the hell are you?! Somebody! Help me!" the elf screamed barbarically. What a failure of a man to begin shrieking like a woman as soon as someone brought him down.

"Souya? What are you—? Whose bow is that? Wha……? Guildmasterrrrr!! Please, come right away!" Evetta walked by, turned pale at the sight of me, and called for the Guildmaster.

"You agaaaain?! What is it this time? Wait, who is that?" His sleepy countenance also suddenly changed into one of alarm.

"This crazed heim pulled an arrow on me out of nowhere! Do something about him, quick!" protested the elf.

"This is not about you. It's about the woman on this Otherworlder's team." He completely ignored the elf. I had no time to explain, so I started interrogating my catch.

"You were meant to have Laualliuna Raua Heuress in your party today. Tell us what you did to her, now."

"I don't know what you're talking about! I've never had someone like that in my party!"

"Hang on; I'll look into it." The Guildmaster suddenly

produced a staff made of human bones that stood as tall as him. "Winds—twirl round, spiral, fly, and gather the dungeon expedition request forms for today." His staff struck the ground, and immediately papers fluttered all around him. "Mertar of the Heuress Forest, correct? Hmm, there is indeed no such record here."

"Right?! So please, hurry up and get this guy off me! This heim's gone mad!"

"No, I mean to say we do not have any record of your entire party's expedition," he explained. "What is the meaning of this? What were you doing?"

"I saw them coming out of the portal. Shall I contact their counselor?" Evetta asked.

"Wha—? No, uh..." The elf shut his mouth under the Guildmaster and Evetta's added pressure.

"Want me to explain it to them?" I offered. "You—"

"Poe will tell you." One of the beastmen in the elf's party spoke up. Some sort of canine, he had a childish face and pointy ears. Though he wore light armor over his lean body, he carried an enormous shield. "Mertar got money from prince and sold elf princess. Counselor knows. Prince's beastmaid stole record paper."

"Poe!" exclaimed the elf. "You little—! Do you know what this will do to us?!"

"Shut up. Don't care. I can't trust someone who sells their own kind. Poe might be next. I never party up with you again. Goodbye," he announced, then left.

"Sorry, we're going to go, too. Don't ever speak to us again, former leader, okay? You're absolute scum." The other members followed suit. I toyed with the idea of sending arrows through their backs but let them go for the moment. My arm had grown tired, so I released the harpoon. It drove straight into the ground with a sharp, heavy *thwack*.

"Ah! Ahh!" Perhaps thanks to the harpoon that scratched his cheek, the elf soiled himself.

"Guildmaster, arrest this man at once. I'm going in to save Lana."

"You know where to find her?" he asked.

"Only that she's on the tenth floor."

"What's the deepest level you've reached?"

"The fifth."

He rammed the elf with the butt of his staff. *Is that magic? I* thought for a second, but he'd simply knocked the elf out with brute force.

"Evetta, go call Pops. Quickly."

"Yes, sir. Souya, please don't do anything rash while I'm away. Promise me." She raced off as fast as a wild beast on four legs.

"Come on, idiot," ordered the Guildmaster. "I'll help you, but just this once. Moron."

I pulled the harpoon out of the floor and followed after him. He stopped before the portals.

"This will only happen this one time as a very special exception. I personally feel for the princess, so I will assist you for her sake. I'm not doing this for you. Don't get the wrong idea, got it?" *As if.*

"Just hurry up."

"I'm going to open an emergency portal that'll get you down to the tenth floor in one go. I have a few pieces of advice for you. Will you hear them?"

"Make it short." I hadn't expected to have access to the tenth floor so quickly. It was a happy accident, but even that might not me get there in time.

"If you realize you cannot save the princess, run. Forget her. The king may be kind, but he is that prince's father. Also, the Guild will leave no record of our assistance, so do as you please. Adventurers are nothing if not free."

"I'll kill that prince if I catch him with his pants down. Does your advice still stand?"

"Never mind the prince. He employs formidable guards. Do not throw your life away." The Guildmaster lifted his staff and tapped the portal, which turned red.

"And one last thing." He leaned in to pose a question. "I am Saorse the Small-Winged, a diminutive miracle born from the ends of St. Deimast's madness. O fierce, wandering, wavering soul, would that I might record thy name in my mind."

"I am Lümidia of the Hidden Name, the terrible fool who shot and killed the Giant Spider, then let the Dragon Eater escape. You have my thanks for your assistance, young man," the great hero inside of me answered without my permission.

You are never to do that again. My body, my will, and my life are my own. Who I kill and who I save are crimes for me to commit. So lend me nothing but your archery prowess. I don't need anything more, and I won't ask for anything else.

Very well. Her will resounded in my heart, and she disappeared.

I ducked into the portal. A torrent of light enveloped me for a moment, and then I stood in darkness. The dungeon's structure was no different from that of the fifth floor, and a dim darkness covered the stone walls from which it was built.

"Isolla, answer me."

After a bit of static, Isolla's voice came through. "Squad Member Souya, exactly how did you manage to come all this way?"

"I'll explain later. Tell me Lana's current location."

"Sending you the map data." A map of the floor marked with a red dot appeared on my glasses' screen. "I must apologize.

I attempted to help while Ms. Lana fled but scared her, and she threw me away."

"Got it. Find me."

"Understood. I'll rendezvous with you at the target destination." Another red dot tracking Isolla's location showed up on the screen, along with a GPS path directing me down the shortest route to my goal. Following the provided course, I moved ahead.

Keeping my body low to the ground, I sprinted through the dungeon as quietly and quickly as I could while not alerting anyone to my presence. The lycan bow had power, but it could not cure me of my weakness, so I couldn't afford to waste energy fighting monsters right now. I turned a couple of corners and passed by walking human bones and lumps of meat arranged into blasphemous designs. The floor was bigger and longer than I'd imagined. The agitation urging me to *hurry, hurry!* piled up and sent cold sweat flowing down my cheeks. At the same moment, my stamina and nerves wore out. I thought about checking my ryvius but figured there'd be no point in seeing a fingertip's worth of anything.

After what felt like an hour, though it actually didn't even take five minutes, I finally approached the rendezvous point. But then—

"Ah."

"Meow."

—I ran into a dark-brown feline beastmaid.

"The area up ahead is occupied. Run along, meow. Huh? Didn't I see you at the bar with—?"

Jingle, jangle, jiiingle ♪, rang several gold pieces as they tumbled to the floor behind the beastmaid.

"Mrah?!"

She turned around, only to find Isolla disguised as a lantern. It gave me the perfect shot. I took out a harpoon, swung it hard at the beastmaid, and clubbed her over the head.

"Eep!" she squeaked. I wasn't going to hold back against more advanced adventurers.

"Bravo," I told Isolla.

"Pleasure to be of assistance." I crouched down and gave Isolla's tiny hand a high five.

Removing all the weapons the beastmaid carried, I gagged her and tied her hands behind her. Then I bound her legs together, too, and pulled them back to connect with her hands to complete the hog-tie. That would probably keep her out of battle.

"Isolla, don't get too close, but don't stray too far, just in case."

"Understood. On another note, the knight in the prince's envoy defeated all the monsters in this area on her own, so you need not worry about them."

"Got it." *So I'm gonna have to go up against that knight, plus two other advanced adventurers?*

"Squad Member Souya, I have a battle plan."

"Of course you do, partner." *Well, I've also got help. No problem. In any case, we'll either get them, or they'll get us.*

I nocked a harpoon and drew back the bowstring. Taking deep, quiet breaths, I shuffled forward. *Don't you dare rush this. You only get one chance at a surprise attack.*

I stole through the darkness like a worm. Eventually, a bright light came into view, emanating from two lanterns lying on the ground. There, before a dead end in the path, stood the lady knight, flawlessly vigilant. She peered through the darkness like a guard on the lookout. Her helmet made it impossible to track her gaze. Though I'd completely blended into the dark, I thought she met my eyes at one point, and my heart raced like crazy. The mage leaning against the wall appeared to be some sort of aristocratic woman who was clearly bored. She held her own staff along with another whose owner I knew very well.

Then I saw Lana. The prince had thrown himself on her and was holding her down to the ground. My emotions threatened to burst in a fiery explosion but immediately did a one-eighty and turned ice cold. If Lana's clothes had been in even more disarray, and if the prince had already whipped out his royal member, I would have almost definitely shot an arrow right through his head without a second thought.

"Oh, come now. No girl has ever put up this much of a fight before. The king is blessing you, a vile wench, with his favor, you know? I can't imagine what reason you have for resisting so."

"U-unhand me! Is this how the son of the king behaves?!"

"Adventurers are nothing if not free. The son you're speaking to can at the very least take his pick of women to bed. Not to mention, you're a wretch who burned her own people to death. How much lower could you sink? Just surrender already." The prince insolently grabbed Lana's thigh, but she flailed her legs and shook his hand off. Maybe she had more strength than I realized, because she struggled with all her might and seemed to keep him from carrying out his deed.

"Rgh! Lanceil, help me."

"I must refuse, Lord Prince. We are in the dungeon. No one knows what lurks in the darkness. I cannot imagine why you would insist on this location."

"What other choice did I have? Uncle Medîm's been harassing me, so I haven't even been able to frequent the brothels lately. You saw what happened yesterday. And before that, he dared punch me in the face merely for teasing some beastbrat. Simply unacceptable insolence, don't you agree?"

"......"

I trained my arrow on the silent knight. *Do I go for it? Or should I aim for the prince first?* As my arrow wavered with my resolve, the disinterested mage spoke up.

"Now, now, dear Prince. If you like, I can work my exquisite magic for you and turn this bumbling princess into a wild harlot. Tee-hee, she'll beg for you like a dog in heat. Only her brain might get just a teensy bit mushy and vacant, but you don't mind, do you?" She placed the butt of her staff close to Lana's head. "This must be so hard for you, Your Highness. First falling into an unfamiliar world, then having one of the heims you elves call garbage ridicule you. But do not fear; that all ends today. I'll help you forget it all. Everyone and everything will become no more than a dream. Your soul will sink into a lustful illusion, and you'll become a pathetic dog who shakes her ass at every man she sees."

"Stop this." Lana grimaced in pain.

"Ha-ha! A dog, huh? Perfect. I'd been thinking about getting another one anyway. Maybe I'll have them lick each other up first."

"Lord Prince?!" the knight turned around and exclaimed in reproach. Just then—

—I released a shot in the dark. The harpoon pierced the mage through the side of her torso and pinned her to the wall, and she lost consciousness without fully grasping what had happened. A beat later, both staves dropped to the floor.

I held my bow vertically, nocked another harpoon on the right, and pulled the bowstring back to maximum tension. In that moment, I was confident that I could land that arrow wherever I pleased.

"Lord Prince! Get down!"

I let the arrow fly from my fingers; the bowstring cracked like a whip and hit the sound barrier. The knight responded in a flash. She took the arrow barreling at her like a cannon directly on her shield. It contorted, and my arrow bounced off and broke. The impact sent the knight flying back a few paces. The spirit in me and

I exulted in the shot from the bottom of our heart and readied the next arrow.

The knight hesitated, unsure whether to go forward or defend. But no such uncertainty overcame me. I drew back the bowstring and released the restraint on the arrow. A cacophony of metal rang through the dungeon, but the knight did not take a step back like after my first assault. Instead, she slanted her shield and diverted the arrow's force; she'd already learned to work around them. *This woman's the real deal. She's better than an exceptional swordswoman; she could be a burgeoning hero.*

"Why don't you show yourself?! You coward!" she shouted, unaware of the irony behind her request, but I used it to my advantage anyway.

"I'd much sooner call the band of trash ganging up on a single woman cowards, wouldn't you?"

"You—you're the man from the bar who—"

"Souya!"

Both the knight and Lana cried out in surprise as they saw me in the light.

"It can't be. The petty weakling that I pummeled back then would never manage such a feat."

I ignored the prince.

"But if you insist on calling me the coward, I have no problem crushing you to your face. I've got four more of these arrows—these harpoons made for hunting great fish—on me. Make it through all of those and you win, my lady knight. I'll slink off into the dark once again. But if you fail, I'll pulverize your precious prince's balls. He gets off to dogs, right? Probably best to castrate him."

"You bastard, you'll—!"

"I accept your challenge," agreed the knight, cutting her prince off.

"Good. Let's begin," I announced, then immediately began firing arrows in quick succession. None had much force to them. The knight effortlessly blocked every shot and closed in on me. Composing myself, I drew, aimed, and released. She ducked and dodged. The unsuccessful arrow lodged itself in the wall right next to the mage. Evidently, the knight had predicted my target from my line of sight.

I see. Still glaring at her, I shot an arrow into the ground. It bounced off the floor and rammed straight into her shield. She couldn't deflect its force from this angle. In a second that moved in slow motion, the arrow smashed through the shield and grazed against her helmet. Her skirt fluttered, and I saw something silver flicker beneath.

Undaunted, the knight tossed her shield aside but refused to stop and closed the gap between us in the blink of an eye. Only six meters of separation remained. You would never know she wore a full suit of armor by the savage speed with which she ran. In a race, she and Evetta would be closely matched. One more breath and I'd be in the range of her sword.

Unwavering, I aimed. If she dodged this, it would hit her prince dead-on. This match would last a fraction of a second. The knight unsheathed her sword. At that exact same instant, I unleashed my arrow. In a superhuman feat, she cleaved it down the middle and both halves fell harmlessly behind her. She then assumed a stance much like Shuna's, though different in thrust and without the same twist. The knight crouched down low, swung her blade at my neck and—stopped a hairbreadth away.

"You've lost. You have incredible skill with that bow. I have never witnessed a marksman with the power to destroy the shield the king bestowed upon me. Truly incredible."

"Kill him! Lanceil! He drew his bow on the king, you know?!"

"Retreat. Advocating for an elf doesn't make you a good person," she said, ignoring the prince once again.

I'll bet she's not a bad person, though she does seem pretty stubborn.

"Thanks. But we're not done yet." I walked straight through her body and shot at the prince. It pierced his shoulder and pinned him to the wall.

"Eeeyyeaaaaaaaaah!" A gnarly scream.

"Wha—?!"

I shot another at the knight, whose focus had now completely shifted. It didn't cleave all the way through but did deal great damage to her chest armor.

"You can stop now."

Isolla's hologram of me disappeared. Then I stepped out of the shadows for the first time. For the record, I'd also lied about the number of arrows I had. I fired another one at the knight's legs. Again, it found no purchase but crushed her armor. The damage from the blow got through to her. Next her shoulder, her knee, and her elbow, but I still couldn't seem to make her bleed. She was a much more advanced adventurer than me, so I couldn't afford to let my guard down for a second. I shot at her, prepared to use all the arrows on me, continuing even after she had stopped showing any sign of resistance.

Though I reached back to grab another arrow from my quiver, I found only air. Kicking up one of the arrows lying on the ground, I drew the bowstring back, way back, then released it. It pummeled into the knight's head. Her helmet shattered and her head hit the floor. Long silver hair spilled out, and I saw her flattened beast ears. Then, finally, she bled. *Good, now I can definitely kill her.*

"I beg you."

"Wow, I gotta hand it to you. You're still conscious?" I'd have died thirty times over by this point.

"Do as you please with my body, but the prince—"

"Screw that." I gave her a kick in the head. She would say no more. And I wasn't about to lick my lips that easily or relax until the very end.

Strong warriors make me nervous even if you're left with nothing but a head. That's why I'll kill you as quick as I can. Hurry up and die already.

After retrieving my arrows, I once again stood before the knight. Just as I notched one—

"Souya, stop this. She'll die if you do any more."

—Lana stayed my hand. I hesitated but then, strangely enough, did as she said. However, just to be sure, I turned so Lana couldn't see and stuck the snapped-off tip of a harpoon into the knight's thigh. Once the poison started flowing, it would probably put her out of commission for a while.

"Lana, are you hurt? Did he do anything to you?"

"No, I'm all right." Though thinly covered in dirt, she didn't seem to have any injuries that would leave a scar. Still, just for good measure—

"Answer me, Lord Prince of Remlia. Did you do anything to her?"

—I asked, an arrow trained on him. I thought it best to hear both sides.

"Do you understand what you've just done? My father will not stand for this. And of course, all my retainers will make sure you and that bitch, and anyone who helped you, pay for this."

That sounds hella flimsy. There's not much use in arguing this, but I might as well hit him with some reason.

"I'm just a new adventurer who hasn't gone any farther than

the fifth floor. An emergency portal brought me down here, but the person who opened it for me has said they'll forget it ever happened. In fact, nobody else saw me use it." The Guildmaster had knocked the traitorous elf out, and even if other staff members had seen me, they wouldn't know where I'd gone. "And as for Lana, one of your party members stole the permission request form, the one I happen to have right here."

I showed him the slip I'd pinched off his beastmaid, then set it on fire with my lighter and watched it burn until nothing but ash remained.

"I'm going to make all the other party members who betrayed Lana disappear, too. Every last one. Then I'll feed your corpse to a monster until not a scrap of you is left, and then it's good-bye forever. Where exactly would your little revenge come in? After all, who would ever believe a single initiate adventurer took down all your super-mighty party members on his own?"

"Y-you…" Even this imbecile finally realized where he stood. *It sure is hard teaching a dumbass anything. Dogs and cats learn a hundred times quicker.*

"I will only ask you once more. Think, very carefully, and answer me. Did you do anything to her?"

"I—I tried but didn't get to. I didn't do anything yet!"

I decided to take the moronic look on his face as proof he spoke the truth.

"Okay, next—"

"Souya, you've gone too far. That's enough. Enough." I hadn't put it past Lana to say something like that, but it still surprised me to actually hear it.

"Lana, this man was about to do something so awful to you that I'm afraid to say it out loud. How can you just forgive him so—?"

"But he didn't because you saved me. Everything is fine now."

"Sorry, I can't back down on this one." I knew very well how stubborn she was, but it didn't matter. Spare this kind of person from punishment and they'd mistake that mercy for good luck and do it all over again. He needed to feel some pain.

"At the very least, the very bare minimum—I know. Let's have you apologize to Lana."

"You're telling me to beg forgiveness while I'm stuck to the wall?"

Seriously, what a piece of shit. After a good old-fashioned fist-fight, I could befriend almost anyone in the world, but even if we had that fight on the most picturesque sunset riverbank, I would never get along with him.

"Squad Member Souya, movement detected. I assume it's another party."

"We'll have you apologize another day. But I'm telling you now, I will make a living pincushion out of you if you dare lay another hand on Lana, starting with, as I promised your lovely knight, your balls."

"……" He said nothing.

I put down my bow and quickly retrieved all the arrows, then removed the one sticking out of the mage and left her body lying carelessly on the ground.

"You bast—!" the prince protested as I held his face down with my foot and pulled the arrow out of his shoulder. "What's this? My body's…"

"It's paralyzing poison. Don't worry; it won't kill you. Probably." The poison seemed to have really sunk in. "Isolla, anything left that could be used as evidence?"

"Negative."

I picked her up and tied her to my hip, then hung both Lana's staff and the bow from my back.

"I'm sorry. I'm still a bit..." Lana's legs trembled. She had no reason to apologize. "Eek!"

I carried the princess away like a princess. *Huh, she's so light. Even I can carry her all by myself.*

"Lana, I know this is awkward timing, but would you please form a party with me?"

"Huh? ......Yes, gladly."

I had gained another partner on my adventure. And then—

—I made my way to the bar run directly by the Kingdom of Remlia's Adventurers Guild. According to the sign that hung outside, it was called the Wild Ox and Silver Fox House. Up until the day before, those letters had meant nothing to me, but I could now effortlessly read them. Did I have the hero to thank for this? Or my goddess?

I walked into the bar still carrying Lana, not giving any shits about what people watching might think. It was still midday, so the place had only a few customers, but all my party members had already arrived. They'd been pleasantly chatting among themselves but started at the sight of us. I walked right up in front of their table.

"Sorry!" I said, bowing my head slightly. Then I turned to exit the bar.

"H-huh?! Souya, wait, wait!" cried Bel. "I don't get it! None of this makes any sense!"

"Please, don't stop me! Take a guess based on what you see! Read between the lines!"

"Not even the God of Perfect Vision could read what you're trying to say! Tell me what's going on!" She clutched at my poncho.

"Yeah, I'm not followin' this, either. Explain," added Shuna, who stopped me and forced me to take a seat. With no other choice, I sat Lana down on the chair next to me.

"First, introduce us, if you would. Who might this be?"

I started off by answering Arvin's obvious question. "This is Her Highness Laualliuna Raua Heuress, princess of the Heuress Forest. Only a few moments ago, I asked her to join my party."

"A princess!" Bel's eyes sparkled. "Shunie, look, look! She's sooo cute. I've never seen a real princess before. A real princess, in the flesh."

"Huh? Yeah. I mean, yes." Shuna blushed red and got nervous. Poor naive scoundrel.

"Actually, while my father does indeed rule over the people of the forest, I am now an adventurer, very much like all of you. That title holds no meaning anymore," corrected Lana.

"H-how noble."

"S-so lovely."

Lana's aura had Bel shivering. She followed it up with a knock-out smile and blinded Shuna. Arvin watched contemplatively.

"Oh-hooo, you're all here, are ya? You're late, you know—?" The boss came over to our table and then, making a great deal of noise, got down on one knee and put a hand over his heart. "I beg your pardon, Princess Laualliuna. I have been informed of the countless affronts my nephew has committed against you. I swear to you that I will make him pay for it one day, even if it costs me my life. My humble bar is naught more than a place for fools such as the ones before you now, but I pray you will enjoy a bit of respite and refreshment here."

"We hope you have a good time," Bel and Shuna, for some reason now lined up next to the boss, chimed together after his example.

"Please do not trouble yourselves. It's really quite all right. Souya, say something."

"Formalities displease Her Highness, the princess. O ye common folk, be at peace."

"Souya." She pinched my upper arm for making light of the situation. She was clearly angry, but it felt like a reward. Bel's smile stiffened for some reason.

"Excuuuse me, but what relationship do you two have?" she asked.

"That's difficult to answer," Lana answered, troubled. It troubled me, too. We looked each other in the eye, equally troubled.

"Shunie, what do you reckon? Think it's a suspicious adult relationship?"

"Hell if I know. But it pisses me off." Bel's question had irritated him.

"So how did you come to associate with an elven princess? Why would you add her to the party without consulting with us first?" Arvin asked, completely calm.

"Well......" I fell into thought, trying to figure out how to start explaining.

"Oh, meow, Mr. Otherworlder. Thanks sooo much for this morning." Tutu walked in wearing her work uniform. She hugged me tight and rubbed her cheeks against mine. She'd gotten way more handsy than last time. After she walked away—

"Ow!"

—both Bel and Shuna kicked me in the shins.

"Boss, I heard quite a story on meow way here, you know."

"Oh? What's that?"

Ah, shit.

"Somebody beat the prince to a pulp and poked a bunch of holes in his retainers with a spear or something."

"Oh-ho, I knew this day would come eventually. Who did it? Not too many adventurers could take Lanceil down."

"That's just it; nobody knows. The prince and his party got poisoned or something and can't even talk right meow. Maybe it's an unidentified Dark Crowned monster."

"Ohhh...... Ahh, sorry for the interruption, everyone," the boss apologized.

Arvin held a harpoon in his hand—one of mine. When did that happen? I always tried to keep three eyes out for pickpockets, so when did he take it?

"Interesting item you've got. This a spear?" he asked impassively.

"It's a merfolk harpoon used for hunting great fish. A friend of mine sold it to me." He tried to touch the tip, and I lunged across the table to steal it back. "That's dangerous."

"Laced with poison?"

"......"

Arvin let out a deep sigh. He was clearly several times more perceptive than I'd given him credit for. The boss's expression also changed; it looked like he'd caught on, too.

"No, um—" My face tensed. I wanted to tell them, but if that got them involved, they could end up dead. In the end, I only had the power to protect whatever I could carry in my hands. Anything more than that would be too much for me. "Lana, let's go."

I stood up. *I'm begging you, take the hint.*

But the boss put both his hands on my shoulders and forced me back down, then said, "Sorry, Tutu, but I'm going to need you to go home today. Here, your wages."

"Wait, seriously?! Meow god! This is my lucky day!"

He handed her a copper piece and sent her on her way, paid off the rest of the customers with money and bottles of booze, and kicked them out, then locked the doors and came back to the table. No one remained in the empty bar but the boss and us.

"Now then, as promised, I'll read your last member's vitae. Come, hand it over." *Really comin' at me, huh?*

Reluctantly, I fished my scroll out of my backpack. For a second, I hoped that maybe it would have gotten wet, but the completely waterproof backpack refused to let that be a problem.

"I, Rasta ole Rhasvah, servant of Lord Windovnickel, hereby agree to read aloud the vitae of—" Etcetera. He unfurled the scroll, shined a magic light over it, then began to read. "Studied under Éa Raua Heuress. Acquired archery skills in the beastfolk line. What's this after that? I can't read these letters. Anyway, after that, it says you mastered Welswein archery. Wait, Welswein?"

"Welswein? I've heard that before somewhere, but where?" Shuna tilted his head in question, which the boss answered for him.

"Lady Welswein was Lady Gladwein's grandmother. Fortune did not shine on her own military deeds, but the warrior line she started produced celebrated knights, adventurers, and heroes. It grew to be the most prestigious line on the Left Continent. I'd heard its teachings had fallen into disuse after many years of extended conflict, so how exactly has an Otherworlder come to master it?"

That question put me in a very difficult position. "Well," I began, showing them the Heuress Gauntlet. "I put this on, and it, like, you know."

"Huh? What? You mean to say our family heirloom had that kind of power? It certainly does possess its own magical energy, but that shouldn't affect the people who wear it. It's only something my younger sister liked to wear as decoration after my elder brother found it worthless and disposed of it." Lana seemed the most confused out of anybody.

A mysterious look came over the boss's face. "I can sense a mystical, albeit weak, force within this. I suspect this item will only reveal its powers to specific races or particular individuals."

"Why would an elven heirloom work on a heim like—?" Bel covered Shuna's mouth before he could finish asking his very candid question. *Good work. You just read the room.*

"I said I would continue, but this is all that's written on the scroll. As such, I'll have you explain the rest to your party yourself," ordered the boss.

Yeah, makes sense. He even went and kicked everyone out of here for this. I've got no other choice but to tell them.

"My name is Souya. I came from another world, from a land called Japan, in order to acquire some sort of resource found on the fifty-sixth floor of the dungeon. My primary deity is Lady Mythlanica, and I am also a Disciple of Lady Glavius, the Night Owl. Apparently, the reason my vitae disappears from my scroll has something to do with Lady Mythlanica. I'm sorry."

"Mythlanica the Malevolent, also known as Mythlanica of the Dark Flame." Arvin scowled. "She is, if I'm not mistaken, one of the gods the Church of St. Lillideas has designated as malicious." He cradled his head in his hands. *Sorry, man, for so much.*

"And I have one more thing to tell you, but promise me you'll never speak of it to anyone, for your own sake as well." Taking the bow from my back, I set it on the table, then placed the harpoon Arvin had stolen next to it. "Today, with this bow and this arrow, I shot the prince of Remlia."

"He did it to protect me. I assure you, he had no nefarious motivation," Lana interjected, but—

"You drew your bow against a monarch of Remlia to protect an elven monarch?" Arvin's expression flew right past cold and ended up completely withered.

"And what's wrong with that?" asked Bel. "It's supercool. Plus, I've heard nothing but bad rumors about that prince."

"Yeah! One of the beastfolk kids I made friends with here told me the prince beat him up. No real prince would do something like that!"

The two kids jumped to my defense. Unfortunately, that's what I'd feared most.

"You two just don't understand. A mere adventurer has no business standing up to a member of the royal family. They'll crush you like a bug. You both came here because you had something you wanted to accomplish as adventurers, right? Are you willing to throw all that away to support this man?" added the mage called, umm, uh…oh, Zenobia.

"Souya. Just guessing here, but you forgot about me, didn't you?"

"……No, of course not." *I just couldn't remember your name for a second. It's been a crazy couple of hours.*

"That's a pretty suspicious pause." Disregarding that, Zenobia laid it all out for us. "Sorry, but I'm not trying to stir up any trouble with the royal family, so I can't agree to partner with Souya. I came to this dungeon to deepen my knowledge and find my future husband."

Arvin continued after her. "Souya, do you have any intention of severing relations with this elf—? No, that's a tactless thing to ask…… I'm against it, too. As I mentioned before, I cannot form a party with an elf."

Shuna and Bel put their votes in next.

"I'm fine with it. Lady Gladwein always says, 'The righteous choose to help.' And it pisses me off to hear this dude is waving his authority around so he can do whatever the hell he wants."

"Me too. That prince is the bane of all women."

The boss turned to me. "Your party has divided. What will you do?"

"I'm against it. I can't party up with you."

""Whyyy?!"" both kids whined. Shuna came around behind and started strangling me, and Bel jumped on my lap and pinched my cheeks. Cornered, I began to persuade them.

"Shuna, Bel, you two know nothing of the world yet. It's a huge pain and a huge risk to turn an entire group against you. Not to mention, I'm up against the royal family and the 'king of adventurers.'"

Lana stared daggers at me, so I removed Bel from my lap. I let Shuna stay draped over my shoulder. I couldn't see his face, but he sounded pouty.

"Then you're gonna need strong fighters, right? I don't think I'm that weak."

"Shuna, you're a strong kid. But you travel with someone who couldn't stand to see you bleed. If someone hurt you, Bel would curse them forever, right? She might even go looking for a reckless fight. And just picture how you'd jump to battle if the opposite happened and Bel got injured. If we take that even further, Disciples of Lady Gladwein might also mobilize to protect you. Once that happens, it'd be full-out war, and war is the one thing I want to avoid at all costs," I explained, trying my hand at a logical argument.

That seemed to make sense to Bel, but Shuna still looked unconvinced. I kept going. "As people I've explored the dungeon with, you two—actually, you two and Arvin and Zenobia—are important to me. If anyone attacked you for some arbitrary reason, I would never forgive them. I'd get revenge no matter what. So that's why I can't be in your party anymore. I don't want to be the reason you get hurt."

He didn't answer for a while. It took time to swallow the bitter truths of human relationships. Even a dog would turn its nose up at something this awful.

"……Hmph, fine." He trudged away dejectedly. Zenobia opened her arms wide, but he ignored her and sat down next to Arvin, who ruffled his long red hair.

Putting that aside: "You four will continue as a group without me, right?" I asked.

"Yes, of course." Arvin's answer gave me peace of mind. I got up from the chair and took Lana's hand, then said my last good-byes to my extremely short-lived party.

"Well, this is good-bye. Please forget you ever met me."

CHAPTER 4
An Otherworlder Too Busy for the Dungeon

Now commencing the first-ever briefing session on explorations in the Other Dimension. Requesting cooperation from project participant."

"Okay."

Isolla's voice echoed through the night. I sat all alone in my tent. Lady Mythlanica had gone over to the sisters' tent, mentioning she had something to discuss among ladies.

"Please provide your report on project progress."

"At this stage, I have managed to explore up to the fifth level, though I did use an unofficial emergency portal to access the tenth floor. However, no record of this descent exists. Due to a bunch of different circumstances, I had to sever ties with members of my first party. In exchange, I have teamed up with a mage, an elven princess.

"She bequeathed to me an item of mysterious power that gave me the skills to wield a bow and arrow. It's insane. I've shot straight through an empty bottle behind me without looking—from fifty meters away! And it felt so natural, like I've had this ability for decades. Perhaps as a side effect of this same power, I can now also understand the official writing system here.

"As for supporters, I have Ghett of Maudubaffle on my side. I've also established neutral relationships with the Adventurers Guild, the Zavah Night Owl Trade Group, and the Ellomere Western Peng Traders. I have an adversarial conflict with the Kingdom of Remlia's crown prince, Kero......something." I'd completely forgotten his name.

"After compiling relevant data and recalculating this project's probability of success, I have determined it has increased to two percent."

"It went up! By a crap ton! We made it out of the decimals!" It felt amazing.

"Yes, indeed! This number represents an incredibly dismal evaluation of humanity, but for you, personally, it is a great accomplishment! Squad Member Souya......you have grown quite strong."

"It's all thanks to you two for helping me out." My chest swelled with pride from Isolla's uncharacteristically enthusiastic praise.

"Now then, dropping that ridiculous farce..." Aaand she ruined it. "...How about you try considering this figure as a ninety-eight percent chance of failure? How does that feel?"

"It makes me want to die." Even the most famous doctor in the world would throw in the towel at those odds.

"Exactly. The first vital step in setting yourself up for success is accurately understanding your current situation. After conferring with Machina, I have decided to respect your wishes to the best of my ability. Or, more like, I've given up on trying anything else. You throw your guns away without a second thought, do what I forbid you from doing, extend your hand to others even though you admit it will cause you all sorts of trouble, expend far too many resources on cooking meals, fly into a rage whenever anyone wastes food, leer at all your female companions with lustful eyes, and—"

"I get the picture." She seemed ready to go on for a while, so I cut her short.

"Nevertheless, you also acquired a power to replace your guns. It is conceivable that no other squad member could have accomplished such a feat. For that, I commend you. However?! ......At the same time, you have gotten yourself involved in a preposterous situation. I would like to explain exactly how outrageous it is, but due to the lock Machina has placed on my vocabulary, I do not have the authority to express its scale, as my words might unintentionally inflict you with a severe mental illness. But I do not have the authority to tell youuu. HA-HA-HA!!"

I wondered if she'd broken down, but maybe this was her true personality.

"My final question for today: Squad Member Souya, do you wish to abandon this project?"

"That's a hard no. I've still got so much left to do. I can think about giving up after I try every possibility."

"I had assumed you would say as much. We have a saying in my country that goes, 'The only man who never makes mistakes is the man who never does anything.' And with that, I bid you good night. The wind will blow strong this evening. Please wear sufficient layers to keep yourself warm."

It had been quite a tempestuous day—I'd acquired a new power, fought to the death, gained new friends, and lost old ones. Almost as if in reaction to that, the night passed quietly and left a chill on my skin. Lady Mythlanica did not return to my tent. *I guess I'll sleep all alone tonight.*

(11TH DAY)

A new day dawned.

"Good morning." Lana's dazzling smile almost purified my soul. Just a little more rot in there, and it would've erased me entirely.

"Morning."

In return, I started preparing breakfast. After a little of this and that, I had a pretty tasty meal ready. Ghett also showed up, and we had our meal in what had become familiar company for me here. I broke bread with a merman, a goddess in her feline form, and an elven princess. Even for this world, this probably didn't count as normal. We made an odd group.

Before long, Ghett returned to the river, Lady Mythlanica went back to bed, and Lana and I started cleaning up. For the record, I did tell her that she didn't have to help, but she wouldn't hear it. We stood shoulder to shoulder washing dirty dishes. If something this simple sent my heart soaring, what chance did I stand going forward? It made me nervous. *Come on, rational brain. I'm counting on you.*

Then, "……Is Éa doing any better?" In trying to get my mind to switch gears, I wound up asking a pretty heavy question. She hadn't gotten up from bed since the night before and hadn't shown up for breakfast this morning, either.

"No."

Lana kept smiling, completely void of emotion. She started giving off a slightly cold aura, a darkness unbecoming of her lovely nature. I debated whether to dig any deeper, but then a horse's neighing cut that debate short. A carriage approached us, driven by a middle-aged man, someone we had no need to fear.

"Lana, go in the tent," I told her. She nodded and hid from

sight. I held my bow at my side, ready so I could shoot at any moment, and hid an arrow behind my back.

"Sorry to disturb you so early," greeted Pops, stepping out of the carriage cabin. "The king has summoned you and the princess. You'll oblige him, right?"

"And if I refuse?"

"More people will come every day to ask until you agree."

Kind of a low-key way to mess with someone. Now then, will the father of all adventurers side with one of his own?

"On one condition. On the way, I'd like to stop and tell everyone I know that you are taking us to see the king." *I could mess with him, too. If anything bad happened to me and Lana, it would tarnish his image, even if just by a speck.*

"Sure. And let me tell you one thing right now. If the king condemns you to imprisonment or execution, I'll risk my life to help you escape. I'll even contract a ship to take you all the way to the Left Continent. But the man I know would not do something that foolish."

"I can't trust you." After all, random strangers had granted him the title "father of adventurers." Gossip always came with exaggeration. Lies found their way even into the poems written about great legends. I could only trust the people I judged for myself.

"Fine by me."

Lana, who had been closely listening, emerged from the tent. We locked eyes for a second, and then I helped her board the carriage first. My bow in hand, I ducked into the tent. I tied Isolla and the quiver around my waist and filled the latter with as many arrows as I could carry. Then I put on all my usual gear and ordered Machina to evacuate Éa.

To my goddess asleep in a corner of the tent, I said, "Lady Mythlanica, the king has summoned me. I'll be back."

"Mm-hmm. Return before lunch," she ordered, then let out a gaping yawn and went back to sleep.

I hopped into the carriage, whose cabin turned out to be simpler and bigger than I'd imagined, then sat down next to Lana as if I belonged there.

"Oh, Pops, are we dressed all right for the occasion?" I mean, I'd basically geared up for war. At the same time, I had no intention of removing any of it, even if he said I should.

"Adventurer manners dictate you should appear in full gear. You're fine."

Lana looked down at her own outfit. She had her staff, her robe, a small pouch around her waist, and other adventurer essentials. The problem was her white robe. Stains we couldn't remove in the wash subtly stood out. It had once been a high-quality piece of clothing, but the fabric had ripped and pulled in several places. An indescribable expression briefly flickered over her face, but not too quickly for me to miss.

The carriage raced over the meadow, then slowed its pace once we entered the city. People crammed the main street as usual. We first dropped by the Zavah shop and got Lana some new clothing. Pops bought it for her. "Don't sweat it," he'd said. "I'll have the king pay me back and then some." It would've been rude to refuse his kindness, so I also got clothes for Éa, daily necessities for the ladies, and a whole load of underwear. Whatever we couldn't carry, I asked to be delivered to the campsite.

Next, we dropped by the Ellomere Traders' shop. After enduring the owner's overly enthusiastic welcome, I bought three rather expensive bottles of booze. One of these I took to the constable at his post. "Is this a bribe?" he asked, to which I replied, "It sure is," and handed it over. Then we headed to the Wild Ox and Silver Fox House, where I gave another bottle to the boss, who said, "If you were going to get liquor, you should've gotten it here."

Afterward, we stopped by Tutu's restaurant. Pops and I dragged Lord Baafre, who had once again been floating in the river, onto dry ground. He drank his whole bottle in one gulp to wake up. I realized then that I should've bought a barrel of cheap liquor for him, not one expensive bottle. I decided to pass the Adventurers Guild without calling on anyone. I trusted Evetta, but officially, she couldn't take my side. It would be unfair to expect her to be neutral.

"All ready. Let's go," I told Pops.

"Aye."

As planned, I'd told everyone I'd met that we were on our way to the king's castle.

Back up—tell me this doesn't feel like a round of final farewells. Wait, wait, wait. I've only gotten down to the tenth level, and that doesn't even count because I went there unofficially, so I've really only made it to the fifth floor—only the fifth. My adventure's just getting started, so why does it feel like everything's about to end?

"Souya, are you okay?" asked Lana. "You look a little pale."

"I'm fine, just disgusted at my own incompetence."

"You should be more confident in yourself. You're doing a good job. And regardless of what kinds of people or gods decide to criticize you, I am grateful to you and will always be on your side, no matter what."

Her kindness hung heavy on my heart. Could I ever repay her? And could I do so while still pursuing my original goal? Ah, was this why my rate of success was only 2 percent?

"Did you two cross that line already?"

"Huh?!"

A weird sound came out of my mouth at Pops's casual question. I would've loved to go there if possible, but one urgent emergency after another had left no room to think about that.

"No we have not," Lana firmly responded. *That doesn't hurt. Definitely, not shocked*, I kept telling myself.

"Good to hear," Pops acknowledged, a deeply meaningful look on his face. I figured he wouldn't tell me why, even if I asked.

My thoughts spun round and round on the topic, and before I knew it, we arrived at the royal castle. The small, moss-covered palace stood in the shadow of the dungeon in the northeastern part of town.

"Pretty dingy, right? Elite adventurers live in classier places than this. Our king couldn't care less about that sort of thing, though," Pops explained. "He also uses a fortress built almost six hundred years ago. As he says, it's all good as long as it can keep the wind and the rain out."

It certainly was dingy. Parts of its walls had crumbled away, only to be repaired with pathetic wooden boards. And it got almost no light, so even though it was still morning, the sun seemed far away. One of the chains holding the drawbridge up had rusted and snapped off. Maybe the only beautiful thing about it was the flag it had hoisted. Its design had a bull and a fox facing each other. I'd seen something similar at the boss's bar, too. Guards did theoretically protect the entrance, but one look at Pops and they let him through without a word. We followed after and entered the castle.

Emiluminite stones lit up the castle's interior, which had more elegance than I'd expected. Maids of various races welcomed us in rows. They all bowed their heads in unison, and I almost followed suit. Three of them led us to the second floor. That's when—

"Lord Medîm, I'd like to have a word with your guests."

—a maid it pained me to look at came around the corner. Bandages were wrapped around her beautiful face, and her left eye had swollen shut. She had long silver hair and black-tipped, pointed ears, and a fluffy tail peeked out beneath her skirt. I hadn't recognized her without her armor.

"Fine, but hurry it up. We've kept the king and his guest waiting for quite a while. I'll go on ahead." Pops turned to us and said, "She has better sense than to start any bloodshed here. Don't worry." He could say that all he wanted, but I still wouldn't trust her.

"Thank you. This way." She showed us into an empty drawing room with a long table and chairs, dilapidated lights, relatively lavish curtains, and iron-barred windows. I stayed alert, ready to fire my bow at any moment.

The maid got down on one knee and bowed her head. "First and foremost, I'd like to offer my sincere apologies for the rudeness we have shown you."

"Please do not concern yourself. It's in the past," Lana replied, but the maid spat back, "Elf, I did not mean that for you. I was speaking to Lord Souya of Japan."

That pissed me off. She'd saved me the trouble of deciding what attitude to take with her. I responded in an icily cutting tone, "Apologize all you like; I'm not gonna let a single thing you've done slide. You don't mind, do you?"

"Not at all. However, allow me to apologize once more. Regardless of the strategies you may have employed, you had the technique, the wisdom, and the tools to defeat all three of us on your own, yet I ineptly accused you of cowardice, thus besmirching your feat. For this, I am truly sorry from the bottom of my heart. If my body can serve to repay you, please do with it as you wish." Her straightforward gaze stared at a very inappropriate place. I considered making a complete mess of her and leaving her in shreds, but I didn't have time for that now.

"Is that all?"

"No. What I'm about to tell you is the real reason I pulled you aside."

There's more?

"It concerns my lord, the prince. He is irrefutably timid and simplistic, a demonic little bully, a skirt-chaser with twisted proclivities; he shows no decency befitting of the royal family and personifies not a shred of what it means to be king. We shoulder some of the blame for this, as we have not had the heart to admonish him since his elder brother's tragic death," she admitted, shitting all over him. "However, he is cunningly intelligent if nothing else. Rather, he believes himself cunning and has a half-baked understanding of debased matters, which he is now exploiting to proceed down a troubling path. My lord prince summoned King Remlia and the king of the elves. He intends to reveal everything that happened in the dungeon and formally apologize to the princess. Can you infer what this means?"

......Wait, so he's going to apologize in front of members of both royal families? Which means Lana's father will be there, too, right? So the prince is gonna apologize to an elf and fess up to what he did. I don't know what Lana's father is like, but most would generally lose their minds in outrage.

"Sorry, I'm not familiar with your customs here. But does that mean......he could start a fight?"

"If it goes poorly, it could devolve into war." I felt the blood drain from my face. "Some among the elves still refuse to admit they have lost to the heims. They are a proud and arrogant race. They would not simply stand by silently if they learned that the prince of heims had trampled over and attempted to rape their princess. Additionally, this last defeat has cost Heuress a considerable degree of the power he had to unify his people. If he responds carelessly to this incitement, other members of his tribe will plot to unseat him. In the worst case, this could spark a civil war among the elves before anything else."

The timid torment others for only one reason: They have no imagination. *I should've made that damn prince into monster meat. But it's not Lana's fault; it's my fault for listening to her.*

"Should his actions spark a military conflict, the prince will most certainly fall under criticism. However, he can wash away any stains on his honor or sins with his authority. The heims have followed this evil practice since the days of old. Furthermore, some adventurers would gladly raise their arms in warfare."

No matter the age or the world, there had always been those who love war, and some who couldn't live without it. And as the merchant's goddess said, "War is a profitable enterprise."

"Elf Princess, do you wish to burn your people to death once more?"

"Absolutely not." Lana squeezed my poncho hard. I would've done anything to ease her pain. The curse had ingrained that desire in me, along with the skill of the bow.

No, let's be real. My own feelings are responsible for more than half of that, aren't they?

"I've got a question for you." One thing I couldn't wrap my head around: the implications behind her apology. It didn't make sense.

"My name is Lanceil. I pray you remember it."

"Lanceil, why do you want to stop this war?" It would surely benefit the prince and this country.

"I fear for the king's well-being. He is advanced in age, and his health has recently taken a worrying turn." *Why would a lowly maid, and the prince's subordinate to boot, worry about that? There's definitely something else going on here. She sucks at lying.*

"Lord Souya, I have heard you are a wise and knowledgeable

man who detests war. Unworthy as I am to serve you, please feel free to use me and my body however you wish. I beg of you, please stop the prince's scheme."

Damn, she's just begging me to use her. It sounds almost sexual. I mean, she does have an amazing body, muscular and sexy, kind of like what you'd get if you gave Evetta a little more muscle and plumped up her chest a bit. Hmm? Their faces look kind of similar, too.

However: "I don't know how to respond to that," I replied. I had absolutely no ideas.

"Lanceil, everyone awaits our guests. Hurry— Ah!" A dark brown feline beastmaid walked in without knocking and with no sense of decorum. She looked at me and pointed. "You! How dare you tie me up!"

"Caroro, we have no time for that now," scolded Lanceil.

"Nooo! The prince got angry with mee-ow because of you! He fired me as his guard! Now you must marry mee-ow!"

"Huh?" What was I supposed to do with this? She jumped and latched on to me, hugged me tight, and hit me with a surprise proposal.

"You little! There you go again!"

"Nooo! I'm gonna marry him right meow! I want a stable life!"

"No honest adventurer seeks a stable life!" Lanceil grabbed the feline beastmaid by the scruff of her neck and tossed her into the air. She made a perfect landing. This time, Lanceil approached me, took both my hands in hers, and looked at me pleadingly. "In any event, Lord Souya, I'm begging you! All our fates rest in your hands. I will do anything to assist you, even if it means offering you my body to—"

The feline beastmaid jumped on Lanceil's back and started to strangle her. "There *you* go again! Not that 'offer you my body' spiel! How many times do you think you've used that meow?"

"Silence! This is but the third time!"

The two started bickering. I finally kind of understood the beastfolk of this world.

The door opened once more and—

"You're taking too long!" Pops stormed in, furious. This wasn't my fault. He dragged us out into the hall. The two maids caught up to us and went on ahead.

I tapped Isolla Pot on the top of her head three times. We'd settled on that as our SOS signal a little while back. Her message appeared on my glasses.

Squad Member Souya, I understand what you seek. You'd like a strategy to avoid instigating a war, correct? Machina and I have spent the past few days considering this question, having foreseen that something of this nature might occur. We ran five thousand simulations and determined......there is no conceivable way to escape this. I sincerely apologize for being unable to provide assistance. I am currently devising an escape plan; please stand by.

It was all over. This had ballooned into something too big for me to handle on my own.

"Souya." Lana tugged my poncho. I could only imagine how awful I looked at that moment. "Would you allow me to handle this?"

"You have a plan?"

"Yes I do." My savior goddess stood right next to me all along. "But I need to ask you something first."

"Ask me anything."

"Do you have a fiancée or person you love in your homeland?"

"No, just a younger sister."

"I see. That's a great help." *How?* I tried to ask, but Pops came to a halt before a room and opened its doors.

It looked almost exactly like the last one. All the rooms in the castle had been built to look alike as a defensive measure against invasions. One elf sat to my left at the table in this room; two heims, to my right. The two maids we'd just spoken to stood in the corner of the room, along with another two people I didn't recognize.

I assumed the elf was Lana's father. He was the spitting image of Éa and looked no older than me. Leaving him aside, I turned to my real problem—the two heims. One was the smirking, idiotic prince. The other wore a crown over his bald head. He looked around sixty, but his chiseled face showed signs of great exhaustion. I could tell he and the boss were related. Perfectly tailored attire and a mantle clothed his flawless physique, and an unadorned sword hung from his hip. This, without question, was King Remlia.

"I imagine the sudden summons caught you by surprise. Forgive me; my incorrigible son insisted on having you come." His voice sounded lower, and more pained, than necessary. Was he ill?

Maids pulled our chairs out for us and encouraged us to sit. Lanceil helped me with mine. She emitted a very strong *I'm begging you* aura from her every pore.

"That said, Medîm, why is it you are here? You are not a man rich in time to waste."

"Lanceil told me she'd been injured, so I came to give her a hand with some of her duties. Don't worry yourself about it." Pops spoke frankly, and very casually, to the king. Only the real deals could get away with that kind of attitude.

The king looked at Lana. "Princess Laualliuna, are you well? I suspect it must be taxing to adjust to this unfamiliar occupation as an adventurer. Please do rely on me for anything you may require to make the transition easier."

"No, Your Highness. I have no......difficulties to report." I sensed a hint of murderous intent in Lana's words.

"You do seem to have lost some weight," the king of the elves said to her.

"You imagine things, Father." Her tone took on an even more terrifying tenor.

Then King Remlia turned to me. "I understand you came from another world?"

"It is a distinguished honor to meet you, King Remlia. My name is Souya, and I hail from a foreign land called Japan. I am currently employed as an adventurer." My voice shook a bit toward the end.

"What fascinating features you have. Young man, should we have another opportunity and more time in the future, I would gladly hear your stories of this foreign land." That did nothing to calm my nerves. "Now then, Georg. Our guests have all arrived, as you requested."

"In such case, Father, Your Majesty, the reason I requested you summon everyone here today was—"

"Wait," the king interrupted. "First, we discuss Lanceil."

"......I will explain that matter at a later time." The prince shrank on the spot.

A terrifying glint in his eye, the king demanded, "No. I have summoned the king of the elves and their princess here at your behest. You swore you would explain how Lanceil came to sustain her injuries if I satisfied this condition. Lanceil is as stubborn as her mother. Once she decides she will not speak of something, a dragon could trample her and still she would not relent."

Something's weird. Why would the king concern himself so much over a single maid's injuries?

"You realize you are disparaging my wishes, do you not? Every day you look upon our family crest: an ox and a silver fox. The ox is drawn in the likeness of the oxen Dark Crowned monster I defeated, and the silver fox represents Lanceil's mother, who in that battle threw down her life to protect me. Can you comprehend the enormous significance behind defiling our country's crest? Do you feel nothing for having hurt the person who would be your elder sister if the laws were any different?!"

All at once, sweat drenched my brow.

Shit. This is bad—especially for me. At this rate, I'll get executed before any war breaks out.

I glanced behind us and saw Lanceil beaming at me with a stunning smile. I returned it with a look no words could describe.

"No, Your Majesty. I assure you I intend no such thing. I simply wish to proceed in order of—"

"What is the point of changing the order of business here? Do you mean to deceive the king?"

"N-no!" The prince comically panicked, but I had no mental space to enjoy the scene.

Lana took my hand. I wanted to ask her why, but she began to speak before I had the chance.

"Souya is the one who defeated Lanceil." *What the—?!*

"Ohhh." The king's eyes shook me to my core.

"The other day, the prince's party and the two of us engaged in a duel within the dungeon. We are fully aware that this is prohibited. However, a very important matter compelled us to proceed nonetheless."

"Then let us hear it. However, Princess, understand that depending on how you answer, I may have to dispose of you both."

Lana didn't even flinch at the king's threat, far from her usual, sheepish self. She sat ramrod straight, and I could feel the strength of her resolve, the kind you might need when deciding one of the most important decisions in your life or—

"We dueled so that the prince would grant Souya and I the permission to wed."

Hmm?

Hmmm?!?!

Hmmmm?!?!?!

My mind went blank at the most unexpected sentence I'd ever heard in my life.

"Heims and elves are forbidden from wedding in the Heuress Forest. However, I am now but a common adventurer, so it is only logical that I defer to the king of the adventurers' will. And yet, I did not wish to trouble you, Your Majesty, with the trivial concerns of a princess turned commoner.

"The prince learned of our quandary and bestowed upon us these words: 'I challenge you to a duel. Should you have the strength to succeed, I shall plead your case before my lord, His Majesty, the king.'"

The prince's face said, *Huh? I never said that.* Mine said, *Yeah, I know.*

"We fought with everything we had," Lana continued. "However, we stood no chance against him. It was bound to be so. We could not hope to stand on equal ground with Georg ole Remlia, son of King Remlia, and his retainer Lady Lanceil, renowned for her bravery. The prince outwitted all my magic, and Lady Lanceil deflected every arrow Souya unleashed at her. However—"

The king ate up her every word.

"—our great hero Heuress imbued our last arrow with grace. Its power destroyed Lady Lanceil's shield and shattered her helmet. We cannot credit our own strengths for this miracle. And yet, the prince magnanimously accepted defeat and provided us the opportunity to speak with you here today."

This was probably how the history books got written. They didn't actually mean much, in the end.

"Lanceil, is this the truth?"

In response to the king's question, Lanceil responded, "Verily, it is so. In the last arrow they released, undoubtedly the very same arrow that vanquished Rhora the Great Spider, I caught a glimpse of the legendary Heuress."

The prince flapped his mouth open and shut like a complete idiot. *Serves you right*, I thought but also realized I risked replicating that same expression and did all that I could to keep it together.

"Georg, you did well."

"Huh? Your Majesty?" The prince regained his senses as the king slapped him on the back.

"You risked your life to honor the wishes of your people. That is exactly how a king should behave. I thought you hateful for acting out of nothing but self-indulgence, but evidently your children can mature before you know it."

"Your Majesty." Tears choked the prince's eyes. What a truly lovely story—all of it bullshit, of course.

"You called me for *this*?" said the elven king, who had carefully watched the proceedings. His voice sounded horribly icy.

"Mellum, I assure you I—"

"Excuse me. I will take my leave." The king of elves did not even wait for King Remlia to finish speaking before he stood from his chair. He spat one last parting shot on his way out. "My daughter is dead. I see only an adventurer before me. King Remlia, I entrust her entirely to your will." A maid accompanied the elven king out of the room, and a heaviness clung to the air after the door closed behind them.

The king cleared his throat and in a cheery voice announced, "I, the first monarch of the Kingdom of Remlia, Remila ole Armaguest Rhasvah, hereby grant my blessing upon your betrothal. Would you prefer to use elven wedding vows?"

"Yes, if it would please you, Your Majesty," Lana answered, completely ignoring my dumbfounded ass.

"Mm, very well. I shall prepare a modest gift to cover your ceremony. As for the paperwork, I shall have the Adventurers Guild draw it up for you. Princess, or rather, Laualliuna, and you, Souya, interracial marriage is not without its difficulties. You two must take each other's hands and embark on this adventure, together."

"Yes, Your Majesty."

"Uh, yes, Your Majesty." I copied Lana's answer. We still held hands.

The king stood from his chair, followed by his son; we bowed our heads to them in unison. Left completely out of the loop, Pops scratched his beard out of apparent boredom. I looked out the window onto the scenery in this foreign land and thought of my sister, so far away.

Yukikazzie. Looks like your big brother's getting hitched.

"Souya, we're here."

"Huh?"

The next thing I knew, we'd arrived back at the campsite. I saw the carriage out on the meadow, returning to the city. My brain had reached its processing limit, so I had no memories of anything after about the time we left the castle.

"Now, then." *Time to make some lunch, I guess—*

"Please forgive me!" Lana got down on the ground in *dogeza*, prostrating on the earth.

"Hmm? Wait, what?!" It all happened so fast that I couldn't take it in. I let out a shrill squeal and bent into a funky shape.

"Lady Mythlanica and Machina explained that in the country called Japan, you assume this pose when you want to make the most sincere of apologies or entreaties!"

"You don't need to know that!" *How dare they go around sharing the worst parts of my country!*

"No, I refuse to lift my head until you forgive me! I'm so terribly sorry! I didn't even ask how you would feel about the matter and did something so preposterous all on my own. The things those beastmaids said to you made me panic, and I seized upon this sudden impulse. You have saved me time and time again, and I still haven't even returned a single favor. How could I dare burden you yet again?! I will do anything within my power to atone for this! I know better than anybody that I am unworthy of being with someone like you! However, we cannot now go back on what we said before the king! So only until you find someone you truly love, just until then, please *pretend* to marry me!"

I see, so you're telling me to marry you for show. Wait, wait, wait, hold on.

"Mr. Souya." Machina poked my back from behind. "How can you let a woman go on like this? Aren't you ashamed of yourself?"

Huh?

"Squad Member Souya." Isolla, at my hip, clutched my poncho. "Prove to us your sincerity as a man. Machina and I refuse to support someone who cannot manage that."

Huhhh?

"Souya," said Lady Mythlanica as she came out of the tent. "I've gleaned the general picture. Good luck, I suppose." *Right.*

I had an elf prostrate on the ground, two AI machines criticizing me, and a goddess in her feline form. Amid this most chaotic of scenes, I got down to one knee and lifted Lana's head.

"Lana, will you……pretend to marry me?"

"Yes, thank you very much."

It would've been a pretty nice scene without the *pretend*. The AI units played the sounds of applause.

"Congratulations. We have a saying in my country that goes, 'Marriage is an adventure.' Isolla and I will do everything in our power to support you two as you embark on your journey."

"I have nothing to add." Lady Mythlanica's comment was exactly on point.

"Whaaat, you're home? Where'd ya gooo?" A sleepy Éa came out of the tent.

Lana smiled as she said, "Éa, your big sister has decided to marry Souya."

"Whyyyy?!"

It took half a day to explain everything.

(12TH DAY)

The next day, I went to the Adventurers Guild and submitted applications for both a new party and our marriage license. When I filled out the permit, I realized that elves practice polygamy. According to Lana, this tradition dated back to the days of old. She said elves have long life spans and low birth rates, which I figured must have played a part. Maybe they'd settled on that custom for lack of other choices.

I made a few errors on the form and had to write it again. For some reason I couldn't explain, I kept making a ton of tiny mistakes. After struggling for about half a day, Isolla took over and used a laser to burn the information into the allotted spaces. It took thirty-five tries, but my paperwork finally passed all the checks, and Lana and I officially became husband and wife. Still, it was only a marriage on paper. I hardly felt anything.

"Congratulations." Evetta looked at me like a doting mother and clapped. I couldn't tell you why, but the Guildmaster collapsed behind her.

(13TH DAY)

We rented out Tutu's place to hold our humble "fake" wedding ceremony. Who knows how they'd heard about it, but the Zavah Night Owl Trade Group and the Ellomere Western Peng Traders dropped by while we set everything up and offered to supply whatever we needed. I didn't want to owe them any favors, but they said something about how this kind of party provided the perfect platform to advertise their businesses. Satisfied, I asked them to handle the drinks, food, and party favors.

After we finished all the preparations, I ran around town to invite our guests. Fortunately, it only took me about two hours to gather everyone. And so, surrounded by not too many but not too few people, we began the ceremony. Lana and I called upon our respective gods and exchanged our vows before them. One was a cervine god named Lord Ezeus; the other, a feline goddess, Lady Mythlanica. The god and goddess offered their blessings and grace to each other's respective devotees and brought the ceremony to a close. Lord Ezeus's speech took up most of this part, but Lady Mythlanica read the room and simply muttered, "You have my blessing."

Next came the banquet for our starving beasts. It turned into a small zoo. Evetta chowed down on an extra heaping plate of food. Shuna and Bel kept apace next to her, heartily devouring their own plates. The young beastmaid who had carried Lady Mythlanica through town before sat in front of them, stuffing her cheeks with dinner.

The Guildmaster, Pops, the boss, and Lord Baafre, who apparently all went way back, cheerfully drank it up together. Ghett sat with the young chairman of the Ellomere Traders and his common-law wife, the mermaid Bambia. The three stayed close to the river and quietly ate their meals. Tutu's stunningly gorgeous friends refilled the young Zavah chairman's cup so aggressively that he almost passed out drunk. Lanceil threw her arms around me, then got into a very entertaining scuffle with Lana. Tutu paid them no mind and came to sit on my lap, then wrote down the recipes for the dishes that had been served.

All the people I'd met from a wide variety of races had gathered here. And yet, no other elves came aside from my bride. Éa had been dead set on attending, but her health had taken a turn for the worse early in the morning, so she'd stayed back at camp, sleeping.

In the way of every world, people who heard the commotion decided they had to join in. Some heard about it through friends, then friends of those friends showed up, then people those people knew joined our banquet, ate our food, and drank our spirits. Predictably, we ran out of both. However, we had two heads of trade groups in our midst. Their moment to let their brands shine had come. And yet, both the piss-ass drunk Zavah chairman and the young head of the Ellomere Traders, eager to impress his wife and her grandfather, went more than a little overboard and brought out carts upon carts of food and drinks.

The sun set, and the riotous banquet full of eating and drinking, singing and dancing, reached its highest tide. I did my best to act respectably at first, but even I gave in halfway through, lost my senses, and became just as idiotic as everyone else. Lana took Lord Baafre up on a drinking contest and had him cornered. A woman in a black dress danced atop one of the tables, a bottle of ale in her hands. Did she know someone here? It felt like I'd seen her before. Tutu's friends started stripping; the middle-aged men howled. Beltriche cuddled up to Evetta. Some faces I knew disappeared, soon replaced by ten times their number in strangers.

The crowd and noise grew so out of hand that the neighbors

started to complain. The constable showed up. I offered him a drink, and he didn't even get halfway through it before he began shit-talking the aristocracy in the Central Continent in a long-winded rant.

Shrieks and angry screams, cheers and flirtatious calls rose to the skies from this feverish, chaotic, interracial feast. I no longer felt alienated like the outsider I'd been when I first arrived. If anything, a sleepy sense of comfort filled my heart.

Ahh, I really have become an adventurer.

(XXTH DAY)

Someone took my hand in the midst of the dreamlike morning mists and pulled me away from the clamor. Walking before me I saw the woman who had just become my fake wife. Dizzily, giddily, we wandered through the streets like a pair of sleepwalkers. We fell in the river.

"*Gasp!*"

The cold water immediately sobered me and woke me up. The river came up to my waist, deeper than I'd thought. Lana splished and splashed as she swam—wait, no, she was drowning. I immediately grabbed on to her and held her as high above the water as I could.

"*Ghah!*"

She put both her arms on my shoulders and gasped for air. Drops of water scattered from her long silver hair. Her eyes shone beneath the light of the three otherworldly moons, gold just like them. Out of some coincidence or perhaps fate, Lana gazed at me through eyes exactly like Lady Mythlanica's.

"Pft, heh-heh, ah-ha-ha-ha-ha-ha!" Then she laughed with an innocent, childlike smile. "You saved me again."

"Damn right I did." Two moons leaned in. Neither of us knew quite what to do, and our teeth gently collided. We connected for the briefest of moments, too short to really take anything in.

"I know those aren't your true feelings. But I have fallen in love with you."

"What do you—?"

Lana hugged my head so tightly, so passionately, I almost couldn't breathe. But enveloped by this pair of infinitely soft globes, I stopped caring about anything else.

"I'm in love with you. I love you. I never want to let you go."

"……"

I couldn't get my emotions in enough order to respond. It felt far too soon to say, *Me too*, and I didn't know for sure if I even had the right to say so.

"I'm only being selfish and pushing this twisted love on you. So I'll place you under a spell. If you ever truly fall in love with someone else, if I come between you and your happiness, or if I die, I will make it so you forget everything about me."

That I couldn't take quietly. "That'll never happen." I wouldn't ever forget the heat of her skin, her warmth.

I saw her smile through tears. "But, you know, in the end—," she started to say, but my mind slipped into darkness. The uproar echoing in the distance slid further and further away, so far I could hear nothing anymore.

Just like when I first came to this world, I fell into a bottomless—

"!"

—I woke up. Glimpsing the sunrise, I frantically reached out my hand and latched on to……Lana's breast; she slept deeply at my side. Its supple softness filled the palm of my hand. I could touch this for the rest of my life and never tire of the sensation.

Huh? I got the feeling that I'd been dreaming, as if I'd tasted a vision as sweet as this moment.

"O-ow." My head pounded. Sleeping on the hard cobblestones

all night had left my body cramped and sore. I glanced around to find guests from the banquet sprawled all over the place like me, each and every one of them in awful positions. On top of that, the place had been so thoroughly wrecked that it made the devastation left in the wake of a typhoon look tidy.

"Oh, Souya. Mooorning."

"Hey, Tutu. Morning."

Tutu, the owner of the devastated bar, curved her back in a refreshing stretch and greeted me.

"Sorry for all this mess."

"Don't worry; that's what big feasts are like. It happens all the time. Okay, Souya, I've gotta go to work meow, so I'll leave the cleaning up to you." She waved her hand and her tail and went off to work.

"……" *I have to clean it up? All of this? I have no words.*

(14TH DAY)

The past few days had been so busy that I hadn't even had time to think about the dungeon. But they'd been fun. I could look back and smile on those days forever, even if I found myself in the lowest rings of hell.

"Was it fun? C'mon, was it fun?"

"Yeah, sorta." If I told Éa how crazy it'd actually gotten, I could see her grumble and pout about it. My bride, by the way, was currently suffering from a hangover. She was out like a light in my tent.

"Aargh, I can't believe I couldn't go to my own sister's wedding."

I'd come to play doctor in Éa's tent. Her pulse had weakened since the day before, and her once feverish body felt icy cold.

"You'll just have to look forward to your own wedding," I told her.

"As if I could last that long."

I glanced over at Éa's ryvius lying next to her bow. No more red remained in the vial. The ryvius didn't normally work outside of town, but it did around our tents. According to Lana, it had something to do with the abandoned dungeon not too far away from here. This campsite sat perfectly on the border. The kitchen marked the cut-off point, and the sisters' tent lay just outside the ryvius's reach. I tried to move Éa somewhere where it would work, but she refused, claiming it would only prolong her suffering.

The ryvius couldn't remove foreign objects from the body or purge it of poison. It healed the damage caused by the toxicity, but as long as the object responsible for the contamination remained inside, it could really only buy you some time.

Machina had scanned Éa and found that the bullet had entered through her stomach and lodged itself in her hip bone. We would need to cut her open, push her organs out of the way, and remove the bullet if we wanted to treat her. This world had greatly advanced magical treatment capabilities, but as a result, its traditional internal medical technologies remained underdeveloped. To make matters worse, it only had a short history with guns, so of course, no one knew much of anything about treating bullet wounds. Every medical advancement required a vast number of sacrificial patients. It would surely still take a long time to reach casualties on that scale here.

On the other hand, we did have some knowledge on the matter. However, the medical program had only recovered 16 percent of its full functionality. Isolla suggested we give her an IV with chelating agents to extract the lead in her blood, but Machina vetoed the plan, pointing out that it would only help temporarily and might cause her wound to inflame.

Only the ryvius and Lana's magic had kept Éa alive since the moment she had gotten shot. That, and her strong desire to not leave her sister alone. Ironically, my appearance had softened that resolve.

"Looks like I finally can't move anymore," she noticed, touching her own legs.

"Hey, maybe it'll help if you put this on again," I offered and showed her the gauntlet. A curse with the will to protect these two dwelled within it. I still hadn't been able to take it off, but maybe I could find a way.

"As much as I hate to admit it, Heuress's grace belongs to you. It didn't choose me. Plus, I don't want anything a heim has put his dirty hands all over." Her insult held no power. She slumped over onto me. "If you ever get tired of that, feel free to hawk it. Also, researchers pay good money for elf corpses, so go ahead and sell my body while you're at it. I don't need a funeral. Just send a lock of my hair back to the forest. If my father or elder brother give you any trouble, tell them I said, 'Go to hell.' I guess that's about all."

"……" I couldn't say anything. There's nothing to say to someone who has accepted their fate.

"So please look after my sister, Brother." She took my hand. I placed both of mine over hers.

"You got it."

"Okay, now I've got no regrets left," she said, smiling peacefully. I leaned in close.

"You sure?"

"I'm sure."

That made up my mind, too. "Then give your life to me."

"Huh?"

"I came to this world to save my younger sister," I said, then left the tent to get ready. I stepped up to Machina and gave her an order, even though I knew she'd probably been listening in the whole time. "Machina, cancel all current operations and deconstruct the medical program. Extract the information and consolidate it. Prepare to commence the laparotomy."

"Understood. I expected this might happen and have already begun preparations. I will finish them in five minutes. Time is of the essence, so I have planned the surgery to begin in one hour."

"That's too soon."

"Mr. Souya, you did not make any specific demands for resource allotment, so I will use the surplus as I see fit." My rough, amateur commands paid off. But I needed to know one more thing.

"Tell me, what's our chance of success with this surgery?"

"You have ordered me to do it, and I have said I will. So we have a one hundred percent chance of success." Very encouraging to hear.

"I also have a proposal," added Isolla as she rolled over. I picked her up. "I followed Machina's example and searched through the records of my previous generations. The emergency medical treatment data I found comes from a surgery performed forty years ago, but I would like you to let me use it to help. With this, I expect our success rate should increase by twenty percent."

The new 120 percent rate began to feel like a measure of how we believed we could make it, as long as we had the will. My partners had spoken. I placed all my trust in them.

"Save my little sister. She's in your hands."

"Please rest assured. We will live up to your expectations; I guarantee it."

EPILOGUE

I wound my way through the city's chaotic nighttime streets. Having finished some errands, I was on the hunt for someone. I checked at the inn, but they told me their guest had stepped out, so out I went in search as well. In the end, I found him at the same bar as always.

"Evening, Souya. It's rare to see you here at night."

"Yeah, I had some things to do," I briefly greeted the boss, then headed toward a corner of the bar. There sat Arvin, slowly sipping a drink. "Mind if I sit here?"

"I have no authority to deny you that." True enough. I sat down.

"Oh, meow, Souya. What'll it be?"

"Fruit juice and stewed beans."

"Okaaay." Tutu took my order, swished her tail back and forth, and disappeared into the kitchen.

"Apologies. I didn't make it to your wedding," said Arvin. I rested my hand on the longsword hanging from my hip. It had rustic embellishments and a blade made of surprisingly high-quality steel. Though it still felt a bit heavy for me, I'd need to learn to swing around something that weighed at least this much if I wanted to be a real adventurer.

"You know, the strangest thing happened. The morning after the reception, I woke up and found this tied around my waist. I can understand losing something, but what do you make of gaining a new item when you're passed out?"

"I couldn't tell you."

"I looked into it, and apparently the Central Continent has a custom where you give the newlyweds their presents when they least expect it." Lana had received a shortsword as well.

"Do we? Sorry, I've forgotten," he deflected, playing dumb. Pushing him any harder on the subject would be tasteless, so I let it drop.

"Anyway, Arvin. How's it going in the dungeon?"

"We still haven't found a new leader. We did try teaming up with an adept adventurer, but he turned out to be a fraud. It ended well, as we walked out of that with more money, but we've made no progress." I'd also heard a rumor of a retired adept adventurer who'd gotten stripped of all his possessions and beaten to a pulp. Actually, that happened all the time.

"After that, we tried working with another guy of a similar standing, but he mistook Shuna for a girl, and they went at each other's throats. Shuna pummeled him until his ryvius ran out. We had to pay a small fortune for his medical expenses." *That's frickin' awful.*

"Arvin, did you tell Shuna off?"

"No, I'm not cut out for scolding children. What am I supposed to do if I reprimand him but he refuses to obey? I don't know how to pull my punches in a fight."

Well, that helps exactly no one. I'm pretty sure Shuna's the kind of kid who'll listen to what you say, but he's at that age where you have to be straight with him for his own good.

"We didn't have much other choice, so I tried leading an

expedition......and got lost. Truly lost. We spent two days wandering around in between the seventh and eighth floors. Shuna wouldn't stop yelling, Bel cried all the time, and Zenobia started talking to the walls. Then we ran out of food and water, and this terrible anxiety took over the whole party. If Pops hadn't shown up and saved us, our adventure might have ended then and there."

Yeah, I was the one who asked Pops to go in after you.

Adventurers almost always descended into the dungeon for two or three days at a time. However, the provisions Arvin had bought stood no chance of lasting more than a day. When they still hadn't come out by the second day, I panicked. They could all fight on an intermediate level, but they woefully lacked any survival skills they'd need to make it down there. Plus, they hadn't learned the value of retreating. That was on me. I'd led them to victory in our first-ever battle, and it had set in as a bad habit. As the final nail in the coffin, Arvin evidently had zero sense of direction. He couldn't read a map at all, and neither could any of the other members.

The Guild did offer survival lessons for initiate adventurers, but they were all the kind of people who jumped right past tutorials. If they had time to waste on the lessons, they'd use it to explore the dungeon instead. It cost money to take those classes, too, so I could understand where they came from.

But I still had to wonder, *Why are they so completely ignorant about this stuff?* The way Machina put it, the answer lay in the standards of our respective civilizations and in the fundamental knowledge I picked up about roaming around dungeons in the period video games I used to play.

Good adventurers caught onto this stuff instinctively. Those who didn't get it just had to get those who did on their team. That's what parties were all about: complementing one another's skills. Faced with all this, Arvin—

"I'm drinking away my insecurities about what'll happen to us going forward."

—chose to escape from reality.

"That sounds like a lot."

"How about you, Souya?"

"We added another party member, but it'll still take us a while before we actually explore any of the dungeon."

"Don't tell me. It's not another elf, is it?"

"It's another elf."

Éa's wound had healed, but I wouldn't call it a miracle. Machina and Isolla had made it happen. They'd taken the bullet out and extracted the lead from her bloodstream, then removed any damaged tissue. Within two days, her health had stabilized. By the third day, she'd regained all her energy. We'd overcome the problem of her wounds, but we still didn't know how her body would react to anesthesia or modern medicines, so we were very carefully observing her for any side effects. Éa, however, refused to sit still and caused Machina and Isolla all kinds of grief.

"I simply can't tolerate elves. They keep stealing the people I need from me right and left."

My order arrived. With very low expectations for how they would taste, I started nibbling on the beans while Arvin spoke of his past.

"You remember the great-uncle I told you about. Well, I owed him a deep debt. I was an illegitimate child, but he pulled me out of the lowest depths of society and raised me as a knight. If he hadn't helped me, I'd have spent my life stealing and murdering in the slums of Ellusion, doomed to drown and rot in its gutters full of mire. My service as a knight didn't last very long, but it was an invaluable honor. I truly felt I had found my path in life......only for it to end like that. And then they took you, too."

The heartthrob revealed his painful past. Ladies two tables over gazed longingly at his deeply troubled countenance. It taught me a bit about when and why women fell for men. "Elves and I truly do not mix."

"Well, that happens." Whether due to luck or fate or history, some races simply did not get along. No amount of flowery thinking could convince me that even humanity could one day come to live in peace.

"I've burdened you with enough idle talk. How about you tell me why you really came already?" Arvin had some really incredible powers of perception.

"I have a proposal." I placed Isolla Pot, disguised as a lantern, onto the table. "Isolla, say hello."

"Hello, Lord Knight. My name is Isolla, and I am Squad Member Souya's partner."

"You sure have some strange equipment. Is this a hidden treasure from the dungeon?" Even the people of this world reacted with surprise at a talking lantern.

"Isolla came with me from my world. I won't lie; she's amazing. She can read maps and give you directions, so you'll never have to worry about getting lost and stuck in the dungeon. She also has a somewhat rudimentary ability to detect enemies approaching. And as long as we're within two floors of each other, she should be able to put you in touch with me through my glasses. I'd like to lend her to you."

"What does this mean?" Arvin proceeded very cautiously with his relationships. He never jumped at tempting bait, perhaps a lesson he had learned through experience.

"I have one condition. Everyone in my party, myself included, are rearguards. If a monster takes us by surprise, we'd all be wiped out with a single hit. We need a shield."

"I cannot accept your condition. I would need to obtain special permission from the popes of Ellusion to form a party with an elf. My country is currently at war with a gang called the Dark Elves from the Left Continent. Some have gone so far as to call their leader the new king of beasts. Even assuming I could abandon my own personal aversion to elves, I would never be able to acquire that permission," Arvin rattled on and on without stopping.

"Calm down, calm down. I'm not asking to join your party. I'm not even asking to form an alliance with yours. Your party and mine will proceed independently of each other."

"Hmm? Meaning? What are you trying to say?"

Explaining this was kind of a pain.

"I'll go through this in order. First, you and your party descend into the dungeon. My party *just happens* to go in after you. We won't get too close or stay too far. If we come across an unrelated party, mine will disappear from sight. We'll rely on Éa and Isolla's detection abilities to avoid battles as much as possible but will leave you to handle any that we cannot escape. You may notice some arrows or spells come flying from behind you, but don't pay them any attention. You and your party can take all the monster resources for yourselves. We'll make money in other ways."

This proposal took both Arvin's situation and my own into consideration. It would clearly prove beneficial for both of us.

"You really think we can fool anyone that easily?"

"Arvin, I impulsively unleashed an arrow on the prince of this country, then used deception and strategy to twist that crime into a beautiful story. Lady Mythlanica is not called the Malevolent for nothing. I promise you now that no foreigners or elves will play a part in any anecdotes, tales of glory, or honor due to Arvin Forths Gassim. What do you say?"

My goddess's cunning plans worked. She had given Lana the advice that led to her drastic move. However, Lana had apparently put her own spin on the plan and added the "marriage" element to it.

"I see...... Understood. I have one condition as well."

"Anything you like."

"We split the resources down the middle. You have close ties to two trade groups, right? We'll store our items there for a while first and then divide the money after."

"Got it." I tightly gripped the hand Arvin extended to me.

"I guess I'll have to get Shuna and the others up to speed on this, huh?"

"Well, actually, you're the last person I spoke to. Everyone else already agreed." I felt bad putting him in a difficult position, but I'd gone around him and told everyone else ahead of time. They'd all gladly agreed.

Arvin gave me one of his refreshing smiles. "So if I'd said no, I'd have been out on my own, right? The others would have abandoned this incompetent leader, wouldn't they?"

"No, I don't think they...would? Oh, yeah, they totally would...... O-ow! Arvin, my hand! My hand! It hurts! My bones are cracking! They're gonna break!"

Friendship in this dimension hurt so much it almost made me cry.

(31ST DAY)

In the morning, I excitedly prepared for our adventure. Thirty-one days had passed since I'd first arrived in this realm, and I had still only made it down to the fifth floor. Time flew by as I watched over my sister-in-law's recovery. Éa complained that I had been too cautious, but I couldn't help it—I was worried.

Now fully recovered, she ate and ate some more. "Looks like we left a hole in your stomach when we opened you up," Isolla darkly joked. Are we sure she wasn't actually made in England?

I knew Lana would also have whatever I made, so I put my heart into it.

I'd also decided to make the lunch we'd take into the dungeon with us myself. The food they sold at the Guild left me at a loss for words. Lumps of flour and butter did not count as food. Those were ingredients! Who could dive into the dungeon on a stomach full of something that gross?!

Anyway.

This would be our first time exploring the dungeon as a joint party. In a way, it was my first genuine attempt to take on the dungeon. However, we'd agreed to take absolutely no undue risks. We planned to descend down to the seventh floor, map the shortest way back, and get out. And just in case, I prepared a bunch of extra provisions.

Those included flour so we could grill some chapati in the dungeon, bacon and dried fish, cheese, and homemade potato chips. I also packed two bottles of the mayonnaise I'd longed for, which Machina had made for me, a bottle of, in this world, incredibly precious honey, a bottle of herb garlic butter, a jar of salt, onions, garlic, herbs, olive oil, and several loaves of deathly hard brown bread to feed a few people in only the most extreme of emergencies. The dungeon apparently had its own water sources, but I also brought water fortified with minerals for several people. I didn't forget to take more than I might expect to need, as well as some strong liquor for cooking and first aid, cooking utensils, and—

"Mr. Souya, that's enough," Machina cut me off. "You could feed seven people for four days with what you have. It's a waste of energy."

"Food is never a waste, you know?!"

"Pardon me. I was entirely at fault, so please calm down. Your entire personality changes when it comes to food," she noted, delivering a shocking dose of truth.

"S-seriously?"

"Seriously."

"Sorry, I'll be careful."

"Thank you."

Begrudgingly, I gave up on the cabbage. I'd wanted to use it to make *okonomiyaki*-style chapati, but I guessed that would have to wait for another time. The condiments and cooking utensils I would carry, and the rest I planned to divide into four and leave with the Zavah Night Owl Trade Group for Arvin to pick up.

"I guess the rest is all set."

"Yes. You have your food and equipment, and breakfast is ready. I really challenged myself today and made miso soup, rice balls, fried eggs, and lots of mini sausages!"

What is this, a cram student's midnight snack? She should be able to make so much more, so why did she go with this lineup?

"Then I guess I'll go wake up my wife and my sister-in-law."

Waking them up was my favorite part of the day. I got to look at two elves in unbecoming states of rest, and nobody would come to arrest me. I didn't even have to pay for it.

"Before you do, Mr. Souya, I'd like to discuss something with you."

"Hmm?"

"The truth is, I've been writing a memoir. Adventures like this are inherently dangerous, and I never know when you may lose your life, so I would like to make sure I get everything down in record."

"That sounds like a great idea." Even if I died, that record would remain to tell someone else in the future about my visit here and the days I'd spent suffering like an absolute idiot. As long as I could pass that information on, none of it would have been in vain.

"I thought about naming it *Record of the Other Dimension File 01*, but Isolla rejected that idea. She said I needed to make it something that would catch people's interest more, or they wouldn't read it even if they came upon it."

"Makes sense."

"Herein lies the problem. Isolla has suggested naming it *The Mythlanica Witch Project*, or *Cloverfield 2*, or *REC: Attack of the Elves*, after documentaries with altogether horrible endings, and I'm at my wit's end. The copyright issues could get tricky, too."

"Yeah, most likely." Though I'd kinda want to watch those.

"I would prefer to not expend any more resources on this. Mr. Souya, please come out and decide on a title! Isolla and I will give up and accept any title you propose!"

So they never trusted my sense to begin with, huh? Well, probably best that way. I don't plan on spending too long thinking about it. I've got a difficult adventure waiting for me, so I don't want to waste any mental energy on this.

I just need something random but easy to understand. A title that gets straight to the point.

I taste-tested the miso soup and murmured:

"The Otherworlder, Exploring the Dungeon."

THE END

AFTERWORD

Good day, good evening, good morning. I am the author, Hinagi Asami. Thank you very much for picking up a copy of *The Other-worlder, Exploring the Dungeon*. I cannot say if you are reading this after or before purchase, or if perhaps you have followed the story from its days on the Web. It would also be impossible for me to know whether you are reading it now or have already read it and in what time period that might be occurring. Maybe you fished this out of the devastated ruins left in the wake of nuclear warfare or some such disaster.

In any event, I am grateful to have this story as a *published* book. Even if I keeled over tomorrow, this book would still remain. I mean, it would still be on the Web also, but that's that and this is this. They're pretty different animals.

In the process of making this book, I did some major correcting and revising on the original work. It's incredible how many flaws I found in something I'd had quite a bit of confidence in when I'd originally published it. I would like to thank my editor and proofreaders for their help with this. I'm also grateful to the illustrator, Kureta, for creating the wonderful illustrations within, to all the members of the video game and planning and book editing departments, and to every one of our collaborators.

And yet, the only reason I managed to publish this book at all was thanks to the supporters who left me their encouraging comments while I serialized this story online. You have my deepest, deepest gratitude. I would be even more grateful to new readers who buy and support my work.

If I had to say what kind of book this is, I'd say it's a light novel whose main theme is *irony*. There is one other hidden theme, but well, it would be tacky for me to point it out in something I wrote myself, so I will seal my lips for all of eternity on that point.

I've worked some near-future sci-fi elements into a tale similar to those in the reincarnation fantasy genre. However, there will be no reincarnation. There are no cheat codes. I've done everything I could to exclude any video game aspects such as skills or status details. This book appears to be one of those recently common fantasy stories but is actually something a little different. I went into this intending to write a story about following the noble path, but based on the reviews and feedback I get from others, it appears it may be a novel about going down the road to evil.

This story won first prize in the Dragon Book Up-and-Coming Authors Fantasy Novel Contest. It's an honor I don't deserve. Honestly, I thought I'd been scammed. That's how surreal it felt.

I started off with this nebulous dream of becoming an author one day and wrote stories I meant to be like novels. Looking back on it now, I don't think I did a good job of it at all. But apparently, I don't like to give up easily, and the longer I kept at it, the more the stories turned into something approaching a novel. The longer I kept writing vaguely novel-like books, the more novelish those stories became. Comments and reviews I received spurred me on, until finally, thanks to this first-place award, I was able to turn this story into a real novel.

No matter what you do, the longer you do it, the more you will grow. I have no doubt about this. It's all about spirit and guts.

I'd like to express my deepest and utmost thanks to everyone who has collaborated with me on this novel—and to those who will continue to do so in the future. If I'm lucky enough to have a second, I look forward to working with you again.